Praise for

PLANET JANITOR

"A rollicking plot-driven adventure... The dangers are intimidating, the wonders evocative and the thread that ties it all together is always just a little more tangled than it seems."

— The Canadian Science Fiction Review

"The novel's got a great energy about it, but also an undefinable maturity that gives it that "Golden Age" feel. *Planet Janitor: Custodian of the Stars* is an accomplished novel of immersive depth and imaginative scope, highly recommended."

— SFBook.com

"There have been other books speculating about what might happen if the Earth were devastated by an asteroid or a space-borne plague. But we really haven't explored the potential of creating an industrial base devoted to managing the environment in the wake of a disaster."

— SF-Fandom.com

"Chris Stevenson is at the top of his game — and genre — in this highly entertaining yet also thought-provoking novel. It's the kind of book you won't put down once you've picked it up."

— Jim Melvin, author of *The Death Wizard Chronicles*

"The highest praise... You would absolutely buy everything else this author had to offer."

— Aurora Reviews

"The controversy surrounding space debris/junk is an innovative and thought-provoking concept for a book."

— SFFWorld.com

"It was an adrenaline filled fast paced adventure."
— Chasity Tarantino, Batty for Books

"An intriguing and exciting cross between *Aliens* and *10,000 Years B.C.* — Stevenson shows us a future filled with proof that we should listen to Stephen Hawking's warnings about alien life forms and what they want to do to us."
— Gini Koch, author of *Touched by an Alien* (12 book series)

"Chris Stevenson's novel, *Planet Janitor: Custodian of the Stars* is highly entertaining. The technology is believable and really grounded in science. This is always an important factor for solid Sci-Fi. The characters are well-developed and their individual storylines will suck the reader right in. There is enough action, humor, and even a touch of romance mixed in to satisfy even the casual science fiction fan. This makes *Planet Janitor: Custodian of the Stars* an easy recommend."
— *Tales of the Talisman* — Volume 8, Issue 1.

"*Planet Janitor: Custodian of the Stars* is a science fiction novel that includes humor, plenty of action, and a lot of heart."
— Sarah Wallace, descendant of the famous William Wallace author of *Heart of Humanity* and *Price of a Bounty*

"FIVE STARS: Chris Stevenson writes a believable Sci-Fi story, not an easy feat in itself. But more than that, he makes the whole thing edge-of-your-seat adventurous from the very beginning."
— Lynda Coker, author of *Stormee Waters* and *The Ocean Between*

PLANET JANITOR

A NOVEL

CHRIS STEVENSON

ENGAGE BOOKS

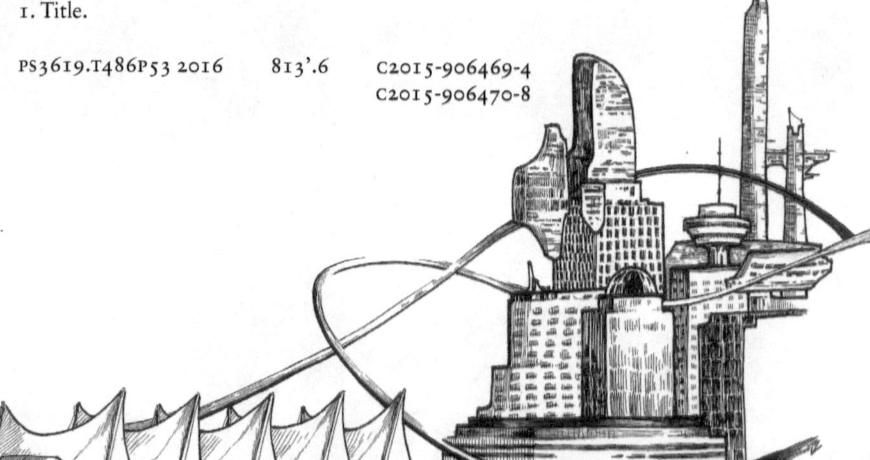

ℓ ENGAGE BOOKS

Mailing address:
Engage Books
PO BOX 4608
Main Station Terminal
349 West Georgia Street
Vancouver, BC
Canada, V6B 4A1

www.engagebooks.ca

Substantive edit by: Andrew Wilmot
Substantive edit by: A.R. Roumanis
Cover art by: A.R. Roumanis
Cover design by: A.R. Roumanis
Illustrations by: Toni Zhang
Edited by: Dayna Martin
Proofread by: Nola Papp

Text set in Sabon.

FIRST EDITION / FIRST PRINTING

Planet Janitor: Custodian of the Stars
Text © 2016 Chris Stevenson
Design © 2016 Engage Books

LIBRARY AND ARCHIVES CANADA CATALOGUING IN PUBLICATION

Stevenson, Chris Harold, 1951-, author
  Planet Janitor : custodian of the stars : with two bonus short stories / Chris Stevenson.

Issued in print and electronic formats.
ISBN 978-1-77226-111-0 (bound).–
ISBN 978-1-77226-110-3 (paperback).–
ISBN 978-1-77226-112-7 (pdf).–
ISBN 978-1-77226-113-4 (epub).–
ISBN 978-1-77226-114-1 (kindle)

1. Title.

PS3619.T486P53 2016   813'.6   C2015-906469-4
                                      C2015-906470-8

PLANET JANITOR

CUSTODIAN OF THE STARS

CHRIS STEVENSON

VANCOUVER:
ENGAGE BOOKS
2016

This work is dedicated to Alexis Roumanis, publisher extraordinaire of Engage Books, for his professionalism and hard work in assembling this small and improved omnibus of *Planet Janitor: Custodian of the Stars*, and the added shorts. He believed from the very beginning, and was relentless in producing a premium SF novel, when other publishers would have let it fade away into the depths of deep space. Thanks, buddy. For EVERYTHING.

Contents

JOURNEY INTERRUPTED

The *New Ulysses* exploratory data probe drifted just outside the open cargo bay door, looking like a crinkled can, only it was the size of a small zip shuttle. Its sensor arrays, solar panels, camera and spectrometer platforms were crushed, folded in on themselves as if it had suffered a catastrophic impact. As deep as they were inside the core of the main asteroid belt, Captain Zaz Crowe had no doubt that it had lost its telemetry functions 15 years ago and run smack into one of the minor asteroids. Exactly as the NASA report postulated. As a result of being reported lost, with no investigation or recovery effort launched, it was fair game for private salvage. Zaz had wasted no time in processing his salvage claim on the derelict space probe.

New Ulysses had a gold film skirt worth 50,000 imperials alone, discounting the other precious metals and on-board systems. "One man's trash is another man's treasure," was a favorite motto of the Planet Janitor Corporation, and the cargo bays of the *Shenandoah* were brimming to near capacity with such discarded treasure from a 27-day sweep of the asteroid belt. The M-type nickel-iron asteroids weighing three tons and smaller, comprised much of the ship's salvaged inventory, and would fetch a nice price on the open market, for both metallurgic and collector value.

Zaz adjusted the targeting laser and pointed it at one end of the probe, while his mechanical engineer, Galoot, targeted his beam to pinpoint the mid-section of the probe at the opposite end. They fired the grappling darts at the same time. The darts struck the craft on the laser points, embedding deep into the metal structure. Zaz flipped a switch, activating the retrieval lines. The lines became taut, then the probe began a lazy drift into the cargo bay. Once the probe drifted to the center of the bay, Zaz spoke into his helmet mike.

"Sammy, close bay C-2 and pressurize the deck. Slow to dead still."

"Aye, closing and pressurizing. Cutting engines. Nice snatch, Zaz. That's about the last of it, right?"

Zaz knew that his navigator and co-pilot, Samantha King, was eager to get Earth-side, as well as the rest of his crew. He was amused by her massive shrub of red hair and way she labored to keep it in place, rather than cut it and simplify her hairstyle. "We're all junked up, Sammy. You can prep for a bang jump home."

"Music to my ears! I'll start the jump pre-flight."

Zaz snugged the probe up against the retrieval armatures, cranking the lines tight. It took 15 minutes for the deck to heat and pressurize, allowing both crew members to remove their pressure suits. Zaz stored the suits inside a deck trunk and wiped his face. When he looked at Galoot, the eight-foot tall 480-pound man grinned at him, conveying an expression of victory. And rightfully so; their recent junk harvest had gone exceedingly well, with no foul-ups, injuries or emergencies. Hell, they hadn't even scratched the paint during any of the retrievals. Nothing but *smooth moves*.

Zaz and Galoot walked a circuit around the *New Ulysses* probe, noting the structural damage. Besides evidence of a collision, the probe was pockmarked with tiny micro meteor holes and contained a thick layer of what looked like basaltic asteroid dust. In spite of the damage, it was nice haul. Just one more piece of trash out of the space lanes, Zaz mused, and gave it an affectionate pat. Five years in the space reclamation business had really panned out, and the Planet Janitor Corporation was beginning to make great strides in financial gains and reputation. If he hadn't inherited the business from his father, none of it would have been possible. At 39 years of age, Zaz was seriously considering an early retirement if things kept improving.

"Galoot, strap her down with the heavy carbon fiber lines, and meet me at the bridge."

"I'll get her cinched down good and tight, Cap'n."

Zaz took the nearest foot tram to the elevator, feeling unusually upbeat and gratified. No incidents, sickness or ship-board malfunctions in just under a month's salvage time. It was a damn miracle. Yet he had a haunting premonition that things had gone too well.

When he arrived at A deck, he'd already formulated a celebratory party in his mind, complete with entertainers, music, six-course meals and enough champagne to drown his crew. He thought about handing out some bonuses once they had their inventory turned in. When he reached the bridge, he was surprised to see his petite botanist, Dendy Dollar, his demolition expert, Carl Stromboli, and Samantha standing in front of the nav console, facing his direction. They let loose with party poppers, showering the bridge deck with colorful streamers. They chorused a cheer and pumped their fists in the air. Dendy ran to him and embraced him in tight hug.

"Yeah, we're going home," said Zaz, grinning. "It hasn't been a long haul, but it's been a profitable one." He looked at Samantha. "What was the weight on that last one?"

Samantha pulled her enormous froth of strawberry blond hair away from her face. "About two point seven metric tons. Nice size, even for one of the older probes." She turned around and took a seat at the nav console, taking up where she'd left off with the pre-flight.

Carl frowned and set his jaw. "Yeah, but as usual I didn't even get to light a match. You don't know what's it's like when a doctor of pyrotechnics can't blow something up. It's the only way to relieve my emotional pressure valve."

Carl Stromboli lived for detonations, impacts and explosions. As a child he used to light a lot of fires, causing his parent untold misery and apprehension. He'd always explained it away, not by confessing that he had a fatal case of pyromania, but that it was an early career move that he one day planned to implement and profit by.

"You just set off a party popper," said Samantha over her shoulder. "And that should be enough until we get home. Then you can stick a tube of C-6 up your butt and blow yourself to kingdom come."

Carl sniffed. "Very funny Ms. Top Heavy. I've got a retort for that but it's – "

"Okay, that's enough celebrating," Zaz cut in. "I'm sure everybody's got something to do. Carl, check on the cyro tubes and program the automechs for routine service and maintenance chores. I'll have Galoot check the bang pod drives. Sammy crunches our numbers, and Dendy..." Zaz tried to disengage from his smallest crew member, but she had snug hold on him, her cheek buried in his chest. He had to admit that he could think of worse things than having a pretty botanist wrapped around him like a boa constrictor. He finally untangled himself and held her at arm's length, gazing at her light brown eyes, heavy brows and thick bangs. If he didn't know any better, he would have thought she was flushed and gushing at him.

"Okay, Dendy" he said, "You check on the hydroponics lab and make sure everything's battened down." She had a green thumb, and by simply talking to plants, shrubs and flowers, she could entice them to thrive and blossom. Admittedly, Dendy put the "fun" factor into the Planet Janitor Corporation, blessing them with an insufferably sweet and positive disposition.

"You bet, Zaz!" she said, and left the bridge with a child-like skip. *She was gushing at me.*

Zaz took a seat next to Samantha at the nav console, looked at the central view monitor, where she had brought up the system's array – hydrogen fuel, deck pressure and temperature, repulser coils, generator output and nuclear pod status. As far as he was concerned, if one data point was off in preparation for a bang pod jump, he'd insist on postponing the return flight until they performed a complete debug and fixed the culprit system. It was the reason he never held the optimism the others did when contemplating a return trip, or any trip. One minor system failure always seemed to create a domino effect, with several minor system failures snowballing into a major catastrophic event. It was always the little things that crept up to bite you in the ass when you least expected it.

Samantha brought up a bar graph showing the continuity in the repulser coils. "Full voltage there," she murmured, then projected her volume. "Ya know, you're going to jinx us if you keep staring at the monitor like that. Relax. You're always looking for gremlins when there aren't any. Everything is checking out."

"Gremlins hide then jump out at you. I never really believed that old saying 'the check's in the mail.' I'm never satisfied until the check's in the bank. Besides, it's the prerogative and duty of the captain to shoulder the worry. That's why I have no fingernails." He gave her a half-hearted laugh, but he was dead serious about his theories. *I'm not a pessimist. I'm a realist. There's a difference.*

"Where do you want to pop in?" asked Samantha, her fingers hovering over a numeric keyboard.

"How about the front door. About 80,000 miles out, directly over Long Beach. That'll let us cruise for a couple of hours, and give us time to get cleaned up and packed."

"You've got it. I'll give the Port Authority our registry and esti-mated arrival time."

"Punch it in and hit send, sweetie."

"Punched and sent. Ya know, I was thinking that..." Her words dropped off, replaced by a whoop-whoop siren. They both looked at the monitor, eyes fixed on the flashing yellow letters, PROXIMITY ALERT.

Zaz flicked a toggle, cutting the siren off. Samantha changed the forward window to optical view, showing fore, aft and side camera views through hull-mounted gun scopes. She punched up the magnification on the monitor and read the right ascension and declination coordinates of the mystery object. She toggled the aft gun scope to come to bear on a pin-prick of light. She watched the spectrometer for 30 seconds and said, "It's moving, whatever it is, and in our general direction."

Zaz sat on the edge of his seat. "Perturbed asteroid? That would be a one in a billion shot!"

"Don't know. The spectral intensity is increasing by fractions, and by timing it, I can get a rough velocity."

Galoot came over intercom. "Heard a siren, chief. What's up?"

A moment later, Dendy and Carl parroted the same concerns. Zaz explained that they had a bogey approaching. He expected them to make a breathless dash to the bridge. He couldn't blame them. Having a proximity alert wasn't exactly an earth-shattering event, since it had happened numerous times. But mostly in the shipping lanes. Astronomically speaking, they were on a dirt road in the core section of the main asteroid belt. The only things that moved in this sector of space were big rocks that had been knocked out of their orbital resonance.

Dividing her eyes between the spectrometer and the chronometer, Samantha danced her fingers over the panel calculator. "Got some rough estimates," she said, nonplussed. "The speed is between 35,000 and 45,000 standard miles-per-hour. That's within the speed parameters of a rogue body, but the spectra and density seem off. We know it's within 10,000 miles of us because that's our warning distance."

The rest of the crew members filed hurriedly through the bridge hatch and took up standing positions behind the nav console. It was fortunate that the two Planet Janitor scientists were Earthbound, or else they would have had a traffic jam on the bridge.

Dendy gripped Zaz's shoulder and said, "Any coronal discharge or tail?"

"It's not a comet," said Samantha, adjusting the magnification and camera focus. "If it stays on its present course, it'll pass within 300 miles of us. Which is against safe traffic distance for deep space. Almost *has* to be a solid body or composite."

"Finally," said Carl. "Looks like I get to blow something out of the system. Don't look at me like that, Zaz. You know it's our duty to stop runaways from entering major shipping lanes and station zones."

"We still don't know what it is yet," said Zaz. "So hold those thoughts."

"We'll know in about 12 to 15 minutes," said Samantha. "It's coming nearly head on."

Zaz groaned, thinking about his revised version of Murphy's Law: *If something can go wrong, it's already happened.* The worst scenario would be Carl's guess that it was a rogue headed for the interior shipping lanes. That would require a trajectory plot to find anything in its path. Then they would have to intercept, analyze and formulate a plan for taking it out. The scenario would delay their jump home, considerably. Not to mention, they'd have to file a report with the International Security Agency, filling out forms and appearing at a hearing.

"Anything on its mass?" asked Zaz.

Samantha answered with a hesitant mumble. "Too small to be a planetesimal, and too large for a meteorite. Somewhere in between, like about starliner size. I'll know more in a few minutes. I can tell it's a shiny little jewel, whatever it is."

Zaz shook his head. "Engage the engines and prepare for evasive maneuvers." Standard operating procedure dictated keeping a safe distance between an unknown flyby and the ship. His next protocol was to order the crew to their accelerator couches, which he did a minute later. Samantha lit the port engines and took them out another 2,000 miles from the path of the approaching body.

"Dead still," said Zaz.

"Aye, dead still," Samantha responded, and then readjusted the magnification and focus. "Well no wonder she didn't look right."

Zaz didn't have to guess what Samantha meant. He could pick up the slightest detail of the nearing object. It had an elongated profile, and it left a barely perceptible contrail in its wake – almost a thread. He wondered what a ship was doing this far out in the main belt under standard propulsion. Unless it was a survey vessel?

Samantha looked over her shoulder, pegging her eyes on Zaz, who sat in the command chair. "It's a craft all right, moving at flank speed. No course deviations. She's emitting some type of ejecta."

Zaz gave her a pert nod. "Hail her on the emergency frequency and tell her she's approaching traffic."

Samantha donned her headset and dialed in the frequency. "Unknown vessel, this is the ore freighter *Shenandoah*. You are in violation of deep space traffic separation. Alter your course and reduce your speed."

Zaz patched into the communication channel from his chair console. "Unknown vessel, this is Captain Crowe of the ore freighter *Shenandoah*, state your name, registration and flight plan."

No response.

Samantha tried several more hails, and set the *Shenandoah's* cameras for automatic tracking of the ship. A photo record would be needed in an inquiry. The ship was plainly in violation on two counts: failure to respond and disregard of proper traffic separation.

Zaz watched a large conical craft take form, bullet-shaped at both ends. What he found amazing was the appearance of port and starboard airfoils, which extended out from the fuselage like delta wings. Either she was a very old craft, or something very new and experimental. The hull looked smooth and brightly copper-colored, containing no weapons platforms or antenna array.

Zaz glanced at his engineer. "Galoot, have you seen anything like this in the shipyards?"

Samantha cut in quickly. "She's coming up abreast of us now. I'm pulling in visuals on some hull markings."

Zaz studied the screen. The image danced a bit, but he could make out INTREPID HWD 553P. The bar scale on the bottom of the screen indicated a length of 1,450 feet and about 400,000 metric tons. The aft end of the ship trailed a fine wispy mist of some unknown gas or liquid. The ship continued at flank speed, headed for the inner planets.

"I'll check the ship registration archives against that ID number," Samantha offered. "The 'P' denotes a private vessel, probably a contractor. That's all I know so far."

Galoot cleared his throat. "She's a triple-hull transport freighter, for sure, boss. Those wings are fail-safe structures for atmosphere insertion. I think she's Chinese. I've seen one before that came into the yard for an engine retrofit. The HWD stands for Hazardous Waste Disposal." Galoot knew his ships. He'd worked at most of the major West Coast shipyards for the past two decades. He'd once jumped-started an ion generator with a paperclip, to restart a satellite.

Samantha looked up from her console. "Galoot's got it right. United States registry, but it was imported from China 15 years ago." Samantha looked at a small window on the main monitor. "The *Intrepid*, current captain, Alexandria Remy. Her ship-board systems are fully automated, and she has a crew complement of four. That's a pittance for running that behemoth."

"Bring up a still shot of the hull. I didn't see a company name, only a small logo."

Samantha brought the ship's side profile into view. Zaz could see a small space-suited figure wielding an overloaded wheelbarrow, superimposed over a radioactive pinwheel. It appeared almost cartoonish in rendering. He told Samantha to look it up under company trademarks. She came back a minute later with the identification.

"Anderson and Wiley Transport, out of Philadelphia. Their motto is 'Don't bawl – We'll Haul.'"

Dendy perked up. "They're in kind of the same business we're in. How come we haven't heard of them?"

Zaz took that one. "They're licensed for Hazardous Waste Transport. That isn't exactly something you want to broadcast about a company. Just a tad off-putting."

"Yeah, but we've done it," said Carl. "And everybody knows who we are."

Zaz rolled his eyes. "We've never been ashamed of it. Some businesses don't like to announce the fact. Sammy, I'll take the helm from here. I going to come up behind her, and I want you to analyze that venting gas. Give me a chemical breakdown. In the meantime, send a message to Anderson and Wiley and tell them what we've found.

"I'm on it."

The captain lit the aft main hydrogen engines and advanced the throttle. The speed of the *Intrepid* clocked out at 37,500 miles-per-hour. That gave Zaz a margin to catch her, and even overtake her, if need be. Gut instinct was no way to run a ship, but something bothered him about the *Intrepid's* hell-bent speed – no response to hails – no course deviation – a systems leak. The ship obviously had a nuclear bang drive, but it hadn't been activated. If the crew needed to reach home port or make it to the Vegan atmosphere to dump their load, they were doing so in the slowest mode possible.

As the *Shenandoah* approached the aft slipstream of the *Intrepid*, Samantha tabulated the chemical makeup of the ejecta. As the ship's sensors sucked up the minute particles, information appeared on the main view monitor in the form of graphs and numerical data points. Zaz waited eagerly for Samantha's analysis.

"Okay," said Samantha. "Chemical composition is a diluted form of H_2SO_4, non-flammable, with a molar mass of 98.079. It looks like – "

"That's sulfuric acid," said Dendy. "Even I know that. They're venting acid, and that's a very unusual substance for any component on a ship."

"Unless it's cargo," said Zaz. "Let's give her the once over." Zaz increased his ship's velocity, crossing over to the starboard side of the *Intrepid*. He studied the hull lines and asked the others to report anything that looked unusual, especially evidence of explosive decompression. Passing over the bow, he could see nothing unusual until he looked at the physical view-screens and ports, which appeared discolored.

"Cabin windows are opaque," said Samantha. "Either moisture or gas. It doesn't look good, Zaz." She tried to raise the ship again, repeatedly hailing. She shook her head. "Nothing. Not a peep, and we can't see any signs of bridge activity through that haze."

Zaz looked at Galoot. "Would a universal entry key work on their hatches?"

"No reason not to. It's standard regulation, especially for non-military craft. You thinking about boarding her, boss?"

Zaz had knots in his gut, and it was from what he was seeing. It was more than suspicious. Something was dreadfully wrong aboard the *Intrepid*. The crew's lives were at stake, or God forbid, past that point. The ship was a runaway, plain and simple – a threat to navigation and possibly carrying a very dangerous cargo. "Galoot, gather up three mini-sleds, three Hazmat pressure suits and a hatch key. I'll meet you at the starboard B deck airlock."

"On my way."

Carl released the air bladder on his couch and made a move to get up. "Finally some action!"

"You're not going," said Zaz. "You'll stay here and assist Samantha. I'll need a response from Anderson and Wiley. Sammy, I want the *Shenandoah* within kissing distance of that ship."

"You heard him, Carl," said Samantha, and slapped a seat next to her. "Plant your greasy butt next to me and get ready to work for a living."

"I always get the short end," cursed Carl, and stumbled to the forward nav station.

Zaz released his seat bladder and curled his finger at Dendy. "You're going with. Any objections?"

Dendy pushed up out of her couch. "Not a one, Cap'n. I need some fresh vacuum anyway."

Zaz and Dendy left the bridge. Besides running the hydroponics lab, Dendy Dollar had served time on the *Blue Peace* marine vessel as a science intern. A fish-kissing, tree-hugging environmentalist, Dendy had her own strict rules about the preservation and sanctity of life. Fiercely independent and smart as paint, she could also hold her own as a medical technician, having served as a nurse when she was eighteen. Zaz had a feeling she had more than a scrap of hero worship for him, but he couldn't deny that the pert brunette at half his age, held a bit more of his interest than just vocational attributes. She had a curious bond of attraction over him, but those feelings were turning into something more serious and intimate which, lately, confounded him.

When they reached the B-deck airlock, Zaz opened up a cabinet and pulled out an emergency kit. He hoped he wouldn't need to use it, but he was about to enter the unknown and felt that being prepared would save himself a flight back to the ship. Galoot joined them a moment later, carrying a mountain of gear. They donned their Hazmat suits, helping each other close the seals and adjust the fittings. Zaz strapped the emergency kit to his waist. They stepped inside the airlock, shutting the hatch. Zaz punched the wall panel for de-pressurization, then watched the wall panel and his wrist display. He spoke into his helmet mike. "Com check." Galoot and Dendy answered back, crisp and clear. Samantha piped in a few seconds later. "Have a clean read on you. Be careful."

Once the airlock panel read green, Galoot opened the hull hatch and held his mini-sled out in front of him. When he activated the small propulsion engine, the sled pulled him out into space. He angled the double-handled sled frame to pull him down toward the *Intrepid*. Dendy followed next, flying out a good distance from the hull. Zaz took up the rear, but turned to close the exterior hatch. The three were now adrift.

"Galoot, take us to a hatch nearest the bridge."

Galoot flew off, his giant bulk propelled gracefully through the vacuum of space. He allowed Dendy to follow next, spotting her from behind. She had a bit of trouble maneuvering the sled, and performed a clumsy zigzag drift. She got the hang of it in a minute, and straightened her course. Galoot reached a rectangular hatch, marked with yellow stripes. He worked the universal entrance key into a slot and turned it, cracking the seal. He flipped the hatch open and waved his arm as an invite. Zaz drifted within a few feet of the hatch opening. The interior of the airlock chamber atmosphere looked clear, a good precursor sign.

One by one they pulled themselves inside the airlock chamber. Zaz fastened the hatch behind them, using the interior locking lever. He next checked the chamber data panel, finding it lit and showing real time temperature and pressure of the ship's interior. The temperature read 74 degrees Fahrenheit, with 20 percent oxygen. The ship's artificial gravity on the other side of the hatch was intact. What he did not like, as he looked through the thick glass hatch portal, was evidence of a pale, yellowish mist in the ready room beyond. The hatch door on the other side of the ready room was cracked open.

Zaz thumbed a panel button and watched the readout. The airlock began to pressurize, returning weight to their bodies. They dropped their mini-sleds to the floor.

"Open her up, Galoot," said Zaz, and stood back while the big man threw a lever and pulled the door open. Zaz took the lead, walking slowly through the ready room, glancing at cabinets on both bulkhead walls. Nothing seemed out of place or disturbed. He pulled the ready room hatch open and stepped out into a pristine white corridor that lead off in right and left directions. He knew he needed to go left toward the bridge, and at least down a few levels. The right corridor lead to the ship's interior and aft section.

"My suit sensor detects high outside air acidity," said Dendy. "It's a good thing we're wearing Hazmats. The substance is corrosive on seals, valves and joints."

Zaz looked at his sensor array on his wrist computer. The concentration was lethal, able to cause respiratory failure in just minutes. He had two major concerns: the lives of the *Intrepid's* crew and the source of the acid leak.

"Galoot, I need you to go aft and see if you can narrow down the source of the acid. It might be engine related – some type of propellant, or associated with the cargo. Watch your wrist gauge. If the acid concentration gets any worse, alert me and beat it back here."

"I can find my way around this bucket. I'll come back chop-chop if things look bad."

Zaz felt the knot in his gut cinch tighter, watching Galoot lumber down the corridor and disappear around an intersection. He pressed on, with Dendy at his side. He noticed a wet film on the walkway, believing it to be acid residue. He came upon a bulkhead placard that showed a schematic of the deck levels, and the precise spot where he stood in relation to the bridge. He followed the corridor and came to a spiral down-ramp, equipped with double handrails. He descended the steep ramp and arrived at a landing, which denoted one level down, then continued on to the next landing. Three hatchways came into view at the bottom of the ramp, but the one marked FLIGHT OPERATIONS, grabbed his attention. He opened the hatch and stepped through. He found himself in a combination galley and dining area, surprisingly immaculate and free of clutter.

Dendy brushed up against his shoulder, obviously preoccupied with the sights. "This ship looks brand new," she said, with a nervous waver in her voice. "I mean, the upkeep is incredible. Not what you'd expect with a used freighter. But I'm worried about – "

"I know what you're worried about and so am I. I'm wondering if they had enough warning to outfit themselves. I think the scrubbers failed and this gas went through the ship's recirculating vents." He wiped a film of what looked like sweat on the outside of his face shield. The acid was already starting to eat away at the protective glass, which he hadn't counted on. But that didn't make sense. Glass was impervious to acid. He hailed Galoot for a report.

"Just entering the main cargo deck now," came the response. "It's pretty thick in here, almost wet. Looks bad, boss. My visor shield is fogging up."

"Don't stay too long. We might have to bug out fast."

"Copy that."

The bridge was not cordoned off from the galley-dining area. Zaz could see straight through to the V-shaped bridge console, and a wedge shaped arrangement of accelerator couches. He saw a slumped figure, out-fitted in some type of protective suit, leaning over from a command chair, head resting on the console. He assumed this was the captain. Ten feet to the right and further back lay the prone figure of a woman, on her back and hands drawn up to her throat. They hurried to the prone woman first. Unable to read the woman's pulse through the suit gloves, Dendy rested a hand on the woman's ribcage and looked for movement. Zaz knew there would be no respiration – the woman had swollen, burned lips, milky white eyes and smears of blood on her nostrils and chin.

"Oh, God, Zaz. She's gone!" cried Dendy. "Massive hemorrhaging of the airways."

Zaz read a breast patch on the woman's company suit aloud, committing it to memory. "Darlene Bentwater, Flight Engineer."

They moved quickly to the command chair occupant. Dendy gently pulled the head upright and gazed into the helmet visor. The back of the suit collar contained stenciled letters: ALEXANDRIA REMY – FC.

"I've got muscular response!" said Dendy. "Her suit controls are active, showing a pulse and respiration, but it's weak. Her oxygen supply is critical."

"Galoot, I need you up at the bridge," said Zaz urgently. "We have a survivor!"

"On my way... I'm finished up here anyway."

Zaz pulled an extension tube from his oxygen valve and connected it to the captain's oxygen inlet. He turned a dial and filled the depleted oxygen canister, giving it a full charge. Within a minute, the captain's eye's fluttered and she took a gasping breath.

Carrying a lifeless body through ship's corridors in a Hazmat suit was next to impossible. Zaz needed some kind of a cart or gurney, and having no idea of the ship's layout, he was at a loss for knowing where to start his search, unless.... *The galley.*

Zaz fast-walked to the galley and began pulling open cupboards and lockers, looking for a fold-out transportation device. He pulled one thin hatch door open, marked LABORATORY, looked inside and saw a body. The woman had sat down with her back against the bulkhead, drawing her knees up into her chin. Her head lolled to the side, eyes closed. A spray of blood freckled her face and chest. Patches of hair lay on the deck, like small puddles of mud. She had her legs half in, half out of a pressure suit. He closed the door quickly and continued looking. He found a small storage room filled with foodstuffs and water containers. A stack of boxes sat atop a four-wheeled, double-tray serving cart. He brushed the boxes off the cart and pulled it through the storage area and out into the galley. When he wheeled it to the bridge, Dendy already had the flight captain sitting upright.

"Samantha for Zaz. I've been listening in. You have one responsive and one decedent. Is that correct?"

"One responsive and two down," Zaz corrected. "I found another dead in the galley bathroom. Sammy, we're going to try and get the survivor out as fast as we can. If we can manage it, we'll transport the two bodies. Any callback from Anderson and Wiley?"

"No callback yet. Jesus, I can't believe we're having this conversation." Samantha sounded hopelessly defeated.

"I need you to keep it together right now, Ms King. Keep *Shenandoah* on course and keep your ears open for that callback."

"We've got three no-lifers," said Galoot, cutting in. "I've brought a gal up from the cargo bay. I just set her down next to the airlock. I just couldn't leave her behind. Looks like she was checking out the damage when she was overcome."

"You did the right thing," said Zaz. "What's *your* status?"

"Just a little tuckered. I can't see too good through this helmet – got to wipe the damn thing every ten steps."

"Slow your pace, then," said Zaz, and gave him directions to the bridge. "Zaz to Carl. Get suited up and prepare to assist Galoot at our ship's airlock. We need the survivor and deceased taken on board ASAP. Bring a few extra helmets to the *Shenandoah's* airlock."

"I'll be there."

The Planet Janitor crew had faced tight spots before, witnessed death, saved lives and come out of it with their sanity intact. This was somehow different – more severe. His crew needed to cap all their emotions and follow protocol to the letter, or more corpses would be added to the inventory. He especially worried about Dendy breaking down on him. He told her to disengage the autopilot while he recovered the body from the bathroom. He set the body on the top shelf of the serving cart. He placed the second body on the bottom shelf of the cart. It was a macabre scene, and he had to use some medical tape to strap the bodies to the frames, keeping the appendages from hanging out.

Dendy soothed the survivor as best she could, incapable of administering any meaningful treatment until they transferred the patient to the *Shenandoah*. "Auto pilot is non-responsive, Zaz. Something wrong with the controls." She pulled the captain to her feet, then assisted her in walking toward the exit.

Galoot entered the bridge with awkward steps, his hands held out before him, seemingly feeling his way along. His helmet faceplate appeared fogged over and wet. Dendy used some gauze to clean most of the heavy film away. Without being told, Galoot took the cart in a firm grip and wheeled it across the bridge and into the galley. Dendy held on to the waist of the captain and, together, they hobbled behind Galoot. Zaz knew the transfer would be difficult without him, but right now he had to wrestle the ship into submission. He had a feeling that the flight captain, the only one who had managed to get fully suited up, had been attempting to gain control of the craft before she passed out.

He took a seat at the command station and stared at the control panel, familiarizing himself with the switches, levers and input keys. The autopilot was easily discernible. He disengaged it, but it remained active. He pressed the main engine cutoff switch. It had no effect. He next tried the directional dial, turning it slowly clockwise to alter the ship's course. Non-responsive. He'd never seen anything like it before – all systems were hot and operational, yet there was no way to cut their circuits. Then he had a hunch and spoke into this helmet mike.

"Galoot, I can't shut anything down. The whole control panel is non-op. Could the acid have seeped into the circuitry and burned something out? Is that possible?"

"Yeah, it's likely. The stuff is pretty corrosive and could eat through any metallic connections. Look for an emergency main cut-off."

"This panel if full of Chinese symbols and characters."

"Look for a ship's profile that has a lightning bolt-shaped X through it."

"Found it. It's under a glass bubble."

"Break it and trip the switch."

Zaz brought the heel of his gloved hand down on the small dome and shattered the glass. He flipped a heavy toggle switch. The cabin lights dimmed momentarily, then flared to full intensity again.

"I already know it didn't work," said Galoot. "Look for a kick panel at your feet. Open it up and start pulling the large plastic-handled relays. If that doesn't work, it means the secondary wiring is fused somewhere between the bridge and the engine-generator area. It would take days to find it, if that's where the problems is. I'll be there directly when we off-load."

"That's affirmative." Zaz saw three pull-out kick panels. He removed all three and looked for Galoot's description of the relays. He found them, and started yanking them out. When he was finished, the only thing he'd managed to do was cut the bridge illumination, sending it into emergency backup. He felt hopelessly lost in knowing how to cut the ship's power. As Galoot guessed, some major juncture had failed in another part of the ship. He dialed up his suit cooler, having broken out in a nervous sweat.

"Samantha to Zaz – Anderson and Wiley reached. They confirmed no communication with the *Intrepid* for 20 hours. They just filed a "Lost Contact" report with the International Space Administration. I told them we were performing an emergency assist operation. They were surprised and saddened by the causalities, but wished us God's speed in the recovery effort.

"Tell them I can't stop this ship. I need a solution. And, Galoot, grab an oxygen charge on your way back."

"I'm on it," said Samantha.

"Copy that," said Galoot.

Zaz looked at the panel again. Several system gauges and lighting displays were out, some flickering. The artificial gravity still functioned, likewise for the air recirculation and temperature. Although he hadn't seen it before, he now noticed a warning display indicating that a nuclear bang pod was armed. He had no idea if the bang pod drive had been activated by the captain in preparation for a jump, or if it had shorted out and armed itself. The disarm switch did not function when he toggled it. With the multiple system shorts, the nuclear propulsion pod could detonate inside the ship, instead of outside of it like it was designed to do.

"Samantha for Zaz. I've got a track plotted for the *Intrepid*. She'll pass by the Exon hydrogen re-fueling station if she remains on present course, give or take in about six hours, and she'll flyby about 700 miles within it's outer safety marker. So I've sent an alert to the station, just in case you can't arrest her flight or alter course. Anderson and Wiley have no engineer at hand to answer your questions."

"Acknowledged. Typical." Zaz had nothing else to say that had a good news ring to it. In fact, things had taken a turn for the worse. They used to call them "hang-fires" or "pellets stuck in the tube." If a nuclear bang pod detonated inside the ship, it could propagate a chain reaction and ignite two dozen or more pods in the track drive, resulting in a three or four-hundred megaton explosion.

Galoot showed up fifteen minutes after Zaz had tried his last disconnect procedure. Galoot had changed out helmets and brought an oxygen charge canister, which he promptly fitted to Zaz's suit, charging his system to full capacity. Zaz let him look at the console and try his hand at shutting off the main engines. Failing at the panel, Galoot ducked inside the kick panels and began gutting the interior wires and circuits. After five minutes, Galoot gave up and turned toward his captain.

"All switching power is dead from this station. And I couldn't tell you where the next main harness fits into the secondary power supply. But it sure has one, because this ship is now on main battery backup. If I had a manual and a week of reading time, I could find the problem. And I hate to tell ya, but you've got a hot one in the tube."

"I know that. What are our options?'

"This ship is carrying a couple hundred tons of old style backup batteries. That was their cargo pickup. From what I could see in the cargo bay, a couple of those batteries exploded, probably from a static discharge or something. The acid got sucked up into the vents and sent it all over the ship, including the nuclear containment area. We're taking about o-rings, seals, valves, wiring and gaskets gettin' eaten up, disintegrating and then causing other failures. We're looking at a – "

"Thermonuclear explosion," Zaz said. "Can we nudge her off course or plant a charge and blow the engines?"

"Cap'n, I wouldn't sneeze on this ship for fear of it going off with a mini-nova. You could blow her drive but she'd still have inertial velocity and keep right on going. Besides, its got so many shorts it could blow any minute. We need to pull out now."

"Samantha, here. Zaz, you've done everything humanly possible. The risk goes off the charts the longer we stay with it. You have to let this thing go – whatever happens is inevitable."

"Planet Janitor can't stomach failure," Carl broke in. "We all know that. Look, you can't stop the thing or push it – it's not fixable. You can't off-load its bang pods. All you've got left is a doctor of pyrotechnics who knows how to set a charge in the tract drive and blow that sucker to slag. You take it out before it takes you or anybody else out. *Premeditated.*"

"We haven't got the time," said Zaz. "We're on our way out."

"By the time you get out of there, I could be in the stern section and have the charge set. The *Intrepid's* captain was able to tell me where to set the charges"

"You're not even ready," said Zaz.

"Still got my suit on, and I took the liberty of packaging a C-6 charge and remote detonator. Got it right with me. Now, you want to turn tail and run or are you serious about punchin' this thing out?"

Zaz looked at Galoot and hunched his shoulders, a useless gesture in the suit. "Okay, Carl. The ball's in your court. Get over here."

"I'm already inside your airlock. I'm heading for the stern now. When I tell you, arm all the bang pods and beat it to the airlock. I'll be bringing up the rear."

"Sorry, Zaz," said Samantha. "I had no idea what he was up to."

Neither did Zaz, but right now Carl's reckless courage was the only solution they had on their menu. Carl Stromboli lived for concussions, P-waves and destruction on a mass scale. He'd often used the analogy that the universe began with a bang and that he was a living testament, in his own morbid pursuit, to that reverence of creation. He firmly believed that the goal of great construction came about only by perfect destruction. Carl would now have to rise up and meet that challenge – to destroy in order to save and preserve.

Dendy's voice, shaky and high-pitched, came through Zaz's headset. "Zachary, I swear, if you don't get back here I'm going to suit back up and come after you!"

"I hear you. I'm coming back – count on it. Right now, you have a patient to take care of. That's my order and your assignment."

Zaz hated to sound terse, but there was no other way to deal with their present situation. "Carl, status report!" Now *he* was feeling the stress.

"Moving as fast as I can. Just found the access to the engine bay."

There wasn't anything to do to rush things. The wait was agonizing. Zaz considered sending Galoot back to the *Shenandoah*, but he knew from past experience an argument would follow and Galoot would stay to the bitter end. Zaz knelt down to pick up a small log book from the deck. It was a hard-copy written account of the captain's last notes. The words occupied less than a paragraph, and they were scrawled by a frantic hand. Some of the words that stuck out were *Leak, Ventilation* and *Chaos*. He couldn't read much of anything else, but realized after a moment that his foggy helmet glass was to blame. *All I need is to go blind right now*. Galoot helped by wiping the helmet face with some gauze.

"I'm a big dolt," said Galoot. "I didn't realize these new Hazmat helmets came with clear shipping plastic. That's the stuff that's melting."

"We were pressed for time. You couldn't get everything right."

"Carl to Zaz – light 'em up!"

Zaz flipped a bank of toggle switches on the panel and turned on his heel. Galoot was already 10 steps ahead of him on his way out of the bridge. The suit would only allow a trot, anything faster caused a misstep. They passed through the galley, entered the corridor and found the ramp. Zaz pulled himself up the ramp, using the handrails. The overhead lights flickered twice then blacked out. They snapped on their helmet lamps, but the small beams barely cut through the acid mist.

"Major system breakdown," said Galoot. "Let's hope the airlock still works."

"You're reading my mind." Zaz planted a foot to push off near the top of the ramp and suddenly became airborne, drifting up toward the ceiling. He saw Galoot float upward, performing an awkward frog kick.

"There's goes the artificial grav," said Zaz. "Carl, what's your status? We just lost ship's gravity."

"I'm swimming, headed for the upper bulkhead. I'll kick off the cross members."

Which meant that he was still in the engine or cargo bay, with very high bulkhead ceilings. "We won't leave without you," said

Zaz, trying to reassure him. Meanwhile, he had his own problems, grabbing for seams in the corridor paneling, trying to propel himself along. Galoot shoved himself hard along the walls to thrust himself forward, but his feet lost traction on the deck. The maneuver threw him into a clumsy somersault. They finally adopted a system by shoving off the ceiling and deck in a series of controlled crashes. When they reached the airlock, Zaz checked the panel and found it operative. The mini-sleds hovered a few feet off the deck. He swung himself inside, Galoot following. They left the hatch door open, then swapped turns wiping each other's helmets.

"Where's Carl?" asked Samantha. "Is he with you?"

"Don't worry about me," said Carl, with a huff. "I'm breaking the breaststroke record. Be there in a second. I can only see out of the corner of my helmet. Thanks, Galoot. If we ever get out of this, we're going to have words."

Before Zaz could say anything, Carl appeared at the hatch entrance, fumbling and reaching out. Zaz grabbed one of Carl's hands and pulled him in. Galoot yanked the hatch closed and stabbed the panel buttons. The panel lights appeared as a smear through Zaz's helmet visor, but he could make out the color change from red to yellow to green, showing de-pressurization. He heard Galoot's grunts, evidence that he was working the outer hatch lever. The next seconds brought a slight buffeting against his suit. *Open hatch.*

Zaz wiped his sleeve cuff over his helmet face but only managed to smear it further. "Gentlemen, I'm blind," he said. "I can't even find a mini-sled."

"I'd help you if I could find you," said Carl.

"Wish I could follow y'all's voices," said Galoot. "But I'm no better off. I think I got a sled handle, though. You're gonna have to grab onto me."

Three blind mice, thought Zaz, ruefully.

"Stop kicking and swinging your arms," said Dendy, loud and clear. "We've got you."

Zaz couldn't believe his ears. "Where are you, Dendy? And who is *we*?"

"Captain Alexandria Remy, at your service," said a raspy voice. "It's my ship. It's the least I could do."

"We're about three feet from you," said Dendy. "I warned you I'd come after you. Hold *still* and extend an arm!"

Ordinarily he would have cursed her out for disobeying his direct order. Under the circumstance, he decided to obey *her* direct order. He felt something wrap around the wrist portion of his suit, followed by a firm jerk. Within a minute he felt the sensation of being towed. His shoulder struck something hard, then he had the feeling of entering a vast open space. He realized immediately that he was on the end of a lifeline and that Dendy and Alexandria Remy had tied the three of them together and pulled them out of the hatch in tugboat fashion.

"That's it girls," said Samantha. "Nice and easy. They're stringing along just fine."

Zaz could do nothing but remain limp and hope that Dendy's aim was precise enough to get them to the *Shenandoah's* airlock. But then he knew how determined and skillful she was at handling emergencies. She'd had her moments of mental and emotional excesses, but when the situation became truly dangerous, she got good and motivated. Currently, he could think of nothing but praise for her quick-thinking and courageous behavior. The feeling was mutual for the *Intrepid* captain, who moments ago had been on the brink of death.

Once Dendy and the captain had herded them inside their ship's airlock, they pulled them together in a solid knot, so they could hold on to each other. Zaz felt the welcome return of his body weight, and removed his helmet. He took several deep breaths and unsnapped the seams and joints on his suit. With his helmet off, he helped Dendy and the captain out of their gear. Free of their suits, Zaz led the dash to the bridge, sweating and puffing all the way. He found Samantha on her feet, waiting for them. She let out a breathy sigh when they entered.

"All accounted for," said Samantha. "Get to your couches – we're outta here!"

Dendy helped the *Intrepid* captain into a couch, activating her seat bladder. Within 15 seconds, the crew were secured and braced under Zaz's watchful eyes.

Zaz slipped into the command chair. He took the helm controls, fired the starboard retro and pulled the *Shenandoah* around 180 degrees. He advanced the throttle to flank speed. "Sammy, I hope you plotted the *Intrepid's* course and found nothing up ahead."

"Nothing but deep space, Zaz. I sent an emergency broadcast with the coordinates. I vectored all ships out of the area."

The Exxon refueling station would be too far downrange to be effected by the blast. The zone was absent of traffic. Now if only Carl's charge did what it was supposed to do.

Zaz figured that thirty minutes would give them roughly 38,000 miles distance from the blast, with the combined opposite speed of each ship. Carl had the remote detonator in his hand, ready and willing. Samantha trained the aft gun scope on the ship, readjusting the focus as it retreated in the distance.

"I don't think you'll have time to outrun it," said Captain Remy, her eyes pink and watery, hair askew. "I know my ship – she's going to blow, and you can't take that chance."

Zaz frowned. "What do you suggest?"

"Find the biggest asteroid on the field and duck for cover. It's faster and safer."

Zaz blinked. "Sammy, anything close that can hide us?"

Samantha split the view monitor into port and starboard visuals, adjusting the gun scopes. "We've got one that size about 20 degrees off our port bow. ETA about four minutes."

Zaz could see it on the monitor. He swung the ship in it's direction, throttles still pegged. It was the longest four minutes of his life. He cut the engines and reversed thrust, dangerously close to a potato-shaped asteroid that dwarfed the *Shenandoah*. He crabbed the ship toward it, firing his retros to bring the hull up against the rogue object. The ship clunked with a shudder, then held steady with a creaking sound.

There's no such thing as the check's in the mail. Only when it's in the bank. "Any time, Carl," said Zaz.

Carl sucked in a deep breath. "Bye bye, you unholy piece of crap." Carl never had the chance to push the button on his remote. The monitor screen lit up with a blinding light. Samantha switched to an infrared filter. The exploding image on the monitor blossomed outward like a chrysanthemum, eventually filling the entire screen. The filtered colors dazzled the eyes, changing from white to yellow to orange, finally resolving into chartreuse. A moment later, a tremor rattled the *Shenandoah*. A piercing, static hiss filled the intercom speakers. Three heavy jolts followed that vibrated the bulkheads. An explosive electromagnetic wave sent the ship's monitor and panel into electronic seizures. The white burning light subsided, leaving a misty aspen glow.

Carl stared at his lap and rubbed his forehead. Dendy closed her eyes. Samantha slumped in her chair, her face filled with anguish. Galoot shook his head sadly.

Zaz had no words of solace. What could he say to soften the blow of what they'd just experienced? If he had found the *Intrepid* earlier he might have saved the other crew members. If the cargo hadn't exploded, three of them would be alive right now. If they hadn't taken on such a dangerous cargo they would have made it home safe and sound. If...if...if. Zaz felt as though he'd done so little, after doing so much. As for the performance of his crew, if it were in his power and station, he'd pin a medal on every one of them for services rendered above and beyond the call of duty. In that measure, they had surpassed victory.

Zaz looked at the *Intrepid's* captain, knowing that she had saved their lives. He gave her a thumbs up and a nod.

Captain Remy returned the gaze with listless eyes, and gave him a weak salute.

"Sammy, set a course for that refueling station. Just take the *long* way around."

"Aye."

THE MOON IS NOT ENOUGH

Captain Zachary Crowe reached Alpha deck and took a small foot tram to the bridge. He was last out of cryo sleep from a 26-hour bang pod jump. After entering the bridge, and much to his delight, he could see that Luna took up a full third of the front viewing portal, with Earth in the background, a swirl of blue and white. They'd come out right on target as planned — perfect telemetry.

Sitting at a horseshoe console at the forward nav station, Samantha King, navigation's officer, crouched over a pull-out counter, adjusting dials on her headset. She wore a cockeyed grin. That's all she was wearing, since she often went straight to the bridge after a jump, to check the life support and communication systems. He tossed a pair of Planet Janitor coveralls at her, averting his eyes while she donned the suit.

The men had always joked that Samantha's wild shrub of auburn hair took up a couple of zip codes, as well as her breasts. She had plain features, except for bright, inquisitive eyes and full lips. Crunching numbers appealed to her, and after missing out on a NASA position, she contracted her astronavigation services to any takers. She answered an add for Planet Janitor and joined Zaz's team. Since then, wherever she pointed the ship, it went there with no questions asked.

When Zaz turned around, Samantha chopped her hand sideways – her call sign for 'quiet.' She tapped her headset, indicating she was in the middle of a message.

Samantha scribbled some notes on a pad and then unhooked her headset. She sucked in a breath. "Well, bend my eyes and eat my hair," she said. "Checking the airwaves, I picked up some chatter ten minutes ago. It was coded and faint but I hacked through."

"So?"

"It's a job proposition – a high-tech corporation soliciting a salvage company. It's a plea for help, with a side-order of desperation."

Zaz looked over his shoulder, making certain they were alone. "How much desperation, and give me the abstract."

"The recovery offer is fifty thousand Imperials. Animules Incorporated, that new nanobot technology corporation, tried to hire Porter Space and Salvage to touchdown at Tranquility Harbor Mining Operations and recover a data case chock full of research material. You know, zip drives, holocubes and original patents and copyrights. Seems Animules didn't have any backups stored anywhere, and all the original soft and hard copy went with a Professor Burgess, who was the inventor and CEO. Burgess had a stall in the shopping mall rotunda, and he was there to solicit investors and sponsorship. You know, set up a display booth and hock his wares to the rich miners. He's missing, presumed deceased."

"Porter begged off?"

"No. Porter never responded, even after two attempts."

"How did you find the conversation?"

"I was scanning the frequencies, trying to pick up any news about the Harbor tragedy when I broke into the communication. You know me, when I catch the scent of money I'm all over it."

"Good find, Sammy."

Tranquility Harbor Mining Operations had just suffered a meteoroid shower less than 50 hours ago. Two thirds of the complex had been breached, destroying major structures and life support, resulting in 42 lost lives, over 500 evacuated, and untold injuries. Zaz was hired to do a fly over with the *Shenandoah*, mapping out a photo grid to record the damage. The International Security Agency would expect him to keep that commitment, and that's exactly why he was here at the moment. The rest of his crew were setting up the aerial survey cameras as he and Samantha spoke. This newer job was an easy drop and scoop, and they could coordinate it with their main mission. It was perfect.

"Raise the solicitor and offer our services," said Zaz. "Since you know what the offering bid is, raise it. You and Carl stay with the ship and perform the mapping survey while I'll take Galoot and Dendy down with the zip shuttle. If we get a green light, I don't see a problem."

"Can do, although I'd prefer not to work with Carl." She looked behind Zaz's shoulder. "Whoops." She donned her headset and began twisting dials and punching keys.

Zaz turned to see Dendy Dollar leaning against the bridge hatch entrance, examining her fingernails. Petite, cute and an environmentalist at heart, Dendy had spent the last two years interning aboard a Blue Peace research vessel. She'd loved the work, anything having to do with the sanctity of life, but her alleged preoccupations with the male crew became legendary – one-sided accounts, mostly from the men. Instead of attaining the competent role of science technician, she became a distraction. She left her Blue Peace dreams behind to take up a position as botanist-nurse with Zaz's crew. She was his newest employee and he had never gotten to the "push" stage with her."

Dendy cocked an eyebrow. "And just when was I going to be informed about this little drop and scoop? I thought we were booked up."

Zaz grinned. "A little side job popped up. It could mesh right into our schedule. How about a nice fat bonus?"

"Awe, cripes," said Dendy and stomped a foot. "I thought we were headed home. Why can't somebody else take care of this?"

"What's our motto, Dendy?" Zaz challenged.

Push.

"Our motto? Every time some corporation, agency or company pisses, we get stuck with the mop and bucket – that's our motto, to be blunt about it."

"No, we're planetary ecologists. Spills, fires, junk, toxins, all catastrophes are sworn concerns of ours. You knew that from the beginning. We owe it to ourselves, more than anyone, to at least query and makes ourselves available."

"Negatory," she huffed. "You want to pick up a bunch of documents for bureaucrats, and that might land you and all of us in a big bucket of stool. It's a junk mission. That's a disaster area down there, Zaz. I don't know if I want to see it."

Push had come to shove. "I'm ordering you, Dendy, because you're a professional and I need your help. Besides, we haven't finalized anything yet."

Dendy glanced over her shoulder. "You hear that, Carl?"

Carl Stromboli, the demolition expert, stepped into plain view from behind the bridge hatch. Zaz guessed he'd been standing there the entire time. They'd both ambushed him.

"I heard it," said Carl, pushing back a flop of greasy black hair out of his face. "You don't want me to go because there ain't no structures to blow or mountains to move. I object."

Zaz shook his head. "Overruled. You stay with Sammy and do the photo grid, and that's *if* we add this job to our roster." Zaz knew Carl had gypsy blood, so he would agree to another drop and scoop without too much fuss. Carl hailed from a large extended family in Italy. He used to light a lot of fires as a child, which gave his parents untold misery. "They didn't understand me," he once said. "It wasn't pyromania, it was a career move." He'd joined Zaz's crew with the express purpose of blowing structures and moving mountains. He christened himself "doctor of pyrotechnics."

The only other crew member aboard was their big mechanic, Galoot, and he went where the *Shenandoah* went. Otherwise he wouldn't know what to do with his hands, and he was the type that could fix a nuclear bang pod drive with a string and a band-aid. And Zaz's Russian ore freighter was often prone to string and band-aid repairs.

Samantha snapped her fingers for attention. She held up a finger, then the thumbs up sign. "Yes, we can provide that," she said into the mike, "just make sure you give us the correct address. And what was that code sequence again? Got it. And you say it's second floor, south wing? Animules Incorporated. Yes, that'll be fine." She turned to Zaz and grinned.

Zaz licked his lips. "We've got it?"

"Uh, huh. Seventy-five thousand. I got the location on the Animules shop, so I'll vector you in there. It has a security vault of some type, so have Galoot take a cutting torch, just in case you have to break and enter."

"Now, you see," said Carl. "I could use some explosives to blow that vault clean open."

Samantha sighed. "Yeah, and you'd destroy the contents of the vault, leaving us nothing to retrieve."

"We'll use gentle persuasion this time, Carl," said Zaz. "We can't risk damaging the vault contents."

"Suit yourself."

They now had a second official assignment, which was an easy drop and scoop. "Take us to Luna, right over the complex – south wing," he said. "We'll shuttle down, then you split off and take care of the mapping job. Stay on our regular frequency."

"Aye," said Samantha, and moved to the captain's chair, where she readied her hand on the hydrogen engine throttles. She flipped a few switches, which sent a shudder through the bulkhead. The *Shenandoah* began to move.

Zaz spoke into his wrist com. "Galoot, slight change of plans. Meet me in the shuttle bay and pack a plasma cutter and breaching tools. You are finished down there, correct?"

"Yeah, boss. We're ready to shoot. You got something else up?"

"A quick drop and scoop at the Harbor. Shouldn't take any more than a few hours – nice bonus."

"That's plum fat. I'll be there."

Zaz walked briskly out of the hatch, with Dendy skipping to catch up. He figured Samantha would get them over Tranquility Harbor in about 20 minutes, which would leave them 10 minutes to prep the shuttle, then fly down and land on a clean tarmac, suit up and exit the shuttle – another 30 minutes. If they ran it right and tight, both missions could be finalized at about the same time.

They took the lift down to the shuttle bay. Zaz deactivated the magnalocks on the landing gear of the zip shuttle, while Dendy entered the craft and began a pre-flight check. Galoot trotted across the shuttle bay, his heavy thuds echoing in the cavernous interior. He'd brought a plasma cutter and tool kit with him. Zaz rose up from the nose wheel and gave the big man a thumbs up, for clearly Galoot had run full out to meet up with his captain.

Zaz had particular fondness for his mechanic. According to legend, Galoot's first baby rattle was a piston from an old diesel engine. As the child grew, so did his interest in anything mechanical. After working in the spaceport ship yards for twenty years, he earned a masters certificate in aerospace engineering and function. When he joined Zaz's crew, Galoot was single, lonely and almost eight-feet tall and 480 pounds. Shunned by those who feared him, rejected by women for his awkward mannerisms, he found his home in the company of true friends aboard the *Shenandoah*.

"Just a slight departure from the job for a few of us," said Zaz, then filled him in on the particulars.

"I'm game, boss.

They entered the shuttle and took their seats. Zaz patched into the *Shenandoah's* bridge, while Dendy pressurized the cabin. "Com check. Sammy, anytime you're ready."

"I'm ten miles out from the complex, and I'm coming in slow and easy – lots of drones out there and a few war galleons in the airspace – don't want to upset the space grunts. I guess the military is doing their own survey of some type, so don't upset them. You can launch now and save some time."

"That's affirmative. I'll be as polite as whisper." Zaz brought the repulser and engines online, then opened the launch bay door. The shuttle lifted, a static corona discharge crackling beneath the ship. He swung the nose around and pulled a joystick back, lighting the aft thrusters. The shuttle passed through the bay door and out into space. Zaz saw the Harbor complex as a spec on the fringe of the Mare Tranquillitatis, and added more engine boost. He didn't want to come in too hot, attracting any unwanted attention. The military presence perplexed him for a moment. He would have suspected to see civilian contractors bringing in heavy industrial equipment.

Zaz dove the shuttle toward the outside edge of a pentagon-shaped structure, knowing that it was the shopping mall area that branched off the larger box-like mining warehouses and hangers. He looked for the south wing marker on the end of the structure, and glimpsed a small tarmac adjacent to a loading dock. He gave the aft engines a quick boost, sending them into a glide. He braked with the forward retros, simultaneously disengaging the gravity re-pulser. They dropped smoothly, braking just before contact. The shuttle touched down on the tarmac, kicking up a cloud of lunar dust. He cut the engines, turned on the exterior floodlights, even though enough sunlight allowed good visual acuity of the three-story-high structure.

It took them 10 minutes to get into full pressure suits. Dendy pulled out three extra oxygen packs from a locker and bagged them up. They performed suit checks, then Zaz opened the pressure lock. Passing through the outer pressure lock door and onto the dusty soil, Zaz checked his suit gauges, noticing the daytime tempera-ture was 190 degrees Fahrenheit. Dendy and Galoot reported full suit functions – normal readings. Zaz led the way, performing an awkward hop-step maneuver in the one-sixth gravity, heading for the nearest utility airlock entrance ten yards away. It was funny as he looked around, he expected to see some kind of outward signs of damage, like spiked craters, breached walls and torn structures. The first-floor viewing windows were dark; the second and third floor windows looked gray or slightly lighter in shade.

"Looks pretty normal, doesn't it?" said Dendy.

As Zaz stepped up to the utility hatch, he could see a small yellow strobe light blinking on and off. It meant the hatch had a fail-safe power feed mechanism. It was currently locked, but it had a touch panel for code entry. "Sammy, we're on the south side and I'm at a utility hatch to the mall area – I'll need that entrance code now."

"You have your shuttle floods on?"

"Yeah."

"Okay, I can see you, and I'm also getting a ping off your suit tracers. The code's alphanumeric – TRANQUITY155B."

"Affirm, I read that tranquility one-five-five-bee." Zaz pushed the touch pad buttons with the tip of his gloved index finger. The door vibrated then popped open. Zaz took the lead down a narrow corridor and stopped before another pressure hatch. He turned up the brightness on his helmet lamp. This hatch didn't require a code entry, so he threw the lever and pulled the hatch open. They stepped through. Galoot shut the hatch after them.

They'd entered a rectangular room, which had a bank of cabinets flanking one wall and utility benches and tools taking up the opposite side. It looked like some type of a ready room. The temperature had dropped to 140 degrees. Zaz approached the end of the room and worked the lever to open the next hatch. Another corridor. At the end he found a placard over a security door that read MAIN MALL ROTUNDA. Dendy guessed out loud that the mall complex was on the other side of the door. Zaz opened it, peered around the edge then swung it wide. They stepped through into the central mall hub, a circular area that contained shops around its periphery. His helmet lamp extended for 50 yards, and he could see a blanket of dust on the walkway panels. The roof extended up nearly 25 feet. He proceeded cautiously for several yards, able to discern large objects in their path. Bits of trash, boxes and papers, littered the interior of some of the shops. Broken furniture, mostly chairs and tables clogged the 15-foot wide walkway. Strewn shards of glass and glossy plastic set off streamers of refracted light.

"Looks like a panic scene," said Galoot. "Customers and shop owners caught in a stampede."

Zaz nodded, a useless gesture. "Sure does. From the reports, they didn't have much warning." Pause. "Sammy, you read?"

"Read you clear. I'm looking at an overlay right now, and you need to proceed to your right until you pick up an auto tram to the second floor. Then continue straight until you find shop 225A – That's the Anamule shop location."

"Affirmative."

Zaz rallied them into a swift skip-trot, following the walkway, dodging bits of flotsam. He saw his first structural damage – a blast hole that pierced the ceiling and gouged out a chunk of real estate, just to the left of the walkway inside the park area. A tree leaned precariously, its branches shattered and stripped of leaves. Three park benches were upended. Plasti-cement mushroomed out from a ten-foot wide crater. The concussion wave alone would have killed anyone near its impact. The atmosphere and oxygen had left the structure quickly, uprooting objects, until the debris had fallen and settled on the ground.

Zaz found the auto-tram easily, and began to trudge up to the next level. The best way up the incline demanded an awkward kangaroo hop, holding onto the tram guardrail. When they made it to the second floor, Zaz counted shop numbers, since he could see them by some of the operational overhead and shop lighting fixtures. It meant the second floor generator was still producing some power.

He found shop 225A after trekking a quarter of a mile around the walkway circuit. The louvered shop doors sat wide open, revealing a long room with jewelry showcases on each side. Some of the overhead track lighting flickered with spasms. Nothing seemed disturbed except for some promotional banners that hung limp from the ceiling, and large glossy marketing posters that sat cockeyed on the wall. Glossy photos, within broken frames, lay on the floor and counter tops. He headed for the rear of the shop, only glancing at the contents of the showcases, which revealed a strange collection of insects, reptiles and small mammals, either pinned on construction board, freeze-dried and propped in various poses, or submerged inside alcohol-filled jars.

"What kind of a shop of horrors is this?" asked Dendy. "What's with the dead animals?"

Zaz kept focused on the rear shop door, quickening his pace. He could swear he saw a blinking LED light on the door panel. "I'll wager they're nanobot creations," Zaz said. "You know, that DNA replication stuff, where they clone cells at super fast speeds. Hyper-linking, I think they call it."

"So they cook up little bugs in a soup," said Galoot. "Makes 'em feel like God to create little critters."

"That's about the size of – " Zaz caught his breath. He read the small door panel keypad display, which said OCCUPIED. He looked through the door portal and could see an anteroom filled with plastic cases and cardboard boxes. A massive stainless steel vault door occupied the rear of the anteroom, leading to another section. *Double air-lock.*

"Sammy," said Zaz, "I've got a double airlock and I'm at the first door. No keypad."

"Just a minute...okay, that's a supply room and it takes a code card. The vault beyond takes a combination, so you might have to cut through both. I have about another hour left on the mapping job."

Galoot opened his tool kit and moved in. Zaz stepped back to allow the big man access, then looked at his suit watch. They had one hour to retrieve the goods and extricate themselves. He felt a light pat on his shoulder, turned and looked at Dendy. She had a code card wedged between her gloved fingers.

"Where'd you find that?" he asked.

"You were standing on it."

"Jesus." He took it and ran it through the entry slot. The door shuddered, then popped open. *Pressurized.* That was a surprise. He stepped in, checked the inside door panel. Sure enough, it had a pressure breaker switch and it was in the "on" position. He motioned them inside and slammed the door. Galoot took the lead and ended up standing a few feet away from the heavy vault door at the rear of the anteroom. Zaz watched Galoot studying it, titling his head, reaching out and smoothing a hand over it.

Zaz checked his suit watch again. "Can we cut through, Galoot? Is it doable?"

"Not an industrial security vault, boss. This is a star liner walk-in safe that's been retrofitted for this complex. There's a another room-sized cavity on the other side."

"What does that mean?"

"It means it's a piece of cream cake. I know this make and model." Galoot snapped an extension on his plasma cutter, screwed in a nozzle and turned a valve on a small tank. He pulled a trigger and lit the cutter. "It's got four rod pistons coming off the central cam – top, bottom and two sides. I cut through the seams and shear the rods."

Zaz stepped back, pulling Dendy with him. Galoot wasted no time in searing slits in the vault door, working from the top and moving clockwise. Sparks flew, slag dropped like thick rope. When he finished, Galoot yanked hard on the vault handle twice before the door snapped free of its seams. Galoot opened the door up a crack. Zaz peered inside the interior, and indeed saw what looked like an enormous walk-in safe. He saw boxes of lab supplies, two electron microscopes, pressure tanks, demonstration kits, a large centrifuge and...

Human legs.

Zaz slammed the vault door closed. "We've got a body! Galoot, check the pressure on the other door. Make sure that pump is working at full capacity." Zaz checked his suit gauges, finding that they had a 19/79 oxygen-nitrogen mix. The inside air temperature read 55 degrees Fahrenheit. The atmosphere was livable, but it didn't mean they didn't have a corpse in the vault.

"Zaz, repeat that last line," said Samantha.

"I say, we have a body in the main security vault. I saw a pair legs protruding from behind a centrifuge and some pressure tanks. Vitals unknown. Alert the corp execs; they'll want to know about it."

"Right away!"

Galoot hurried back. "We've got standard pressure and it's holding. Temp and oxygen is okay. If that person is alive, how we gonna get 'em out of here?"

Zaz hadn't prepared for a rescue. If that was a corpse he had only to report it and give the coordinates to a recovery team. But to get a body out would require some fast and innovative techniques, if said body was hanging on by a thread.

"Galoot, as quick as you can, weld a brace over this seam to reseal it. That way we won't destabilize the vault atmosphere when you open the first hatch. Then beat it back to the shuttle for one of the generic pressure suits."

"Aye." Galoot picked out some welding rod from his tool pack and leaned his shoulder into the vault door. He told the others to do the same, putting what weight and strength they had against it. He burned a large glob of slag in the seam, letting it coagulate. He shoved hard on the vault door, testing it. It would have to do. He dropped the kit and headed for the first hatch with a lumbering skip, which left Dendy standing next to Zaz, her eyes wide with inquiry and apprehension. She sat the extra air packs down and splayed her hands in submission. "What do we need to do? Do you think that person is alive?"

"I'm going to need your help with this. Can you function?" Her face was a pallet of anguish.

"I think so," she said, drawing her shoulders back. "Tell me what to do."

"I have no idea what condition this, presumably a man, might be in when we gain entry. I want you to follow me in and provide a quick diagnoses – you're trauma qualified. He might be in shock or mentally unstable. He might be near death…or deceased. If he's alive and unconscious, I want to get him suited up and transported out – ASAP."

She blew a foggy sigh against her faceplate. "If he needs aid I'll know what to do. If he's beyond hope and gone…I'll let you know that too."

"That's fine." He patted her helmet.

Twenty minutes later Galoot appeared with an extra suit in the crook of his arm and another air pack. Zaz took the suit and stood poised at the vault door. Galoot checked the other panel and offered a thumbs up when the pressure stabilized to Earth-normal. Zaz backed off and let Galoot cut the brace out. He pulled on the vault handle, swinging it wide. He took Dendy's hand and pulled her through. As a precaution, Galoot slammed the vault door shut.

Zaz and Dendy performed three bunny hops to get to the rear of the vault, where a man lay in a fetal position with a lab smock pulled over his head. Zaz knelt and pulled back the smock, then made room for Dendy to squeeze next to him. She pulled back on the man's forehead, propping his eyes open, then brought her helmet light to his face. Next she lowered her face shield near his nose and watched for exhalation.

"Eyes responsive and he's breathing," she said quickly.

Zaz pulled on the man's ankles to get him clear of the wall. Dendy laid the suit down and opened up the quick-release torso seam. She twisted the helmet off, setting it aside. Zaz removed the man's shoes, and with a coordinated effort with Dendy, lifted the body up and onto the suit. They tucked the legs and arms into the openings, pulling, shifting. Zaz flipped a lapel back. The man wore a lab smock; the breast patch read Albert Cunningham.

"Samantha, here," came the voice. "We've got a major problem, Zaz."

"You can say that again," said Zaz. "But he's alive and we're getting him suited up. You don't have to tell me that we might be a little late. Did you inform corporate headquarters?"

"I just got royally chewed out by a Commander Ellison, 12th fleet space marines. I had to verify that we had permission to conduct a photo survey. They're not through with me, either. I'll get right back to you on the other. Be safe."

"Will do. I don't know who I have here. Could be the professor, could be an assistant. Want my helmet cam visual?"

"No. I'm running three visual-audio feeds right now, and I'm all thumbs."

"What's Carl doing?"

"He's asleep on an accelerator couch."

"That dumb, lazy bastard."

"Give me a physical description, so I have something to go on."

"Uh, Caucasian of average height, about 170 pounds with a fair complexion. Looks to be about sixty or so. He's wearing a smock with the name Albert Cunningham."

"Got it. One second...okay, according to corporate there were two assistants: a Reese Daily and an Albert Cunningham. You have an assistant there. Any sign of the others?"

"Not a peep. The shop, in fact the whole mall, looks deserted. We're going to evac this man out, hoping that he hangs on."

"Core temperature is down and his pulse is weak," Dandy threw in.

"Understood," said Samantha. "I'm still on the survey shoot. I'll give you a ding when I'm finished. Commander Ellison's back on – gotta go!"

Zaz had nearly forgotten their prime directive when he happened to glance at the vault corner and see a large stainless steel case. He retrieved it and read a small placard embossed on its side. ANAMULES INCORPORTED – TOP SECRET – EYES ONLY. Zaz grabbed the case, noticing that Dendy had the man suited up and his helmet on. She dialed in the oxygen and thermal life support controls on the suit. They pulled the man to his feet and dragged him to the center of the vault. They used the extra air packs to charge their suits. Before Zaz could agonize over how they would transport Albert Cunningham back to the shuttle, Galoot picked up the semi-comatose man and slung him over a wide shoulder, then headed out of the vault with a low stoop. Zaz and Dendy followed in the wake of Galoot's long, skipping strides. Zaz grabbed the torch-tool kit on the way out.

"I'm sorry I put up such a fuss," said Dendy. "I had no idea."

"We're not out of this yet," said Zaz, trying to keep his footing without going down.

"Zaz, priority, come in," said Samantha.

"Read you."

"Zaz, I've just been rudely informed that the Tranquility Harbor Mining complex is under martial law, declared a disaster area. I'm cleared to finished up my survey. But no one is supposed to be down there. I'm going to try and smooth this over somehow. I haven't admitted to anything yet. I'm so sorry. I should have gotten status on this from the beginning. It's my fault."

Dendy exhaled a small shriek. "I just *knew* it! Right from the start. Now we're in a bucket of crap."

Zaz felt his heart drop into his stomach. If the military caught him on the premises, he could be prosecuted for criminal trespass and looting, or even fired upon. Tranquility Harbor was a disaster area. The last thing the International Space Administration wanted was a bunch of privateers rooting around a catastrophe site. His next decision determined the fate of his crew. Have Samantha lie or admit to nothing, or tell the truth and take their swats. There was time when wearing the captain's bars provoked a feeling of respect, pride and accomplishment, where, seemingly, nothing could go wrong and all the stars in the universe were gloriously aligned. Now, because of a trivial oversight, he'd put his crew in danger by neglecting to cover his ass. He knew what he had to do.

"Sammy, admit to the truth. Which is total ignorance of the situation. Tell them we have a live rescue in progress and we're on our way out with the patient. Offer them my head if it'll gain us any leniency."

"I'm on it, Zaz!"

They ran into a snoop drone on the second floor walkway. The turkey-sized flier pulled in front of them, hovering and adjusting its optic eye. It flew backwards, keeping pace with them. Zaz used one hand to support Albert Cunningham's legs on the way down the auto-tram. Galoot nearly pitched forward and lost his load. The military drone circled their heads, opting for the best angles to view the four civilians. Zaz would have liked nothing better than to swat it out of air, but right now it had more authority to be where it was than he. At least they would see the confirmation of a bona fide rescue.

They stopped after entering their first service corridor. Dendy checked the man's vitals and confirmed that he still looked weak but was beginning to stabilize. They continued on, passing through the hatches until they emerged outside. The snoop drone had disappeared momentarily, reluctant to follow them through the confines of the service corridors. It appeared again outside the complex, but kept its distance.

When they reached the shuttle, Zaz pressurized the airlock, and ushered them inside. They wiggled out of their suits, then freed their patient. Dendy pulled down a wall bunk and opened up a first aid kit. They soon had Albert Cunningham strapped in and resting under blankets, with an IV drip taped to his arm.

Zaz hurried to the pilot's station and prepped for lift-off. Galoot strapped in, wiped his face on his shirt sleeve. Galoot was hot and soaked from the trek, but right now a change-out was not possible.

Galoot blew a whirlwind sigh. "Well, they're ain't anybody big enough in prison to beat me up. Just one of the little blessings, I guess."

Zaz raised Samantha. "Precious cargo aboard. What's your coordinates?"

"North end of the Harbor complex at the moment," replied Samantha, "coming your way. Don't grav-lift until you see the whites of my eyes. I'm flanked by two war galleons, and they're watching my every move. I think we get to live, but we're headed for a royal ass-chewing – full investigation style."

"That's affirmative, chick waiting for mother hen. Good job, Sam. If we make it out of this alive, tell Carl he's fired."

"You mean for the sixth or seventh time? By the way, expect a little bonus for your passenger. Corp's paying an extra fifty thousand for his safe return."

Zaz mimicked Galoot, "Well that's plum fat. That might just cover our trespass fine. Too bad we didn't get the professor; that reward would have gotten us some great lawyers."

"Yeah we'll need 'em to get out of this pickle," said Samantha, "They had a standing reward of a half a million for the professor's safe rescue. Would have been a political feather in our cap, too."

Zaz looked up through the roof portal and could see the bulk of the *Shenandoah* braking under hydrogen engines just above them. It blacked out a wide section of the star field. *Missions accomplished*. Maybe the last ones.

Zaz poised his hand over the repulser toggle. Before he could grav lift, he felt a pat on his shoulder and turned. Dendy stood behind him, wearing a jaw-stretching grin.

"What's up, little cakes?" he asked. He gave her hand a squeeze.

"Our patient has come around – he's responsive and talking. He says thank you profusely for his rescue. He didn't think he was going to make it. By he, I mean *Burgess*. We have the professor on board! Seems he grabbed an assistant's smock to cover up."

Zaz's hand slipped from the toggle. He tried to speak but the words wouldn't come. He could only see Galoot's and Dendy faces, two of the most incredulous expressions he'd ever seen.

PLANET JANITOR

CUSTODIAN OF THE STARS

CHAPTER ONE

MISSION OF MERCY

TEN THOUSAND MILES out of Triton's atmosphere, Captain Zachary Crowe was running a final systems check for the jump home when the nav panel lit up – incoming message. Samantha King, navigator of the *Shenandoah*, stiffened in her seat when she caught sight of the flashing signal.

"Are we available, Zaz?" she asked.

"Not really, but it might be important. Put it on intercom so Dendy and Carl can listen in."

Samantha accepted the subspace priority call. The image of a man with a gray crew cut appeared on the grid. Commander Tobias Ellison of the 12th Fleet, Air Assault Marines, sat in a float chair, facing the camera. A long scar cut a trench down the front of his neck.

Zaz eased up from his deck chair and stood out of courtesy, wondering why he was being hailed by such a high-ranking military officer.

"I've reached Captain Crowe of the *Shenandoah*?" said the commander, his speech slightly garbled.

"You have, sir," Zaz responded.

"You're not representatives of Blue Peace, I hope. I had a difficult exchange with them last year. It seems they're adverse to taking risks where lives are concerned."

"No, sir. We're Planet Janitor, environmental custodians, though we've been contracted by Blue Peace before."

"We found your location on the KED. You were chosen because we have no other vessels in that sector. One of our deep space observation platforms has picked up an inbound stray asteroid of approximately three-point-two million metric tons. Preliminary calculations indicate it's on direct trajectory with two of our flight corridors. The Houston-International Space Complex and the Lunar to NASA Observation Platform are in a direct line for transit. Probable contact-interception is one hundred percent."

Zaz frowned. They weren't looking for another job at the moment, but he didn't want to sound indifferent or unsympathetic. Still, he had a few nagging questions and concerns. "Why can't traffic be diverted from those flight corridors until the object has passed?"

"You ask the organizations that question. They're running passenger, supply, and maintenance flights to those locations. You can't shut down those corridors indefinitely. Besides, the International Space Authority is likely to throw a fit if they discover we allowed a rogue object to approach so closely to our space infrastructure. This is Space Defense Directorate business. We want this handled."

Yeah, it's your business and that's why you're calling me. Although, his façade began to crack. "How much time are we talking about?"

"A little over two hours standard before it passes your vector point. We dispatched two cruisers and two heavy galleons from our Mars base. They're on an intercept course in case it gets past you."

"Half my crew is Earth-side," said Zaz. "You've caught me shorthanded. We've just come off a Triton mapping expedition and were expecting to make the jump home. I don't know if we're the proper solution to this, or if we have the – "

"According to our records, you have munitions onboard," said Ellison, ignoring the objections. "A strong enough C-6 charge will deflect the solid body asteroid. We're talking about at least a two-degree shift in course trajectory – a very simple maneuver. We're asking for your voluntary enlistment to perform a low hazard task for your government."

Which meant this would not be a hire-for-profit mission. The last minor asteroid he'd knocked out of the solar system netted him 50,000 Imperials. However, there was something more to consider than just monetary concerns. The situation tugged at his moral center. There had to be a compromise.

"Twenty-five thousand Imperials," said Zaz. "Compensation for the cost of fuel, in addition to covering the workload and effort put forth by my crew."

"I would hate to cite the Humanities Act at this point, Captain Crowe."

"The Humanities Act also indicates that a crew should not risk bodily harm under any circumstances."

Ellison frowned. "I didn't expect you to barter over this. I'll agree to the terms. However, I do so reluctantly."

Zaz gave him a pert nod. "Send us the coordinates and telemetry data patch. We'll set up an interception."

"Very well. After a mission-accomplished entry, you can expect a transfer of funds to your account and a written commendation, which will be added to your civilian record. Apprise us of your progress and any new information you glean from the encounter. We're sending the data patch now. We're counting on you. Ellison, commander 12th Fleet, out."

Zaz let out a gale-force sigh. This would not sit right with his crew. The remaining crewmembers were Earth-side, waiting at the Long Beach Port facility. They had been expecting the *Shenandoah's* immediate return. Both groups had been anticipating some well-deserved time off after having spent the last seven months (off and on) in the solar system. In that time, they had managed to stack up nine missions: four space debris removals, two ore transfers, two satellite retrievals, and one mission of mercy. The *Shenandoah*, a converted Russian-built ore freighter, was long past due for a scheduled maintenance check; her hydrogen tanks were low – a prolonged burn would sap their fuel supply.

Samantha flipped back a wild lock of bright red hair. She ignored the data input, turning to face her captain. "I can't believe you agreed to this, Zaz. You heard it yourself – they have a bead on the rock and are fully prepared to take it out. That's what our orbital Defense Directorate is for – eliminating imminent threats."

He wasn't listening. He could only think of the threat an impact that size would have plowing through traffic lanes, and the destruction it might wreak if it fragmented.

A few minutes later, Dendy, Planet Janitor's petite botanist, scurried through the bridge hatch and curled her fists on her hips. She gave Samantha an accusing glare, even though she had clearly heard Zaz making the deal over the intercom. "Say it ain't so, Sammy. I thought we were making the pod jump for terra firma."

"Don't look at me. I'm only the nav officer. Better talk to your captain."

Dendy sidled up to Zaz. She put one hand on his forearm, like she always did when addressing him.

"Aren't you getting a little tired of riding in on the white stallion every time someone sends out a distress call?" she asked. "It's not like you can't afford to be choosy. We've more than filled up our quota for this year. Haven't we earned that vacation?"

He gazed into her light brown eyes, losing his train of thought for a moment. "It's not a question of what I want or need. That commander could have pulled rank on me and enforced the Humanities Act. Besides, you know our mission statement – we're stewards, sworn to preserve and protect any habitable environment against all threats. That includes defending the sanctity of all humankind in matters of peril or suffering. Sometimes we have to take it on the chin."

"Take it on the chin?" said Samantha. "Zaz, I'm punch drunk from taking it on the chin."

Zaz leveled a hardened stare at each of them. "You tell me how it would feel, knowing that any station or ship took a direct hit because we, or the Defense Directorate, failed to stop an incoming asteroid. I'm sure you would have no trouble arranging the funerals and replacing destroyed property."

Dendy closed her eyes. "You would have to put it that way, wouldn't you? I guess it's the right thing to do, even if we are pulling the short straw."

Carl Stromboli, the demolitions expert, stomped through the hatch, puffing hard from his dash to the bridge. "Out-fucking-rageous," he said. "Looks like I've got a BB to blow. You crunch any numbers on this thing yet? Why is everybody standing around looking like shell-shocked mutes?"

Zaz was the first to move, taking a seat in his accelerator couch. "Sammy, get our gun scope and sensors on this object. See if you can verify dimensions – size, velocity, density and trajectory. I need rendezvous estimation, but I need some really tight numbers first."

"Aye." Samantha swiveled back around and ran her fingers over a keypad, but not without giving Carl an I-can't-stand-you look. "Just give me a few minutes and I'll have the numbers for you."

Dendy hurried up to the forward station and took a seat at the console. "I'll monitor our performance and engine data," she said, looking to the others for approval. "I don't want to be a fifth wheel around here."

Zaz nodded. "PSI and fuel are critical – watch for redlines on the performance gauges."

Samantha keyed in the scope and sensor data, bringing the information up on the main viewer. "Okay, got her," she said. "She's coming in fifteen degrees off our starboard bow. Mass is 3.2553 million tons, with a diameter in excess of eleven hundred feet. That's awfully light for a nickel/iron body, and spectral analysis confirms it. Density is undetermined at this point. She's got a perceptible wobble about her linear axis, about twenty revolutions per minute. But she's coming in very hot. Velocity is about twenty kilometers per second, or about forty-five thousand two hundred and ninety miles per hour."

Zaz knew that such speed would push the limits of the *Shenandoah's* engines. Catching up to the beast would be a problem, even if they had a lead.

Carl whistled. "Damn, at that size she'll need two megapack charges, and we'll have to use one of the big drones to get in there for a standoff shot." He rushed toward the exit. "So much to do, so little time!"

The explosives expert was now in his element. Carl Stromboli lived for igniting combustibles, setting off charges, and imploding structures. He wouldn't waste any time rushing down to the pyrotechnics lab to pack his charges and rig the detonators.

Zaz fired the retros, bringing the ship around in a stable profile by using the stars as a reference. He cut the drift, bringing the ship to a halt. The huge port and starboard viewing windows gave him an unobstructed view of space so he could confirm what the gun scope and sensors were seeing. He ignored the brightest stars and picked out a small pinprick he suspected was their target rock. There was a slight variation in its position after a few minutes, proof that it was moving toward them, nearly head-on.

Samantha swiveled in her chair. "We don't have enough fuel for the burn we'd need to catch it. Even with a lead and punching her in the guts, we can't do it. Remote detonating a bouy is out of the question – not precise enough."

"This is already starting to look bad," said Dendy.

"We'll use gravity assist and slingshot around Triton," said Zaz. "Calculate the burn for orbit and intercept."

Samantha slapped her forehead. "I didn't think of that."

"That's why he's captain, Sammy," said Dendy, almost swooning over Zaz.

Samantha worked fast. She calculated the telemetry data for an orbital burn around Triton and programmed the data into the computer guidance system, setting up the autopilot for the maneuver. Zaz felt a vibration travel up through the deck. The ship turned. The edge of Triton came into view as the ship accelerated into its gravitational arc. They could see three quarters of the moon, its water, ice and nitrogen make-up obvious; it looked like a blotchy, multi-colored snow cone. There were active geysers on its surface, tiny smudge-like plumes that mushroomed up into the atmosphere.

"How are we looking, Sammy?" asked Zaz. "My head's vibrating. I can't see the grid lines on the screen."

"We're tight in the pipe. Just about ready to end one hundred and fifty-two seconds of burn..." She squinted as she read the data. "On my mark...engines off! Approaching thirty-eight thousand and climbing."

"Gettin' the whip," said Dendy

The task would be staying in tight synchronous orbit, while making a steady climb in velocity. The crew took their stations: Dendy readied the gun scope, training the sensors on the object; Carl prepared the bomb drone; Samantha manned the ship's engine console. Zaz remained in his command chair, his hand poised over the three slide-lever throttles on the armrest.

"Approaching periapsis," Samantha called out. "Fifteen second auto burn for maximum velocity."

As the moon's gravitational pull intensified on the ship, the digital velocity readouts on the screen climbed in a dizzying blur. Five minutes later they were traveling at optimum speed, barreling around the far end of moon.

As the *Shenandoah* snapped out of the gravitational field, they were traveling in excess of 49,000 miles per hour. Whether it was a computer miscalculation or a gravitational anomaly, they'd jumped the gun and come out in front of their target. It meant a breaking burn – more fuel expended.

Dendy said, "Okay, target is one degree off our port stern, seven-point-three thousand miles out, and moving fast. Velocity is now forty-five thousand, two hundred and fifty. She's slowed down a bit – must have shed some mass."

Zaz watched the graph as he toggled the reverse retros for a tempered burn. He tapped the throttles back gently, incrementally slowing the *Shenandoah*. The object behind them closed the distance. Dendy brought up a visual of the object on the screen. Carl swore. Samantha gasped. Dendy remained dead quiet, her attention fixed on the data readouts.

Zaz could not believe what he was seeing. The asteroid looked like a fat dumbbell, flipping end over end. The edges of the thing were hurling dust, ice and larger chunks of debris in a bizarre figure eight pattern around the object. It emitted a blue plasma disruption – and every so often threw off static discharges that looked like miniature lightning strikes. He'd seen contrails on comets before, but nothing that resembled this fireworks display. He couldn't believe that a stone object with such a radical, unbalanced configuration could maintain its shape without flying apart or disintegrating – unless it had a super dense core and a heavy gravitational field.

"Jesus," said Samantha. "It's the first time I've ever seen a flying soup bone. Dendy, I hope you're recording this."

"I have been the whole time. It's one for the books."

They watched as the object passed slowly in front of their port viewing window. At a thousand yards, the sight of it took the breath away: a lopsided tumbling mass of blue plasma on a reckless ride through deep space.

Zaz flicked the throttle once, twice, thrice. He shut the retros off and held his breath. They were now even with the object, running a parallel course. "What we have here, folks is an asteroid with a sublimation coma. That's the remnants of a comet on its deathbed, burning off all its gases until it's nothing more than a solid core. We caught this one in its transition period."

Carl grimaced. "I don't care if the fucking thing is a baby buggy with chrome spoke wheels. I've got a package to launch filled with enough C-6 to knock that whatever-you-want-to-call-it into the next galaxy."

Dendy looked up from her console, her face pensive. "I don't think you want to do that. No, I *know* we don't want to do that. It's crosshatched. I've never seen so many surface irregularities – cuts, fissures, mounds. Zaz, we have a rubble pile here! Correction – make that two rubble piles connected by some kind of equatorial mass, possibly an oblong iron core."

The news could not have been worse. One could not detonate explosive ordinance on or near a rubble pile – a collection of compacted stony meteoroids – without it flying apart. Dangerous shrapnel would be sent in every direction, possibly knocking out defense platforms, satellites, and even commuter spacecraft.

Carl's face pinked. "Check your sensors again. There's no such thing as a bunch of rocks flying around space looking like that."

Dendy glared at Carl. "That's not a solid asteroid, Stromboli. It's a compacted mass of hundreds of objects."

"We'll defer to Dendy's judgment on this," said Zaz.

Carl reared up from his chair. "Don't tell me I went through all that for a goddamned hang fire! Now what the hell are we going to do? Cuss it out of the system?"

"You're just pissed because you can't blow something up," said Samantha.

"Shut up, the both of you," said Zaz. "Samantha, get Ellison on line and tell him what we're up against. We've got one maneuver up our sleeve that might work."

Samantha relayed the message, but like the other crewmembers, her eyes were drawn to Zaz with what looked like terror. No one said anything for a long while, until Carl couldn't stand it any longer.

"You're not thinking about ramming that bitch."

"Nobody said anything about ramming," said Zaz, knowing the *Shenandoah* weighed almost two hundred thousand tons and packed the equivalent of a hundred and fifty million horsepower. "I say a good strong shove would do the trick."

"Zaz," said Samantha, "the son-of-a-bitch is somersaulting end over end. It'd pound our ship into a tin can if you got the wrong angle of attack."

Zaz was on the verge of losing his temper. He knew what he had to do. He had no tolerance for hesitation or paranoia right now – he was committed.

"Zaz knows what the heck he's doing!" Dendy shouted. "We can come in at the midline – there's less rotation there. Besides, stop and think about it – we know the structural makeup and behavior of this beast. If we let this thing get past us, the military is bound to do something real stupid, like fragging it into a bunch of pieces."

Carl and Samantha exchanged fitful glances, but made no further protests. Zaz set his jaw and lit the retros. He used minute pulses to move the ship laterally, careful to watch the ship's profile on the viewing screen. It amounted to a precise choreographed maneuver, side-slipping the ship toward the revolving mass.

As the asteroid loomed closer, its menacing size put the crew on edge. It nearly made Zaz dizzy to look at it through the huge window panel. It was no easier on the equilibrium watching it on the screen graph.

The 1,200 foot-long bulk of the *Shenandoah* inched closer to the behemoth. Debris struck the hull, igniting in tiny pyrotechnic sparks. The nav console began to hiss with an electrostatic white noise. Zaz gave the bow retro a squirt, bringing the huge nose of the ship in toward the center mass of the asteroid.

Samantha called off proximity data: "Ten meters and closing… five meters. Two meters…initiating contact on my mark…now!"

The ship gave a jolt. Zaz fired the outward jets, shoving the ship's starboard bow into the rotating mass. A nauseous vibration traveled through the hull. The deck plates rattled. The interior of the bridge filled with a sound like a giant bell ringing. Zaz knew the double hull would hold up against the friction. He just prayed that the asteroid would not break into two smaller bodies.

"No course deviation," Samantha shouted above the noise. "We have full hull integrity, but it won't last."

Zaz gave full power to the outboard retros – a twenty second burn.

"Negative deviation," Samantha cried out. "It's not enough."

Of course, it wasn't enough. The retros were attitude thrusters. He needed a lot more juice to shove this hulking pig off course. "Brace for main engine start," he called out, knowing that there was no time for his crew to transfer to the accelerator couches.

He shoved all three engine throttle-levers forward. The ship wobbled and lurched. There was a muffled roar inside the bridge, combined with a terrible wrenching sound. Still, he increased the power to the main engines, listening as Samantha warned that they were exceeding the limits of their hull's integrity.

"We've got a course shift!" Dendy cried. "One-point-seven degrees. Kick her in the guts, Zaz!"

He maxed the throttles, certain he was pushing redline.

The ship cocked dangerously, puncturing through the asteroid's surface. Part of the rotating mass came around to pound the hull. The crew's necks pounded back against their headrests. Carl's harness snapped, nearly pitching him from his seat.

Zaz ignited the retros, simultaneously cutting the main engines. The *Shenandoah* shuddered with a last violent jolt. The hull ripped away from the spinning mass, awash in a storm of ice chunks and dust. A sudden quiet came upon the bridge. Everyone was silent, still frozen to their consoles. Zaz noticed his hand white-knuckled on the controls. He tasted blood on his lip.

Dendy broke the silence: "Two-point-four degree course shift! I repeat: the foreign body is now on an adjusted course change. Sensors indicate that it is intact."

Carl straightened in his seat, fingering the torn harness. "Promise me you'll never do anything like that again."

"No promises," said Zaz. "Although next time, I'll give it a few more minutes thought. Sammy, any damage?"

"We didn't get out of it unscathed. I'm reading an outer hull breach. I'm guessing we've got some nasty scratches and dents too – you can throw in a paint job."

Dendy put her head down on the console. "In case anybody's morbidly curious," she muttered, "we don't have enough braking fuel for the trip home. That last burn sucked our tanks. You can forget about a jump to anywhere – that's out of the question too."

Zaz slumped in his seat. He knew from the start such a possibility existed. It was an equitable trade; they were adrift at the edge of the solar system with no gas station in sight, in exchange for the privilege of having freed up two important flight corridors. At least that's the way he looked at it.

"Ain't that just peachy!" said Carl. "We're stranded out here like chumps in a broken down ship."

Zaz sighed. "Sammy, hail Commander Ellison and tell him the objective has been met. Then give him the object's new trajectory– they need to divert all sub-space cross traffic. Tell him to expedite a fuel barge to our location ASAP."

"Aye, I'll call it in as a code yellow – vessel assist."

Dendy unbuckled her seat harness. "Well, tag us late for home, guys. Anybody up for a game of spider-checkers?"

CHAPTER TWO

DREAMS OF AVARICE

Captain Zachary Crowe sat with his crew in the spaceport bar. He fumbled through his hardcopy ledger, absently sipping from a bottle of champagne. His geologist, Lyle Wagner, peered at him through the multiple lenses of an Optipak, strapped to his head. His eyes looked like two blue saucers behind the contraption.

"Why couldn't we make a few low Earth orbits and haul some more scrap, skipper?" asked Lyle. "If you're still considering that nickel rock out there, I'd give it another thought. It might be too labor intensive to cut her up in piecemeal chunks." He took a drink and raised his glass in salute. "By the way, nice job taking out that rogue. We knew it was something important when you didn't show up on time."

Zaz had had his eye on huge nickel-iron mass wandering on the fringe of the asteroid belt. It would garner a small fortune if they could lasso it and splice it up without too much trouble.

"Give thanks to the military on that; they took the credit for it."

"Damn shame," said Lyle.

Zaz flicked his index finger in the air. "For one thing, every trash collector who has a shuttle is snatching metal scrap out there. It's a crowded sky." He flicked his middle finger next. "Second, you're talking about a nickel-iron asteroid that's free for the taking – we can carve it up piecemeal. We stick an owner's flag in it and it's ours, and just like a bank, we can make periodic withdrawals." Another finger. "Third, the *Shenandoah* is no bucket, thank you very much. I don't care how smart you are, Lyle. There's no reason to insult your ride. She's your home too."

"Sorry," said Lyle. "Wrong choice of words."

Zaz might have seemed terse, but it was not without reason. Sure, the *Shenandoah* was 40 years old, but she was a stout Russian-built ore freighter. There were only three surviving in existence, and one of them reposed in the Wisconsin Aeronautical Museum.

"Fourth," continued Zaz, "that little asteroid can help serve as a down-payment on something else."

Carl stared at his missing fingers. "You thinking about buying another ship, Cap? If so, I'd consider it a privilege, if you were to ask me, to this bitch to slag. I mean, I'd give her full ship's honors, with an epitaph and everything. You have to admit, she's old and draggin' her ass." Carl looked down at the bar table then pushed his greasy black hair from his face. He couldn't meet Zaz's glare.

Another insult directed at his ship!

"I'm not buying another freighter," said Zaz, "and I'm really surprised you'd enjoy taking our grand old lady out like that, Carl. I've got nearly a half million imperials, two pounds of raw diamond crumbs, and another three hundred thousand in alloy. I can pick up Alph, the asteroid for – "

"Oh, gawd." Samantha pulled up from her seat. "Ride me hard and put me away wet, he named the fuggin' rock!" She stabbed a finger across the table. "Okay, Carl, pay up. That's fifty you owe me – none of your IOU shit."

Carl winced as he counted out the bills into her open palm. She stuffed them in her cleavage without another word and then fell back into her seat. He stared angrily at her, his frustration heightening as his eyes drifted to her hefty bosom.

"Like I said," Zaz continued, "that asteroid is a pure pot of gold, and so far it's escaped notice. That will give me enough leverage to make my bid." Zaz pulled a galactic real estate pamphlet from his jumpsuit pocket and tossed it on the table.

Paddy, the ship's zoologist, narrowed his eyes on the dog-eared brochure. He pulled a dirty yellow tam from his head to scratch at his buzz-cut scalp. "Okay, I'll bite, Zaz. What is this big purchase? Care to enlighten us?"

Zaz took a pull on his champagne, licking his lips. "It's ninety percent terra-formed, with a habitable target date of two years from now. Of course, there are only three prime locations suitable for settlement. That just makes it all the more exotic. I figure a combination refueling station and theme park would pull the most potential out of the investment."

"Damn," said Carl. "Spit it out so we can lick it up."

"Titan," said Zaz, opening the brochure and jabbing his finger at the survey map. He looked from face to face, trying to read the expressions of his crew. They looked like they had a case of collective indigestion; none seemed too thrilled with the proposition.

Lyle broke the spell, looking over the rims of his lenses. "You want to purchase a moon?"

"No, not the whole thing."

Dendy wobbled to her feet and put her hands on her hips. "Heck, Zaz, if you wanted to buy a small body, why didn't you just ask me? I'd charge you a lot less than millions of imperials." She sat down and cocked an eyebrow at him.

Samantha was not to be outdone. "For that kind of cabbage," she said, her hands lifting her ample breasts, "I'd let you tie me up and have at it." She let loose with a peal of bird-like squawks. The others joined in with chortling fits. Someone gagged. Carl slapped the table, nearly upsetting the drinks.

Zaz didn't understand it. They weren't laughing at their meal ticket, were they? His crew had received fifty percent of everything he had made in the past four years. All he wanted was a little respect and understanding.

"Awe, lighten up a little, Zaz," said Dendy. "If you get any stiffer you're going to burst out of the top of your head."

Maybe he was taking all of it too seriously. They *were* celebrating the success of the asteroid intercept mission. His demeanor easing somewhat; he allowed himself a small chuckle. The girls had offered themselves to him, even if it had been a joke. He kind of had a thing for Dendy – she'd used her wiles on him in the past year, strutting around with that perfect little body and nuzzling him when they were alone.

Carl slapped Zaz's shoulder. "That's better, Cap. Hell, it's the first time you've ever told us about any life-dreaming things. But I was serious as a heart bust for wanting to scuttle the old gal."

Galoot clomped through the bar in their direction. The old-style neon lights shined off his baldpate. He took up as much room as two men and made no excuses for it. The giant bulled his way through the crowd, carrying a small blonde girl over his massive shoulder. The girl's dangling feet struck the faces of several patrons as they passed. But no one insulted him or complained; not to Galoot. Weighing almost a quarter of a ton and nearly eight feet tall, the man carried a small gravity field around him.

Galoot pulled two stools up to the crew's table, then twirled the girl around and plopped her on his knee like a ventriloquist's dummy. The girl giggled, looking cross-eyed at Zaz.

Space trash.

Galoot peered at the table's occupants. "Who told a joke without me?" he asked, looking from face to face. "What's so pee-in-your-pants funny?"

Paddy removed the dirty yellow tam from his head again and furiously scratched the gray crew cut. It had to be lice, thought Zaz.

"Our captain has gone lunar," Paddy volunteered.

Galoot yawned. "Lunacy? That's ok; we're all a little nuts. What do you think of Carybell?" He held her up like a toy doll. "She can't walk too well right now because she took a cheap moon flight. They didn't have any artificial gravity in the shuttle bus, so it made her a little muscle dumb."

Carybell's head lolled to the side. She keeled over, heading straight for the floor. "Whoops," said Galoot, snatching her up before she hit the deck. He propped her in the crook of his arm then uncapped a bottle of Demon Whiskey. Carybell let loose with a raucous burp.

Zaz watched as Samantha and Dendy exchanged knowing glances. They knew damn well that Galoot hung around the spaceports eyeing little wobbly girls that had just come off short flights. He'd exaggerated about the girl being muscle-dumb from a recent flight – she was too drunk to stand. But the port authorities never messed with him, and so far, Galoot had never violated the respect of any women that Zaz was aware of. Planet Janitor's policy was one of decorum and self-restraint. The giant had always kept those rules sacred.

Lyle wiped his Optipak lenses off with a napkin. Without looking at Galoot, he said, "Captain Crowe wants to buy the moon, Titan – lock, stock and barrel. What do you think of that, your Prodigiousness?"

"I am not buying the entire moon."

Galoot screwed up his face. "You mean one of Saturn's pebbles? Well, that sounds plum cool. When are we going? Don't we have another gig to do? Wait a minute." Galoot looked struck down for a moment. "Gee, Boss, don't we get to go with you? Are you going to be a king or president out there all by yourself?"

"I want to go, too!" said the blonde Carybell-doll.

Galoot put a slab-like hand over her mouth.

Zaz waggled his head. "No, no, we're not headed out there yet. I'll admit that I'd like to retire soon. You're all invited to join me if you want, but talking about this is a little premature, don't you think? I still have some fines to pay off and a few court appearances to make." He stood up and raised a glass. "Let's toast to Planet Janitor, celebrating the strides this little company has made. We have more to be thankful for than we realize. To my crew – a motley bunch of junkyard jocks if ever there was one!"

They bolted to their feet, raising their glasses and bottles. The Carybell-doll hit the deck.

"To Planet Janitor!" they chorused.

They sat back down. Galoot picked up his prize and attempted to feed her a sip of moon brandy, but she scowled and pushed it away.

Samantha put her hands under her chin, looking wistful. "Remember when we were called out to the barrier reef to arrest that run-away algae propagation? We air-dumped six hundred tons of chlorine on the reef. We sure killed that bad jelly!"

"Yes," said Paddy, "at the expense of decimating a small fish population, not to mention some healthy corals, crustaceans and kelp beds. I couldn't believe Australia demanded a formal apology."

Lyle titled his head. "It hardly compares with the havoc Carl caused in Southern California. He says, 'Hey, a little controlled back-fire is the way to neutralize the main bug nest.' So what does he do? He lights a backfire that gets out of control, then drops napalm on another line that goes up, then the two merge into a firestorm. It was a good thing we got retard on it before the National Forest burned to the ground."

"Ah, so what?" said Carl. "The drought made all those conifers anemic – they were already dying by the thousands. Got rid of the critters though, didn't we?"

"Yeah," hiccupped Dendy. "And got rid of twenty thousand acres of timberland. We're lucky we weren't fined."

"We *were* fined," said Zaz. "It cost me twenty-five thousand imperials."

Galoot's face brightened. "Hey, remember when we tried to capture Kepler 2 and we knocked it back into a decaying orbit?"

"Yes," said Lyle. "She entered atmosphere and came flaming down over Quebec. We only got written up for that one."

"Aw, big deal," said Dendy, running her fingers through her black curls. "At least we took that hunk of crap out of the sky before it rained on somebody's parade."

"Au contraire; it rained on a farm house," corrected Paddy. "Thank your bloody Gods it didn't kill anybody. Except a horse, or was it an alpaca?"

A new round of laughter erupted. Several customers backed their chairs away from the rowdy crew. A knot of awe-struck patrons watched Galoot light a napkin on fire and hold it up, only to drop it to the floor with the words, "There goes that nasty Kepler now. Quick, y'all had better duck! Too late – whoompah!" Galoot hugged Carybell hard, forcing out a squeak.

Carl folded up a paper jet from a menu then tossed it across the bar. "Five by five – down the pipe!" he said to anyone who was listening.

Dendy clapped. "Oh, make another one! I want to hit that hunky little shuttle pilot in the keester."

Zaz smiled as he thought of those memories. The incidents did not tarnish the fact that Planet Janitor had received three international accommodations for Excellence in Environmental Preservation. Regardless, it always seemed that the press was hoping to find a chink in their company armor. Bad press, bad luck, and bad breath seemed to be their lot in life. Just one glorious accomplishment might put them back into the graces of the public eye.

Zaz felt a tap on his shoulder. Their waiter, Andreas, clasped his hands between his knees and bent over close to Zaz's ear. The slim man reeked of rose petals and starch.

"Mr. Crowe, your affiliates are frightening some of the patrons. I wonder if you would be so kind as to downshift this to a dull roar. I know you are celebrating; if you would like a private booth in the back, I could arrange it."

Samantha pulled her elbows from the tabletop but left her breasts resting there. She looked cockeyed at Andreas. "What's the matter, babe? Got your little testes in a twist?"

"I am only asking that you keep the noise factor down to an acceptable decibel level, *dearie*," said Andreas. Then to Zaz: "Please help me contain this – I should not like to bring this to the attention of the bar police. As for another important issue of priority, I have a very promising lead for you. I would be willing to divulge this source for the usual monetary consideration."

"How hot is this tip?" asked Zaz, above the din.

"Positively nuclear."

Zaz had used Andreas for a score of past jobs. For a fifty-imperial tip, he could land a job that would net around forty thousand – even more for complicated assignments. Andreas had an uncanny knack for finding lucrative clients who were apt to keep their mouths shut about certain legal issues that city, state, and federal governments might find compromising in nature. But Zaz would never do anything blatantly illegal. They had already had enough bad ink and cyber-flogging to last a lifetime.

Zaz glanced around the room. "Is the client here?"

"Yes. Would you like an introduction?"

Zaz slid him a 50-spot and eased up from his seat. "Sounds good. Take me to him; we don't have the proper setting here for a business discussion."

Andreas ushered Zaz to the back of the establishment where he seated the captain at a private booth. Sitting directly across from him was a dapper young man dressed in a white formal tuxedo with blue lace trim. He had a braided jet-black ponytail that hung over one shoulder. The man was speaking rapidly to an older female as she took electronic dictation. They paused when they saw Zaz.

"Sir," said Andreas, "this is the esteemed Captain Zachary Crowe, of the Planet Janitor Corporation."

"Henry Gable,"said the dapper man, "vice president of Orion Industries Real Estate and Development." Gable dismissed the woman from the booth.

A scream, followed by a crash came from the front of the bar. Andreas winced, excused himself, then rushed to the front of the establishment.

"I've heard of you," said Zaz, admiring a face that Michelangelo could have carved out – young and glowing with a flawless complexion. "Orion took over the third phase settlement of the moon. You sold timeshares for the Tranquility Harbor project. You've also expressed interest in Titan and Europa. I've seen your face alongside your father's. Can't say it's changed much in twenty years."

"Extended cryojumps have curtailed the aging process. One day it will catch up to me." He laughed at his own joke. "But let's forget about that. I seem to remember you as well. You've had several write-ups and network appearances. Some of your work-for-hire expeditions have met with less than stellar reviews. Then again, I am also impressed with the accolades. But I'm not here to dally over track records. What I propose requires more guts than brains. I need a capable crew and ship for a mission."

"What kind of assignment?"

"Me first. What kind of references can you give me?"

Zaz pulled a small wafer out of his breast pocket and handed it to him. "Download that into your KED. It contains our company profile – the straight dope: we're a new company – we've made mistakes. But we're likely to take on any job that won't appeal to another outfit with twice our resources. We were the innovators of the first space debris reclamation market, so we've got the experience. We're not cheap, but we are competitive; Planet Janitor won't price itself out of the industry. Now, what's the nature of the job?"

"If you don't mind," said Gable, "I'll ask the questions. I need to know the size and make of your ship, and I'll need an inventory roster of her components, drive and hardware. Furnish me with a heavy equipment list, in particular, earth excavators and movers. You'll need survey gear. I want to know if you can clear twenty square miles of settlement then put up a permanent retaining wall to cordon off the property."

"She's a class-D Russian ore freighter, over a thousand feet long. I can give you her gross tonnage and registry, but that's all on the wafer. She has an Ultrinium hull – that's the metallic glass variety – and a bang-drive power source; she'll do light's end. We have a full range of maintenance automechs, two medium-sized grapplers, three dozers, two graders, a metal mill and processor, assorted trench diggers, some front-loaders and six tractors. We have a cargo of demolition pyrotechnics, in case you want us to shoot a structure or move a mountain. We can drain a lake with our Phillips pumps, detoxify soil, or corral an oil-sludge spill. The equipment is second-hand, but our automechs keep everything serviced to specs. In truth, we've had some glitches with them lately, but we both know that's normal. Is that enough?"

"For now. What about your complement?"

Zaz detailed the qualifications of his crew, along with their stations of expertise. He exaggerated some of it, but he figured Gable wouldn't expend the energy with background checks, since he'd already acknowledged their "less than stellar" reviews. Besides,

Gable was just a corporation kid – a placeholder. He'd report to his father, the owner of the Orion conglomerate. Gable could decline and nix the deal if he wanted to. Zaz wasn't worried – the solar system was full of deals.

Out of courtesy, Zaz waited for Gable to speak first.

"Mr. Crowe," said Gable after an uncomfortable silence, "some of your qualifications are marginal. It seems like you're running a skeleton crew instead of a full team. I'm willing to overlook that if you are willing to overlook the inconvenient particulars of this mission. I'm asking for a sacrifice that will test your resolve. It is not the nature or difficulty of the work. It will be the decision to leave Earth and travel a long ways out. You'll no guarantees, except by your own hand, to make it to your destination and then return safely. This trip has irreversible consequences. Your emotional losses could be staggering. We've revised a non-standard contract to compensate you and your crew for any possible loss. We're offering five billion imperials – half up front and the rest upon return. We're including five percent of the global mineral rights. I don't have to tell you that you could buy your own planetoid with that kind of bank."

"You're talking about a cryo sleep – a jump that's going to last for more than a few years. That could mean a Life Extend program for our loved ones. I know my parents – they'll be against it. I can't speak for the others."

"If it's any comfort, your second payment will be installed in an indestructible account. Barring global war, economic collapse, or the complete dismemberment of Orion Industries, you will have access to it upon your return. From then on, you'll be gliding under a platinum parachute for the rest of your lives. Not to mention, the lives of your children, and your children's children."

Zaz wrinkled his brow in thought. Something didn't make sense. "Your company has all the resources to accomplish this mission. You're more qualified, have a larger workforce, own the latest technology and ships. You could wrap this thing up much faster than I could. So what's the catch?"

Gable didn't miss a beat, "We're union. The workforce majority ruled to decline the contract by a three-to-one vote – they're afraid of the jump. We cannot force our people to go. Two other developers have also turned down our contract. I won't mince words, Mr. Crowe; we've scraped the barrel's edge."

"You mean, bottom." Zaz suddenly felt very uneasy. Gable nearly implied that he needed expendable personnel, people who wouldn't be missed if they vanished from society for a very long time. He wondered just how much digging Gable had done before he'd decided to offer his mysterious contract to a bunch of "less than stellar" individuals. This was no chance meeting. Henry Gable had come looking for Planet Janitor – more to the point, he'd stalked Zaz to this very bar.

"Mr. Gable. Henry. So, one of your deep space probes has found a planet, dropped a dart flag of ownership, and now you want to send out a tech team to develop a plot of land. You wouldn't be so interested in this world if it weren't ready-made in a habitable sense. That probably means it has a G-type star, a breathable atmosphere, weather, minerals and water. Okay, you've found yourself a real jewel and you want me to trail-blaze it for you. I get that. It's what you're not telling me that gives me pause. Why do you want a retainer wall around a twenty square mile land-division? Animals? Toxins?"

"Nothing like that at all. There are no large indigenous life forms, much less anything else of a threatening nature. The planet has two large salt oceans, and two connected continents with numerous freshwater lakes and streams. We would simply like your team to clear a specific area for settlement. The contract includes a confidentiality agreement that deals with the nature of the assignment and the destination."

"What's wrong with it?" Zaz pressed.

"From our photographic grid survey, this area would pose psychological problems if not cleared. The condition of the ground surface in its present state would serve as a deterrent to livable conditions. We want you to locate, bury and destroy these unfavorable features."

"I'm not very good at riddles. Bury and destroy what?"

"I can't tell you. Suffice to say, upon you're arrival upon the surface at the precise coordinates that we provide, it will become obvious as to what has to be done. There will be no question in your minds about your job. Furthermore, I plan to continue my search for a company that will agree to the contract and have them follow you out within a year's time. With any luck, you will be on your return by the time they occupy the area. If you haven't completed your assignment, you'll have company, numbering four construction battalions."

"You've got to tell me what the project entails. The safety of my crew is at stake. I'm not flying across the galaxy on a dare or a riddle. Play it straight with me and I'll play it back."

Gable blew out a long sigh and loosened his tie. "The danger is psychological. There is no other way to describe it. To maintain the secrecy of the details is of profound importance. That is all that I can tell you until you are on the planet's surface. We are not asking for miracles or guesswork. You'll know exactly what to do and accomplish it with ease. To see it is to believe it."

"That still wasn't an answer," said Zaz. He tried another question: "How many Earth years are we talking about, round trip?"

"Have you been drinking, Mr. Crowe?"

"I've tipped a few tonight with my crew."

"It's best that you learn such information when you're sober. Read this in the morning." Gable slid a small wafer across the table. "Everything you need to know is recorded on that: atmosphere, geography, ecology, weather and survey maps. You won't need bio suits – she's nearly Earth-like. That's why we're so interested. This beautiful blue marble we're sitting on has a pretty little twin sister out there. If we don't claim it, somebody else will. My number is on the company wafer. Call me tomorrow afternoon with your decision. If you decide this mission's for you, we'll patch you the planet and star coordinates. Thank you for your time, Mr. Crowe. I hope we can reach an agreement."

Gable extended his hand. Zaz hesitated before accepting the gesture. It felt clammy – almost inhuman.

Zaz left the booth, tucking the small wafer in his vest pocket. When he got back to his table he found his crew festive, bordering on reckless. He took a seat, pushing his chair back to watch as Dendy danced on the tabletop to some rock-a-bop tune, much to the delight of the crowd. His eyes swam as he tried to follow her gyrations.

Zaz called her Tiney Dancer, and Dendy Dollar lived up to the moniker. She was single, but he'd heard she'd had many admiring boyfriends within the Blue Peace organization. At twenty years of age, She was the cute little sparrow that the eligible young men of the world had failed to clap shut in their hands. She was a flirt, but he wasn't sure if she was a real flirt or simply a practicing flirt. She never mentioned her parents or other siblings, and Zaz had assumed that the departure from her household at a very young age had not been an amicable split. She had always been a tree-hugger and marine life advocate. When speaking out about crimes against nature, her voice could crack the hull of a ship. As well as her background in botany, she fancied herself a nurse (in training), which meant that she could also apply a Band-Aid and use a thermometer with the best of them.

Dendy performed a little skating motion to the end of the bar table, as she shook her hips, she looked down provocatively into the eyes of her captain. She suddenly spun around, took a wide stance and then dropped her head to gaze at him upside down from between her legs.

"Wanna take a ride on the Dendy express tonight, Cap'n, gorgeous?" she cooed.

"I'll pass, Tiny Dancer." He felt a sudden heat on his face. He shifted uneasily on his stool. From somewhere deep inside, he felt a mysterious tremor which had nothing to do with her. If she only knew just what kind of express ride they were being asked to take.

Thirty minutes later the bar police frog-marched the Planet Janitor crew to the exit and sent them out into the street.

CHAPTER THREE

FAIR WEATHER FAREWELLS

Zaz paced with nervous anticipation in front of the conference room door. His crew sat inside; he'd given them the Orion Industries. Zaz had already seen the contract assignment in solitude, but he'd promised to let them watch it so they could make their own decisions. As the captain, he had no wish to influence anyone's vote. They would be more uninhibited without him in the room, able to speak freely amongst themselves.

He noticed a bail of wire, a broken armature, a puddle of hardened slag, and several brackets lying on the deck. "You want something done right, you have to do it yourself," he muttered. He spoke into his wrist-com: "Blue Five, Blue Six, get up to the conference room corridor and pick up this trash. While you're at it, vacuum up the shavings and silver solder, too."

"We're on our way, sir."

He knew the decision would be an individual one; some crewmembers would no doubt be reluctant to tear themselves away from loved ones. Those who had elderly parents, aunts, or uncles stood to lose them with a long jump. Zaz would not force their participation. If he had to, he would replace any reluctant crewmembers.

Zaz' father was 60 years old. His mother was 58. It was possible that one or both of them wouldn't survive his absence. He would take measures to enlist them in the Life Extend program, where their odds of living until his return would be drastically increased. The program was costly and required a full body rebuild. He could afford it if Planet Janitor accepted the deal.

He stopped pacing, allowing two pearl-blue bipedal automechs to pass and begin the cleanup. They were fully robotic, insectoid-looking, autonomous and remote machines, whose duty was to serve as maintenance workers aboard the *Shenandoah*. Their color designations denoted their job function – Blues were reserved for menial jobs associated with low-level hazards. The silver models functioned as smart bombs. The greens took care of the high-level repairs.

The two Blues bent over and collected the loose junk via magnetic arms and clasping pincher-like fingers. One of them sucked up the small slag bits through an attached hose. They lumbered down the hall to the main reclamation hold.

Zaz paused. *Maybe they're going to me him down. Maybe they're stuck like a hung jury desperate to break a deadlock. Maybe they…*

Another automech clunked down the corridor toward him. It was a silver model carrying a backpack. It stopped next to Zaz, its multiple optic eyes zeroing in on his face.

"May I assist, sir?"

"I didn't ask for you," said Zaz. "Do you even know who you are?"

"Silver Two, smart bomb. I'm responding to the call."

"I said, *silver solder too*, not *Silver Two*. Forget it. Cancel. Go tuck yourself back in your cradle." He looked at the backpack it was carrying. "Wait a minute. Are you armed?"

"Just carrying, sir."

"Get back to your cradle."

Zaz watched the departing silver mech until it disappeared around a corner. Now his automechs were hearing things and dispatching themselves to follow orders that hadn't been given. That one had a bad voice recognition transceiver. He made a mental note to tell Galoot about the goose-chasing Silver Two. For now, he sidled up to the bulkhead door with his ear to the metal. At first he couldn't hear anything past his own nervous breathing. Then he heard steps approaching and the latch mechanism clicking. The door swung inward.

Paddy waved his arm, ushering the captain inside. "I'm gob smacked you didn't have a bloody glass up to the door," he said. "Sammy's going to give us a mission statement. We know you'd like to hear it."

Zaz took a seat at a grungy Lucite table and looked at the faces seated around it. Not one of his crew looked up from the tabletop. Lyle ran a finger across the edge of a cup. Samantha scribbled in a note pad. Dendy had made a pillow out of her forearms and was hunched over, drumming her long fingernails on the table. The rest of them looked equally disassociated, bored, or hung over. He had prescribed oxygen and stim tabs earlier.

"Well, kids," Samantha began as she looked at the printout in front of her, "let's go over the hard stuff first. The destination is a second orbit rock in the habitable zone of Tau Ceti. Tau is a yellow dwarf with a spectral class of G8V. It's eleven-point-nine light-years from here, and that's one way. It has a solar mass of zero-eight; it's a twelve billion-year-old main sequence star. Our destination planet sits in a rather narrow habitable zone of zero, six–zero, nine astronomical units, and has a non-eccentric orbit, just like its parent star. Mean temperature variations are from twenty to one hundred thirty degrees Fahrenheit at the equator. That translates to extreme hot and cold. With a twenty-two hour day, we could probably get by wearing the cold collars and britches. If we worked at night, we could suffice with half-bio suits. It's an oxygen/nitrogen mix, so we won't need scrubbers or breathing gear."

Lyle referred to some notes; he flipped up his optical magnifier, gazing over trifocals. "Why would they pick the equator for this development? It looks like a massive desert plain. The more favorable climes are evident in the northern hemisphere."

"That's the boundary of the vegetation line," said Paddy. He scrubbed his fingers through his gray crew-cut then pointed to the wall projection that showed a Mercator representation of the planet. "It's because they won't have to clear an area devoid of flora – they can build without heavy clearing. They'll probably dam some of those rivers for a reservoir then run aqueducts into the settlement. It also looks like the climate is milder at the equator, which negates hard weather.

Carl peered at everyone through pink eyes. Zaz could see a lot of it had gone over his head, but Carl was not to be ignored.

"They just want us to go into that desert and do our jobs. As soon as we blow up the mess, level and fence-off the property, we can pull out. We don't belong in the trees cutting down a forest."

Zaz stiffened. "No one said anything about blowing things up, Carl. Even if we don't do anything more than strike a match out there, it doesn't mean we can't use you on the site. Please, forget about pulverizing things for the moment."

"What kind of gravity are we looking at?" Galoot asked. It was a fair question – he had a lot of extra body weight to be concerned about.

"You won't have to worry," answered Samantha. "In fact, you'll be a little lighter on your feet, Galoot. But we'll pay for it when we get back. I just hope it won't mean a loss of bone mass. We can add some additional resistance training during our stay on the planet."

Lyle took over, referring to his notes again. "We'll get more precise atmospheric measurements once planet-side – the company probes that did this survey got about seventy percent of the survey correct. There are other variables that weren't recorded, like the ocean currents, anomalous weather patterns, solar flare activity, radioactive hot spots, and quake activity. You all saw the seven most obvious volcanoes – two of them were erupting when photographed. As far as I can figure, we're dealing with a pretty normal molten core planet. I don't think it will throw us any surprises. Especially when Orion Industries intends to follow us out there with a big construction company."

"They haven't found that company yet," said Zaz. "They're *assuming* they'll have somebody lined up. Which leads me to believe that this is a rush job."

"I got that impression too," said Dendy. "I used to be involved in surveys that sometimes lasted years for any kind of environmental impact study. Orion Industries ran a couple of low-level probes on this rock that just reported back after a long lag. A lot of things could have changed since then. What about plate tectonics and major shifts leading to some unforeseen cataclysm? Maybe it took a comet or asteroid impact five years ago."

"That's right," said Paddy. "Once we arrive planet-side, we'll will be ignorant of any environmental changes that have taken place. A lot can transform in twelve years."

"Once we enter orbit," said Samantha, "we shoot our own science probes down and get an accurate picture of what's up. If the planet isn't fit for habitation when we arrive, we've just blown a quarter century of Earth time."

Zaz shook his head. "We wouldn't get a real time project cancellation."

"Sounds like a big damn gamble all around," said Galoot. "I've only jumped to the asteroid belt with you five times, boss. But this ain't a short walk down the block. Do you think our cryo-pods and tanks are going to hold up? Our sleeper gear is the older model. That's a number one concern on our li'l hit parade."

"Would you like to know something?" asked Paddy. "We will need re-certification, with a retrofit to get our sleeper gear up to compliance. You can't skimp there – one miscalculation or en-route mishap and we'd end up permanent snoozers adrift on the bloody spiral arm."

There was no denying the complexity and danger of the trek. So many things had to fall into place for there to be a chance at success. Zaz was beginning to think it was all a bad idea. There were too many 'what ifs' to be considered. A ship and crew that was ninety-nine percent capable was a ship and crew that would not make it back – or survive. A jump that long required a one-hundred percent success prep.

Zaz wanted to know their gut feelings about the mysterious assignment. He asked them specifically if they had any clue about what the company might be hiding.

"That's a good question, mate," said Paddy. "That is the greatest paradox of the whole proposal. They want an area surveyed then cleared. But this cleansing involves something distasteful. What could be distasteful enough to deter settlement? They want a retaining wall. It stands to reason that once we rid the area of the phenomenon, the retaining wall is designed to keep it from coming back into the compound. I'm thinking of a pest or animal of some sort."

Lyle polished his glasses as he spoke. "They so much as said that they were not aware of any indigenous life forms that posed a threat. You all saw the presentation. What if it were something non-organic? Perhaps we have to tear down some old alien structures. It would be very bad publicity to claim ownership of a planet with evidence of its previous occupants still lying about."

Dendy made a face. "Maybe the area contains a residual swamp or a moat? They're not exactly aesthetically pleasing to the general public's senses. I understand the significance of a marsh or tidal area – it is a full ecosystem, one that is self-sustaining and vital. I think these developers come off as a bunch of yahoos who couldn't give a care about science or ecology."

"It is a desert plain, Miss Dendy," said Lyle. "It is unlikely that it contains wetlands."

"Something gave 'em the heebie-jeebies," said Galoot. "If it scared their pants off, they figured it would do the same to a bunch of colonists. They need some numb nuts to go in there and get rid of it."

"I'll betcha it's just a bunch of poison plants," Carl interrupted, "or something like that. Maybe it's drug weeds, like poppies or marijuana plants – something that would make you go nutzo. Whatever it is, I say we just blow it into the next millennium and be done with it. There's nothing that half-a-dozen thermite charges won't fix. Hell, we could do it from orbit so we wouldn't have to get face-to-face with whatever's down there."

Samantha rolled her eyes. "Carl, why does everything have to be annihilated? This might be an operation that requires a delicate or careful touch – like a slow, methodical surgery. Maybe it requires great expertise and, quite possibly, that's the real reason why they chose Planet Janitor. I admit that this secrecy mandate irks the hell out of me, but maybe they know something about us that we haven't considered. Are we underestimating ourselves?"

Zaz grumbled. "When was the last time we won a Schubert Prize for science? We might have some kinks, but we can change that. On the basis of what we know, do we feel like this is something we can do with certainty?"

No one offered a comment. Once again, all eyes fell to the tabletop.

"All right," Zaz continued, "I know that twenty-five years is a big lifespan chunk. We have people around us that we love and care about. I don't see why we can't offer Life Extend to anyone wanting it. We can afford it with the first down-payment and we'll still have the lion's share left over."

Carl threw his head back, tossing his hair. "Now it ain't about that," he began, taking on the role of de-facto spokesman for the group. "We all agreed, to hell with everybody else – if they don't want to wait on Life Extend for us, then we aren't going to force the issue. We're ready to red-shift outta here. We haven't got a problem with doing the job or leaving some folks behind. We all want to go."

Well, forgive me for being the oversensitive one. His crew was not a heartless lot, but Zaz had expected to hear a few more arguments. It occurred to him that they might be reluctant to make the trip on the *Shenandoah*. Once again, his ailing vessel would be a target for scrutiny and damnation.

"I promise to get a full refit for the *Shenandoah* out of my share," said Zaz. "I won't have a crew that thinks their ship is a liability."

"Oh, we will need a refit all right," said Lyle. "That's not the most important issue."

"Yeah," said Dendy, biting her lip. "We want more money. We're getting cheated. We don't want the regular deal. We want equal shares. We'll divvy up the expenses."

Zaz rose to his feet, studying the faces of his crew. They gazed back at him with open defiance – expressions he had not seen before on any of them.

Galoot smacked his palm on the table, scattering some papers. "It wasn't my idea – they made me vote that way!"

Zaz strolled around the table, his hands laced together behind his back. He stared at the back of their heads as he passed each one. Their heads moved in a wave, watching as their captain circled them like a bull shark waiting to strike. Dendy's grin gave way, showing the first signs of a frown. Paddy's eyes rolled to the back of his head.

"I'm ripped to shreds," said Zaz. "How is it that the most controversial part of this job doesn't happen to include the missing twenty-five years? I thought it would be the most important consideration."

"We are of the loner taxon," said Paddy, giving the explanation a zoological bent. "The only emotional connections we have are with each other. We'll deal with the extended separation in our own ways, but we are putting *ourselves* in jeopardy – not our loved ones. We don't want the carrot dangling out in front of us – we want the whole bushel. If they really want this Shangri-La planet, I believe we can bargain – knuckle them under."

Zaz took his seat, now looking at his crew in a different light. He had to appreciate the fact that they weren't blowing methane out of their asses. They were at least honest in their appraisals and needs; it was "gimmie all the cabbage now." So be it, if that was the most important issue for them. At least it simplified things.

"Okay," said Zaz. "What kind of figure are we looking at? We've got one hour before I have to finalize the deal. I'd like a head-start on the bartering end, so let's hear it."

"Nine billion," said Samantha. "That's one each, and a little bit more for you."

He nodded, thankful it was not going to be a drawn-out negotiation. It was probably one of the first things they'd set their minds on. Nine billion. Jesus.

Zaz rose from his seat. "Samantha, use the direct line on their wafer. Call up Henry Gable."

She keyed into the table console. Zaz watched the wall screen for a connection. It came up in a moment, the image of the vice president of Orion Industries materialized.

Zaz skipped the pleasantries: "We'll take the job for nine billion – nothing less. We'll need twenty-four hours to get our personal affairs in order, then six days to prep the ship. We want half the deposit today so we can invest or stockpile the salary."

Henry Gable held up one finger and said, "You'll have to excuse me for a moment." The screen went dark. Zaz knew it was a ruse so that the employer would not appear to be hasty or seem as if he was giving in too soon.

Gable came back on the screen. "We'll meet the demands," he said. "We would like to tour your ship and approve it. We have some excellent technicians that can assist with the shakedown and retrofit. I'll need your bank access code so we can make a deposit. I can deliver the contract this afternoon, say, around three?"

"Samantha King has my power of attorney. She'll approve or make any necessary amendments on my behalf. Just come aboard; she'll be expecting you. We're docked at K-Island, Long Beach. You want slip one-twenty-one. I'm sure you'll recognize the *Shenandoah*. I have to travel across the state on an urgent matter, so I don't expect I'll see you in person before we lift. Consider your hand shaken." The screen went blank.

"Slap me, 'cause I'm dreaming," said Carl. "Those suckers bit!"

Zaz gave his crew a stern look. "You know that once we commit to this there's no backing out. I would suggest you make peace with your family and friends – offer the Life Extend program to them. If there are any family members that you care about or need your help, I suggest you show your generosity before we depart. I'm leaving to see my parents now. I think you should make similar plans. I would also suggest last wills and testaments, making your banks available to beneficiaries. If there are any of you who have a change of heart and don't wish to participate in this venture, let me know now so I can find a replacement."

"It's not like turning down one job with the option to come back," said Paddy. "Refusing this job would mean giving up Planet Janitor. I think we're in it for the long haul."

All heads nodded.

"Then that's it," said Zaz.

*   *   *

Zaz took the bullet bus from Long Beach across the state into Nevada. He had to transfer once he reached Henderson. He found the Drowsy Hollow housing community via a short air cab ride. The cab took him to the front of a massive housing compound, where he used a keycard to enter through the main gate. He walked up a flagstone path until he reached the third residence on his right and continued along a narrow footpath to the front of his parent's home.

The residence was an old-style two-bedroom stucco with a large loft. The property occupied two acres, lined with exotic trees and shrubs. A brick planter was at the side of the house; it was filled with daffodils, marigolds, carnations and roses, a veritable fruit salad of colors with a cacophony of scents. The house hadn't changed much since his last stopover visit three months ago, only now everything seemed to be in full bloom. The grass in the yard was cropped short and finely edged. He noticed the addition of a few volcanic rock water fountains that filled small ponds. It was still as beautiful as he remembered it.

He heard the chatter of laughter coming from the rear of the house. Of course, on such a day his parents would be in the garden. They had grown all of their vegetables for the past twenty years. Not for the economy of saving a few imperials, but for the health benefits owed to organic gardening. "Do it yourself," was one of the Crowe family mottos. His mother had no equal in the culinary arts when she worked with fresh produce. She made the best vegetable pizzas he'd ever eaten. His father seemed to think that every square foot of the property needed a fruit tree. He had a riot of them planted around the property; his favorites were peach and avocado.

Zaz walked around the corner of the house and found both parents crawling in the rows. They looked like two mischievous children in a sandbox, digging up little troughs of dirt. They had a pile of carrots between them. As he watched them, he realized they were picking the vegetables then showing each other the deformed shapes, commenting on what the likenesses represented. His mother was saying, "Now this one looks a little like you when you're in one of those moods." She cackled and tossed the tiny carrot into a pile.

"That's not fair," her husband said. "I can't find anything in here that's riding a broom. And besides, you'll find me over in the zucchini patch."

Zaz stepped up behind them. "I hope you don't find anything in there that resembles me."

They both turned around on hands and knees. Don Crowe's face broke into a wide smile. "Zachary, what a nice surprise!"

Ruth used her husband's back to push up to her feet. She wiped a strand of wind-blown hair from her face then clapped the dirt from her thighs. She held out her arms. Zaz embraced her, kissing her dirt-stained cheek. She held him off at arm's length.

"Still not eating right," she said. "I can see that right away. C'mon, papa. You look like a prairie dog down there."

She led her son to a small table that sat under a red and white striped umbrella. Don followed, taking seat with them. Ruth poured lemonade from an ice-filled pitcher. His parents looked tan and fit, happy and still in love with each another. Their fortieth wedding anniversary had just passed, but they still had a lively step and sparkle in their eyes.

"You weren't standing there very long, were you?" asked Ruth, guardedly.

"Just long enough to know that dad thinks he belongs in the zucchini patch." Zaz took a long pull on his cup.

She flushed crimson. "Oh, lordie."

"You caught us frolicking," said Don. "We're guilty as charged. It's nice to see you, son. You here on business, or is this a social call? How's the company treating you?"

"I guess you could say it's a business minded social call. PJ is coming along as expected, barring the occasional negative media shots. I'm sure you've seen some of the news."

"What do they know about a new upstart company?" said Don. "Planet Janitor is innovative, a David amongst galactic Goliaths. I'll bet the government could use some bacon to go with all that egg on their face for not even thinking of such a concept, let alone the lucrative entitlements. You did right by taking it off my hands. We'd have had a gang of imitators today if you hadn't expanded the company. Then where would we be?"

"No one can fault you for coloring outside the lines," said Ruth. "Many of our greatest inventors faced ridicule and insult."

Zaz could always count on his parents for their positive reinforcement. They could never find fault with him. They were always there with a "that's my boy" shout when the storm clouds brewed.

His father had started Crowe's Reclamation and Salvage twenty years ago, selling out to a competitor before the company hit the skids. Don Crowe had never really known ridicule or opposition in the true sense of the words. He'd played it smart and left the business at the top of his form. At age 60 he'd taken an early retirement, but had no desire to involve himself in Planet Janitor, even though his business expertise would have been welcomed. His parents had resigned themselves to a retirement lifestyle. That was just fine with Zaz; any business failure belonging to Zaz would have indirectly reflected back on his father's, and he had no wish to complicate their lives. He *was* grateful for his father's loan to get Planet Janitor off to a start and obtain new patents.

While they sat in the shade exchanging small talk, it became more difficult to drum up the courage to tell his parents about the true reason for his visit. Though they would be happy for his new contract, it was the other particulars that gnawed on him. He knew he would have to lay it all out.

"Mom, dad, I've got a very lucrative deal in the works right now. Actually, it should be finalized by now. It's one of those once-in-a-lifetime opportunities – I would go so far as to say it's groundbreaking in every way. My crew unanimously decided to participate. It's the kind of deal that will set us up for life – maybe even a few generations into our future."

"Then why such a cross look on your face?" asked his mother. "You should be ecstatic over such a thing."

"Just a moment, mamma," said his father, putting his cup down and leaning forward in his chair. He stared at Zaz. "Something tells me this is a deep dive into a shallow pool, son. I can see it on your face. If this is such a great contract, what's tugging at you? How can I help?"

How about you're agreement to live longer so I can see you when this is over? How about setting aside your religious convictions and conservative ideals so I won't feel so guilt-ridden over my decision to leave you? Will you allow me to test your love and give me your blessing?

He would have to start slow, ease them into it. Then he would let them cruise with the idea for a while before dropping the big bomb.

"It's really a great job," Zaz began, "and, interestingly enough, it's with Orion Industries. It is totally legit, complete with a premium contract loaded with perks. In fact, it's an astronomical deal – pardon the pun."

"Then what's the problem?" asked Don. "You've only mentioned money. What's the rest of it?"

"I've got to take a leave of absence to fulfill the guidelines of the contract. The leave of absence is the most difficult part of the job. You see, it's more than – "

"We're going to be here for you, son, no matter how long it's going to take," said Ruth. She refilled his cup.

Her husband shushed her. Don narrowed his eyes pointedly. "This is a star jump, isn't it? How far out are you going?"

Not only was his father a good negotiator; he was a better interrogator. There would be no easy way to tell them.

"It's a hellish long ways, dad. I'm afraid we're talking about a quarter of a century – a full generation." There. It was bombs away.

"Oh lordie," said Ruth, spilling her lemonade as she bolted to her feet. "Oh, lordie." She bit a knuckle then began pacing over the sun deck.

Don poured another cup of lemonade and drank it down in two gulps. He pulled his collar down angrily, stretching the fabric. "I'm feeling a little sunstroke. Isn't it hot out here? Let's say we go into the house."

"Dad, it will be just as hot in there. Nothing will lessen the impact. I want you to know that I will be installing enough into your account to purchase two Life Extend programs. I want you both, I mean, I'm begging you to participate in the programs."

Don shook his head ruefully. "They acid wash the circulatory system. They lung-scrub. They do synthetic reconstruction and bypass surgeries that aren't needed. It's unholy – intrusive. Besides that, the cost is prohibitive!"

"Cost is not the issue," said Zaz quietly. "I can't leave knowing that there's the possibility that – "

"That we'll never see you again!" cried Ruth, suddenly turning on him with muddy rivers streaming down her pink cheeks. "How could you ever consider doing something like this?"

"Mom..."

His father kept his tone civil. "Look, our scientists are on the verge of FTL. I hear that antimatter and electrogravitic drives are just about on the shelf. Surely you can wait for one of these vastly superior innovations. Jump drives are a thing of the past."

"Dad, those new drive concepts are a bit further off than you realize. Besides, I have a time constraint on this project which allows no wiggle room. It's an immediate work summons."

His mother bit her lower lip. "Why won't they let you wait? I think they are being unreasonable and selfish!"

His mother was inconsolable, frightened and on the verge of a tantrum. He'd seen her like this once before when he'd gone hunting and brought a young white-tailed deer home. She caught him dressing the animal out in the work shed. Of course the place looked like a shop of horrors, with all the bloody deer parts hanging from hooks and scattered on a wooden table. She'd been deeply ashamed, saddened by his decision to kill another living thing. She fixed him with that look now.

His father massaged his temples. He said nothing, seeming to be caught short of breath. He looked like he might burst internally, which meant he was near the end of his emotional limit.

Zaz waited patiently for them to recover, or least regain a somewhat fitful calm. It took ten minutes. He went on further to explain more details. His father listened attentively. Ruth disappeared briefly into the house, only to reappear a moment later with a small bottle of straight rum.

"I'm sorry," said Zaz, "I would tell you more but there's a confidentiality clause. I know it sounds clandestine, and that a lot of it is open to interpretation, but we've decided to accept the conditions.

I admit that the money had a lot to do with it. I didn't do this to cause you any heartache – I didn't come here for that."

"So this is a newfound planet?" asked Don. "I assume it's safe and non-hazardous Or have these bureaucratic buffoons left something more out of it? I don't know. The whole thing stinks, if you ask me. And what kind of experience do you have making a leap like this? Do you think that old scow is up to an out-of-system trek across the galaxy?"

Zaz picked up on the instant confidence reversal. Now he was not a David amongst galactic Goliaths. Now, the *Shenandoah* was a scow and Orion Industries were buffoons, when at one time his father spoke very highly of them. Zaz was not a mature 40-year-old adult sitting across from his parents. He was 16 again, and about to be lectured on the misgivings of giant corporations, impulsive, foolhardy decisions that would leave his parents devoid of his company for a generation. The next thing he heard was the dreaded "selfish" word applied to him. It made him cringe.

Zaz spoke for another hour, trying to explain his motivation for taking the job. He begged them to see the advantages inherent in the Life Extend program.

"I'm sorry I'm putting you through this," said Zaz. "I've thought about it and I still keep coming back to the same conclusion. With a record of so many mishaps and near disasters, I thought it was about time I tried something challenging, a way to redeem myself. I want to know that I can do this. It's the only way I can see of getting out of this rut that I've been digging myself deeper into."

"You don't have to prove anything to anybody, son," said Don.

"Only to myself, dad. I can take this sabbatical away from society. But I can't turn my back on you and mom. I've got to know you're with me on this – that you'll at least consider the option."

His father peered at him. "You're dealing with one of the Gables. Who is it? Give me his number. We can get this all straightened out. This is nothing more than a big misunderstanding."

Zaz slapped the tabletop, the cups danced. "Damn it, dad, there is *no* misunderstanding. It's too late for any negotiations, dealings, amendments or refusals. I'm leaving. But I want to leave with the knowledge that you're willing to wait for me. To do that you'll have to subscribe to the Life Extend programs. I'm not asking you to deny your faith and convictions, or submit to eternal damnation. I'm pleading with you to consider a wonderful alternative, as opposed to letting the tide of nature rule your physical destiny. I'm asking you to make this leap of faith for me."

"That's precisely why we cannot honor your request," said his father more forcefully. "This is not a leap of faith you're asking for. You want us to trespass across a forbidden threshold. You are asking us to deny God's wisdom and power over us – asking us to defy a natural law that was intended to keep the existence of humankind in balance. Your own principles by which you founded Planet Janitor – to make this world a better place to live in without disrupting the natural flow – have now become, by your own definition, an opportunity to disrupt life's flow, all for the sake of some grand adventure that rewards you with limitless comforts and monetary gain. What price you pay if you should gain the world, my son, were you to lose your soul in the taking of that gain?"

His mother, fortified after a few gulps from the bottle, softened her face. "I've loved you, Zachary, from the moment you opened your eyes to this world. I always knew that I would part from you – that you would carry on. That is the way it was meant to be – the cycle of existence, in its natural function, has always been the great scales that weigh the burden of life and death. It has been that way since the beginning. There's no reason to question the 'whys' or 'what ifs'. To follow the harmony we must all obey the cycle."

Zaz paused in thought after his mother's words. Her convictions ran deep, and she never said anything that did not have some prophetic spiritual message. It made him feel so unethical and superficial proposing such an idea. Yet, he did have his own life goals and direction to think about.

"I don't understand your resistance to this, but I'll respect it." Zaz rose up and hugged them both in turn. Each embrace seemed to go on forever. He was caught in a moment of eternity that he wanted to soak up and remember for as long as he lived. He hadn't realized or appreciated it as much as he had at this very moment. He knew now

that he was about to leave his best friends. His parents were idealists –
staunch defenders of their faith. Zachary Crowe was an extension of
that faith. Everything they stood for resided in him. They would never
ask him to surrender to anything he didn't believe in. What if things
were reversed? Would he abandon a lifetime of beliefs just because
there was a convenient way out? Was he asking them to agree to an
easy way out because they weren't strong enough to stand the test?

Somehow he'd known all along that they would reject his
plan. Yet, he had denied it, holding out for their acceptance.
He felt like that deer he'd shot so many years ago was now
representative of his parents. Only he'd missed a clean kill and
left the animal to suffer.

He couldn't prolong their suffering any longer – he would run,
get away from the pain. That would be the heart shot, the end of it.

"Surely you're going to stay for dinner," his mother insisted.

"I'm afraid I can't," Zaz said softly. "I need to get back to the
ship and make her ready." He turned to leave, feeling a knot in his
stomach, his eyes misting over. He walked away, resisting the urge
to turn around and take one last glimpse of his world, knowing
full well that another called out to him. He stopped once, rubbed
his face hard. He couldn't believe that he'd actually walked away
from his parents, leaving them wondering if they would ever see him
again. He thought about the word "selfish", and how he so totally
deserved the moniker.

He took a huge breath, thought of his crewmates, and continued
on. It seemed he was barely able to put one foot in front of the other.

As he made his way around the house and onto the footpath, he
heard his father call out after him.

"We'll meet again, son. Godspeed to you and your crew. We
love you!"

CHAPTER FOUR

SHAKEDOWN FOR AN OLD GAL

ZAZ STEPPED UP to the security gate for slip 121 at K-Island, Long Beach. He ran his security card through the gate lock then stepped through. The *Shenandoah* sat like a hulking beetle on multiple legs, its mass taking up all 1,200 feet of the docking slip. Cargo elevators suspended by cables were already ushering goods into the ship's underbelly. Technicians, supported by mechanical scaffolding, ran their beam welders over the damaged hull. Lifts at the rear of the ship off-loaded scrap metal and recycled ores. Dozens of dockworkers grappled loads from a warehouse and sped them across the tarmac, depositing them on the elevator cages. The activity confirmed that Samantha had authorized the purchases and loading of supplies; she had taken it upon herself to sell the scrap and buy the shipboard necessities.

But why had they started so early?

As Zaz walked closer, the long, shadow of the *Shenandoah* loomed from overhead. He studied the massive cylindrical coils that ringed the bottom of the ship. He hoped the gravity repulser lines could take the powerful electromagnetic surge required to lift her fully-laden weight. They couldn't risk a short or generator failure in that system – she would never gain orbit. Worse, she could gain vertical altitude, quit, and pancake on the surface. Such an accident would likely kill everyone on board, in addition to taking out a good chunk of the spaceport.

Zaz headed for the pedestrian lift, a tube extending down from the bottom of the hull. He saw a man dressed in a white lab coat and clutching an electronic notebook run across the tarmac. He slipped in a puddle of lubricant and fell face first onto the tarmac with a sickening thud. He got back up and limped along, intercepting Zaz at the bottom of the lift.

"Now that's exactly what I'm talking about!" said the Port Inspector. "Your freighter is leaking in fits and starts all over this slip."

Zaz noticed the man's chin was bleeding and a corner of his VisiPad had a nasty dent in it.

"It's just a little hydraulic fluid," said Zaz. "Just give me the damage report; I'm a busy man."

The Inspector showed him the VisiPad screen, pointing to various code inscriptions. "You've got four violations for emitting hazardous substances, one infraction for over-extending your slip perimeter, and you are currently venting a gaseous anomaly from your starboard bulkhead near the aft stabilizer jets. Furthermore –"

"Where do I sign?"

The inspector looked barely restrained, a large vein throbbing on his forehead. "Give me your thumb signature on the screen next to your registry."

Zaz smudged his thumb on the screen then started off again. "The check's in the mail." Then, from under his breath: "Bureaucratic parasite."

He took the lift up into the bowels of the *Shenandoah* to A-Deck level. Once there, he switched to a foot tram that took him to the bridge at the nose of the ship.

The bridge was a half moon-shaped command deck that bore a striking resemblance to an executive suite that had had coitus with an oil refinery. Two old-fashioned viewing windows took up the port and starboard bulkheads, wrapping away from a center-mounted screen that displayed the main navigation visuals. An array of sub-computers had been installed on a support shelf just under the main screen. Portable seat bladders sat behind the shelves, accessible for anyone needing to operate a sub-station. Ten larger command chairs, designed for seated, recumbent, or full reclining positions, took up half the command deck space. A small galley and head occupied the rear port corner. The left starboard corner contained built-in cabinets stocked with survival gear and pressure suits.

Samantha had pulled out a chair at the forward station just under the large nav screen. She had a pre-flight roster in her hand and was checking off systems on a control panel that resembled an organ keyboard.

"How goes the battle, Sammy?" asked Zaz.

She swiveled in her chair. "Oh, I didn't hear you come in! It goes – we've got several Orion techs on board checking everything from our sleep pods to the Bang Drive. I was about to bring the anti-grav repulser on line, but decided to hold off until those dock workers got out of the field."

"Yes, let's not make radioactive puddles out of the help." He stepped up behind her, gently laying a friendly palm on her shoulder. "Anybody on leave?"

"No one, Zaz. They're all here. Lyle and Paddy left together earlier but came back about twenty minutes ago. I signed the contract when Gable arrived and took the liberty of installing the first advance payment into your account. Then I withdrew equal shares for the crew so they could bank their amounts. I didn't want to waste any time, so we started in early on the repairs, prep and loading. How was the visit with your parents? Rather brief, wasn't it?"

He didn't answer right away, still feeling flogging pangs of guilt. He had failed to convince his parents that the Life-Extend program was a positive option. How was he going to explain that to his crew?

She patted his hand on her shoulder. "Look, it didn't go real great for the rest of us either. My uncle told me I was a damn liar and to sober up the next time I came around with tall tales about flying across the stars in a scrap heap. Sorry. I think we're of the same mind to turn mother's picture to the wall and get the hell out of here. There's a running joke at the spaceport bar about whether or not the 'planet wreckers' will ever get off the pad. It's ten-to-one that we implode on the slip the minute we fire up. That reminds me: I hope you haven't run into the Port Inspector."

"Too late. I signed for the violations. Seems we're pissing volatiles all over their precious tarmac. What's the mood like amongst the crew?"

"Well, Galoot is running around behind the FAA administrator saying 'yes, sir' a lot. The administrator is the one who'll have the final say whether we take this trip or not. They can't really scrub the mission If we pass all the regs. We always manage to limbo under the rail. Lyle and Paddy are busy organizing the science station. Dendy is in the hydroponics lab making sure the auto feeders, thermostat and water pumps are going to stay online without any hiccups. Last time I saw her she was trying to fix a busted timer."

"Where's Destructo?"

"Carl is in the forward hold strapping down anything that might go boom. He's also directing the automechs to perform the preflight maintenance chores." She sucked in a breath. "And I'm here trying to bring up the right charts to see how difficult this jump is going to be. This is a number-crunching nightmare, Zaz. One of the Orion astronavigators wanted to punch a preset sequence in for me but I told him to eat comet dust."

"Sammy, they just want to help. Are you sure you can handle this? It wouldn't be such a bad idea to take a little advice, especially for something like this."

Samantha King had once told him that she had a face that would make a child cry, a body men would die for, and a brain that was a couple chips short of a motherboard. She'd graduated from Cal Tech with a degree in astrophysics, but failed to get a position at NASA when she never received the coveted acceptance letter. She had been an accountant for 10 years, until she answered an ad for Planet Janitor and agreed to try her hand at navigation. She was in love with space, but fed up with numbers. She had the wildest shrub of red hair that Zaz had ever seen. He didn't know much about her family or friends. The *Shenandoah* was her home, as it was for the others; she seldom ventured far from the familiar hulk.

"Zaz, "she said, "Do you trust these people entirely? I mean, really? If they're going to leave so much information out of the mission's objective, how much could they leave out of our nav computations? I did play it safe, though. I told him he could double-check my figures when I finished the program. We have a week, don't we?"

"You take however long you need." He pointed a finger at her head. "Our mission's success depends on that little computer you have up there. Just make sure all the little terabytes add up in that pretty little skull. If it's any consolation, I'll be here to triple-check the figures. Just pray we don't end up in another galaxy."

She laughed, clapped her thigh. "You are just too baaad, captain corn dust!"

Dendy brushed into the bridge holding her hips. "Okay, I caught you both red-handed having fun aboard the *Shenandoah*. You should be written up for it."

"Fine," said Zaz. "Just spell my name right."

A silver automech appeared behind Dendy, clomping up to her side. It looked at Zaz then placed its hands on its hips. It rocked on its heels and said, "Gak, gak, gak."

Zaz narrowed an eye. "Okay, Dendy, who's your boyfriend?"

Dendy pursed her lips. "He's been following me around for the past two hours. It has to be a glitch or something. He won't listen to me. I called Carl, but he's busy."

Zaz looked at the stenciled monogram on the automech's chest then spoke into his wrist-com. "Galoot, drop what you're doing right now and get up to the bridge."

Zaz approached the silver biped robot, stopping just short of it. He could see that it was wearing the same backpack it had on before.

"Silver Two, are you armed?" Zaz asked, wanting to know how many screws were loose in this machine.

The automech turned its palms over several times. "I have two arms," it said.

"Are you armed three times?"

"No, sir, I don't think I am. What can I do for you?"

"Stay right where you are. Don't move." Zaz backed up to the forward station, while waving for Dendy to do the same. They stood there in silence for what seemed an eternity. Galoot finally arrived, ducking under the doorway.

Zaz gestured toward the automech with a head nod. "Galoot, unplug that backpack and pull it off of him. Use force if you have to."

Galoot stepped up behind the biped machine, yanked a harness from a jack, put a knee into the automech's back, and tore the pack from his frame. He threw it on the deck.

Zaz rubbed his hands together. "Now pick him up and take him to the first charging cradle you find. Magnalock him into it."

Galoot slung the machine over his shoulder and stomped out the door.

"What was that all about?" asked Samantha as she wiped a bead of sweat from her forehead.

"It's bad enough we have to do a complete preflight," said Zaz, "but when we've got smart bombs running around with busted gidgets, it ups the paranoia factor. If either of you see any more automechs doing things they're not supposed to be doing, call me so we can lock them down. Come to think of it..." Zaz called up Carl. "Look, I need you to recall all of the Silvers and lock them down with a power cut."

"That's affirmative, Cap. I'll get on it."

Zaz retrieved the pack from the floor and shoved it inside a storage locker. His wrist-com beeped. "Crowe here."

"Yes, this is Lyle. Did you have a nice trip?"

"Everything went as expected. What do you want?"

"That bad, eh? Anyway, we never recycled our last load from the septic tanks. The bi-valve opened somehow. We got a gusher. I'm afraid it shot up, spraying all over the ship's hull and down on the – "

"Let me guess, the tarmac?"

"That's affirmative. An inspector and a few dockworkers got caught under the deluge. I think that counts as a monetary fine."

"Tell him the check's in the mail." Zaz clenched his fists and kicked an accelerator couch. *Damn it all to hell*. This whole thing was turning out to be one giant spill.

"Okay. I'll inform the inspector."

Zaz paced in a tight circle around the bridge deck. Was it to be just one damn thing after another? Six days to get ready and he already had more system malfunctions than a blind three-legged dog with rabies and a bad case of diarrhea. He would need fifty-two weeks to get ready. Was the *Shenandoah* truly a daughter of the stars, or just a misguided call girl from another galaxy? *Surely, old gal, you have just one more long trip left in you. Please tell me that you can make this jump without disintegrating into a billion slivers.*

Carl buzzed him on the wrist-com, "Captain, I'm gettingg all the Silvers locked down now.

"Fine, Carl. Keep all the Blues and and Greens online. Just make damn sure the Silvers are disarmed and completely deactivated."

"Yazzer."

Whoever said that running a ship was easy because it was a management position? Whoever said that running a ship that hadn't even left the slip was easy? Whoever said that running a ship that might *never* get out of the slip was easy?

"You don't look so good, Zaz," said Dendy. "I have to go down to hydroponics to fix some pumps. You can come with me and we can get frisky behind the raspberry bushes. Might put things in a better perspective."

"Thanks for the offer but it would only complicate things."

"Suit yourself."

He watched as Dendy left, then turned back to Samantha, who had resumed her systems checks. Without looking up, Samantha said, "You know it wouldn't hurt you to bat an eyelash back at her. She's a little smitten with you."

"She's just flirting to pass the time. I'm convenient. Maybe it's the captain complex."

"She might come off a little crass, but that's her nature. She doesn't know any other way to get a man's attention other than to offer herself up. I think she's had an inferiority complex ever since Blue Peace let her go. The way she explains it, it wasn't her fault, and I believe her."

"What would you know about an inferiority complex?" Zaz said, half-jokingly. But his smile dropped when she turned around to look into his eyes.

"Ever heard of the term 'Plain Jane'? Well, I'm the 'it's a shame, Jane' version. It's bad enough to be a woman sometimes, but when you're saddled with a mug like this…well. Then I get the stares at these." She indicated to her breasts. "*That's* how I know, Zaz."

"Look, don't sell yourself short. Besides, when was the last time I held a conversation with your breasts?"

"Yesterday at lunch time. It's all right. I'm rich now. I'll find me a cabana boy." She laughed, the sound resembling a parrot squawking.

The only relationship Zaz was looking for at the moment was a better one with his ship. He had a crew to think of, which negated personal delights. The furthest thing from his mind right now was a romp behind the raspberry bushes.

*   *   *

Twelve major components had to be certified to pass inspection. The nuclear drive capsules were triple-checked to make sure the timers were operable and would reliably ignite. The secondary hydrogen drive was tested for thrust, along with all the retro jets. After the dock was cleared, the gravity repulsers were activated – the ship lifted, allowing measurements to be taken to determine the coil load. Galoot serviced the sleeper pods, installing new parts. The gel tanks were flushed, then refilled with new bio preservative.

Every suspect valve and seal had been replaced to guard against leaks and catastrophic decompression. The internal artificial anti-grav generators would be checked under the vacuum of space, but the field coils were inspected and rebuilt where needed. The hull shield generators were tested and, in spite of a poor startup glitch, they attained full intensity, surrounding the exterior of the ship with a plasma field that would serve as an impenetrable barrier to any space debris or asteroid impacts. The hydroponics timers were cycled to make sure they would auto feed, seed and water the organics.

The oxygen tanks and CO_2 scrubbers were purged, the seals checked. The waste processor received a rebuid. Galoot and Carl made sure the automech's processors functioned properly, and that they were accurately interpreting transmissions via voice commands. Three malfunctioning automechs had to be scrapped.

Galoot ran the proximity warning system through a series of mock scenarios. The warning system would wake the captain upon the event of a field distortion, harmful gamma ray burst, or random object impact. Every safety concern was addressed; there would be no miscalculations, slip-ups, or negligence of any kind. If Zaz found anything to be amiss, or thought that any crewmember couldn't perform their duties, he would scrub the mission.

*   *   *

The Reliability certificates were awarded at the end of the week. The FAA administrator had signed the flight documents, pronouncing that the *Shenandoah* had met compliance. The flight plan was approved. The only negative write-ups concerned the overall age of the ship. The administrator stated that there were no guarantees that one or multiple systems would not fail due to unknown circumstances. The connotations were noted as "Act of God" component failures beyond the control of the crew." Zaz signed the certificates, which absolved the FAA of any and all liability.

The hour of lift-off arrived.

The crew strapped into their accelerator couches in the recumbent position. Zaz sat at the forward sunb-station with Samantha, making the necessary last-minute computations. He checked the figures of the Orion navigator, who had gone over Samantha's figures. The numbers checked out.

Zaz called up the Port Authority, asking for a confirmation of their slip dead weight. The figures came back a moment later. He checked the weights on the cargo ledger, noting their fully-laden weight. He found a discrepancy. He knew the digital port scales were never off – they were finely calibrated, digitally controlled, accurate to within fifteen grams, even with a ship the size of the *Shenandoah*.

Zaz turned to Samantha. "I've got the dry weight and dead weight down to an ounce. I'm showing one hundred and five pounds over gross, Sammy. Do you read the same?"

She looked preoccupied. "We always accumulate extra dust and moisture on the hull when we're sitting in port. You know that."

"Not anywhere near that much."

"You forget," she said, "that we blew a septic valve that sprayed our hull. I would guess that we're full of shit, pardon the reference."

"Delightful. Please adjust for it." Now they were full of shit. He dialed up Port Traffic Control. "This is Captain Zachary Crowe of the ore freighter *Shenandoah*, five-nine-nine-tango, requesting liftoff clearance for outer-planetary jump."

"*Shenandoah*, five-nine-nine-tango, this is control. You have clearance for a grav lift to seven hundred thousand feet, then lateral flight to a nuclear ignition safe zone. The slip is clear of souls. Permission to activate repulsers. Have a good flight."

"*Shenandoah* five-nine-nine-tango, that's a four. How long is our window, control?"

"Control here, *Shenandoah* – that window will close up in forty-five minutes; you have two Starliners on approach eighteen hundred miles out. You better get while it's clear. Control out."

"That's a four. *Shenandoah* out."

Zaz and Samantha strapped into their main deck chairs. Security bladders snuggly fastened them in. Zaz placed his hand on a round pad equipped with two attitude levers, three dials, and a dozen touch pad buttons. The large forward viewscreen crackled to life, displaying a matrix of symbols. The lower right corner of the screen split into a quad view, showing exterior camera shots fore, aft, port and starboard.

He punched in the repulser drive. A yellow bar graph appeared on the digitized screen, showing a climbing voltage surge. First came a tingling in the toes, then the tingling started to radiate upward. The generator whined, gaining rev momentum. Tiny sparks flittered around the bridge. The sky outside the window hazed with a purplish hue. Zaz watched the bar graph until two line indicators spiked. He turned a dial. The massive craft began to lift.

On K-Island, slip 121, the cement tarmac began to rattle. Nearby offices and loading docks wobbled on their foundations. The air seemed to stretch like fabric. A seagull flew too close to the plasma field, disintegrating instantly.

Zaz felt the ship's nose cock forward. He straightened it out, then retracted the giant centipede-like landing legs. He spun hard on a dial. The *Shenandoah* picked up speed, climbing straight up the flight chimney, dragging bits of trash in its wake. A crack of thunder split the atmosphere.

Zaz's jaw rattled, but a smile stretched across his face. Nothing compared to the thrill of breaking free with a huge craft. Experiencing a grav lift was a sensory overload. Only the mighty Starliners had given Zaz as much excitement. But where the Starliners were powerful and smooth, the *Shenandoah* was old-fashioned and brute-rude.

They hit 700,000 feet in six minutes. Zaz dialed the repulser generators down and then cut them out. He took a fix, keyed in a command. The *Shenandoah* continued with a new heading under hydrogen engines out into the safe zone.

"Holy grabbing guts," said Galoot. "I might have crapped myself."

Zaz waved a finger at him. "You weren't supposed to eat for twenty-four hours. Everyone better be purged for the pods."

"Wow," said Dendy. "My teeth are ringing. I can't feel my gums."

"Welcome to the ionosphere," said Samantha, "compliments of the express elevator."

"That was bloody invigorating," said Paddy, who began scratching the small patch of gray turf on his head. He'd lost his filthy hat during the acceleration.

"I'll have to agree with that, sir," said Lyle. "You really punched her in the guts!" He waggled his head, looking for his Optipak.

Carl sniffed. "Yeah, you've got to stop treating this heap like a hotrod, Zaz. You didn't have to scorch off the line like that."

"Just seeing what the ol' girl has," said Zaz as he dialed up the artificial gravity. As he accelerated the hydrogen engines, a small grin appeared on his face. *Scow and bucket, eh?*

"Just take her panties down if you want to see what she's got," said Dendy. She climbed out of her couch and stomped around the deck, testing her weight. Satisfied, she walked in a bow-legged gait to the nose window to look out. She sighed breathlessly. Zaz could tell she was marveling at the view. It was something you never got tired of – watching the stars arc in the heavens. He could see Orion's belt and its fuzzy nebulae. He felt the urge to join her there. He knew that she was out there flying amongst the stars, like Wendy in Peter Pan.

Make a wish, Tiny Dancer.

It took over eighty minutes to reach 50,000 miles altitude – the safe zone. Samantha took up a seat at the forward station to run some last minute checks. She swiveled in her chair and snapped her fingers for Zaz's attention.

"I don't believe it," she said. "She's humming like a Swiss watch. Just say when, Zaz. We're in the pipe – lined up straight as a laser shot."

Zaz got out of his seat and stepped up behind Dendy. He put his arms around her, leaning her back into his chest with a gentle embrace. "Whatcha see out there, little one?"

"Oh," she said, arching her head back to look up at him. "Bright and beautiful things. Why?" She seemed confused for the moment.

"Kind of the same in here," he told her, rubbing his hands together vigorously. It was time to address the crew.

"Sammy, give us a thirty minute countdown. Carl, bust the first shift of Greens and Blues out. As for the rest of you, this is your last chance. Speak now or forever hold your peace. We can drop back down in Long Beach and you can walk off this ship with no regrets. You'll have to surrender your share, though."

"What," said Paddy, "and get left out of Planet Janitor history?"

"Okay. Get to your sleep pods, chop-chop. Galoot, hang back with me for a minute." Zaz waited for them to leave. Dendy gave him an admiring smile over her shoulder as she left, nearly walking into the bulkhead. Satisfied they were alone, Zaz looked up at the towering figure. The large man shuffled his feet and picked at a fingernail.

"Tell me, Galoot. Were you going to let her walk the corridors for twelve years, play spider checkers with herself, and eat raspberries? I'm sure you didn't have anything like that in mind. Now why didn't you just come out and ask me?"

"How did you know?" Galoot stammered. "Look, I was going to tell you, boss, really I was."

"I just knew we weren't carrying one hundred and five pounds of crap on the hull. I hope to God she hasn't eaten anything, so she's clean to make the jump. I suppose you had that planned too."

"Yes, boss – Captain Crowe. I did. I mean, she's okay for the long jump."

"Then go get her out of the locker you stuffed her in, or wherever you hid her. Get her into a sleep pod."

The giant took Zaz's hand and pumped it vigorously. He rushed out the door, nearly taking his head off on the overhead. It looked like Galoot had finally rustled up a girlfriend, Zaz mused. He just hoped he hadn't kidnapped her.

Galoot was easy. He'd always pined for a mate, believing that he was just as normal as the regular guys. Only he'd never taken his physical dimensions into consideration. Somehow he'd blocked that out – thrown that part of his makeup out the window. Denial. He was always trying to demonstrate how compact he was by trying to fit into tight spaces, small float cars, or standard-size chairs. If something broke under his crushing weight, he was apt to throw a fit and blame the manufacturer.

Galoot had been with Zaz from the beginning of Planet Janitor. He had been originally hired on as the chief mechanic and systems technician, responsible for the maintenance of the ship. He abhorred the title, convinced that being a mechanic denoted a lower status than the others. Zaz, with one swing of his magical employer's wand, had given him the title of chief security officer. It kept Galoot from thinking about his menial position and, though it was an honorary title, much like the one given to Doctor Seuss, he'd taken it to heart. It was funny, though – Galoot spent most of his time in the ship's hold, wrestling with the machinery, doing what came so naturally to him – wrenching. The giant could reassemble an airbus that had gone through a shredder.

Galoot was alone. The *Shenandoah* was all he had. No one had ever come to visit him, except to gawk. Some had regarded the giant as a perversion or a freak.

Zaz took a last look out of the viewing window, then keyed the final program sequence into the nav console. He left the bridge and walked briskly to the pod chamber on A-deck. When he got there, he could see that the crewmembers were nude and waiting for their insertion.

Zaz waited for Galoot to appear with his friend, Carybell. When the two finally arrived, Zaz looked at the small girl and said, "I'm Zackary Crowe, captain of the *Shenandoah*. I'd like to officially welcome you aboard, Carybell."

"Um, thanks." She looked around timidly, her hand grasping Galoot's in a tight clasp. When she saw Dendy, her eyes brightened. They were both tiny women, able to look at each other eye-to-eye.

Dendy shook her hand. "Pleasure to meet you. Just follow me."

Dendy made sure Galoot and Carybell disrobed, then placed them into their pods. She fitted them with catheter needles in their arms and heart stimulators then closed the lids after they climbed into their pods. She did the same for the others.

Before Samantha's lid was closed, Zaz spoke to her. "You should be ashamed of yourself. You knew all along we had a stowaway."

"Night, Cap'n," Samantha cooed, blowing him a kiss.

Zaz stripped down and entered his pod. Dendy slapped his forearm and inserted the needle into a vein. She placed a small barbed electrode over his heart – the stimulator.

With a wink Deny said, "Don't let the bedbugs bite,"

"See you in Never Never Land, little one."

The pod bubble came down over him with a pneumatic hiss. He could see the blurred image of Dendy's face just outside. She watched him for a while before she turned and entered her own pod.

He felt the chemicals surge into his arm. His muscles began to feel like cardboard. A small pump flicked on at his feet. A thick gel, the consistency of rubber cement, oozed up over his ankles and crept past his knees. It smelled like acetone. He felt the dermal preservative rush faster up his abdomen, giving him a thousand jellyfish stings. He could feel nothing below his ribcage now. An overwhelming sensation of drunkenness overcame him. His eyelids fell like iron doors and his heart fluttered once. Then it stopped.

*   *   *

Somewhere in the recesses of Zaz's last cognizant thoughts, his synaptic responses spilled out a small and fleeting memory. He was Peter Pan, and he'd lost his shadow – it was somewhere in the universe a million parsecs away. He thought he heard it call out to him from some distant dimension. He wanted so badly to find it. Wendy Darling was there, but she was afraid to fly and couldn't find him in the void. Then he felt himself pulled further away, speeding faster into oblivion.

He was ageless now, just like Peter Pan. Time was a comforting friend – an ageless old man who'd come to stay for a very long time.

Somewhere in the vastness, he heard a far off voice. *We'll meet again, son. Godspeed to you and your crew. We love you!*

The first nuclear capsule rode down the track drive toward the stern of the *Shenandoah*. It exited aft of the ship's transom, like a pellet disgorged from a barrel. A timer clicked. The capsule detonated with the force of a seven-megaton atomic bomb. The force slammed against the massive driver cone, kicking the ship out into the vast black reaches. The stars seemed to curtsy as the *Shenandoah* sped by.

CHAPTER FIVE

IT'S ALL OR NOTHING

THE PRESERVATIVE GEL flushed to the bottom of the pod tank. The canopy lid snapped open with a *whoosh*. The cardio stimulator delivered a burst of electricity to the long-dormant heart. Another jolt. The heart muscle contracted, then flexed outward. The heart picked up speed, like an old, heavily-weighted truck on a downhill grade. Skin pores glistened – the grayish flesh began to glow a soft pink.

Zaz' chest rose with the first intake of breath. The first exhalation let loose a nasty odor from between cracked lips. Tiny body arm hairs lifted up like wind-blown blades of grass.

An eyelid fluttered. Then the other.

The first thing he noticed was the weight of his head. It felt like a boulder. His neck gave a muted *crack* when he tried to move. Zaz swung his arm over the lip of the pod, grasping for the oxygen mask. He brought it to his face and inhaled, coughing up a thick string of mucus. His head began to clear, but his limbs were still numb, doll-like.

Zaz threw one leg over the pod, twisted upright, straddled it for a moment and then fell to the floor. He crawled around for a few minutes, letting his eyes adjust. They wouldn't focus. He saw indistinct images through a mirage-like glimmer. He realized he'd broken the catheter needle off in his arm. He plucked it out, wincing in pain.

Once he felt stronger, Zaz stood up, the lip of the pod supporting his weight. He could see the life monitors on the other pods. They were all in the green. Thanking the star gods, he looked across the chamber to the digital chronometer. The date on it confirmed they'd made the jump sequence. He stumbled to a nearby console and flicked several toggles on, not wanting to wait for the auto cycle. The rest of the pod lids snapped open, emitting the same powerful acetone-like odor. He watched the bodies stir, then began to extricate the rest of his crewmembers.

He pulled Dendy out first. She hung onto him like a small child "What time is it?" she asked, her voice thick with sleep.

He massaged her shoulders. "You mean what year is it? You're now thirty-two-years old, Dendy Dollar, but you don't look a day over twenty."

Zaz looked down the corridor. He could see a Green automech standing guard, its bulbous metal head swiveling back and forth. Farther down the same corridor, another Green passed through an intersection on its way to a checkpoint station. Normal onboard ship operations were in full swing.

The rest of the crew popped from their pods like bugs from cocoons. There was much swearing and stumbling. Carl, feigning blindness, fisted Samantha's breasts, for which he got a sharp crack across the cheek. He'd tried those moves twice before on shorter jumps. It had never panned out.

They all managed to struggle into their jumpsuits – except for Paddy and Lyle, who almost put their legs into the same jumpsuit before they corrected their mistake. It figured; they were practically joined at the hip in whatever they tried to do, so it was no surprise that they were the last dressed. And yet they stood there in the pod chamber grooming themselves and talking about subjects that no one understood or cared about. They were a couple of brother scientists on the same wavelength.

Galoot was unsteady on his feet, fawning over Carybell, who wore an anguished look on her face.

"I have a headache," said the tiny blonde.

"We all have headaches," said Zaz. "I hope we didn't scare you." He wondered what kind of ship's function she could serve to remain content without going onboard-bonkers. To downplay her significance would hurt Galoot's feelings, and Zaz did not intend to prick those tender sensibilities. Galoot had told him in confidence that Carybell was desirous of a life-change, something that would restore her dignity and give her a sense of worth. Zaz had a fair idea of what her past profession had been. He asked Carybell what she liked to do in the form of recreation or activities.

She rubbed her temples. "Well, I like to sing and take rides. But I really like flowers."

"Flowers. Then it's official. You're our new assistant botanist. You can help Dendy in the hydroponics lab. What do you think of that?"

Zaz looked at Dendy and read the five-alarm fire in her expression: *Now you're saddling me with a little bimbette who probably doesn't know a weed from a magnolia.*

"Shall we?" he said, ignoring Dendy's stare as he led them down the corridor to the bridge. Half of the bridge deck was illuminated in a soft, refracted light that came in through the view windows. Though he couldn't see it yet, he hoped that the light came from their target star, Tau Ceti. When he checked the instruments and maneuvered the ship around, a small sun glowing like an ember came into view. The spectral analysis matched. Though they were a little far out, they'd nailed their mark. It was Tau Ceti.

Zaz lifted Samantha with a hug. "My God, Sammy, we did it!" The others flocked to the windows, crowding the forward station.

Lyle pulled down some masking filters over his eyes and scrutinized the star. "She's not as bright as our sol," he said, almost in a stupor. "She seems almost lonely, sir. Like a little star that got kicked out of the constellation."

Zaz sat down at the forward station next to Samantha. "Sammy, put our gun scope in her orbital plain. See if we can pick up her two babies. We want the second rock out."

Samantha dialed in the telescope. The image came up on the screen via a solar filter. Two tiny specks appeared almost inline: one was very close to the sun's equatorial plain; the other was slightly above it, farther out. It was a stroke of luck to have both planets in orbit on their side. But it wouldn't last long. They would have to set their trajectory for the second planet out then intercept it.

Samantha fired up the hydrogen thrusters.

Zaz looked down at the console. He noticed a yellow warning light. Samantha's eyes found it a second later. They exchanged troubled looks. Zaz keyed in a prompt. The information flashed up in the lower left hand corner of the view screen.

CAUTION: YELLOW STATUS — NON LIFE-THREATENING. EXPLOSIVE DECOMPRESSION — STARBOARD CARGO HOLD, DECK C, SECTION 9B. REPAIRS PERFORMED AT 23:00 HOURS, 11 YEARS, FOUR MONTHS FLIGHT TIME. INTEGRITY REGAINED.

Carl tried to whistle through numb lips. "I'll check it out, Cap."

"Well, something hit us or we hit something about nine months ago," said Zaz. "It was a double hull penetration. It looks like the Greens got to it and sealed the breech." He looked over his shoulder. "You reading an impact location, Galoot?"

"Yeah, boss. It looks like we took a shot in our underside next to the side bulkhead. That's a bad place to get a golden BB. Mucho bad."

Zaz got up from his chair. "Carl and Galoot, you come with me. Sammy, take us in but stand off from atmosphere until I'm back. Dendy, get some stim tabs, Aspriprofen, and fire up the galley. It sounds like everyone has gravel in their guts. Oh, have Carybell help you."

Zaz led the way to the lift. They took it to the bottom cargo hold, stepping out into an immense cavern. The roof bulkhead loomed fifty feet overhead; the hold spanned four hundred feet at its widest. They took the centerline foot tram down the length of the ship until they reached a point one thousand feet from the stern.

They crossed between two ore bins, heading on foot to the side bulkhead. That's when they saw it.

Sticking up from the hull deck, wedged tight into the ragged hole, were the upraised legs of a Green automech. Around its hip joints was a huge glob-like puddle of metal glass — the material used to plug catastrophic leaks. Rope-like strands of solidified metal glass were all over the deck — evidence of a frantic emergency.

Zaz took a wild guess. "The missile came through the hull, poked a nasty hole in the plates, the alarm went off then the Greens responded. This Green's magboots weren't strong enough to keep him anchored; he got too close to the vacuum and was sucked in. His frame was crushed, but there were still micro-leaks. The other Greens arrived. They emptied their patch guns right onto their buddy and sealed up the pinholes."

Zaz looked at the angle of the crinkled legs to determine the trajectory of the projectile. He gazed overhead, trying to find the impact point, but could only see a shiny spot where something had struck the ceiling plates before disintegrating into a spiked star pattern.

"Must have been a nickel-iron bee-bee, probably no bigger 'n a walnut," said Galoot, shaking his head sadly. "Came in here like a bullet, flayed her open, then ricocheted around to beat all to hell."

Carl wiggled one of the automech's limp magboots. "Hell, if it wasn't so tragic it would almost be funny. This dumb bastard sure gave his all for the cause."

Zaz looked at the deck plates. "I'm more worried about what it hit before it got in here. The gravity repulser lines run just below this puncture."

Carl licked his lips. "Want me to suit up and take a look-see?"

"No, put a remote crawler with optics out there. No sense in risking a space walk right now. But we'll have to know before we reach atmosphere. See to it, will you? Shoot the pictures to the bridge. I can check the repulser line connections at the console. Once we have the images, we'll know for certain. Don't tell the others until I know what we're dealing with."

Zaz left with Galoot. They rode the tram back to the bridge in silence. Neither of them wanted to talk about what they'd just seen. A dozen scenarios ran through Zaz's head; chief among them was Murphy's Law of Space Travel: one system failure is usually the result of multiple system mishaps that invariably lead to multiple failures. The domino effect.

The bridge smelled of steaming food when they returned. Zaz took a seat at the forward station, noticing that Samantha had brought them within the troposphere of their target planet. She'd sent two probes down to the surface and they had reported their findings. The atmosphere checked out – no anomalies. He felt her eyes on him.

"What's wrong, Cappy?"

"Don't ask," he said. He accepted a plate of dinner from Dendy, who told him that Carybell had prepared the entire menu. He gave Dendy a warm smile and looked around the bridge. Paddy and Lyle were gone. He supposed they were prepping the science station in anticipation of an immediate landing. Carybell lay asleep in one of the deck chairs. Dendy had turned around and was on her way back into the galley. Galoot was in earshot but the was okay. The coast was clear.

"Sammy, fetch me a constellation chart from the locker."

She walked to the back of the bridge and began rummaging through the chart logs.

Zaz brought the repulser system online. He sent a maximum voltage pulse through the coils. A continuity reading told him there was high peak resistance – a dangerous level. He quickly shut the system off and took a bite of hydrated chicken from his plate, unsure if anything could get past the knots in his stomach. Samantha came back to him with an armload of charts and wearing a perplexed expression, one that he was getting unfortunately used to seeing lately.

"I don't know why you wanted these," she said. "You know which constellation we're in. So what's up?"

"Just doing a little double-checking. Nothing serious. Can you line us up?"

"I'll take us around to the sunny side of the planet and time us for a daytime drop at the coordinates they provided. We want the larger landmass in the northern quadrant. What the heck is the name of this rockoid, anyway? They didn't give us an official designation for it. They just called it 95-Tau-B."

"Huh? Oh. That's because Orion Industries didn't want to go through the official naming board of the International Astronomical Union. I figure they swept this baby under the carpet. You know, Hershel was voted down when he proposed the name, Georgian Sidus, for Uranus. Let's kick it back to him in tribute. Sidus, for short."

"Hmm, Georgian Sidus," she said, rolling it around in her mouth. "I like the sound of it."

The screen view changed. Zaz looked up to see outside camera shots transmitted by the crawler. He toggled the controls, increasing the size of the image on the screen. Samantha blinked when she saw the detail.

A large rope-like structure, the coil, could be seen imbedded in the bottom of the hull. It was as big as a sewer conduit, full of super-voltage filament fed by the gravity repulsing generators. The camera view showed a five-by-five-foot section of the coil. A smooth hole the size of a fist had punctured the middle the middle of it. The edges of the impact hole showed obvious scorch marks. Whatever had hit the line coil had done so at extreme velocity without breaking up before penetration. Of all the places for an object to hit, the grav repulser coil line was the worst.

Samantha slumped in her seat, interpreting the image in a nanosecond. "We are so screwed."

Zaz felt a warm breath over his shoulder. Dendy stood behind him, her palms resting on his shoulder. "We got hit, didn't we?" she said. "That's what you're looking at."

Zaz sighed. "Somehow, some *when*, the force-field around the hull hiccupped and went offline. We took a strike while the shields were down, then the force-field blinked back on again. The foreign object got us with our pants down; we never got an auto-alarm wakeup. What are the odds of that? Anyway, it shows a terminal disconnect. That means a power loss. We still have seventy percent repulsion strength. As big as this ship is, with the load we're carrying and the planet's gravity…well, I don't know."

"We could go in for a drop, lose it and pancake," said Sammy.

"Can we repair it?" asked Dendy.

Zaz shook his head. "Those lines are ten feet thick, filled with super-conductive composite. What are we going to use, a pin torch and solder? I don't think so. It's a continuous line; it's not meant to be patched or beam welded. A hairline weak spot in the patch would blow apart under the electromagnetic load." He looked at each of them. "We scrub. We turn around and go home, park in orbit then wait for emergency evacuation."

"Bullshit. We vote on it," said Dendy, sternly. "I'm sorry, but we came to do a job. There has to be a way, Zaz. I don't want to turn tail and run for home. I say we go for it."

Samantha's face brightened. "Wait, say we go down using that seventy percent while kicking in the hydrogen attitude jets for repulsion assist. We point all our thrusters down and give them full burn all the way. I can crunch the numbers. I think we could make it down and at least do the job they paid us to do. The environment down there is survivable. We have enough shipboard supplies for two years."

"Maybe they could repair our ship, too," Dendy offered.

Carl walked in a few minutes later in time to hear the tail end of the discussion. He had his own ideas. "We got holed all right, smack dab through the line core," he said. "I think we could tie up our big machine equipment with those old surplus drag chutes, approach atmosphere and then kick the load out of the cargo doors right over our landing zone. The chute canopies are big enough to handle the loads. That way we can lighten the gross weight so it takes some strain off re-entry."

"Then we'll vote on it," said Zaz. "I vote to abort."

The captain called Paddy and Lyle back to the bridge. When the scientists arrived, Zaz filled them in on the problem. A show of hands tallied the results. The captain lost, seven to one.

"Well," said Zaz, "I didn't know you wanted to bury the ol' girl in the dirt *that* bad. All right, we go for a landing."

Carl and Galoot went to the hold to rig the chutes and park the heavy equipment machines near the cargo hatches. They would drive the machines off the ship by remote once they opened the doors.

Dendy took the rest of the crew to batten down all of the loose gear, which included securing a hatch over the hydroponics aquarium.

Zaz guided the ship in close for the cargo drop. Reaching altitude at the fringe of the atmosphere, he activated the repulsers. He gave Carl and Galoot the command to drop. Zaz watched his gauges, noting incremental weight drops. When it was finished, he ordered the hatches sealed and everyone to the bridge.

The crew strapped in extra tight. Zaz watched the screen; a belly camera showed a downward angle toward the planet's surface. He could see the huge profiles of multiple chutes descending. A scan showed calm winds at their position over the equator. At least their equipment wouldn't drift dozens of miles from ground zero.

The *Shenandoah* began to freefall. Zaz redlined the repulser power, simultaneously activating the hydrogen retro jets. He adjusted the attitude of the ship for pitch and roll, nearly having to fight the controls. *Now any landing that you can walk away from is a good landing.* He deployed the landing gear early to force more drag on the ship. The *Shenandoah* began to rock and shimmy.

"We're coming down the chimney," said Samantha shakily.

Zaz gave her a worried look. "Yeah, but it's a really fat Santa coming down that chimney."

The landmass below grew on the screen. He magnified the image to show the condition of the soil. Or sand. Or whatever it was. Hopefully there wasn't some jagged rocks below them. It was too dry down there for a freak quick moat or swamp; he knew that from the information survey. The dryness meant heat – heat meant a solid surface. But heat meant less dense air to slow the ship's descent. Jesus. Now he was thinking about thermodynamics!

The retro jets began to overheat. Zaz knew they were not designed for prolonged burns, or to slow massive ships down in atmosphere. It was akin to trying to stop the fall of a lead bucket with flares strapped to it.

At a thousand feet altitude Samantha called out: "Seventy-five kilometers per hour descent. Everyone brace, exhale, clamp your teeth and put your heads back!"

Zaz closed his eyes, counting the seconds down, waiting for the impact. He knew it would be nasty. The landing legs would not take the impact force. The entire hull might even buckle or crack wide open. Would his precious ship crumple like a can? Would *they* survive the impact? Was this the last trip he'd ever make?

Then they hit.

Zaz felt a severe jolt that traveled from his buttocks up through his spine and into his neck. His arms flailed wildly up in the air, then slammed down on the armrests. It felt like his head had plowed down into the seat cushion. He nearly lost consciousness.

Outside, rocks, gravel and sand blew out in a flower pattern, twisted up over the ship in a plume. The P-wave shot out across the desert floor at over one thousand miles per hour. Dust devils shot up from the surface creating small artificial tornadoes. .

For a moment, Zaz thought his retinas had detached. After blinking several times, his sight came back in a wet blur. Someone was screaming. Another sound: gagging. Glancing at the windows, he could see a gray and orange sandstorm, pebbles pinging off the view screen with a loud racket.

He freed himself from his seat harness and looked around. He could see Carybell pitching her head back and forth, gasping and turning a shade of light blue. Galoot fought his way out of his restraints. He was at her side in a moment, blowing hard into her mouth, inflating her lungs. She'd had the wind knocked out of her, having not paid attention to the "no inhalation" rule before they hit.

Dendy, compact and muscular, hadn't suffered from the impact like the others. She grabbed the med kit and began to assist the crew. First she took care of Samantha, who had bitten her tongue. The bleeding was not excessive, requiring only a cotton ball to stop the flow. Carl and Lyle were both unconscious. She revived them with ammonia tabs.

Zaz stumbled across the deck. Carl was moaning, complaining of a kinked back – a possible vertebrae compression. Zaz gently eased Carl's restraints and told him to remain immobile in the chair. Dendy finally made it to Carl. She adorned his neck with an inflatable neck brace and administered a painkiller. She gave Zaz a quick glance.

"You okay, gorgeous?" she asked.

"Just fine," he replied. "What are you, some sort of indestructible superhero?"

She palpated Carl's spine, running her hand up and down. "Heck, Zaz, I once fell off the stern of the Blue Peace Adventurer, forty feet to the water. The crew was more concerned about me landing on the helpless fish." She gave a little chuckle.

Wonder Woman. What other surprises did she have in store for him? She was a superb medic; it was the first time he'd ever seen her pressed into serious action. Her speedy response showed a maternal side to her that Zaz hadn't expected.

An orange dust plume swirled outside the window in a fierce maelstrom, as though the Earth itself had been suspended in midair. Awake now, Lyle took wobbly steps across the deck to look at the disturbance outside. Zaz knew that he was trying to understand what they'd hit to cause so much airborne havoc. The professor had the answer a moment later.

"It's volcanic ash," said Lyle. "Fine silicates suspended in the air. When we crashed, we kicked up a mushroom cloud. Judging from the sand ridge on the bottom lip of the window here, we buried the hull in this material. The impact most likely crushed our landing gear."

Zaz looked out the window trying to fix on something solid. "You mean we're up to our eyeballs in planet Sidus. That's a good thing. That extra cushion kept us from totally breaking apart. I'd rather hit a sponge than lava. It saved our lives." *But it destroyed my ship.* It was an equitable trade – the ship for their lives. But there was an unsettling new problem to be reckoned with.

Zaz spoke to no one in particular. "If the lower half of this ship is buried, then all of our cargo and egress hatches are underneath. We have no exit out of here."

Galoot patted Carybell's head with comforting strokes. Without turning he said, "That's not exactly true, boss. We got one utility hatch and one emergency hatch on the roof. They are only big enough for a normal person to slither through – that leaves me out. Unless you want me to take a beam torch to cut one of them nose windows out."

"We'll do whatever's easiest," said Zaz.

Carl, staring up at the ceiling, said, "It's no big problem for me to set some cutting charges and blow a hole through the hull right in line with the sand level. Probably at Deck B, considering how deep we're buried. I'll make a door you could get a front loader through."

Zaz nodded. "Okay, I like those ideas. But one thing at a time. Carl, you're staying put for now until Dendy gives you a clean bill. I'm going outside. Lyle, Paddy, I could use you out there if you're up to it." They both answered in the affirmative. Wild horses couldn't keep them from exploring an alien planet.

Samantha spoke over the cotton ball in her mouth. "Out-thied temp ith one hundred twenty-one degrees on tha fairy thide." Translation: Outside temperature is one hundred twenty-one degrees Fahrenheit.

The realization of what had just happened came upon Zaz like a sudden nightmare. He marched to a bulkhead wall and began punching it with the palm of his hand. He pounded over and over again until the skin split. Then he began to kick at the dash panels until his foot went numb. He fell to one knee, exhausted.

"Damn you! Why? You filthy stinking..." He pushed himself to his feet, took some even, measured breaths, trying to quell the fit. No one dared say anything, except Dendy, who knew what he had just gone through.

"I'm so sorry, Zaz," she said. "I know what she meant to you. She was truly a daughter of the stars. We wouldn't have made it here or lived through it without her."

He swallowed dryly, took a gulping breath. "Sorry for the outburst. I wasn't expecting anything like this. Now, let's get to work."

Zaz and the two scientists stripped down to shorts and boots. They donned cool collars and britches to keep their core temperature down to a safe level. They donned standard issue coverall. Both scientists retrieved shoulder bags packed with their instruments.

Galoot led them down A-Deck to a midpoint in the hull and then turned down a narrow shaft. He stopped at a service ladder that led up to the roof. It was funny, but Zaz had never known about the hatches. He chalked it up to ignorance; he'd never had to use them before now. Mechanics always seemed to know every cranny on a ship.

Galoot disappeared for a moment and returned with a coil of safety line. He handed it to Zaz. "I'll tie the end off on the ladder rung. Just for safety, boss."

Zaz started up the ladder with the line over his shoulder. It was a long climb. When he reached the top, he found a small panel box with a magna lock switch. He pushed a button. A hiss and a blast of hot air struck his face. He threw the lid back, climbed out and looked around.

The *Shenandoah* sat buried, nearly up to her amidships. Volcanic ash carpeted the entire length of the hull. Overhead the sky remained hazed with dust; it was almost a smoggy brown. A glint of blue sky fought through, like a sapphire peeking through the dust. He turned in a slow circle. He could tell they had crash-landed in the middle of the desert flatlands. In the direction of what he considered to be north, he saw distant foothills, and several craggy mountain ranges beyond that. All other directions produced nothing significant, aside from a horizon that contained small lumps, and what looked like the fringe of a tree or vegetation line in the distant south.

Directly next to the ship, extending four hundred yards out from it was an orange-colored deposit of mineralized soil. Further out, the ground consisted of gray and mottled irregularities – evidence that the concussion wave of the falling ship had blown a layer of ash outward.

The heat was stifling. Breathing through his mouth, Zaz's tongue became gritty with sand particles and ash. Still, the air seemed well oxygenated; he was not huffing for breath, even feeling a little light on his feet as he moved. He activated the switches on his cooling garments then threw the line coil down the hull where it landed in the soil. While Zaz waited, he looked over the vast plain and could see two small white moons just above the horizon. Higher up at the zenith, he saw another smaller planetoid that looked broken in half, as though it had been torn apart by some titanic collision.

Lyle and Paddy came up through the hatch. With wobbly feet, they stationed themselves next to Zaz. Lyle pulled his optical filters down to examine the landscape, cutting out the harsh glare. "Inexplicable," he said, bending over to look at the surface.

"Would you like to know something?" asked Paddy. "It is not unlike Mars, except that it has no massive crater deformation. And my word... could that be snow on those distant peaks? Why, yes, it is!"

Zaz took a few tentative steps down the slope of the hull. "Well, gents, it's not too steep. Shall we – "

He didn't get another word out – Zaz's boots skidded out from under him. He came down hard on his hips and began a swift toboggan slide down the incline. He hit the spongy soil with both feet, but the momentum pitched him forward, throwing him face down into the powdery sand. No sooner did he get to his feet than another body slammed into him, knocking him down again. A third body rolled down the hull like a sack of rocks and thumped in the dirt.

Zaz glared at the two disheveled scientists. "Blow a horn next time, for crying out loud!"

The professors waggled their heads in unison. "We lost our footing whilst attempting the descent," said Paddy, spitting sand from his mouth.

The scientists helped each other up. The three of them looked about. Zaz could plainly see why the soil had cushioned their landing. It was covered with thousands of brittle tree limbs, tangled in a great mat. The entire area looked like the remnants of some great flood, or lahars that had washed an entire forest down from some higher point, tumbling it onto the desert plain. To walk over the shattered debris looked precarious at best. There were no rocks or craters as evidence, just an endless expanse of the bleached white branches, mixed with shards of chalky tree bark.

Zaz took the toe of his boot and dug a trough next to the ship. A full third of the *Shenandoah* had drove into the desert soil – evidence of a tremendous impact. He imagined that B-Deck level lay even to where he stood, give or take a few feet.

Lyle bent down and fingered the bleached white branches, scooping away loose ash. He pulled something out of the soil that looked like a tube with knuckles on the ends. "Oh, my," he gasped, dropping the object.

Paddy fell to his knees and scooped his hands through the soil. He looked from side to side, muttering indecipherable words. He dug deeper into the sediment until he reached a depth of two feet. The bleached branches continued downward to an unknown depth.

"What the bloody hell?" said Paddy. He pulled out a molecular analyzer, waved a small wand over the soil, shading the small screen with his hand to read the instrument. "No isotopes. No iridium layer – that rules out an asteroid impact. No toxins, just silicates, some iron oxides – common sand."

"What's up with you two?" Zaz walked over to them, objects crunching under foot. He looked down. A giant face gazed back at him from the dirt. Two empty eye sockets the size of his fists stared blankly from a large oval-shaped skull. A huge lower mandible gawked open as if in a scream. Teeth the size of small rocks gleamed in the sun.

Zaz took a step backward, examining the ground more closely. He saw identifiable curves, arches, and conical shapes that looked instantly familiar. Some of the shapes resembled skeletal body forms. Others were scattered in pieces. The entire desert floor was littered with them. Not only did they completely cover the surface, but they were imbedded in the soil to an unknown depth.

It was a graveyard – bones beyond count and measure.

With shaking hands, Paddy began to reassemble one of the skeletons. Lyle helped him.

Zaz watched the two, totally mesmerized. Paddy began to speak to Lyle in a haunting monotone, "There, that's the fibula, then the tibia. Those vertebrae are already in line, no need to move those. Here's the right femur…now the left. Yes, that goes there. Oh, my, look at this pelvic girdle! Have you ever seen one like this, my dear colleague? I thought not. This must be the clavicle."

When they were finished, the scientists stood up and backed away from the shape they had assembled. Dumbfounded, Zaz looked at it from several angles. It looked vaguely human, but of gigantic proportions – almost ten feet long. The skull was most peculiar, long yet robust. The teeth resembled types that he'd seen in a horse's mouth, but this creature did not have a long muzzle, only a rudimentary one. The hand and toe bones numbered four each. The ear canal sat higher up on the side of the head, where a bony ridge ran from the huge nostril area over the forehead then around to the back of the skull. The leg bones were as large as Zaz's fleshed legs.

"Giganthopithicus Blacki?" asked Lyle.

"No," said Paddy. "Not sasquatch. Not a primate. The dentine and pelvis are wrong for an ape. Nothing Neolithic. The skull has no similarities there. But it is bipedal, upright with the correct femur head and pelvis for a human-like gait. The phalanges indicate a primitive grasping ability. Do you see the small opposing thumb? Right. It's mammalian-like; the skull is almost bovine in fashion. I should like to take one onboard to examine it more thoroughly. A full DNA analysis is in order."

Zaz began a slow walk out into the plain. He tried not to step directly on the skeletal remains, but it was unavoidable. He heard the crackling footsteps of Lyle and Paddy behind him. Everywhere he looked there were bones in heaps, some piles almost three-feet high. When he stopped to use his boot toe to scrape away the dust on the many lumps, he found skulls. There were thousands of piles. He walked further out into the desert, oblivious to the heat. Somehow he hoped it would stop, all of this death, all of these bones. But he found only more of the same. Miniature skulls materialized. Adults and children? They were identical in shape.

Zaz finally stopped and turned around. He could see the ship as a football-sized shape in the distance. He stood now in gray volcanic ash. His footsteps in the thick dust bore witness to his passing, as though someone had traipsed over a carpet of dirty snow. The skeletal remains continued out as far as he could see.

A profound level of sadness and revulsion overwhelmed him. It was hard to grapple with. The scene bespoke of a terrible catastrophe, an incalculable loss of life on such a scale that it defied reason. It reminded him of the books he had read about global mass extinctions, and the fourth great Middle Eastern genocide between Iraq and Iran. Whatever deity these poor creatures might have known or worshiped, if they were capable of such a thing, had certainly abandoned them to an unmerciful end.

When Lyle and Paddy caught up to him, they were dragging their feet. Tears spilled from Paddy's eyes. Lyle patted his shoulder and said, "There, there, my dear friend. Whatever has taken place here is over now. These wretched souls feel no more pain."

Zaz looked affectionately at the zoologist. Paddy was very close to Lyle. Where Lyle was solemn and reserved, Paddy was more talkative and gregarious. Paddy swore to the possession of a degree in cryptozoology, but the crew had laughed off the claim, knowing full well that there was no such thing as an accredited degree in that field. Paddy's zoology degree had come from a 20-week cyber crash course, paid for in weekly installments. He was self-taught, having studied zoology and biology since the first day his mother had rolled him into a zoo in a baby carriage. Originally born in England, Zaz only knew that Paddy Jackson came from a small town with a "shire" on the end of it. The zoologist never spoke about his background, but it was rumored that his mother had been admitted to a nursing home on the outskirts of London. By now, she would have likely passed on. Other than her, he had no other social ties. His only real occupation lay in his work – the classification and love of fauna.

Some type of flying animal skimmed over their heads, beating its wings in the hot air. Paddy, who would have normally erupted with excitement upon seeing such an animal, gave it a dismissive glance. Zaz and Lyle did the same. At the moment, none of them cared if there were insects or worms in the soil, or flying creatures in the skies above. They didn't care about finding a flower or blade of grass. They were not interested in the minerals that beckoned to them with dazzling colors. They felt something perversely morbid around them. They could feel it in the silence, while contemplating this terrible scene that seemed to go on without end.

Zaz felt tightness in his throat. "What the hell happened here, Paddy? This can't be right. What could have caused something like this?"

Paddy slapped the tears angrily from his face. His voice was a shaky octave higher. "I don't know. In all my years of devotion to God's living creatures, I have never seen anything like this before, save for the extinction records on Earth." He cleared his throat. "This is recent, in a geological sense. The ash layer is not sufficient to have caused this. It was no pyroclastic flow, nor was it a flood. There is not enough sediment or ash fall for that kind of disaster.

These creatures dropped where they stood, in unimaginable numbers – they are literally heaped upon one another. There are males, females, young adults... I even spied several fetal skeletons within the pelvic cavities of their mothers."

"Would you agree that they are all of the same species?" Lyle asked.

"Entirely," said Paddy. "I see no other taxon here."

The captain looked out over the desert, squinting against the glare. He could just make out a small speck in the mirage-like waves. One of their huge construction machines had floated down, landing on the desert floor. He pulled a portable scope from his back pocket and scanned the horizon for more small objects.

"I'll be damned," said Zaz, spying more machines in the distance. "At least our equipment made it unscathed." He pocketed the scope then turned to the other two. "Maybe we should be getting back. The others are probably wondering what happened to us."

"Huh?" Paddy looked at him, but his mind had taken a light-year jump somewhere else. He finally said, "Yes, entirely. We should be off." He looked at Zaz. "Would you like to know something? I do not think there is any doubt as to what our task is, do you?"

Zaz's voice came just above a whisper. "Remove and bury the dead."

They started back slowly, lifting their legs high to avoid stumbling over the macabre remains.

Orion Industries had warned them – no, they had *informed* them that they would know the job requirement when they reached the coordinates. Gable had known all along what had happened here. The deterrent – is that how he'd described it? An aesthetically unpleasing sight? It was something that would deter a normal settlement, Zaz remembered Gable saying. The unmitigated gall. Such arrogance and subterfuge was to be expected from a company that sent probes around the universe, planting ownership flags on any terran planet that would fetch an imperial. Damn the past inhabitants. Just hire some naïve team from a planetary janitorial service to sweep the sad evidence under the carpet and move in a million residents so they could laugh and play over the bones of a forgotten civilization.

The sad part about all of it was the deception. Sure, one could cordon off twenty square miles, construct a twelve-foot high retainer wall to keep the settlers confined. The fact remained that there would still be thousands of corpses just outside the walls that couldn't be hidden. One couldn't keep the people from finding the ghosts. No one could prevent the new settlers from discovering who the real inhabitants of Georgian Sidus were and what had happened to them.

When they got back to the ship and struggled up the line, Galoot was waiting for them with his head popped out of the hatch, looking like some oafish prairie dog. Zaz went down the ladder in a daze. Instead of taking the foot tram, he walked the distance, deep in the throes of thought. His crew gave him a happy greeting when he arrived on the bridge. He collapsed in his deck chair and wiped the sweat from his face. "Whiskey!" he shouted to no one in particular.

Dendy found a bottle of old Scotch in the galley that hadn't broken. She poured him a four-finger shot, which he swallowed in one gulp. He followed it up with another.

Carl sat on the end of his chair with a heat pack strapped to his back. "What'd you find out there?"

The captain shook his head, waving the question off. He snapped his fingers for another shot. He got it.

Dendy bent over to gaze into his eyes. "You look like you've seen a ghost."

"I've seen thousands of ghosts," he said. "Maybe millions."

Dendy hefted the bottle to her lips. She gulped down several belts. Nobody cared that she drank from the bottle.

CHAPTER SIX

GRAVEYARDS AND PARADISE LOST

Sidus Log, Rotation 1.

I've decided to keep an active log, though my writing skills are somewhat lacking. I can liken my attempts at scribbling to twittering on the piano keys while being tone deaf. This will be a hardcopy ledger, since I can take it with me out into the field and it will not be subject to electronic failure.

I slept fitfully last night, the first night on the surface of this planet, Georgian Sidus. Our touchdown did not go as planned. We struck hard. I don't want to write about it - the incident is too painful to recount. Suffice it to say, the *Shenandoah* is no more.

We discovered a grisly scene on Sidus - thousands of skeletons from some unknown race. Something devilish has occurred here, but I cannot hazard a guess. I'm sure Lyle and Paddy will have some answers after they have finished digging up the evidence. My curiosity is piqued about this unforeseen discovery. This will not be the difficult job I envisioned. This task only disturbs me from a psychological perspective. Once I am past those reservations, the work will go on as planned.

I'm struggling against the urges I feel for Dendy. I have no prerogative to do anything about it. The emotional cost is too high. If I remember right, I'm the one that imposed the fraternization rules. How hypocritical is that? I'll stow the feelings for now.

The crew is in good spirits, in spite of our crash landing. There are no serious injuries or illnesses to contend with, which is amazing since we are stuck here until Orion Industries or their representatives show up to relieve us. The crew does not discuss our plight. We know that we have a contract to fulfill - there is plenty of work to be done.

Captain Zackary Crowe, PJ.

CARL HAD PLANTED a dozen cutting charges on the side of the hull just as he'd promised. He blew a ragged hole in the side of the ship that rocked the crew off their feet and then fabricated a ramp so the heavy equipment could roll into and out of the cargo hold.

The atmosphere of Sidus was still a mystery. The first night produced a temperature drop in the high twenties. The first day the mercury hit 122 degrees by the early afternoon. The sky was cloudless over the desert plain, except for some stratus-like sheets to the north hanging over a large range of mountains that looked similar to Earth's Grand Tetons. There were no wind flurries or dust devils, but Zaz knew that did not mean they wouldn't come. A sandstorm on the desert plain would kick up tons of volcanic ash and orange sand, enough to clog machinery and sandblast the ship and anyone caught outside.

A few water lines had broken upon the landing impact. Galoot repaired them and a slow leak in the main water tank. Once finished he went in search of Carybell. She was out a few hundred yards from the ship, picking small weeds that she thought might be baby flower stalks.

Paddy and Lyle had dragged a collection of bones aboard the *Shenandoah*; only a field museum could have held as many. They'd vowed to study the alien creatures and find the source of their demise, no matter how long it took. Lyle had scooped up a crate of soil and rocks on which to perform microanalysis. But studying the alien physiology was on their number one hit list.

The Green and Blue automechs were sent to their workstations to clean up the spilled components. A few of them were let out onto the terrain, but they had trouble navigating over the unstable ground. Several of them had snagged on the protruding bones and fallen down. Zaz ordered the ground cleared and flattened around the ship to provide a more stable platform.

Carl used a scout buggy to find the construction machines that had been scattered over the desert plain. He'd cut the chutes loose and remotely piloted the vehicles back to the ship, parking them in a staging area. One large grader had suffered a broken axle which Galoot was able to fix with a beam torch and a hoist.

Zaz stood under a shade canopy among some camp chairs, their first workable outpost on the jobsite. He could see the professors erecting the last part of the large base camp tent next to him. Carl, acting the part of a foreman, paced a few feet away, looking out into the bleak expanse. He flipped his black, greasy hair over his head, only to have it flop back down. He did not hide his frustration over the assignment's priorities.

"This is the filthiest job detail we've ever been given," he said, his face an expression of disgust and contempt.

Zaz looked at the ponderous Cat-F-9 Fence Driver. It held two massive spools of nylon-composite fence material twelve feet in width. It could be programmed to run a double line of fence while simultaneously pile-driving support poles into the ground to fashion the perimeter. Following it, the Gun Truck would spray expanding foam between the fence sheets, filling up the aperture, which would then produce a 12-foot-high rock-hard retaining wall. The Cat-12 super grader led the procession, leveling a 20-foot wide swath of earth in one pass.

Zaz spoke up before his foreman put himself into a deeper mental rut. "Okay, Carl. They want a twenty-mile square area cleared and leveled. The first thing is to grade a perimeter road four-by-five miles – a rectangle. That will be your fence area. Use the

Shenandoah as your reference point. Be sure you go deep enough to gouge up the bone material. Next, send your Fence Driver onto the road and start laying down the barrier. Follow it up with the Gun Truck. Run your rectangle. That's the first part of it."

"Yeah, I know. I'm not fretting over that part of it. What are we going to do with this mess?" He stepped on a brittle rib protruding up from the dirt, cracking it.

"First, show a little respect. As for the rest, plan out a grid, doze it up into piles, then have the front loaders transport refuse outside the settlement area. The backhoes and grapplers can dig up deep trenches to bury it. Make sure the holes are deep enough. It might take dozens of trenches; it depends on how deep this bone bed goes. It's not all that complicated."

"It just seems like a lot of trouble."

Carl's mind was an easy read. If the man could use explosives to get the job done, he would have suggested it already. But he knew that Zaz wouldn't go for such a radical approach, not for something that called for logical earthmoving techniques. Tops, it might take them one to two months to finish the job, which they'd been allotted a year to complete.

Zaz blew a hot sigh. "You've already got your cookies creamed by blowing the side out of my ship. Let's say we do the rest of it the conventional way."

"Her back was broken like a horse anyway. It's okay to put down a horse that's got its back busted. As far as this here, it's a lot of work, that's all I'm saying."

"You know, eighty years ago, Carl, they used to sit up there and drive those machines. They called them heavy equipment operators. They got a lot of cabbage for what they did. All we have to do is punch some program buttons and turn them loose. We only bring them into the cargo bay for periodic maintenance. We'll have to watch the armatures on the big motors, though. They'll get hot out here during the day."

"Then why don't we run them at night?"

"We're going to sleep at night and work the day shift just like a regular construction crew. We can keep the generators off at night thanks to the cooler temperatures – we have plenty of insulation. Besides that, I want to see what I'm doing out here."

"Okay, I'll do a four-by-five-mile rectangle and lay the wall. Then we go deep enough to level and clean up this inside real estate. I'll start the survey now. Wait a minute – maybe later."

Zaz followed Carl's eye line over his shoulder and turned around. Dendy and Samantha were tromping across the sand, carrying ice buckets, containers and portable cooling jets. They stepped high to avoid the bone ruts. The women wore boots, collars, and the standard cooling britches – and nothing else.

"Mama Mia," said Carl, trying to keep the hairy mop out of his eyes lest it spoil his view. "Now that's the kind of scenery I'm talking about. C'mon over here, Sammy, and let me catch some shade under those."

Dendy trudged up, wearing boots three sizes too large for her feet. She set her containers down. "I'll stand over you, Carl. That way your face will get good and sun blistered. And with any luck, maybe the sun will blind those lecherous eyes of yours."

Zaz frowned. "I thought we had a policy about showing crew skin unless we were jumping or showering together."

Samantha bent over to drop her load. The heavy sway of her breasts did not go without notice. "Oh, lighten up," she admonished. "We aren't Earthbound or onboard a ship, so the rules don't apply. Besides that, we're wearing E-Z Sun Block so we won't get toasted."

Zaz caught Dendy giving him a coy smile while she poured some Freezie Slush. She stepped up to him, extending a cup. He took it, but could not avert his eyes from her muscular thighs, rippling with a sheen of oily sun blocker. She looked to him like a stout little earthmover.

Samantha reared her arms up and savagely raked her fingers through a gigantic bush of hair. The image it conjured would have driven Leonardo DaVinci in a frantic search for brush and canvas. Dendy was more modestly built, so it would have been unfair for him to order Samantha to wear a top. *Oh, the hell with it all, anyway,* he decided, *just another hazard to navigate.* Which reminded him...

Zaz brought the small scope to his eye. Looking out over the plain, he saw a tiny, rice-sized figure. "Now what is Carybell doing that far out? I thought I told her to stay around the ship."

Galoot crunched into the jobsite, ducking under the canopy roof. "I got that other dang leak fixed. Now it's official – we have two years of water." Galoot looked around, but his eyes passed over the two females. "Where's my Carybell? Have you seen my little woman?"

Zaz pointed a finger. "She's that-a-way. Bring her back and tell her not to wander off so far. I don't care if she's picking flowers, weeds, or whatever. She could pass out from heatstroke." He sat down, the furnace-like heat making him weak in the knees.

"That's a four, boss. I'll fetch her now. Oh, yeah, Lyle and Paddy said they want to see you about something important." Galoot marched off out into the desert, heading for the tiny speck of Carybell.

Zaz wanted to finish his drink before visiting with the scientists. Those two could be insufferable bores at times; they were capable of tying anyone up with a two-hour dissertation, and before a person could walk away from one of their lectures, they would have already forgotten the subject. Zaz hoped they wouldn't be too caught up in the alien archeology of Sidus. He had a nagging suspicion that the mystery of the skeletal remains might interfere with their regular work shifts. He couldn't discourage *some* type of investigation. All they really had to do was monitor the machines and program the Blues and Greens to help out. The only physical work required was routine maintenance on the machines. Any analysis of the ecosystem would be pure gravy.

It did not mean there was ample goof-off time. It just meant that some other points of interest were available. Planet Janitor did have qualified professionals that could perform scientific investigations, and Sidus was a brand new discovery that screamed for analysis. Who cared what Orion Industries thought they were doing with their spare time!

The planet certainly had potential; it had a 22-hour day with an unknown seasonal cycle, and a dry, hot equatorial belt, with some numbing night time lows. There was evidence of obvious vegetation. Snow-capped mountains were a sure sign that there were streams, creeks, and lakes. The two oceans were a mystery: what kind of sea and plant life did they possess? Perhaps they harbored something exotic, or contained life-curing chemicals or anti-toxins.

He also wondered what kind of minerals Sidus hid deep in her sediments: what precious veins of ore flowed through her mountainous interiors? Was Sidus a cruel and toxic world, or was she full of hopeful new vistas waiting to be discovered? The planet was an explorer's haven to be sure. She could bring out the crusty adventurer in anyone who walked over her soil or gazed upon her for the first time. But she was also a nagging question mark. Something terrible and unforeseen had happened here. Until that puzzle could be solved, Sidus was an unwitting merchant of death – a serial killer.

Zaz got up and headed for the ship. Dendy crunched along, asking if she could go with him. He took her hand, swinging it playfully. She looked up at him with those bright, black eyes. Zaz knew that right now everything seemed to be in perfect harmony. He felt an ever-increasing need to be with her. His time had always been devoted to entrepreneurial pursuits – finding his niche, discovering his calling. It was somehow comforting to know that he had someone who admired those traits, taking an interest in him. Damn, he hoped he wasn't falling in love! He was intrigued with the possibility but scared of the prospect.

They went straight to the science lab on A-Deck. The place looked like an old mortuary, with heavy black drapes cordoning off small anti-rooms that held chemicals, instruments, meters and containers filled with questionable substances. A long stainless steel table occupied the middle of the deck floor, filled with surgical-like instruments. A complete, articulated skeleton lay stretched out upon it, with a number of skulls lined on the table's edge. More bones had been strewn across the deck, some packed in boxes, others on the floor, impeding foot traffic. The place smelled old and musky, like a preparator's backroom in a museum.

Lyle and Paddy were bent over in serious examination, their noses nearly pressed to the table. Each held a magnifier in front of their faces. Paddy scratched caked dirt from one of the leg bones with a dental pick. Zaz and Dendy took up stools at one of the table ends. The two scientists, engrossed in what they were doing, had not acknowledged their presence.

"Inexplicable," Paddy whispered, "I'm finding more of the same on this side."

Lyle picked through one of the piles, spilling several bones to the deck. Finding something that caught his interest, he held it up against the overhead light and brought it flush against a large magnifier. He cocked his head, trying to get a better view. "Hah! I've found another one," he said. "This metacarpal definitely shows a defensive wound. The lacerations are lateral. This appears to be a sub-adult. It is unanimous – they have all been compromised."

"Hmm. Would you like to know something? The adults possess more of the trauma per square inch than the smaller specimens. It indicates a parental defensive posture, perfectly in keeping with family unit behavior."

"Agreed, sir. They are undeniably mammalian-like, very protective of the juveniles."

Paddy tried to stretch a kink out of his back. "Yes, but where in the bloody hell is the evidence for the instruments that inflicted these injuries?"

"What type of instruments are we talking about?" asked Zaz.

Startled, Paddy pitched his dental pick over his shoulder where it stuck in the fold of a heavy drape. He held his chest, feigning a heart attack. "Good Lord, Captain Crowe. Give a care. Would you kindly sound the horn before you let loose with a note? Now where in the Chuck Dickens is that...oh, rot the thing anyway! Yes, now what is it that I can do for you?" He squinted across the table. "Miss Dendy, I must say that the climate agrees with you. You are looking quite fit and lovely."

"Why, thank you, professor. You should get some sun, yourself. Are you studying the poor creatures?" Dendy was making polite conversation; she admitted as much in the past about humoring the scientists aboard the Blue Peace expedition ship. It was the kind of respect she offered to all the senior academics. It had been the deckhands that frazzled her nerves.

Paddy answered, "That we are. Ah, Zaz. I sent a message that – "

"Galoot told me. That's why we're here. Have you found anything interesting?"

Paddy looked at him gravely. "I should say that we have. I have taken the liberty of naming this species Maximus Paddymous Sidus, if that it not too presumptuous."

"It's the prerogative of the discoverer. Go on."

"These Paddymous creatures have all sustained trauma in one form or another. None are exclusive from the injuries. The adults show the greatest signs of contact, implying that they were protecting the younger ones. There are lacerations about the sternum, hands, arms, and most predominantly, the cervical vertebrae. Many of the neck vertebrae show obvious signs of decapitation. Even the massive skulls show signs of cutting wounds. Truly, they are violent injuries – injuries that would have induced rapid blood loss."

"We didn't see the striations, sir, until we brought them under the glass," said Lyle. "Once we used magnification we were astounded to find these numerous slashing marks. They give every indication of being knife cuts, something akin to a medieval clash of warriors. There even appears to be arrow-like punctures in some of the long bones and skull areas. There are also crushing injuries associated with the arms, but particularly the ribs. Clubbing injuries, most likely."

"What is not present amid the carnage is the use or evidence of what weapons could have caused such injuries," said Paddy. "The opposing force must have overwhelmed these creatures then carried their weapons out upon leaving. It could not have been a fair fight, but appears to have been a decisive, one-sided rout."

Zaz pinched his chin. "What about dating analysis? Can you estimate the time of this war, or the deaths of these things?"

"I used the old carbon fourteen and cross-checked it against the nuclear analysis," said Paddy. "We can estimate a tad over thirteen years, which is spot on. There is no mistake that this was a recent event. We have found some mummified soft tissue. Together with the marrow samples, we're running a complete DNA profile, which should give us the results soon."

Dendy asked the question they were all contemplating: "So, where are the things that killed them?"

"Orion Industries never mentioned anything about an indigenous life form on the planet," said Zaz. "Their planetary survey showed nothing. Judging from the number of corpses out there, we're talking about a huge population – with numbers large enough to have wiped our giant friends out. This must be similar to what Homo Erectus did to our Neanderthal. They beat them with intelligence – superior technology."

"That fits to be sure," said Paddy. "These Paddymous creatures were herbivores, simple vegetarians with a limited technology base. I wouldn't rank them higher than a primitive Stone Age level of development. It would not take much to annihilate them. The question is: where are these conquerors? Are they holding up in some other part of this continent, or the next one over? Why weren't they seen? How could they avoid detection?"

Lyle sat down. "We excavated the area around the ship but could not find any other skeletal remains belonging to a different species. Certainly casualties would have resulted on the other side, as is the case in all wars. But, damn it, sir! There is nothing, not one sliver of bone belonging to another animal. It's quite baffling."

Zaz winced. *Don't tell me I have something else to worry about on this rock. Please don't suggest that there is some unknown anonymous killer stashed away deep in the guts of this landmass that could pose a threat to our existence. Could they be spying on us now? Or, God forbid, within earshot?* He did not need another concern right now. There was a heavy workload and a schedule to meet. The safety of the crew was priority.

Zaz thanked Lyle and Paddy, excusing himself. He took Dendy with him down to B-Deck and jumped inside the nearest available vehicle. They drove the six-wheeled buggy out onto the plain and parked next to the jobsite camp. "Where're Galoot and Carybell?" he yelled to Samantha.

Samantha turned. She had been finalizing machine programs for Carl, who was out on the perimeter checking the first stages of the fence line construction. "Uh, let me see," she answered, cornering a small tent. She looked out toward the north. "Got 'em. They're out there, almost in line with the construction train."

Zaz punched the accelerator, heading north. He kept the buggy's speed down, to monitor the ground condition. The bone bed extended out as far as he could see; small islands of skeletons pock-marked the ground, making it dangerous to navigate. It was disquieting to know that such a mass could have no end to it, with no idea how far out it extended.

After five minutes, he found Galoot and Carybell sitting Indian style in the dirt. Zaz pulled up to them, noticing that they had collected a pathetic handful of brittle shrubs and dried weeds. Carybell was nude, pink with sunburn.

"You two, in the buggy now," said Zaz. "Carybell, those coolers are designed to lower your body temp through the femoral and carotid arteries. Don't ever come out here without them, or sun block. You hear that, girl?"

Zaz didn't mean to seem so harsh where Carybell was concerned, but Galoot had told him in private that the young woman had not led a life prone to responsible behavior. She'd been a spaceport junkie from an early age, having run away from step-parents to explore a world of adventure. Those forays had landed her in nameless men's cabins, hopping from one bunk to another all over the solar system. Zaz figured the least he could do was offer her some form of moral direction and support. She needed to belong to a constructive group that valued her for more than just her carnal talents. That meant some form of discipline.

The two piled into the buggy. They took off, heading for Carl's fence line. Arriving at the site, Zaz pulled ahead of the work train and waved for Carl to join them. He had to give Carl the swish across the neck sign, telling him to shut the machinery down so he could be heard over the roar.

Carl shut the line down then strolled toward the buggy. Zaz walked out to meet him, but he stopped to pan his pocket scope over the terrain leading to the mountains. He wasn't sure what he was looking for, but he had an unsettling feeling in his gut.

Carl stood by, clearing his throat several times. "Well, do you like it so far? I'm checking to see if she's running a straight line. So far so good."

Zaz made one last visual sweep then pocketed the scope. "Yeah, it looks fine, Carl. You don't have to be out here, you know. All you have to do is perform periodic checks."

"You know I've got to watch my automation. Hell, I don't like it anymore than you do. You always have me watch the line anyway. If something goes haywire it could screw the grid."

"Look, I don't suppose you'd have any personal protection weapons? I know you've got some antiques stowed in the maintenance bay, but do you have anything functional?"

"Do you want to do some target shooting?"

"Not that. It would be nice if you had something on you, just in case. Listen, I can't say it any other way – Paddy and Lyle seem to think that something killed all these giants out here. They're convinced it was another type of thing, only a whole lot smarter and carrying some type of weaponry. To be honest, I don't know what to think. But after what I've seen and heard, it would be best if you were armed."

"You're kidding me." Carl gave him a double take. "You're not kidding me. You're saying we have something out here that's dangerous? I mean, besides that little armadillo thing I saw running around earlier and those weird birds?"

"That's exactly what I'm saying."

"All I have is an antique .45 army pistol with about a thousand rounds of ammunition. Then there's an automatic twenty-something rifle that I'm not even sure works. It's really old stuff, Zaz. I'll have to clean them up, figure out how they work. If you want me to tote the damn things out here, I guess that's fine with me. What the hell are we talking about? I mean bogeyman wise."

Zaz stared toward the north again, feeling the sun bake his forehead. "I don't know, Carl. Maybe it's nothing. But if it is something, I'd feel better if we were ready for it. No surprises."

"Okay." Carl shrugged his shoulders then turned and walked back to the fence line.

Zaz hollered after him: "I mean, right now, Carl. I want you armed right now. Jump in. Leave your buggy here."

They headed to the job site at a swift pace. Zaz became annoyed with the bones that flew up, getting jammed in the undercarriage. It was a morose feeling having to traverse over every square foot of Sidus real estate, cracking something under boot heel or tire that had once been alive.

They assembled at the jobsite, under the cover of the shade canopy. Zaz imposed the hydration rule as a first order of business. After they'd consumed their liquid quota he told them to take seats on portable chairs. Lyle and Paddy were still in the science lab, but Zaz dialed them up with his com and told them to listen in.

"There's going to be some new rules around here," the captain announced. "There will be no exceptions. First, no one is to travel any farther out from the ship than one hundred yards in any compass direction. That's unless you get my permission or have a partner accompany you. You'll wear your coolers at all times and re-hydrate every two hours, whether you think you need it or not. I want you to find some type of metal rod that can be used as a walking staff, something to carry with you at all times."

"You want me to have a rod, too?" asked Carl. "I thought you said – "

"No, you carry that .45 and give me the other rifle. Teach me how to operate it. Sammy, I'd like you to put three long-range snoops in the air. Head one north to the tree line, another one south, and the third one toward one of the oceans. I don't care if it's the east or west. I just need some kind of a layout of this place. The survey maps that Orion gave us are too grainy and non-specific."

Samantha nodded. "I'll run them in grids and get you a layout."

Zaz looked at Galoot. "You damn well know what I want you to do."

"I'll get right on it, boss." Galoot picked up Carybell in the crook of his arm like a piece of cordwood and headed for the ship.

Carybell waved to the crew. Zaz knew that Galoot intended to outfit them properly with cooling gear.

The flash oven dinged – lunch was done.

Samantha arm-wrestled her hair into a ponytail then took the precooked food packs out of their containers. She passed them around, holding back two for the professors. Everyone ate in silence, glancing occasionally at their captain, no doubt wondering what had brought on the sudden precautionary status. The only times Zaz had been stern with his crew was when it was job related. Since everything was in order and they were on schedule with the work assignment, the faces around him showed mild apprehension.

Samantha pointed a fork at him. "Has this got something to do with what happened here? Do you think the weapons are necessary?"

"Sammy, you know I'm not paranoid. I just don't think there's any harm in precaution." Zaz decided to change the subject. "How's the trenching coming along?"

"We've got two ditches started over on the south perimeter," Samantha replied. "Both are forty deep by thirty wide. The front loaders are starting to fill them up – the retaining wall will be up ahead of schedule. We might finish this whole project in three months. What will we have to do until the developers arrive?"

Zaz gave her a nervous smile. "Barring that none of our equipment breaks down, we'll take a really long vacation." He took a spoonful of something that looked like creamed potato, thinking about his next directive.

A sudden explosion rocked the *Shenandoah*. The concussion wave hammered the jobsite, blowing the shade tarp from its moorings. The ground shook. Two tent pegs snapped free, nearly collapsing the structure. A small dust plume rose up from the bottom of the ship. Dust and debris fluttered out of the large hatch opening.

Zaz got to his feet, upending his plate in the sand. The rest of the crew jumped to their feet, equally perplexed. All eyes were drawn to the ship. Zaz started off at a sprint for the hatch, knowing that Galoot, Carybell, and the scientists were in the ship. As he ran toward the hatch ramp, he fought back images of his crewmembers lying about in mangled pieces.

Galoot stumbled out of the hatch, carrying Carybell in his arms. The large man had a flash burn on the left side of his face. Zaz nearly ran into him.

"It came from B-Deck at the stern," Galoot coughed. "Don't know what it was. It sent a fireball down the hull."

Zaz pushed him, propelling him down the ramp. "Just get clear right now. Are you injured?"

"Nah, me and Carybell didn't catch the main blast."

The rest of the crew caught up with him at the hatch. Together they ran up the ramp and turned right, heading down the cavernous interior. Other than their boot strikes on the grated floor, there was a haunting pall of silence as they trotted hurriedly toward the stern of the ship. Something smelled very foul on B-Deck – a ghastly odor.

Zaz waved his arm for a halt, realizing that the stern of the ship held the nuclear bang pod capsules, the explosive mechanisms used for propelling the ship. Though they had to be armed before they could be ignited, there was no telling what the explosion had done.

The captain eased them to a slow walk.

In the excitement, it never occurred to him to take the foot tram. Right now, he felt more stable on his legs. They passed by a Green automech that lay motionless on the floor plate, blown there by the explosion. Zaz's boots sloshed in a sloppy liquid – fowled water. They passed by another automech, a Blue this time. It lay twisted around itself in a grotesque pretzel-like configuration.

When they came to the source of the blast, Zaz's shoulders sagged. The huge torpedo-shaped freshwater tank had been blown in two at the middle. He could hear the sound of water cascading down into the lower C-Deck cargo hold, where the blast had ripped through the deck plates. Flying metal shrapnel had blacked out most of the overhead lighting. The port side of the ship's bulkhead had imploded outward and mashed against the primary outer hull, but had not penetrated to the outside.

Located on the stern side of the water tank sat a smaller tank that had ruptured on its end cap. Streams of sludge poured onto the deck from the ragged opening. Some of the thick quagmire fell down to splat on the lower C-Deck. It was the septic tank. Though it had been pumped out before the flight, a hundred gallons of surplus had remained in the bottom, caked to the insides. Now the septic refuge had contaminated what water might have collected in pockets or pools. The standing water had also combined with a carpet of ore dust, dirt, sand, hydraulic fluid, grease and oil. The septic pump motors had taken through and through shrapnel hits.

Dendy kicked the side of the tank, making no effort to mask her anger. "We are so totally fucked now! Every goddamned drop of water we had was in that tank. Ninety thousand fucking gallons." It was the first time anyone had heard Dendy really let loose.

Zaz found himself temporarily speechless. He watched as Carl stepped up to the tank to examine it more carefully. He knew what Carl was looking for. If anyone knew pyrotechnics and blast sources, it was Carl Stromboli. Carl had once enlightened him on the subject of forensic metallurgy; much like a fire inspector had to find a fire's point of ignition. A man skilled with explosives had to determine the source-origin of freak blasts.

Carl stepped backward slowly from the ruptured water tank, measuring his steps until he stopped to turn around. Then he walked slowly in a bent over crouch, toward the bulkhead. He halted at the bulkhead seam and picked something up. It was a shiny piece of chrome-colored metal with a partially stenciled monogram on it.

Samantha ducked down into a tangle of water pipe and pulled something out. She studied the silver chunk of metal in her hands, which they all recognized. It was half of the head section belonging to a Silver automech.

Carl reached for Samantha's piece then held the two fragments together. After a moment, he dropped them to the deck. They were a match. He swallowed dryly, glancing at his captain.

Zaz felt an incomprehensible rage grab hold of him and shake him right to the bones. Of all the damnable mishaps he could ever remember, this one had taken the grand trophy.

"Carl," Zaz said between clenched teeth. "I'm not even going to remind you what I asked you to do before we lifted off. I told you we had a problem with one of the Silvers. Remember something about cradling them and shutting them down – complete disarmament? If that is Silver Two, I am going to choke you within an inch of your life."

Carl toed a piece of breastplate on the floor. "It's not Silver Two. I recognize the call number on this one – it's Silver Nine. I did exactly what you told me to do. I don't know how this one unsaddled and got loose. It somehow got by me."

"Check it out, Carl. Run a complete diagnostic on all the demolition mechs. Find out what the hell happened. We don't need a repeat." He lightened up a bit. He couldn't throw all the blame on Carl – that would have been a cheap shot. Automechs were sophisticated automatons. The manufacturers had been having problems with them for the past 15 years, and there had been more recalls on the Silvers than any other.

Carl looked stunned, guilt-ridden.

Zaz digressed. "Carl, I didn't mean it like that. In case I didn't mention it, if it wasn't for your idea to drop-chute our heavy load, we'd never have made it." He felt he owed Carl that. He never took any of them to task unless it was a deliberate screw up. This had all the hallmarks of an accident.

Samantha turned to Zaz. "I think we have about thirty gallons of drinking water in the bridge galley. What are we going to do for the rest? Maybe we can rig something up with the hydrogen generators, to distill some down. It's crude but it might work."

"We'll be out in two days flat," said Zaz, "at the rate we have to consume it. And that's not including bathing water." He knew the recycling tank was empty since little had been processed since their touchdown. The hydroponics aquarium held salt water that could be desalinated. But there would be hell and damnation to pay from Dendy if they so much as dared pull a water molecule from her precious fish. He called for suggestions.

"The chart shows that those ice capped mountains are about four hundred and fifty miles to the north," said Samantha. "We might find a gorge there – maybe some stream runoff. We can drag the small water trailer behind the six-wheeler. That's four thousand gallons. We can take any other containers we can scrounge up in a few more vehicles. It's worth a shot. We don't have any other options."

Zaz gave her a pat on the head. "You just solved our problem, Sammy. That's exactly what we're going to do. No choice in the matter."

Dendy frowned. "It will take us a couple days to prepare if we want to do this right."

"We'll take those days," said Zaz. "There won't be any mistakes. It's a long ways out across this plain. We'll convoy in multiple vehicles; if something breaks down we switch rides. Make sure there's a full charge on each battery pack. We'll take the big hydrogen truck with us for tow support. We'll pack light – camping gear, mostly – in case we have to spend a couple nights out. The job line will have to be shut down."

Nobody argued with the plan.

CHAPTER SEVEN

MAXIMUS PADDYMOUS SIDUS

Sidus Log, Rotation 4.
"We're heading north toward some ice-capped mountainous peaks for water. We sent one snoop ahead, watching its survey results from a portable viewer while en route. It might help us to trail blaze, making our passage easier once we reach the foothills.

From the very little I've seen of it, this is a hellish planet. I hope my opinion will change once we enter the lowlands, where there appears to be a tree line. Anything would be better than this featureless wasteland. I am already sick of it and it's only the fourth day. I find the mass quantities of skeletons around us disturbing. It's a feeling that pulls at the most morbid realizations of one's inner self. There is a finality here that wreaks havoc with my belief system. I can't put it into words.

We've decided to shut the construction line down for the duration of our absence. It will not cost us any noticeable time. We would not be able to monitor the grid work if something went offline, anyway."

Captain Zackary Crowe, PJ.

ZAZ THREW A LEG UP into the six-wheeled rover and climbed into the seat. Dendy sat in the passenger seat, while Paddy and Lyle took up the rear bench. Carl took the driver's position inside the hydrogen-fueled tow truck, with Samantha sitting next to him. Galoot would be driving the smaller, four-wheeled buggy, co-piloted by Carybell. Everyone wore sun goggles to stem the glare and ultraviolet light.

Zaz took off in the lead, dragging the large water trailer. The other vehicles fell in place behind, like ducks following their mother. The tires furrowed deep grooves in the desert floor, bones cracking under the weight of the vehicles. Zaz put a music cube into the dashboard player and turned the volume up to drown out the noise. Dendy began doing her version of the rocka-bop in her seat. He now knew why *Tiny Dancer* was such a prime-time persona aboard Blue Peace. It was hard to take one's eyes off her.

It was a short jaunt to the north fence wall. Zaz pulled up thirty yards short of it. He waved a circular pattern over his head, the sign for "we're going around this thing." Carl pulled up next to him, stood and fingered a remote control. A section of the wall blew out. Pieces of fence and foam rained down on the stunned passengers.

Zaz stiffened. "Was that necessary? Damn it, Carl, we could have taken the long way around."

Carl shrugged. "I set the charges yesterday – we needed a way out."

Zaz punched the accelerator, driving the larger vehicle through the ragged opening. He picked up speed, aiming a straight course for the snow-capped peaks.

"You've got to hand it to him," said Dendy. "He's a time-saver, that Carl."

"Yeah, and I'm beginning to think I know who was responsible for the Big Bang fourteen billion years ago."

They drove on, watching for ruts and ditches. Dusty piles of bones caused Zaz to swerve occasionally. He passed by a small gray armored-type creature, and it curled into a perfect melon-sized ball the minute it felt the presence of the vehicle. He craned his neck, watching to see if it would uncoil. Paddy nearly fell out of the cab gawking at the thing. Lyle had to pull him back into his seat.

They watched the landscape for other creatures. Occasionally Zaz saw a birdlike animal, but they flew too high to see their features. He noticed some type of hopping insect that vaulted in the air away from the oncoming nose of the six-wheeler. It was some type of locust, he surmised, because they were very still and hard to see until roused. He kept watch for lizards or spiders, but nothing like that showed itself. Damn the desert, he thought. Even Earth's deserts were mild by comparison. He wondered if it was just too hot out on the plain. Nothing could really live on the Sidus desert for very long without burrowing for shelter. What possible creature could survive the intense heat without having its bodily fluids boiled away? It was nine in the morning and already 115 degrees Fahrenheit, or "Fairy" as Samantha liked to call it. It confounded him – not a breeze to be had from any direction.

He knew the big oceans lay to the east and to the west. They did not drive an inland wind over the great equatorial plain. It was unknown whether or not the big planet pushed tides or currents. Sidus had three moons to swell the tides. Did it have any current conveyors like Earth? Did it have poles and glaciers? He suspected it might be so. They were titanic oceans; roughly seventy percent of the globe held water. The two largest Sidus landmasses were equal in size, close to the surface area of Earth's Australia and America. For there to be a substantial atmosphere, there had to be major weather fronts, complete with currents and precipitation.

As a child, Zaz often went fishing with his father. They used to delight in catching catfish and trout the old-fashioned way, without dropping electro lines into the water and zapping everything that came within range of the high-voltage simulated lure. They'd preferred to bait their hooks with worms or cheese chunks. He wondered what kind of life existed in the great oceans of Sidus. Would he hook something that he could show off and eat on a barbecue spit? Or would he capture something that would make scream and run for his life?

Zaz noticed the two other vehicles pulling up abreast of him. Carl signaled with a hand over his mouth, indicating they were eating too much volcanic dust to follow directly behind.

They passed the 100-mile mark when Tau sat at its zenith. The temperature pushed 118 degrees. The cooling collars and britches helped, but given the speed of the vehicles, the hot wind was like a blast furnace on the face. Zaz's cheeks felt like they were on a grill. Dendy passed out more of the sun block, lathering up the captain's arms and face as he drove.

There was an absence of bone beds when they reached the 350-mile mark. There were scatterings, but nothing like the amount they had seen before. The soil looked more powdery. Evidence of tiny shrubs struggled to gain meager rootholds in the soil. He saw more of the tiny armadillo creatures scurrying about. When they approached them, the animals balled-up like the others had. They took on the likeness of rocks as camouflage, compressing to protect their sensitive innards. To protect them from what, though? None of them had seen an alpha carnivore, at least he thought.

At 380 miles out, they came across a delta fan of broken branches and tree limbs that had been woven into great mats and tangles of roots – evidence of a flood plain. A precipitous gorge loomed in the distance. It was no doubt the source of the run-off or flood that had littered the plain. An obvious tree line was now visible that separated the lowlands from the flat prairie, a line cut cleanly as though by an axe stroke. It would make a great settlement site if not for the threat of volcanic activity, and the topography of the valley suggested a possible lahar area. The last thing a deep space colony needed was the risk of a pyroclastic landslide.

Zaz called for a halt, stopping his vehicle. The buggy and truck pulled up on either side. They got out to stretch their legs and take a drink. Lyle and Paddy dropped to their knees, examining the dwarfish plant life. Carybell skipped off, Galoot trailing in her wake.

"I want everyone to stick around," Zaz yelled. He could feel a very slight breeze on his face. He tongued his finger and held it up. The draft came from the gorge.

It was no wonder. He estimated there was a cleft of rock on the left rising to at least 3,000 FEET. On the opposite side, the walls ran up a sheer 4,000 feet in height. It resembled an Earth formation he had once glimpsed, but he couldn't recall where he'd seen such grandeur. It looked like some age-old titanic force had thrust them up – a tectonic upheaval.

Lyle shuffled up next to him, puffing his chest out. He also caught site of the formation. "Have you ever been to Yosemite National Park, sir?"

"*That's* where I've seen it," said Zaz. "Now I remember. Only in a catalogue, though. I missed a scout jamboree trip there when I was a child. Regretted it ever since."

Lyle swept his arm up, pointing to the features. "Half Dome and El Capitan, only they are reversed from this end. It looks like Yosemite Valley. Quite a bit of uplift activity. Odds are she's limestone and granite."

Zaz could always appreciate Lyle's assumptions. He trusted his judgment; the geologist had worked at the United States Geological Survey in Menlo Park, California, and had received numerous awards and accolades. Lyle had a terrible time with females, and avoided the topics of dating, marriage and casual sex. He had a living mother who was on her second marriage and retired somewhere in Canada. Lyle always wrote posts and cyber messages aboard ship, but they were secretive in nature, so no one knew to whom they were meant for. If he didn't have his eyes to a microscope, he had his ear to the ground or his nose in the dirt. Like geology, Lyle was a collection of layers and sediments that ran deep into his inner core, and if he was stingy with anything, it was with his emotions. He'd always worn that damnable Optipak headset. When asked why he did so, he said it came in handy for examining precious stones, because everybody in the world wore Earth's precious gems somewhere on their body.

Zaz burrowed his boot toe in the soil and dragged it. "What gives the dirt this reddish appearance?"

"Most likely iron minerals that have rusted. The rusty color comes about by ongoing interaction of an oxidizing atmosphere with the surface rocks. Sidus has clays, carbonates, salts and other minerals that formed in the presence of water. The big salt plain was once inundated completely. It appears to have been a freshwater lake at one time. I found evidence of diatoms and tiny skeletal shrimp."

"Orion Industries really got their money's worth."

"I think the real prize," said Lyle, "lies beyond in the canyon valley."

Zaz put his pocket scope to his eye. He could just make out some of the characteristics of the plants and trees. He saw lots of blues, greens and grays. The sloping sides of the canyon walls contained a sparse type of timberline. But the trees were most peculiar. He handed the scope to Lyle with the comment: "Looks like something straight out of one of Poe's descriptions. Look at those trees and scrubland."

Lyle brought the scope to his eye. "You are so right, sir. Most peculiar flora!"

Galoot thudded across the sand, toting Carybell under an arm. The small girl hung there like some straw-stuffed doll. She made no move to drop to her feet, but grinned at everyone as though she'd found a new mode of transportation.

Samantha stepped up to Galoot, after shutting the case on her portable viewer. The large man stood there, legs bowed, staring off toward the gorge and sniffing the air.

"You know," said Samantha, "I'll just bet you that Carybell's legs work real good. I've seen her stand before. She does a pretty decent job of it.

"Guh?" He looked down at Samantha. "I was just trying to help her. She's little. She might fall down a lot."

Samantha blew a blowtorch sigh. "If she doesn't start using her legs she's going to lose them from atrophy. Then she'll be falling down *all* the time."

"Oh, all right." Galoot set her down.

"It's okay, I like it," said Carybell. She playfully fingered a necklace around her neck.

Zaz wanted to lay into both of them for wandering off but he moved in to study the object around Carybell's neck. It was a necklace made out of what looked like tiny seashells and woven fiber. He asked her where she got it.

She pointed over her shoulder. "Out there in the dirt. It was on a broken head."

Lyle stepped up to her, and with a hesitant hand said, "May I?"

She allowed Lyle to examine the piece, but when he fingered it too vigorously the strand broke and the shells fell to the dirt. Carybell screwed her face up, but Galoot calmed her before she threw a fit.

Lyle picked the pieces up and showed them to Paddy, who studied them carefully.

"Oh, my," said Paddy. "Primitive craftsmanship. Look at the holes, the weave of this grassy fiber. It is akin to Paleo-Indian artistry, a bit cruder perhaps, but shows obvious signs of intelligence." He gave the others a quizzical look.

Whose intelligence? What kind of intelligence? Zaz gave the gorge a furtive glance then checked the trunk compartment of the six-wheeler. He pulled out the rifle he'd stowed there and slung it over his shoulder. "I want this done by the numbers, he said. "We'll proceed straight toward the gorge in a wedge formation. I'll ride point. We'll take it at fifteen miles-per-hour. Watch this fan area for ruts and soft spots. Carl, keep that pistol ready to fire."

Samantha said, "I've been watching the progress of one of our snoops on the viewer. It's the one in the north, right up that gorge. It shows a stream about forty miles in, so we're definitely going to meet up with it. I'll need to recall all three snoops since their fuel charges are running low. There's nothing significant to report from the other two."

"That's fine, Sammy. Bring them home and park them in our lap. Let's head out."

They started off again – slowly this time. Small branches and dried roots cracked under the wheels. They started a slow incline. The progress slowed even more. Zaz pulled up over the top of a small bush-choked arroyo to gain higher ground. The others had to fall in behind given the narrowness of the track line.

They reached another plateau. It was an eerie landscape to be sure. Small cactus-like plants appeared in an array of rope-like designs. They passed by a grove of gnarly mesquite, for that is what it looked like. Its spindly branches resembled bony fingers ready to grab and gouge. They rolled past some small succulents that exhibited a peculiar blue-green hue. Zaz saw tiny purple blossoms on the stalks of a stunted variety of sage.

The six-wheeler rolled down into a steep gully, gaining the next rise. Here the lowlands rippled like a rough sea with high waves frozen in motion. Six miles farther, almost at the mouth of the gorge, the wheels splashed over the first mud puddles. It looked like the last gasp of a creek. The water source came straight down the valley floor from the north, just as Samantha had claimed. Zaz kept the six-wheeler out in front, breaking a trail for the others to follow.

Three more miles in, they fell under the first shadow of a cliff wall. Zaz had to look up, angling his neck to see the canyon tops. The temperature gauge read 99 degrees. A drop! He felt a pronounced breeze on his forehead – not much, but it was there. The canyon acted as a funnel, producing a draft – a nice reprieve, considering where they had just come from.

Dendy turned the music off and stood up, holding on to the roll cage. She pointed to a lone tree that had a rope-like trunk which had twisted up into ornate spirals. It wasn't the tree she pointed at, but a large bird that sat precariously on one of its limbs. It cocked his head and narrowed a quizzical eye at them. Zaz stopped the six-wheeler to study it. He saw something that looked like an enormous turkey vulture, only it was mottled brown with white spots. It had two fore claws and an extra pair of wings on its hind legs. Its tail was a large fan with multicolored streamers, like that of a peacock.

Paddy leaned over the seat, nearly tumbling out. He gazed at the animal, trying to whistle, but his mouth was dry. "If Microraptor GUI were alive today, it is a fair bet it would look like that. He's positively prehistoric. He resembles something straight out of Sir Arthur Conan Doyle's scribblings."

"He's quite possibly the predecessor of archaeopteryx," said Lyle to anyone who would listen. "This planet is in its evolutionary infancy, except for Maximus Paddymous Sidus, our giant mammalian friend. They were on a fast track compared to the rest of the fauna. The bird and the armadillo creatures seem to be the predominant subspecies so far. By present accounts it is only a microenvironment."

Zaz drove on slowly. He was not about to enter into a paleontological debate about species and microenvironments. Sure, the news was intriguing – there was no denying they had stumbled upon some zoological mysteries – but the priority was finding fresh water and monitoring the safety of his crew. Anything that fell outside those parameters were liabilities – wasted effort. He would have time for secondary thrills after he met his safety goals. Another mystery called out for his attention – another creature that had murder on its mind and could still be lurking in the planet's haunts.

Dendy gave him a nervous smile and patted his thigh. "I've got the creeps too," she said. "I know how you feel and what you're thinking. I just wanted you to know that you're doing everything right, like you always have. None of us could shoulder such responsibility."

He didn't know whether that was an admission of guilt or a confession that she was frightened. He decided it was a little bit of both. Dendy was tough and could be oblivious to softer emotions. She wasn't callous, though. She did have vulnerabilities and concerns. One of them was self-preservation. Fear affected the ingrained primitive response in all humans. In her case, they might truly have been the thoughts of a frightened little girl.

He gave her hand a squeeze. "Being leery of the unknown is nothing to be ashamed of. I'd rather err on the side of caution than perish with an act of foolishness. One of my old Boy Scout mottos was 'Be Prepared.'"

"I didn't know you were a Boy Scout." Dendy looked at him admirably.

"I made Supreme Eagle with fifty-four merit badges."

"At least that tells me you are aware of your environment. I'm a camper and hiker myself. I went up Mt. Rainier before it blew its top."

Zaz stole a glance at her legs. "It shows, Dendy." *Damn those legs!*

"I never got to join the Girl Scouts, because we moved so often."

"You did eventually find Blue Peace. Three years was it?"

"Yeah, I loved it, too. It made me think about becoming a marine biologist. But I was having too much fun to go to school."

"Hah! You're still so damn young. I mean, you've got plenty of time, Dendy. Plenty of time for an education."

"Should I order you a mobility chair now, or later? Or have you been considering Life Extend?"

"I'm sorry, I didn't mean to sound like I'm coming from an ancient perspective."

"Yes you did and I know that it bothers you. I wasn't thinking about it until you brought it up. You relate to me like a daughter, the way you hold my hand and give me pats. That's okay; I'm not fazed by it. I am a woman, you know. Everybody else knows that but you."

"I just need to catch up a little bit," he said awkwardly.

"You go backwards in time and I'll catch up to you. That way we can meet in the middle somewhere. How's that?"

"Hmm." He swung the wheel hard to avoid a large rope-like tree. He topped a rise and, looking over the dash, spied a small creek flow in a gully. It was their first evidence of running water. They were now on the left side of the gorge entrance, where he could see small boulders and rocks in the creek wash. It was hardly a puddle. He knew the source came from the north where the flow would be more intense. A water sample would be less diluted there. He hoped the six-wheeled truck wouldn't bog down with the extra weight of the water trailer in tow. They might get in all right – getting back out would be another thing.

He steered the vehicle for a flattened area that skirted the gully. It almost looked like a trodden path the way it was mashed down and devoid of shrubbery. The others followed directly behind him, motoring along in single file.

Paddy leaned over the front seat. "It is well worn and compacted. It looks rather like a game trail."

Game trail? He just had to say that. *Now what kind of animal would blaze a trail through this valley?*

They passed by what might have been their first alpine hardwood tree. It had the rope-like spiral twists as seen before, but it was more robust and taller. From the trunk hung spindly branches, and on their ends small twigs held fat conifer needles. The needles bore a strange blue hue. Some of the dried needles were gray and brittle. When Zaz drove directly under the low hanging branches of one specimen, Paddy and Lyle stood up and wrenched fistfuls of the twigs in their hands.

"Sit down!" said Zaz. "We can collect later. Strap yourselves back into your seats."

Ten miles later, and still on the same path, they found great swaths of saw grass (or something like it) on the creek embankment. New varieties of trees stood out in stark contrast; some were sprouting white three-petaled flowers; other varieties held peculiar nuts and fruits. Zaz snatched a fruit from a passing tree. It resembled a very small banana in shape, only it was red with orange stripes. Some palm-like trees had nut clusters hanging in large cocoon-shaped bells. One of the four-winged Microraptors busily picked at one of the nut clusters as they passed by.

Dendy was more accurate with the identity of the shrubs and trees she saw. "That one looks like an Asian Rose Apple, and its pod fruit looks edible. See that one? It bleeds red sap just like a dragon tree." She pointed excitedly. "You could almost call that a cork oak!"

They fell into the shadows of the gorge walls in a narrow section. A rise of overburden and slide material rose up to meet the cliff bases. Farther up they could see crags and rain gullies etched in the steep canyon walls. There were numerous fissures, cavern-like holes, and cracks in the ancient rock. Some of the mineral colors in the cliff face were striking; there were reds, browns, and oranges and a bluish lichen that grew in the darker crevasses. Zaz could see yellow-green moss encroaching on the stream stones, looking all the while like algae on a reef. It was all too much to take in – the eyes gulped, hoping to catch it all.

The rush of the creek became faster farther in. Now they could see eddies, swirls, and tiny whitewater rapids. With the rush of water came a pleasing sound like that of wind over dried leaves. The only other sound was the vehicles and their electric hum, although the hydrogen-run vehicle made a muffled *pap-pap-pap-pap-pap*, echoing off the steep canyon walls. The dash thermometer read 88 degrees, another noticeable drop.

Zaz pushed the convoy another 10 miles into the interior, when he suddenly found what he was looking for. A sandy slope that led down to the stream's edge looked accessible. It flattened out in a large, level clearing. Here the water had collected in a great pool, coffered by a natural rock and debris damn.

He pulled around, backed the trailer down to the water's edge and then got out. The other vehicles parked in a wide semicircle. He told Paddy and Lyle to take samples of the water, knowing they could check for toxins and acidity-alkaline levels. They could purify it if they had to. Orion's survey said it would be safe, but he had to be sure: it looked good, flowed fast, and smelled fresh.

They unloaded their breakaway tents, setting three of them up in the middle of the sand clearing. The gently rising slope of the canyon wall began 15 yards away. The perimeter of the campsite held a cornucopia of colorful trees and vegetation. Massive sheets of sandstone and limestone boulders blocked the way to the north. It looked like the path they had taken up this way continued over the slide area. This was as far as they could take the vehicles without knowing what was on the other side.

Paddy and Lyle trudged through the sand, offering their report.

"I give it a clean bill of health," said Paddy, "although it is a tad alkaline and – "

"Whoopee!" yelled Dendy, stripping out of her clothes. She poised in a crouch then shot across the sand. With a high leap, she splashed into the pool sending up a small geyser.

"And forty-two degrees," finished Paddy, removing his yellow tam to scratch his head.

Dendy resurfaced gasping, spitting water. "Holy crap-o-moley!" She clutched her small breasts.

"Now that's what I'm talking about!" Carl followed her in. Samantha skipped to the water, struggling with her cooling britches. Galoot grabbed Carybell and strode to the pool. He pitched the small girl in like a rubber toy and followed, wading up to his chest.

Zaz walked to the rear of the water truck and threw a four-inch line into the pool. He started the small pump, then dropped a purification cake in the bottom of the tank.

"C'mon in, Zaz," said Dendy, splashing the water.

"I'm old and fat and I shall avert mine eyes," he said back playfully. He spent his time between watching his crew frolic and keeping an eye on the bubble indicator on the tank, waiting for it to peg in the full position. They had other large containers packed in the vehicles they would also need to fill. They could top off and return with enough clean water to drink and bathe now that they had a source. He thought about the requirements of Dendy's hydroponics lab. He hoped they would have a surplus, enough to keep some of the plants and vegetables alive. If they had to, he would make a special trip out here to refill for that purpose.

Zaz shut down the pump just as his crew exited the water and dressed. They popped open some portable chairs then sat down to take in the surroundings. Carl cleaned the pistol he had thrown in the sand. Carybell began making a small sandcastle. Galoot sat cross-legged like a big child, sticking small twigs in Carybell's creation. Samantha broke out her portable screen, looking for the two snoops that were due back at any minute. Dendy toweled her hair dry and gazed at herself in a small pocket mirror. And that left...

Zaz did a quick body count. "Where in the hell are those two?" His voice carried with a faint echo. "Goddamn it. I turn my back for one minute and those two Cretaceous cretins are off dinking around someplace!"

Dendy pulled him down into a chair. "Relax, Captain Zachary Crowe. Where's Zaz, have you seen him? I thought I saw him just a few minutes ago. I think it looks pretty safe around here. I don't think they're in any danger."

How ironic, he thought. She wasn't feeling that carefree a little while ago. It must have been the water.

Samantha's snoops appeared overhead and hovered in a small holding pattern. "There's momma's babies," she cooed. "Come, come." She urged them down with the remote. They landed next to her. She picked them up, shook them gently. "Yep, they were just about out of fuel-charge. The south snoop picked up some rolling hills and veggies like these. The ocean snoop never made it – didn't have the range, so I called it back. Nothing out that way except more desert anyway. You can watch the playbacks, but they're boring."

Zaz ordered a hot meal. He hoped that the smell of the cooking would tweak the scientist's noses enough so they would throw down their instruments and come running. He didn't have the mind or energy to go hound dogging after those two. Hopefully, they would exhaust themselves then slither back into camp, offering apologies.

They ate in silence, not including the soothing rush of the stream. The temperature dropped another five degrees. It was a good thing they'd brought extra clothes and heavy sleeping wraps. Zaz had a feeling that, with the change in latitude, they were in for a chilly night. The drafty gorge, with its proximity to the ice-capped mountains, could put them into a deep freeze if they weren't careful.

After finishing the meal, they filled the additional water containers then strapped them to the vehicles. They broke out their sleeping gear and spent a few moments discussing tent partners.

Zaz paced nervously in the sand. He looked at his watch again. It was 5:00 PM Sidus time. That meant the sun would be down in two hours. He gathered the crew in the sand circle, just about ready to order a search party to find the scientists, when Paddy slid down from the slope. The scientist was filthy from head to toe, his face blackened by what looked like soot.

"Where in the hell have you been?" Zaz demanded.

Paddy gulped, trying to catch his breath. "We decided to trek up the rock slide to gain the other side of the gorge. That is when we noticed a deep cleft in the cliff base. It looked unusual – not natural. We decided to investigate. We entered the cavity, or cave, if you have a mind to call it that. We found obvious signs of habitation! There are woven mats and bedding, crude stone implements, even a fire pit with bits of wood coal. But the most *astonishing* thing is – "

"Where's Lyle?" Zaz cut him off.

"He is there now. I came back down for some more lighting. My penlight is insufficient to – "

"Never mind about that. You didn't ask permission to leave – you just went." He turned to Carl. "Get a few pocket lanterns and those walking poles." Then back to Paddy: "We're all going with you. I want you to take me exactly to the spot where you left Lyle."

Paddy nodded, clapping the dirt from his knees. He might have felt guilty about his unannounced departure, but the expression was lost on his face. He had another kind of gleam in his eyes – the thrill of discovery, crossed with lunacy.

Carl passed the poles out. Zaz took a mini-lantern, switched it on. As a group, they followed Paddy up the steep shale embankment. It was hard going, trying to keep their boots from sinking in the rubble. But it was easy enough to retrace the prior tracks of the scientists. Once at the top of the rise, they continued down to a path that led off toward the creek, but Paddy turned left between two huge boulders. They began a climb back up the cliff slope then stopped before a black cavernous maw. The opening was not a natural one. There were gouges and tool marks on the edges of the cave entrance. Splintered rock lay in piles on the outside of the entrance, but the path into the opening was impacted, smooth as though worn flat by the passage of something heavy.

Zaz aimed the lantern beam into the opening. He saw the figure of a man bent over near the back wall. It was Lyle, standing there engrossed with something unseen. Zaz stepped into the truck-sized opening.

The inner dimensions of the cave resembled a small cathedral. It was twenty yards wide and just as deep – a deliberately excavated hovel. The first thing Zaz stepped over was a large fire pit with a ring of stones. In its center sat a large collection of volcanic rocks piled in pyramid fashion. The fire pit was enormous – 15 feet in width. Zaz stumbled, kicking something that rolled across the cave floor. He aimed the light upon it and saw that it was a tightly woven circle of grass. Another few steps brought him standing over a second woven object. He picked it up and held it close. It resembled the crude shape of a bipedal (or human) character. A doll perhaps?

He stepped farther in, measuring his steps until he approached the spot where Lyle stood. He saw large woven mats on the floor, objects that looked like stuffed beds. A half dozen more beds lined the base of a wall a few feet away. Three planed tree trunks placed near the beds resembled tabletops.

Lyle wiped sweat from his face. He had that same peculiar look in his eyes Paddy.

Unbridled lunacy.

The scientist spoke with urgent words. "Yes, yes. At first I thought I had stumbled into some type of ground-based gorilla's nest. I was so wrong. Notice the interlocking weave – precision craftsmanship. It shows great intelligence. I see you've already found the toys. But look here, this is to be pondered over!"

Zaz shone the light on the back wall. Pictographs. Etchings of figures carved in the rock. The rock face itself had been dressed and polished to receive the artwork. As he played the light gently down the length of the wall he could see hundreds of symbols, figures, and representations. They were in neat rows, like a kind of Sanskrit. The hand that had wrought the images was precise, showing great organization in the pictures. The amount of time needed to complete such renderings staggered the imagination.

Lyle looked on the verge of tears as he brought a trembling hand from his pants pocket to give Zaz a seashell necklace. His words were soft: "Is there any doubt that this indeed belongs to Maximus Paddymous Sidus? I found it here on the floor. It is identical in design to the one that we found on the desert plain." He pointed a trembling finger. "Go to the south end. You will find even more to believe in."

Zaz shined his light across the floor then trekked to the other side of the cave. He found a profusion of crudely sculpted wood items – cups, bowls, platters, chopping and mashing implements – all of it plainly recognizable. It looked like an old medieval kitchen or scullery. He saw very clumsy etchings low on the wall, which reminded him of what a six-year-old might do to pass the time had he a collection of crayons, but little talent to use them. Then he looked back at the ball on the floor and the doll he held in his hand.

Dendy came up behind him, gently placing her hand on his shoulder. He turned to look at her. Tears streamed down her face in the refracted light. Samantha stood next to her. She was no better off, frozen in shock. Carl, who usually had something to say at any occasion, held his tongue. The others shuffled idly around, too perplexed to touch anything.

Zaz backed away from the wooden objects, brushing up against Paddy. He spoke to the professor softly over his shoulder. "I'm sorry I yelled at you back there. I had no idea. To think that these creatures actually possessed intelligence and might have been aware of their own deaths is just too much."

"They were sentient beings," Paddy said reverently. "They were fully aware of their existence and place in the universe. It shows in their renderings – they have written their history upon these walls. I have found flint cutting implements, toys, eating utensils, furniture, decorative jewelry, and other assorted items that clearly belong to an active culture. Had there been more large herbivores on this planet, I would have expected to see hides fashioned into clothing material. It seems they exploited what resources they had. It was a noble effort, considering what Georgian Sidus has to offer. Alas, no metallurgy – they had not progressed to that station. Perhaps an Iron or Bronze Age was written in their future, but they were not given the chance to experience it."

"Can you imagine," began Zaz, his voice a hollow ring in the expanse, "the realization that they knew what was happening to them and couldn't defend themselves? It seems like they were so helpless. Did you find any weapons in here?"

"Not even a sharpened stick. Only mashing rocks that I suppose they used for grinding grain, nuts, fruits and other edibles. The flint cutters might have been used to cut the woven materials. They were totally in tune with their environment, using it to its maximum potential. There is no indication of coprolites within this dwelling, which presupposes they must have been hygienically conscientious and buried their waste outside. They appear to have been quite civilized."

"They were a gentle sort, weren't they?" asked Zaz. But he already knew the answer to that.

"Quite so, from all indications," said Paddy. "Following along this evolutionary line, and from our own Earth history examples, it is a fair bet to say that they had some form of communication, or dumb-speak, to have acquired and maintained these organizational skills. Be it growls, whines, chirps, or snorts; they must have had some way of pronouncing their intentions – a dialogue. Rather than saying that I would have liked to have seen them, I can now say that I would have liked to have *known* them. Would you like to know something else?"

Paddy led Zaz back to the entrance. He pointed across the gorge to the cliff face on the opposite side. "From this vantage point you can see hundreds of excavations in the rock abutments. They are all at the base level of the cliffs. This afforded them protection from the elements, along with proximity to the watercourse and vegetation."

Zaz could see small black dots peppering the base of the cliff side that ran down the entire length of the valley. He supposed it was the same on his side. It was the home of the troglodytes – evidence of a vast, thriving community.

"I imagine that it goes on for hundreds of miles into the side canyons and even beyond," said Paddy. "This is the valley of the giants – the homestead of these beings."

Lyle came up behind them with his own bit of news. "I make it out to be fourteen to sixteen individuals. Perhaps it was two families, or possibly three. But it was definitely a collaborative unit. It appears they slept three to a bed or thereabouts. There were at least four or five kids in this group."

Zaz took out his scope and looked across the gorge again. Judging from the number of caves he could see, it certainly accounted for their vast numbers. A question nagged at him.

"Then how did they end up on the desert floor?"

Perhaps it was a rout," offered Paddy. "Maybe it was mass panic. In all likelihood, they were chased or herded there. It would have been much easier to have dispatched them out in the open, given that they were unarmed and unable to defend themselves."

Paddy's remarks brought forth images of genocide, the tactics used in the old world wars, where the conquerors gathered great crowds out into the open for the purpose of mass slaughter. What kind of entity had such callous reserve to commit mass executions on Sidus? Once again, the fear of the unknown gripped Zaz. He felt vulnerable, like a child hiding in a closet waiting for some unseen monster to open the door and spring upon him.

Zaz had one last question: "If they ended up south, out in the desert, would it be possible that the threat came from the north, up this gorge?"

"It is hard to assume that," answered Paddy. "It could have been an attack from the north. Who is to say that Sidus was not populated from the south as well? There could have been numerous strike points. To think that this entire planet is loaded with Paddymous corpses is mind-boggling. The question to ask now is: how many millions, or billons, of Paddymous beings inhabited Sidus? This could be global in scale."

Galoot drove his iron pole into the cave floor, puncturing the rock. "Them rotten sons-o-bitches. Killing these poor big folk like cattle. Well, I got something to say about that – they best not come near Galoot with designs on cuttin' him up, I can tell you. They won't find the slap-down on me so damn easy!"

Samantha gestured to the cave's interior. "Something like this has to be reported to the Interplanetary Council. According to the Stockholm Treaty of 2065, any encroachment upon a semi-intelligent galactic civilization is prohibited, subject to legal punishment. What has happened here is more than an encroachment. It's blatant evidence of planetary genocide, the likes of which has never been recorded in the annals. I am aghast at wondering if Orion Industries knew about this catastrophe and deliberately ignored the evidence. They sure knew about the graveyard out in the desert. What if it doesn't stop there? Is it possible they knew about a global genocide and decided not to report it?"

Dendy hissed. "Those planet-grabbing pigs. It makes us accessories to the crime. Stop and think about it. We *know* what happened here. At the very least, we're guilty of complacency. We're engineering for future settlements on Sidus and hiding the evidence of a galactic felony. Who are we working for? For Orion Industries, that's who. I don't suppose you really know what happened to the American Indians, do you?"

Silence.

She went on. "They were gathered up and relocated, only to starve or be shot out of sport, or hanged. The American natives were nearly driven to extinction, and you can liken their case to what has happened here. Only this is more monstrous. Do any of you know why I'm called Tiny Dancer? It is my heritage – my Indian name. I am half Sioux on my mother's side, and yes, we did all the fighting and dying for our freedom." Dendy burst into tears and turned away. Zaz tried to console her but she slapped his hands away. "Leave me alone!" she cried. Samantha went to her side and held her. Dendy had now put a cultural face and lifestyle to the skeletons, tripping an emotional overload within her. Realization hit the others with the same hammer blow.

"Carl," Zaz said, "thoughts?"

Carl swept his hair back over his head. "Well, the way I see it, the Orion probe sent a light-speed message back to them. Now if this happened less than fourteen years ago, how would they have known about this big war or fight? It could be they are as dumb as we are. I say their probes picked up on the aftermath – all those bones. So..." He took a large breath. "We signed on to do a job, right? We've got maybe less than a year on this dirt ball before we get relieved or get some visitors. Now what the hell are we going to do besides work? Are you thinking about camping out there in the desert, waving a protest sign and cussin' about corporate planet grabbing and whatnot? Or are you planning to get busy and leave all of this behind us for the sake of our sanity? This shit will eat us up, man. I don't want to walk off this planet in a straight jacket. I think we can handle whatever comes at us. As long as it comes head-on, giving me a chance to defend myself."

"With what, sir?" asked Lyle. "We have no weapons, besides a few antique relics and some long poles."

"I wouldn't say that," said Carl. "You're looking at the doctor of pyrotechnics of this company. I've got enough C-5 and C-6 to make a smokin' black hole out of half this planet. Do you even think I'd let anything happen to us if I knew some barbarian menace was going to overrun us?"

"There he goes again," said Samantha. "His answer to everything is to fire a bomb off, because that solves everything. You only have so many fingers, Carl. What happens when you run out of those? Who is going to light your firecrackers for you?"

Carl stiffened. "That's a damn cheap shot coming from you, Ms. Dog-faced girl, who can't even count up the facts of what's going on here. I suppose you'll just swing those big boobs of yours and we'll all stand behind you for protection."

"My breasts never seemed to bother you before."

"Shaddap!" shouted Zaz. "Carl has a point. We didn't ask for this. So maybe we're accessories after the fact – we're guilty on that count. Dwelling on this is not going to solve the issues at hand. It's too late for that. We'll have to deal with some unknown force if it comes our way. We're forewarned, so we'll be prepared. I don't exactly know how yet, but we've got some great minds here to figure it out. For now, let's get out of this place."

Dendy turned on the group. "It's against Galactic law. We have no right!"

"And who's going to enforce the law out here?" demanded Carl. "I claim ignorance."

"Ignorance is bliss," said Dendy.

They exited the cave and headed back. Though Zaz was grateful the scientists had discovered the cave with everything that it revealed about the recent occupants, he now had to question the ethics of his job assignment and all the dirty corporate slime that went with it.

As they gained the rise of the slide and hiked down toward camp, the sunlight faded, eaten up by the shadows. With the darkness came another chill to add to the one they already had. They passed close to a Microraptor that sat on a long branch. The bird squawked then excreted a bubbly stream of guano on a flat rock.

That's exactly how I feel about it. Everything is going that way right now.

High in a rock chasm, two enormous eyes followed the downward descent of the humans until they were lost to sight. The scent the tiny things gave off was something different and foreign. It was not a disgusting or terrifying odor, but then again, it was not very pleasant either.

CHAPTER EIGHT

THINGS THAT GO BUMP IN THE DAY

Sidus Log, Rotation 5.

I awoke early this morning to Dendy's fitful snores. She's bedded beside me. It's a great comfort to know that she's near. It's still dark; my watch reads 3:00 AM Sidus time. There is a nasty chill in the air. The temperature is 18 degrees, brisk by anyone's standards. I've heard falling shale outside near the cliff base. I lie silent, listening, wondering if some small creature was curious enough to approach our camp. I gave up after the noise abated.

We've stockpiled as much water as the vehicles can hold, and we'll be heading back to the *Shenandoah* early this morning.

Yesterday we found the home of the Paddymous giants. Paddy and Lyle believe this discovery to be of such importance that it should be recorded in the annals of planetary exploration. I allowed them to reenter the cave and digitally record the interior so they will have some record of it to study. They will announce and publish their findings upon our return to Earth. Out of all of us, the two scientists seem the least perturbed or agitated. It has to be owed to their preoccupations with the geology, flora and fauna. I can't say that I blame them. I would like to have such blinders on to keep the other negative thoughts out of my mind.

The rest of the crew is tense and divided. Samantha is not talking to Carl, and he flips her the three-finger when he wants to upset her. Dendy is saddened by the circumstances that killed the Paddymous. She is also upset with our participation in Sidus development plans. I gave her some whiskey, hoping she would sleep numbly and forget.

Galoot watches his little Carybell closer than ever. I believe this is the first time that he has fallen in love. He is obsessively over-protective, but I don't think he really knows how to behave in such a situation. Carybell is simple - uncomplicated. She seems to adore the attention Galoot gives her, and stays just out of his reach, testing him to see if he is aware and paying attention. I don't think she does this in a hurtful way, but enjoys the attention and sees it as more of a game. She is a peaceful and quiet type. When she is alone, she sings quite beautifully - haunting, melancholy melodies. She's decidedly harmless.

I think of the future. I wonder what we will do to pass the time once the work is completed. The morale of the crew is paramount to a healthy existence. We will have a long go of it, living in this bubble. If we rise up against each other, I'm afraid we might burst that happy bubble. I've also considered a move to the gorge after the work has been completed. But right now that seems impossible. All of our technology, components and stores remain within the *Shenandoah*, not to mention our construction equipment. God forbid we leave Dendy's hydroponics lab behind with all of her fish, seeds and sprouts. And who would keep our generators serviced and running to charge all the battery packs? Not to mention the risk of volcanic activity.

I often wonder if Robinson Crusoe had such thoughts as these, in his own more primitive way. I am afraid for the future. I don't know why.

Captain Zackary Crowe, PJ.

IT WAS A HELLACIOUS RIDE back to the *Shenandoah*. The six-wheeler got stuck twice in the sand, owed in part to the additional weight of the water trailer. Due to the slower ride back, the heat became that much more oppressive. The crew members fell out of their vehicles exhausted and near heatstroke after the short stops. The return trip had taken eight hours.

Zaz rolled up to the jobsite first. He held off driving the vehicle into B-Deck, to unhitch the water trailer and hook it up to the ship's lines. He stopped dead, noticing right away that something was amiss. When the others pulled up alongside, they saw it too.

Zaz exited the vehicle and walked over to the jobsite. The tent and tarp had collapsed. Equipment lay scattered, as if thrown by some great windstorm. He noticed great rents and tears in the tarp material. The aluminum poles were bent over themselves, as though some heavy weight had crushed them. Two small cooling conditioners had been crushed into finger-sized pieces. Food and beverage containers were broken, mashed flat.

Galoot and Carybell headed for the open hatch to check on the inside.

Carl put a palm over his eyes, shading them from the sun. "What the hell is going on around this place? It better not be those damn armadillos."

Zaz looked at the sand. There were peculiar tracks pocked over its surface. "What are those?" He stepped around to the other side of the shredded tent. A sweet, heady odor tweaked his nostrils. It smelled like perfume. "What's happened here?" Then something caught his eye.

He saw the small dot move at the stern of the ship. He adjusted his sun goggles to get a better view, and then took them off as they became filthy with dust. Squinting against the glare, he made out what looked like a giant black cat taking loping strides. He watched it stop every so often to lean down and sniff the ground. He fumbled for his scope, but dropped it to the sand.

"My word," said Paddy. "What type of creature is that? Most peculiar."

Zaz picked up his scope and slapped the dust from the lens. He brought it to his eye, zoomed in to see the creature more clearly. The sight gave him a start.

The creature was a very large bipedal animal. It had enormous forearms with small sickles for nails. The hind legs were muscular and sported retractable claws. The head looked wolverine-like, equipped with a great lolling slab-like tongue. It had the pelt of a skunk – black on top over a white midsection and black underbelly. As it strode, it swung a large paddle-like tail for balance. It had upright ears that swiveled independently, tuning like sound dishes. The sharp teeth extending from the long muzzle did not suggest this creature was a plant eater. The thing was enormous, reaching at least ten feet high and might have weighed as much as 500 pounds.

Zaz watched it with a horrifying fascination. The creature suddenly changed course, following the line of the ship. It stopped, bent over in a crouch. Then it picked up speed as it headed for the ship's hatch, its huge legs kicking up a fan of dust. Carybell had nearly reached the hatch opening, with Galoot twenty strides behind her.

"Look at that thing!" said Carl, then he began yelling at Galoot.

Zaz shouted and waved his arms.

Galoot, eyes fixed on Carybell, did not see the approaching animal.

"Carl, with me!" Zaz shouted. He sprinted, un-slinging the rifle from his shoulder as he moved. He managed to get a sweaty finger into the trigger guard and fired once in the air. Carl pulled the .45 from his waistband. Galoot turned around, cocking his head, trying to understand the frantic gesticulations. He followed the pointing hands and heard the word, "Luggout!"

The animal went straight for Carybell, its mouth frothing. It passed over the sand at an unbelievable pace with long, muscular leaps.

Galoot turned and saw the animal closing the distance. He bolted for Carybell. Carybell turned just as the creature became airborne. She crouched into a small ball. Galoot threw a running body block on the animal just as it lunged at the cowering girl. Galoot and animal went end over end in the sand, kicking up a cloud of dust.

The animal gained its footing hurriedly. Galoot got to one knee just as the animal plowed into him, clawing with its forepaws. Galoot spread his arms wide, throwing up a barrier. The animal bounded from one foot to the other, attempting to find a path through him. It barked once and charged.

Galoot reared a fist back to punch the animal, but it jumped before he could do anything and brought up its right hind leg, raking him across the stomach.

The large man froze and looked down at himself. For a minute Zaz thought Galoot had been disemboweled. The animal backed away and began circling. Galoot countered and gave out a chesty roar.

Zaz pulled up short. He couldn't get the animal in his sights with all of its maneuvering. Likewise, Carl had raised the .45 but could not find a still target.

The animal leaped into the air. When it hit the ground it did a death spin, bringing the tail around like a small wrecking ball and catching Galoot in the thighs, knocking him away from the girl. Galoot fell to the sand, his body convulsing.

Zaz pulled the trigger repeatedly. He saw tuffs of fur flying with every point of impact. Carl took a two-handed aim and let loose with a volley of automatic fire. Bullets went through the creature and ricocheted off the ship's hull. The animal weaved, trying to dodge the incoming fire. Its jaws clacked with such speed that it was hard to see the movement. Momentarily stunned, the animal stood in a bowlegged crouch, its ears pinned over its head, closing off the loud racket of gunfire. Carybell took a chance and ran from it, heading toward the open hatch.

Galoot, suffering from a bleeding stomach wound, rose up, doubled his fists and marched toward the animal.

"Don't fight toe-to-toe with it!" screamed Paddy. "Give a care!"

"Back off, Galoot!" Carl yelled, edging closer and holding his fire.

Galoot did not heed the command. He dove at the animal, crooking his massive arm around its neck. They fell to the sand.

Zaz lowered his rifle and ran up to the two rolling figures. Galoot tried to flip the animal with a Sumo wrestling hold, but it kept kicking out of the grip, tearing at him.

The flailing tail caught Zaz in the shins, bringing him to his knees. He took the rifle by the barrel, waited for an opening, and swung down with all his strength. The rifle stock cracked in half over the animal's head.

Carl leaped into the fray. He held the muzzle of the .45 to the animal's gut and let off two rounds. Finally, with one mighty yank, Galoot broke the animal's neck and threw its head to the sand. The beast's great muzzle blew a spray of blood. The animal's chest contracted then it gave one last sigh and was still.

Galoot fell off the thing with a roll. He couldn't get up. He'd been shredded from groin to chin, showing great tears in his flesh. Dendy fell on her knees next to him with a med-kit ready. She pulled out several compresses, trying to ebb the flow of blood. Samantha joined her, fumbling for painkillers and antiseptic.

Carybell ran back to where Galoot lay on the ground. She hugged his neck, tears falling from her cheeks onto his face.

The rest of the crew trotted to Galoot's side. Dendy shot Zaz a glance and asked if he was okay, noticing that he'd taken a hit to the shins. He didn't feel anything broken, and only admitted that his legs would be black and blue soon enough. Everyone wanted to help, but Dendy waved them off. "I've got it," she said. Then to Samantha, "Get the portable stretcher from the infirmary."

"I'm on it." Samantha ran toward the ship entrance.

Carl turned on the zoologist. "What the hell is that thing, Paddy?"

The scientist took great, gulping breaths. "I don't know. It is bloody well not in my taxonomy books. I've never seen anything like it. Even in the records of cryptozoology, I've never seen such a thing. I don't know what you would call it. It looks marsupial in a morphological sense, but it obviously possesses some type of carnivorous traits and behaviors. It is truly ferocious."

Pulling his magnifiers into place, Lyle said, "I might add that it looks like something sired by the mother of Romulus and Remus – almost wolf-like. Do you smell that sickly sweet odor? I would bet that it is a pheromone secretion, although it usually has a more pronounced muskiness."

Carl spat in the sand. "That's all we need around here – a skunk-wolf."

"More of a marsupial lion," Lyle corrected.

"What I want to know is whether or not there are more of these things running around." Zaz groaned as he got to his feet. "Don't wax poetic – give me the facts." He looked out into the mirage-like vastness, scanning the horizon for movement.

"I would not know if they exhibit pack behavior," said Paddy, "but it is likely. With no objections, I would like to perform an autopsy on this specimen. That way I can find out precisely what it is and where it might have come from. It could hail from the other side of the continent."

"Fine. Run the damn thing up to the lab on a dolly cart. I have to know if there are more of these around here. It damn near killed Galoot and Carybell. Find out how to kill it easier."

Samantha returned with the stretcher and then headed for the job. Carl left to inspect the damage on the fence line. They transported Galoot up to A-Deck, where they put him to bed in the one-room infirmary. Dendy stapled the large man's lower stomach then put him on an IV drip. After a full body scan, she gave him a double sedative and wrapped him in a sheet. Carybell threw down a sleeping pad and sat on the floor, staring up at the bed where Galoot rested in recovery. Dendy shut the door quietly. She joined Zaz outside the room; they headed down the corridor toward the lift.

"How bad is it?" Zaz asked.

"I've seen worse where shark bites were involved, but it's right up there. He has some deep epidermal lacerations and torn musculature – nothing that couldn't be put back together. There's no tendon or nerve damage, but he's got a hairline fracture on his right femur – he's not going to be chasing his girlfriend around for a couple of weeks or so. I'm surprised he wasn't killed. The only thing that saved him was his size and strength."

"He's Herculean. Not one of us would have done so well." Zaz embraced Dendy and gave her a soothing hug, massaging the small of her back. "You know, when you don't have reason to be frightened, you show fear. But when you're involved in an emergency, you're fearless. You just act."

"Thanks," she said. "You're not so bad yourself in a fix."

"C'mon. We've got to check out our damage."

They walked to the wrecked jobsite. Samantha had just finished reassembling what was left of the tent and tarp. The computer had been set up on a small table; she was busy checking the program, getting ready to start the construction machinery.

She offered the two a grim smile. "How's Galoot?"

"He's going to make it," said Dendy. "He's too stubborn to die."

Zaz looked out toward the fence line. "Is Carl out there by himself?"

Samantha sighed. "Yes, he's brooding again. I suppose he's waiting for me to put everything back on line. The computer was banged around a little but it seems to be functioning. There! I just sent the master command. We should be up and running now. Have a look-see."

Zaz used his pocket scope to look north. He could see the massive fence driver moving at a steady four miles per hour, like a lumbering dinosaur. The gun truck behind it was filling the fence cavities. Looking to the south, he could see the trench diggers descending into their ditches. Everything was online.

"Good work, Sammy." Zaz pocketed the scope. "How long do you think it will take to get the perimeter barrier up?"

"Well, at the speed they crawl, with nearly five miles of north wall up, that would be thirteen more miles, which would be about five or six more hours of straight staking and filling. But we have to reload at least two more spools then mix up the chemicals for three more batches of foam. That's what takes the time: the reload. In two days, barring any problems, we should have it up. We'll have to cut some access panels so we have an exit. That's if asshole out there doesn't get a bright idea about blowing any more holes in our fence line."

"Don't be so hard on him. It's the only thing he knows how to do well. If you take that away from him he thinks he's just some – "

"Dumb Italian meatball?" Samantha finished. "I tried to apologize to him but he just thumbed his nose then flipped me the three-finger."

Zaz thought it best to change the subject. "Can we send out the snoops again?"

"We never packed a lot of high-octane propellant. I can send one out for surveys without burning up too much of our supply. Any more than that would empty them fast. Right now, I'm thinking about rationing for the future. Zaz, for the last year we urged you to get a scout shuttle. We wouldn't have this problem now if we had that vehicle."

It was true enough. The biggest regret Zaz had was never investing in a small craft for transport and surveys. They were so god-awful expensive that it was prohibitive. Of course he could have bought one just before their departure with his Orion funds, but it was too late to beat himself up about it. One snoop would have to be enough for now.

Zaz called Carl on his wrist-com, but there was no answer.

"I tried that," said Samantha. "He's turned his com off. Like I said, he's brooding. He'll cool off and come back in after he figures that he needs to brag about something."

Zaz thought it best to leave him alone for now. "Try to keep the peace, Sammy. We're all we've got. If we can't pull together this whole operation will unravel."

*   *   *

That night the crew slept in their deck chairs on the bridge. The liquor cabinet stayed open longer than usual. Zaz dreamt of his parents and their little house in Henderson, Nevada. It seemed a trillion miles away. His parent's smiles seemed even further off.

Sidus Log, Rotation 7.

"A vicious animal invaded our camp. It was like nothing we've ever seen or heard of before. There was not supposed to be indigenous life on Sidus. Obviously this thing got in under the radar.

The fence barrier is finished. We have a south and a north entrance to leave the compound. The front-end loaders are still emptying their contents in the trenches. I expect this to continue until we clear the entire settlement grid. I ordered the immediate area around the ship dug up and graded first.

Our automechs now have an easier time negotiating the terrain around camp. I've stationed some of them around the outside of the ship and fence line to serve as first-warning guards. I know this is ludicrous since their visual acuity doesn't last beyond a mile, but it provides some comfort. They are to report if they spy any non-human entity in or out of the compound. There have been a few false alarms due to them spotting the armadillo creatures, but nothing else of concern. The automechs don't function well in this environment - what can you expect when their cooling fans and heat sinks are subjected to these high temperatures?

Galoot is progressing slowly. He wants to perform shipboard chores, but this is premature. Carybell remains with him and sees to his recovery.

Sammy and Carl are still at odds with each another. The funny thing is I really think there's something between them. I feel a shipboard romance slowly taking wing, but I won't admit it to any of the crew since I'm guilty of it as well. This place does strange things to human emotions.

Dendy has begged me to visit her hydroponics lab, eager to give me a tour of all her new sprouts and blossoms. I gave her a water allowance for her specimens, since the backup hydroponics tank has been depleted. Our water recycler is taxed to the limit, trying to keep up. Fortunately, none of her plants have succumbed to dehydration. I warned her that her plants rank below the crew's immediate needs. She understands the stipulation and says she intends to abide by the quota.

Presently, my attention is required in the science lab. Lyle and Paddy have been working tirelessly, examining all manner of flora and fauna on Sidus. Lately, their obsession has been with the marsupial lion, or whatever it is. I've ordered the crew to attend an assembly in the science lab, with the exception of Galoot and Carybell. And as usual, I'm late to get there."

Captain Zackary Crowe, PJ.

Zaz entered the science lab 10 minutes after he'd called the meeting. Whatever it was, Lyle and Paddy had said it couldn't wait. Carl, Samantha, and Dendy sat at the far end of the examination table, no doubt to keep their distance from what lay on it. Paddy looked up from a small electronic microscope. He had a five-day beard growth, in addition to what looked like a pound of chopped liver under his eyes, so pronounced were the bags. Lyle appeared no better off; he was holding himself up by propping one arm on the table. He seemed lost, disoriented. A rank smell arose from the room. It was debatable whether the odor originated from the dead animal or the two scientists.

Paddy removed his sweat-stained yellow tam and scratched his head. Zaz wished the man would rid himself of the psoriasis or head lice.

Paddy spoke in a tired voice: "What we have here is some type of collaboration between a marsupial and a canine. The skeletal morphology follows that of an upright marsupial lion, with the pelvic girdle and running apparatus of a therapod dinosaur, or raptor. It is quite evolved and fit to this capacity. It has other features that are almost Lupus. The muzzle, binocular eyes, teeth, ears and forepaws are very dog or wolf-like. The sickle-like claws are decidedly sloth-like, and would be more appropriate for digging, although they are quite effective in a secondary offensive posture. I believe this creature normally roots out burrowing prey. It appears to be carnivorous, but it might also be omnivorous; we've found a meaty substance in its digestive track that is unidentifiable and will require further analysis.

"If you are familiar with the temperament of the wolverine or Tasmanian devil, then you can rightly connect that behavior with what you saw two days ago. It's the most ferocious biped I have ever encountered. The only thing that might even come close to this does not exist anymore. This coloring of the pelt is most unusual for an animal this size. Smaller, venomous or toxic animals typically have such a striking pattern. It is a warning for larger predators to stay away. I can't imagine what might out-size or out-class this beast that could threaten it. Unless there is something else on this planet we have overlooked, which I rather doubt." Paddy slumped in a chair.

Lyle continued. "Moving along, ladies and gentlemen: this creature, that we have named 'Jack,' has the most acute senses extant. The nose receptors alone give it a smelling range of up to twenty miles. The ears are like collecting dishes, and I should think that it could hear a pin drop at two hundred feet. Their eyesight is also extremely developed."

Paddy stood up. He picked up the animal's tail. "This is almost a beaver's paddle, but it has a knot of bone in the end which gives it some weight when swung. It is more like a whip with a small mace on the end. You saw it in action. Jack performs a defensive spiral when surrounded, typically lashing out with this projectile. It is a bone-breaker, to be sure."

Paddy thrust his hand into the rump of the creature, working his arm back and forth. A white substance spurted from the rear and into Paddy's face. He wiped the substance with his tam then threw it on the floor.

"As I was going to say," said Paddy, a bit agitated. "It has a secretive sack near the anus that contains some type of brood scent. There, can you smell that?"

Zaz noticed a sickly sweet odor in the air. It was very pungent, almost unbearable. It was the same odor he'd smelt when fighting with the animal. Now the scientist had it all over him.

Paddy proceeded, unperturbed. "I believe this marking scent is a pheromone of some type which might relate to the herd or pack. Surely there is no other reason for Jack to have such a gland other than to mark a territory or attract a mate. I don't think this is a solitary animal. I think it might belong to a larger group, or even a herd. Then again, I cannot prove that."

Carl raised a hand like a student; it was the first time anyone dared to interrupt the scientist's explanation. "I want to know why we couldn't kill that thing," he said. "I put at least six shots dead into it."

Paddy took some forceps and splayed the chest cavity open. "That is because the major organs, particularly the heart, liver and kidneys, are all tucked away much lower in the thorax. Your shots penetrated the lungs, which was not immediately fatal. Also, this animal possesses a very large adrenal gland. In short, Jack was so filled with adrenalin he had no idea he was injured. Some large bears are not aware of fatal injuries and will continue running or fighting until they collapse. There is also a five-inch layer of fat in the abdominal region that I interpret as a water storehouse. Hence another reason for the bullet's inability to easily incapacitate. A very potent defense."

Zaz couldn't contain his curiosity any longer. "So you're saying there might be more of these.If so, where would they be?"

Paddy looked frustrated. "It stands to reason that there could be more. Honestly, I couldn't tell you where they are. This one happens to be male. It has six testes, so I know that it is capable of breeding. I should like to also have a female in order to study the reproductive organs."

Samantha leaned forward to look at the animal's innards. She ran her hand over the silky pelt. "This thing has fur that looks like a skunk. What is an animal like this doing out on a desert plain? It should die of heat exhaustion out here."

"It does have a temperature regulating system," said Lyle. "It pants like a dog to dispel heat, but surprisingly, it also has sweat glands under the belly. I think it can withstand the heat, but not for a prolonged period. It must cool down somewhere, near a water source or in the shade. We're only following logical assumptions from what we know of our own planet's animals."

"I would like to say," Paddy continued, "that nature produced such a species, but I am not altogether certain of that. Its DNA profile looks superficially arranged. I mean that it has additional strands – codes that I cannot account for. Given that we are in a different star system, perhaps this animal is quite normal. However, the chemicals, minerals and enzymes that make up our body are usually a product of our home planet. For instance, we contain iron, potassium and other elements that are parent minerals of our planet. We are carbon-based."

"What are you saying?" asked Dendy. "That it doesn't belong here?"

"I'm saying it does have trace elements of this planet, but the traces are so minute as to rule it out as a native. I cannot explain how or why this creature shouldn't be here, yet it is here much to my befuddlement. It belongs here in only a small way, yet it doesn't by the most major definitions."

"Maybe the damn thing is dying out," suggested Carl. "Maybe it's going extinct and we nailed the last one left. Maybe they came from that other continent where the rocks and chemicals are different."

"That's highly unlikely," said Lyle. "Planets evolve uniformly with a common dispersion of elements. Unless the sister continent took an enormous asteroid or comet impact and rearranged the molecules and minerals in that locale. That is doubtful."

"Yeah, but it's *possible*," said Carl. "If those things are running around here, I'll bet they came from the other side of the world."

No one said anything. The scientists looked fed up with the fantasy postulations. Zaz could see it in their expressions. He had every reason to believe that they knew what they were talking about. Carl was the fly in their ointment.

"Look, sir," said Paddy, bending over to throw his soiled hat back on his head. "We won't know until a complete mitochondria DNA sequence is performed. I wish that this creature were a doppelganger or a gross figment of my imagination. It is not. And would you like to know something? This animal appears to be over forty years old. That would place it well within the time period that involved the Paddymous extinction. If I can find a correlation between the two species, perhaps deep in the genes of this creature, then we will have another problem on our hands."

"Don't double-speak," said Carl. "What are you saying?"

Paddy marched through a draped partisan, disappearing inside an inner office.

Lyle held his hands out in a pleading gesture. "My colleague is quite beside himself due to fatigue. Please forgive us. I think we're finished with this presentation." Lyle collapsed in a chair, looking so haggard he might have been taken for a 70-year-old man.

Zaz gently put a hand on Lyle's shoulder. "I want you guys to knock off and get some sleep. I appreciate everything you've done. We wouldn't have a thing to go on without you. Shave, bathe. And if you don't," he added jokingly, "then I'll get Dendy and Sammy to wrestle you into the aquarium tank."

"What, and kill all my fish?" said Dendy. "I'll give them sponge baths first."

Lyle nodded and took off his Optipak.

Zaz moved to leave, but turned suddenly. "Why did you guys name that creature Jack?"

Lyle mumbled, "Suffice it to say, it was to honor two little known professors, Jacob and Wilhelm Grimm." Lyle stumbled to the curtain, threw back the flap and disappeared.

Zaz dispersed the crew to their duties. Dendy stayed behind with him. They stepped just outside the science lab into the corridor. Zaz pulled on his chin trying to put it all together.

Dendy looked equally perplexed. "Zaz, are they going crazy? Those two are really giving me the spooks. On one hand, I can believe what they're saying – but did you get an eye on them? They're a mess! What's *wrong* with them?"

"I don't know, maybe too much stress, lack of sleep – frayed nerves. I wouldn't take it too seriously."

"You couldn't take anything seriously!" The voice came from behind them in the science lab. The huge door slammed with a clunk.

Dendy crimped her eyes shut. "Oh, crud, now we've done it. Let's get out of here. Come with me to hydro – we need a change of scenery."

He walked with her down the long corridor. When they entered Dendy's lab, Zaz was surprised at the number of new plants and flowers in full bloom. The different specimens were housed in elevated plastic troughs that held all manner of flora and shrubbery in neat rows. Larger troughs held vegetables, tomatoes, dwarf corn, peas, and assorted melons. Radiant light spilled from overhead. Some of the flora samples swayed under cooling jets to keep their temperatures down. Affixed to the side of the hull was a large plastic tank, alive with several varieties of saltwater fish that had been auto-hatched during the last part of the journey. There were only a few game fish in the tank; the rest were colorful reef varieties. It was nice to see something so beautiful and exotic. Dendy had had to salt the fresh water.

"Well, I'm impressed," said Zaz. He followed Dendy's leading hand as she took him to each trough and described the plants. She had pet names for many of them. He could almost see the flowers soothe to her touch when she patted them. This was Dendy's element. Her face noticeably brightened as she walked down the aisles, pointing to her favorite species.

She said, "We lost about sixty percent of the stock in stasis; I've had to re-germinate the smaller varieties. When the *Shenandoah* hit the ground, it made a mess out of the whole deck – turned it into one big mud hole. Carybell helped with the clean-up and we were able to put it all back together. I've turned the temperature down a little so they won't require so much water. For the soil plants I've set up drip pans to catch the runoff."

Zaz felt a tad guilty. He had not paid a recent visit to Dendy's lab. She'd invested her own company profits in most of the components and hardware. He could see where she had talked Galoot into beam welding the newest troughs to the deck. She had included some additional overhead mist sprayers. The lab's water source came from the recycling system and the nearly depleted hydro tank – she must have been bringing up hand buckets since the explosion. He made a mental note to hook her back up again so that her plants might have a chance of surviving. That meant multiple trips to the gorge.

"Aren't they lovely?" she asked, pointing to a dandelion. "I was thinking that maybe I could transplant some of the heartier vegetables outside and use a sun screen canopy to mask the intense radiation. I could rig a small gravity flow tank. It wouldn't really take that much work and it would give us a small garden."

"I think it's a wonderful idea," said Zaz. "I'll help you with it. Either we'll find some larger tanks to store extra water, or we'll fabricate something." He thought that bringing a little Earth-like flora to Sidus might help keep the crew's spirits up. Wasn't there something about music and plants that soothed the savage breast? Or was it beast?

He followed Dendy to a far corner of the lab, where she squeezed between a small hedgerow of shrubbery. The larger trees and shrubs grew here. They'd taken root from an elevated dirt box that kept their roots anchored two-feet down in the soil. It looked like a miniaturized forest vale, complete with a small pathway.

They came upon a tiny clearing; Zaz looked down and saw a sleeping mat, an empty cup, and an old dog-eared paperback book. He bent over to look at the title: *The Collected Short Stories of R.H. Brentano*.

"What's all this?" he asked.

She sat down on the mat and patted a spot next to her. He obliged, relaxing in the small clearing surrounded by a mass of shrubbery.

"This is my happy place. I call it the 'glorious glen.' I come here to get away from my work, although my work is right around the next big bush." She gave a little snorting laugh.

"What's this book about?"

"Have you ever read Brentano? No? Ah, flights of fantasy – an escape hatch. It puts you somewhere else, another time and another place."

He gave her a quizzical look.

She went on. "You know, fables and stories? My mother used to read to me. That was until I stopped listening because I found other sources of amusement. That was chiefly boys." She looked away.

He liked the profile of her face in the dappled light. She had raised cheekbones, heavy, seductive brows. Her face was an expression machine. He was glad he'd turned the expression machine button on.

"I was wondering about that," he stammered. "If what I heard about you was true, that you were more than a little popular aboard Blue Peace. I mean, it doesn't make any difference…" He trailed off, embarrassed by his own words.

"I don't mind talking about it. I had a couple of shipboard encounters that I ended up breaking off. The rest of the crew thought that I might be more than willing to indulge. You know how men are with locker room talk. Anyway, word got around that I was an easy conquest. The more I refused the advances the more aggressive they became. Suddenly, the shipboard news was that I had a taboo disease. They couldn't read the 'no' on my lips. The ones that I rebuffed were the ones who started the rumors."

"They sullied your reputation and lied about your health."

"I was asked to leave my internship. It was noted that I was a distraction, in addition to being a potential health risk. I never told you because you never asked. I was curious to know if you had passed judgment on me."

"Did I?"

"You passed the exam, Zaz. I never saw anything hurtful in you. Thanks for that."

He picked up the book and read some of the cover blurb. He was nervous, and knew she sensed it.

"It's just like all other books of stories and fables," she said. "You should read it sometime. I have others. You might like *Cinderella*. There's a lesson in there about finding things out about people that you never expected. Kind of like what we're talking about now. Then there's Hans Christian Andersen, Roald Dahl, and the Brothers Grimm. Some of them fall into darker territory."

"Yeah, grim, that's me. Only I don't have a brother. Weren't those guys professors?"

Dendy blinked. "Now that you mention it, they did have some type of honorary doctorate. Hey, that's it! The Grimm brothers!"

"What do you mean?"

"They had a story called *Jack and the Beanstalk*, but that... no, wait. It was also called *Jack the Giant Killer*. Do you think that's what Lyle meant? That the Jack animal is the – "

"I don't think so. It's probably just a coincidence." He reached out to a bush and plucked a small knob of black seed-like bulbs. He rolled them in his fingers, noticing that they left a stain. "What are these?"

She smiled knowingly, shifting her legs. "These are raspberry bushes," she said under her breath.

He brought his lips to hers. She blew a hot breath across his cheek. He found her neck and snuggled his face in it. They kissed passionately.

"Oh, Zaz, whatever took you so long?" she breathed into his ear.

His wrist-com buzzed. He ignored it.

The buzzing became a screeching alarm; whatever it was, it was an emergency.

Zaz quickly caught his breath. "What is it?" he said into his wrist-com.

"We have an urgent matter that requires your presence." It was Samantha.

"Yeah, well right now so do I. What's up?"

"We have some intruders in the compound."

Zaz got to his knees. "Say again?"

"We have some unwelcome visitors inside the fence barrier. You know, the big black and white types? Looks to be about three of them, just inside the west wall."

"I'll be right there!" He leaned down and kissed Dendy. "Please put it on hold for me – we've got a bad one going down." He left at a fast trot down the corridor, with Dendy just behind.

He retrieved his broken rifle from the bridge, where he'd left it. They took the lift to B-Deck and made it out of the ship's hatch in record time. Lyle and Paddy were a few boot steps behind them. Everyone had heard the message.

Zaz made it to the jobsite tent first. Samantha had a scope to her eye, pointing it to the west wall. He brushed her shoulder. "Sammy, where's Carl?"

"He's on his way in from the fence line."

Zaz spotted a dust trail rising on the desert sand in the northern quadrant. Carl had been out there inspecting the blast opening when he'd heard Samantha's message.

Zaz brought the scope to his eye, his breaths coming in heaves. He had to steady his arm to keep the image from dancing. It was hard to see them at first; the tiny figures blended into the dark fence wall. But he had no trouble seeing them when they jumped around in a frenzy.

Samantha dropped her scope. "We have an automech just outside that wall. His motion sensor went off – that's how I got the alarm. They actually *leapt* over the fence! What do you think we should do?"

It wasn't a question of what to do, but how to do it. The Jacks were about two miles out. They still had time to formulate a plan.

Carl could be seen in the distance, approaching fast, his buggy kicking up a dusty wake.

Paddy tugged on Zaz's shoulder. "There are three of them this time, sir. They are no doubt following the scent of the first one. Either that, or they have picked up our presence upwind. It is suicide to stay here and fight them. We should enter the ship and use it for cover. Perhaps A-Deck, where they can't reach us."

"Agreed," said Zaz. "I'll never doubt your word again, professor." Zaz looked around the immediate vicinity, noticing that the gun truck was a dozen yards away. It was the only vehicle that had a small cab for manual operation, with heavy-gauge shatterproof windows on the front and sides, all protected by a mesh cage.

Zaz waited for Carl to pull up before he ordered everyone into the ship. Dendy stomped her foot, refusing to leave. Zaz gave her a forceful shove then turned on the others, who looked equally stubborn.

"I want all of you to take cover in the ship! Carl and I can handle this. We'll hold up in the truck and pick them off. They won't be able to get to us. I'm not going to give up one square foot of our settlement to these things." He raised his voice to a bellow. "Now get going, and I mean now!"

They turned around and trotted off. Dendy threw hurt eyes over her shoulder at Zaz, but then she mouthed, "Be careful!"

Carl walked up to him. "How many shells do you have? I'm only carrying about twenty rounds."

"I have about that or more with me. Let's go; I've got a plan." They ran to the gun truck and stepped up on the running rail to enter the cab. Zaz took the left side, Carl took the right. Putting the scope to his face, Zaz could see the three Jacks making a beeline for the job site.

The animals had assumed a tight formation, no doubt picking up the sight of the tent and ship. Zaz studied their movements. It wasn't easy to get inside the mind of a creature you'd never seen before, much less an alien one. Even as he watched them, the animals picked up a faster pace.

Within moments, the Jacks entered the jobsite, their slobbery muzzles to the ground. Picking up the human scent, they began snapping at the tent poles, darting about like boxers in a ring. Two of the Jacks pounced on the tent, snapping at it, tearing great chunks out of the fabric. The third one snuffed at the dirt, then leapt in the direction of the ship's hatch.

"They're worse than goddamn polecats," said Carl. "Get their attention."

Zaz rolled the window down, waved his arm and screamed. He put the rifle barrel through the mesh and fired a shot. The Jacks perked up, turning their heads, trying to find the source of the commotion. They saw movement in the truck cab and went after it like charging raptors , taking great leaping strides. When they reached the gun truck, the Jacks reared up on their hind legs to look into the cab. Their faces were just above the lower window lip, rabid and snarling.

Zaz lined up on the closest one before it knew what it was looking at. He aimed between the two black eyes and pulled the trigger. There was a loud *crack* and the sound of a bullet ricocheting off the Jack's face. The creature's head bucked backward, but the Jack shook off the bullet strike and let out a barking snarl. The others leapt recklessly at the cab, hitting the doors at full force. Carl leaned around Zaz to let off three rapid shots. All three missed. One of the Jacks hopped to the top of the roof and began pawing furiously at it; the sound was piercing, like that of a grappler shearing metal.

Zaz couldn't get the right angle and had to wait. His ears still rang from Carl's shots. When a Jack bounced off the cab and landed in the dirt, he aimed low, firing rapid shots into its lower gut. This time he knew he'd hit it square, for the creature jerked spastically with each bullet. It stood there for a moment, licking its stomach before it whined and fell on its side.

Carl had another Jack on his side that was trying to get in to the cab. It jumped up on the running board and shoved its muzzle through the wire mesh. Carl rammed his pistol in its mouth and pulled the trigger. The back of the animal's head erupted in a bloody mist. It flopped to the dirt, kicking with spasms.

They reloaded, dropping several spent cartridges on the cab floor. The last animal above them continued to tear at the roof. Zaz watched the metal buckle with the heavy pounding. He glanced at Carl. "On the count of three...okay: one...two...three!"

They shot straight up into the thin roof metal, scattering their shots until they were out. They reloaded – once again, they tried to dislodge the beast by firing up through the roof. The racket was deafening in the confines of the cab. Soon they were breathing acrid gunpowder smoke and coughing, swiping at teary eyes.

"I'm out," said Carl as he tried to slap the smoke from the cab.

"Me too." Zaz hit the manual ignition switch. The truck's electric engine hummed to life. He took the small joystick in his fingers and swung the discharge boom over the cab roof. There was a *thud* – a black and white blur flew past the front window and landed on the desert sand. The Jack was still for only a moment before it shook off its addled state and stood up again. By that time, Zaz had brought the discharge nozzle directly over the animal's head and hit the flow button. A heavy froth of insta-dry foam gushed out of the nozzle and washed over the animal. It tried to kick its way out of the goop, but the foam set immediately, trapping it in a crouched position. Ten seconds later it froze, rock-solid, posed like a stone sculpture. The Jack suffocated within a minute.

Zaz used his scope to scan the area. He wanted a clear field, even if he did have three Jacks lying dead on the desert floor. He opened the door and jumped down. Carl followed a moment later. They walked hurriedly to the ship's hatch, glancing over their shoulders as they moved. Zaz felt great sheets of sweat running down his back, as if heat stroke would scuttle him at any minute.

They'd just made it to the edge of the ship when the rest of the crew came out to meet them. They jumped joyfully, forming a circle around Zaz and giving him hearty backslaps. The captain staggered and fell on his side, completely exhausted. He had one word for them. "Whiskey!"

Samantha got a buzz on her wrist-com; an alarm from the automech sentries stationed around the perimeter. She ran to the demolished jobsite and retrieved her program computer. She tried to read the shaky screen as she ran back.

"We've got another bogey," she coughed. "Same location – just leapt over the fence!"

Carl ran to his small buggy. He jumped inside and gunned the motor, spinning the tires. He rushed straight out into the saltpan, aiming the buggy on an intercept course with the intruder.

Zaz rose to his feet and waved his rifle overhead. "Carl, you dumb bastard!"

It was too late. The buggy accelerated, throwing up a rooster tail of sand. Carl sped out into the compound to wage a one-man war. Zaz knew that Carl had mayhem on his mind.

CHAPTER NINE

DOWNWIND OF A NIGHTMARE

ZAZ COULD ONLY WATCH, helpless with the rest of the crew. Carl had taken it upon himself to act instinctively, with no concern for his own safety. Samantha would have called it "macho bravado," swearing aloud that the man had no concept of deductive reasoning. Carl might not have had much in the way of brains, but he had provocation.

Carl hailed from Sicily. Both his parents had died in an accident when he was very young. Stepparents who'd immigrated to the United States adopted him, but he'd lost track of them after running away from home at the age of fourteen. He'd returned to his homeland, served in the Italian army and tried to make a career out of it. He was discharged after assaulting a superior officer – but not before he'd signed on with several tactical military demolition programs, both underwater and on the surface. He found his way back to the United States and hooked up with Zaz through an ad for employment that called for an explosives expert.

Carl believed that most conflicts, infestations, harbingers of terror, and even bad dreams could be solved with explosives. There was something straight forward and no nonsense about his personality, but there was also a brutal side to his nature. It was rumored that Carl Stromboli had over a dozen blood brothers and sisters, along with adopted siblings. He'd never admitted to seeking out any of his relatives; he fancied himself a gypsy – a loner.

Everyone could understand Carl's provocation: the Jacks were relentless – they were bullies and had to be met head on. Retreat meant weakness; it was like a large, vicious dog that had you on the run – the faster you ran, the more incensed it became.

As Zaz brought the scope to his eye, he could see the two converging. Carl had the buggy floored, holding the speed upwards of 80 miles per hour. The vehicle went airborne as it hit the largest ruts. Zaz thought about running to the big six-wheeler to give chase, but realized there was no way he could get out there in time to help.

Just as a collision looked imminent, the Jack pushed off in one mighty leap and came down in front of the speeding buggy. The four-wheeled vehicle hit it with such force that the Jack somersaulted end over end in the air and landed on its back. The buggy shuddered with the jolt and went out of control, rearing up on its side. Carl corrected, braked hard, skidded 180 degrees and headed back the other way. He ploughed straight into the fallen Jack again, flattening the creature as it tried to stand. The buggy pounced, taking to the air until it landed with several rebounding thumps. Carl stopped the vehicle and looked over his shoulder, checking to see if the animal was dead. He brought the buggy back slowly, stopping at the ship's hatch. The front of the vehicle had tufts of hair and flesh sticking to it; the grille was demolished.

"That's how we used to do it in the army," said Carl, slapping away the dust from his arms.

Lyle, stepped up to Zaz. "I suggest we keep our eyes peeled for any more of them."

"Quite so," said Paddy, doffing his filthy hat.

Zaz considered the advice. The fact that four creatures had now easily come over the fence proved that his crewmembers were vulnerable out in the open. But they had to remain out in the open to monitor the trenching operation, with all eyes on the machines in case they broke down. They would also need to make a trip to the gorge for fresh water; they could not remain locked up in the ship like prisoners.

The *Shenandoah* had it merits. It was an impregnable fortress made of Ultrinium glass-metal, the strongest mineral composite known to science. The Jacks would not be able to get through it by chewing or scratching. It meant closing off the ragged opening that would allow egress. Doing that would prevent bringing the construction machines inside; all heavy equipment would have to remain outside unless they fashioned an opening large enough to get the tow truck through, seeing as it was the largest of the transports. Their castle fortress now had to have a gate.

There was still the question of defending themselves if the situation came to close quarter fighting. There were no weapons stored on the *Shenandoah*. They'd never before had a need for them. Planet Janitor's crew did not carry plasma guns or laser cannons – they were environmentalists and caretakers. Oh, they'd had their spills and out-of-control fire scenarios, but they had never deliberately injured or killed a living thing, except for some bark beetles. Jacks were not bark beetles. One couldn't shoo them off. If there were more of them, like he suspected, they would be hard or nearly impossible to exterminate.

"Listen up," said Zaz. "Sammy, if you haven't already, put a snoop in orbit around our compound. I want to know where those things came from. The rest of you I want assembled in the conference room for an emergency PJ meeting. We're going to have to come up with some defense plans, since it looks like this menace isn't going away."

Zaz strode up to A-Deck, straight to the infirmary. He found Galoot sitting up and drinking some broth that Carybell had made. He put a hand on his friend's shoulder. "Galoot, if you're up to it I would like you to attend a meeting in the conference room. No heroics. You don't have to participate – just listen."

"I can do that, boss. The little one and I will be right along."

Carybell gave Zaz a snappy salute.

Zaz thanked them. He went to the bridge and opened some cabinets. Inside he found some chart paper, which he gathered up in a large roll. He grabbed a large bag of drafting pens then headed out the door. When he got to the conference room, everyone was already in attendance, including Galoot and Carybell.

He spread the supplies on the table and gave instructions for everyone to arm themselves with the utensils. He knew they might not have another chance to meet and organize. They were safe for now; even if the Jacks got inside B-Deck, there was no way the animals could use the lifts to reach them.

Zaz directed his first question to the scientists: "Do you gentlemen have any doubts as to whether or not we have a sizeable population of these creatures in our area?"

"I have every reason to believe that there are multitudes of the Jack creatures on this planet, most likely in our immediate area," said Paddy. "They are highly aggressive, actively seeking us out. A confrontation is certain."

Lyle nodded in agreement. "Sir, my worst fear is a mass swarm. I am convinced that those were scouts following pheromone trails. They have discovered our scent. Once the brood is alerted to our location we will likely be overrun."

Zaz found no need to question their expertise – he only asked the next question for the benefit of everyone listening: "On what do you base this information, and why have you given the name 'Jack' to these animals?"

Lyle said, "Because they are unadulterated killers. The connotation 'Jack' was derived from the story 'Jack the Giant Killer.' These animals are responsible for liquidating the Paddymous giants. The biting and cutting injuries upon the bones are identical with the forensic evidence on their anatomy. We were mistaken about the infliction of cutting weapons upon them. The Jacks are the weapons. I would stake my reputation on it."

Zaz nodded. "What kind of numbers are we looking at?"

"Hundreds," said Paddy. "Maybe thousands. It must be a breeding population – the alpha dominant type. Furthermore, I have done some extensive research in the Pleistocene records. This species closely resembles a Thylacine – Thylacaleo carnifex. It was called the marsupial lion and dominated the Australian continent. It possesses a similar tearing thumb claw. Only our Jack is exclusively bipedal, larger and much more highly evolved. It is beyond ferocious."

Zaz let the information sink in. The crew's expressions went from sober reality to terror-stricken. That was exactly the effect he was looking for; he needed fear to drive the point home – not a mindless fear, but a healthy one based on facts and current evidence.

"As you all know," Zaz began, "we've got problems – maybe a lot more than we ever dreamed. These Jacks, as Paddy calls them, are natural born killers. That's all they do – destroy anything they come in contact with. We've got issues as to what's to be done about it. First: Carl and Galoot, I need some ideas from you two on how we can seal this ship off without hampering our movements. In particular, we need a movable door of some type that can accommodate the six-wheeler, tow truck, and the other smaller vehicles. I need something that will open and close in a moment's notice. I want a complete blueprint design so we can build a functional model pronto. Ideas?"

Carl threw his hair back, but it flopped back down again like dirty linguini. "Well, three things come to mind: we can lay up some fence net and foam it shut then cut out a large panel that will take a hinge arrangement."

Galoot said, "I can find some scrap and beam-weld a cover – but that might take a day or so; then there's that big ol' fence driver that we could park right in front of the opening, moving it only when we have to. Except the fence driver isn't big enough to plug up the entire opening."

Zaz picked the foam cover as the best alternative. He told Carl and Galoot to draw up a preliminary sketch and to includee the proper measurements ASAP.

Zaz continued: "You know we don't have any weapons. The guns that we have won't stop a dozen of these things in full charge. I need some ideas now on how to inflict mass injuries on these Jacks. We've got enough C-5 and C-6 on board to start a war, but those are plastic explosives. What's the best way to use them? Carl? That's your area."

"I'm thinking that we could set up minefields, covering a bunch of grids. We remote detonate the mines to take out anything near them."

Zaz sniffed. "That sounds like a waste of explosives. You can't count on your enemy walking right over your bomb grids. Besides that, how would you know if your target was over the device? What if a large group of them came through a space *between* the mines?"

"We set charges up on poles, or maybe trip-wire certain areas."

"Okay, maybe tripwires at a far enough distance could do some good. What do we do for a medium distance? Say five hundred to one thousand yards? We need to concentrate our firepower at the heaviest population point. If they rush us in a large stream we want to be able to hit that mark and take that line out."

"Excuse me, boss, but I think I might know a way," said Galoot. "We already use our Silvers for smart bombs to blow obstacles. There isn't any reason why we can't pack bombs on all our automechs so they can do the same thing. Once we see a concentration of these things coming, we can move our automechs out to that spot then set them off. Hell, they aren't doing us much good around here except to clean and service things. I say we let them wipe out some of those critters for us. Counting the Greens and Blues, we have about forty-five total."

"I like that idea," said Zaz. "They're mobile and we can direct them. I think it's level enough out there for them to maneuver. What about closer in around the ship – say a hundred yards or so? Why couldn't we fabricate some type of projectile weapons with some pipe or carbon composite tubing? Say we run some scrap metal through the metal mill to make thumb-sized pieces. We can pack it in a tube with a C-5 charge capped at one end and fire it like an old gun."

"Like a blunderbuss," said Dendy. "Or like grape shot in a cannon. That'd rip 'em a new one!"

"I could rig those easily," said Carl. "I could put a magna-cap in the mold and remote click voltage into it. Have to be damn careful, though. I have to figure out the breech stress and the perfect sized charge. But it's doable."

"That's perfect, Carl. Draw up some prototypes that we can mass-produce."

"I have another suggestion," said Lyle. "These Jacks might have a natural aversion to fire like any other animal. If you could lay a trench with something combustible, we might keep them at bay for a very long time."

"All we have is about seventy or eighty gallons of old diesel fuel for some of those antique generators," said Galoot. "We'd have to add some high octane fuel to it. Then it would fire up real good. Maybe we could make something up in the lab."

"I'd rather save the old gas for later," said Zaz. "You're talking about a fire line and we haven't got enough wet fuel for that."

"Wait a minute," said Carl. "We have those small oxygen pressure tanks. We put some high-pressure nozzles on them then fill them with hydrogen from our main tanks. Then we tie up a portable beam torch to it for an ignition source. Then you – "

"Would have a flamethrower," said Samantha, keeping her eyes on her portable snoop screen. She glanced at Zaz. "Nothing yet. It's clear out there."

Zaz nodded. "Start drawing it up. I want everyone's renderings of these devices. We need the quickest way to make them; so keep the designs easy to follow."

Dendy looked hesitant for a moment, her hand half-raised. She spoke up, "Now, if they get to us, I mean, if they run us down, or maybe we can't make it back inside the ship..." She hunched her shoulders. "I'm sorry."

That consequence had crossed Zaz's mind as well. He knew the only way to save them would be a retreat to the highest deck of the ship. Then they would be trapped. There was no telling if the Jacks would surround the ship and wait them out or not. He could not get into the creature's mind to know its behavior. The worst scenario would be to get cornered and stalked – or dying of thirst while stuck in the ship and unable to go for water.

Zaz looked at the professors once more. "I know that we can't fight toe-to-toe with these things because you said so. But if it comes to a last stand, so to speak, what final option do we have?"

"Blunt force trauma," said Paddy. "I would go for the snout with a club or a cutting implement. You would have to have something with reach or length. They can gut you with a kick within a yard or less."

"Carl, can you forge us some flat swords or hacking weapons? Something lethal, but light."

"That's the ticket," said Dendy. "Axes, pole arms, and long swords. You can't bull your way through a swishing axe so easy."

"Yeah," said Carl, pinching his chin. "That stuff would be the easiest of all to make. I knew somebody that had a collection like that."

"And I've seen lots of them in my books," said Dendy. "I can draw them just fine."

Zaz gave each of them a duty and a specific workstation, assigned according to their knowledge and skill. Carl would take up the task of foaming the ship closed and designing a large swing door. He would also set out the pole bombs and design the shrapnel and cannon charges. Galoot had insisted he could do his part, so he would fabricate the small cannon tubes. Samantha had to keep her eyes on the snoop screen, her ears open to any perimeter alarms. she would also help pack the automechs with explosives when she had free time. Lyle and Paddy would construct the flamethrower and some of the small arms. Carybell and Dendy would act as "rag wrenches" and "gofers." Zaz had his own idea of what he was going to do.

They had all the plans drawn up in one night, hitting their bunks after dinner. No one slept well. Samantha confessed to pacing the corridors and then laying with her screen next to her head, periodically jerking awake to check it.

```
Sidus Log, Rotation 12.
We are at war, having been attacked four days ago by
more of those damn Jack creatures. I feel like we have
been gripped by some kind of madness, or a bizarre
nightmare from which we cannot escape.
   There has been little time for sleep or regular
duties, owed to this frantic schedule of arming the
camp. Nerves are frayed and tempers have been lost.
```

I've had to shout down several arguments, one of which erupted between Paddy and Carl, almost to the point of trading blows. Things are calm now, but pensive. If we do not function as a coordinated unit, I believe all coherency and cooperation will deteriorate.

Owed to the distance that we are from our home planet, an emergency beacon is useless. To be stranded is bad enough. To be under a possible siege by a vicious outside agency is mind numbing. I've been visiting the whiskey cabinet more than I would like to admit. I hope it doesn't show. My crew needs a competent leader - not some vindictive and delirious Bligh.

I have allowed Dendy a brief respite, permitting her to plant some seedlings and young sprouts in a small garden in front of the ship. She has a fine net mesh over her 'precious babies' to keep them from perishing in the direct sunlight. It might help calm the nerves and restore a sliver of order to this maddening ordeal that is fast testing our collective sanities.

Love you mom and dad - miss you more than ever.

Captain Zachary Crowe, PJ.

Zaz headed for the ready room next to the bridge. Once inside, he opened a cabinet and took down his survival suit and helmet. It was a customized carbon-reinforced suit that the crew wore for spacewalks. It had full pressurization capability with life-sustaining and recycling hook ups. He left the oxygen pack behind, knowing that it would be useless. He pulled some beam shears from a utility drawer then headed for the conference room.

When he arrived, he locked the door against entry and then commenced his work. First, he cut the suit straight across the knees then sheared off the long sleeves and gloves. He cut out any unnecessary plug or fastener, knowing that the extra holes would provide ventilation. He stood for a while, thinking about what was to be done about the helmet; it was so large and heavy he knew he had to trim it down without sacrificing strength. He decided on removing the chin guard starting at the ear region. He left the pull-down half-visor intact to protect the face and shield from the sun's glare.

When he was satisfied he had the right cut-down style, he stepped into the new custom suit and fastened the straps. He pulled the half-helmet over his head and walked around the room, bending at the waist, swinging his arms, simulating a mock battle with some unseen adversary. Short of vigorous calisthenics, he put himself through every move he could imagine, including falling down and trying to get up quickly. It worked. It was flexible and afforded protection at the same time.

He took the lift down to B-Deck and went in search of Galoot and Carl. He found them at the ship's hatch, which had just been fitted with a foam cover. The men were in the process of fashioning a smaller access door in the large patch wall they had already installed. After watching them for a while, Zaz admonished Galoot for lifting up the weight of the small door they were installing.

"I don't want you busting your gut, big guy."

Carl, who had a hammer and drift pin in his hand, turned to look at Zaz. Both men openly stared at the strange costumed figure of their captain.

"We're finished with it anyway," said Galoot. "Boss, I hate to tell you this, but your pressure suit is all busted up."

"Not busted up – modified. I want all of you to cut your suits down just like this one. Wear it at all times. That looks good, by the way. I see the big door works on a cantilever system. Good thinking."

"Yeah, it's a big hinge," said Carl, pushing his cutting goggles over his forehead. "But you're kidding about the suit, right? Those things run ten thousand imperials apiece."

"You're not going to be doing any spacewalks out here, Carl. The suit has got some tough carbon fiber in it. It might afford some protection if one of those things gets in close. I'm calling lunch in the bridge, so drop what you're doing. Are Dendy and Sammy outside?"

Carl nodded to the door. "Yeah, they're out there. Step right on through."

Zaz waited for them to pull the small door open. He stepped out into the stifling heat. He wondered if the suit would be too much cover and might cause him to rapidly overheat. He walked normally, heading out to the jobsite tent and testing his peripheral vision by turning his eyes from side to side. He had only a slight problem with a side of the helmet that cut off some of his field of view.

Samantha cocked her head as she saw him approach. "What the heck are you all made up for?"

He expected the reaction. He knew he looked a little silly, walking around in triple digit temperatures outfitted in half a spacesuit with a cut down helmet. He *would* get past the sarcasm.

"For your information," he began with an edge to his voice, "this is going to be standard issue from now on. As soon as you have a chance, cut your suit down to this style. What's up out there?"

"Nothing yet. I did get the bright idea of following those animal tracks since they stood out so well in the ash. The snoop lost them about ninety miles out where they disappeared into the southern tree line. I couldn't pick them up again. It's a heavily forested area, a lot like the north but not as rugged. If they're out there, that's where they're hiding."

"Keep on it. But for now, bring your screen with you to the bridge – lunchtime."

Zaz scoped the terrain, noticing that some poles had been planted very far out near the fence line. He didn't see a lot of them. They'd put out tripwires yesterday, covering numerous grids at every compass direction within the compound. There was a lot of acreage out there – 20 square miles of it. Could they anticipate the direction of an attack From Samantha's prints?

To the south, near the fence line, he could see the plume of volcanic dust stirred by the trench diggers and bulldozers. The front-loaders were dumping the bone material over the wall in massive loads.

He walked a third of the way down the length of the ship toward the stern and saw Dendy and Carybell attending to some garden rows. They'd dug down past the bone bed and toweled up some rich soil. Dendy walked up and down the rows with a makeshift water can, sprinkling the tiny shoots that had barely taken hold. He watched the girls for a while, before they turned and saw him.

Dendy pointed a hand spade at him. "You shouldn't sneak up on people looking like an outer space geek. You're going to kill my plants. Or make them cry out in fright, one of the two."

"I couldn't resist – you were bending over again. Look, I'm going to call a quick lunch on the bridge. So pack it up for now and head that way."

Dendy nodded. Carybell clawed her fingers at him in a girlish wave.

Zaz headed back to the ship, speaking into his wrist-com. "Paddy, Lyle, are you two together? If so, where are you?"

"Yes we are, sir," said Lyle. "We are aft on B-Deck, metal-smithing. Paddy impacted his thumb with a mallet when he – "

"I don't need to know the details. I want you two to break and get to the bridge for lunch. Have Dendy look at the thumb when you get there. Have we got enough of those swords and hacking weapons for each person?"

"Yes, we have some fighting implements ready. We will meet you on the bridge."

Zaz made the announcement on his wrist-com again, making sure everyone understood the urgency. In the past, his crewmembers had been inclined to procrastinate or forget a command. There would be no more of that. He wanted them to function as a unit – one mind, one body. They weren't military enlistees, but that didn't mean they couldn't snap themselves into a more disciplined mode.

He arrived at the bridge deliberately tardy. He had no mind to "chew his recruits" for being late. They were tired, on the verge of heat prostration, and at times hardly able to put a few sentences together without forcing it.

Most of the crew lay sprawled on their chairs in the full reclining position. Dendy stood at the small galley, flash-cooking instant meals. Even she looked wobbly on her feet.

Zaz dialed down the thermostat to make the bridge more comfortable. His crew seemed unusually quiet, until he realized that Samantha and Carl were exchanging dagger eyes. He thought that if he looked hard enough he could almost see the brimstone and smoke in the air between them. They had been at it again.

"I'm just saying it ain't a bad thing you have to cover up now," said Carl, breaking the silence. "It won't be a distraction. You don't see me swinging the salami around to cause a ruckus."

"It wouldn't be a question of swinging," said Samantha, "but more of an act of bobbing."

Zaz stepped in front of Carl and snapped his fingers. "Carl!"

Carl looked at him. "Yeah, Zaz?"

"Please leave that young woman's breasts alone. It's not a fair fight anyway. Either one of them is smarter than you."

Paddy and Lyle chuckled together. They'd taken the time to clean up a bit, looking better for it. Zaz hoped Paddy had used some soap and water on his hair to rid himself of the annoying itch that bothered him. Better yet, an acid wash shampoo would have done a fantastic job of killing the nasty bug population in his scalp, or whatever the hell he had crawling around up there.

Dendy passed around the plastic plates: syntho-beef, beans, garden carrots, and a bread pudding. Everyone received a pint of water. Carybell apologized for not assisting in the meal prep, but Dendy excused her due to the attendance she was showing Galoot.

Zaz ate with his helmet on, wanting to get used to the feel. He hoped the others would follow his lead and get to work on their suits soon. For now, he needed their individual reports.

"How's our progress so far?" he asked.

Galoot wiped his mouth. "We were thinking that all the automechs should be kept outside with their bomb packs. That's to make sure that nothing happens inside, boss."

Zaz nodded and watched as Paddy picked up an object at his side. The scientist took a couple of swipes at the air with it. "Lyle and I took some of those thin poles and put them in the hydraulic press to smash them into blades," he said. "We used adhesive and packing string for the pommel grips. We have some ideas for a crossbow that might be affective; we are going to use some old leaf springs and wire to fashion one. We also have a few ideas about arrows that we think might work."

Carl grabbed the blade, whipped it through the air a few times then handed it to the captain.

Zaz felt the weight of the weapon; it was a manageable three-feet long. "This is going to work fine. One for each of us – we'll carry them in makeshift scabbards. The crossbow is another good idea. Don't rush it – make it simple, easy to use."

Zaz handed the blade to Carl, who wedged it under his chair cushion. Carl slapped his seat "That's for close encounters of the worst kind," he said.

"There is just one problem," said Lyle. "After doing some further research on the Jack creatures, Paddy and I have come to a startling conclusion. Since these marsupial lions do not seem to be well adapted to this environment, the heat, I mean, it points to the possibility that they could be nocturnal. The fact that four of them showed up during daylight hours could have been a fluke. Or perhaps they were expendable scouts. Considering the physiology of their eyes, they seem to be well suited for night vision. I am not saying this as fact. But the possibility remains that they could come in the night. We might think about setting up the large stadium floodlights to illuminate a wide perimeter around the ship."

"We've got both hydrogen generators in full operational status," said Zaz. "Even with one out, we can still run all the ship's functions, plus the extra draw from the lamps. I agree that it would be a good precaution to set them up to illuminate the compound. See if you can rig them up on top of the ship's hull – cut the emergency hatch opening to make it more accessible."

Carl nodded. "Okay, after we've got that done, I was wondering if I could do some modifications on the vehicles, like beam-weld some pokers or blades onto the frames. It was pretty easy to run that one down. I don't think the dumb sumbitch knew what hit him."

Zaz looked at the scientists. "Just how smart do you think these Jacks are? You've seen them react to us. What does their behavior tell you?"

Paddy lowered his plate to his lap. "I did not observe them long enough to get a complete sense of their intelligence. When they were struck or shot, they reacted with surprise and confusion. It is almost as if they never expected such counter-violence. If they have near the intelligence of a dog, I would think they could learn from their mistakes and not be likely to repeat them. Then again, they might be aggressive dolts."

Carl waved a plastic spoon. "Well I say we kicked their sweet-smellin' asses. It's too bad there weren't a bunch more around to learn the lesson. That one I ran over sure didn't know what a buggy was! Maybe we ought to root 'em out and draw a line in the sand."

"We're not leaving the compound or the safety of the ship," Zaz stressed. "And we won't be going out any farther than our tripwires near the fence line unless we're packing up to go for water in the gorge. We're damn lucky our vehicles can outrun anything on this planet. I just hope they don't give chase, or are smart enough to follow tire tracks."

Paddy got to his feet. "Every person alive has trillions of skin cells. Thousands of the skin cells slough off our bodies every day of our lives. We breathe, we drop sweat, and we sprinkle these skin cells all over our environment. With vigorous activity, it is accelerated. Animals that have olfactory senses like these only have to follow a few skin cells to find you. And if they are determined to find you, they will go over hill and dale, day or night to do so."

"That's just great," said Samantha. "Now they can sniff us out wherever we go."

Zaz saw a shadow in the sand just outside the nose window. It was visible from both portals and approached from the north. The cabin light began to dim, growing increasingly dark. The overhead lights blinked off – the turbine hum of the ship's generators wound down. Total blackout. Zaz couldn't see his hand in front of his face. A plate dropped on the floor. Something hit the deck and clanged loudly. He could hear Dendy's voice from 15 feet away.

"What the heck is going on?"

"It must be a cumulous cloud," said Lyle.

That made no sense, thought Zaz. "We haven't seen a cloud over this desert since we've been here, much less a breeze. We're in the equatorial belt of this planet, remember? The only clouds I've seen are in the north. We've got a power cut too – the generators are down. Just don't make any sudden moves – stay where you are for now."

Zaz looked over his shoulder. He could not see the bridge hatch. Then, as gradually as it had vanished, light began to filter back into the bridge. Outside, a line of sunlight crept over the sand, chasing the black away. He could see the faces of his crew again. He looked at his watch – it read 2:30 PM. The bridge lights flickered once before coming back on again. Zaz felt the soft hum of the generators through his feet. *Auto restart.*

Lyle picked up the plate he'd dropped. "Was that an eclipse? Or a planetary transit?"

Samantha looked baffled. "The inferior planet is orbiting twenty-five million miles from the sun. I don't think it has a sufficient diameter to cause a total eclipse like that. It never crossed my mind to study this system and its orbital paths. That was more than spooky."

Zaz picked up his rifle and walked out of the bridge to the lift. The crew followed closely behind. He took the lift down to B-Deck, looking through the cavernous hull for any sign of movement or something out of place. Once the lift had stopped, he crept across the hull deck. He reached the small access door and opened it, peering out into the daylight. He cautiously stepped out onto the sand. He took his helmet off and looked up into the sky. There were no clouds. Not even a bird flew overhead.

Lyle swiveled a lens over his face and gazed up at the sun. He stood there for a long while without saying anything. Finally, he dropped his head and flipped the lens up away from his eyes. "I can see absolutely nothing up there. If that was a slow transit I would have seen the planet; it could not have moved that far out of alignment."

Zaz turned to Samantha as she studied her portable screen. "Did you pick up any anomalies out there? Like a ship's signal or frequency?"

"Zip, nothing. There was no detection of movement on the outside markers, either. The scout snoop is still out in the southern quadrant, but I have no visual targets from it. We've just had a planetary blackout and there is no evidence for it. What am I missing? Could that have been a slow-moving comet that skipped our atmosphere? That would jibe with the electromagnetic disturbance."

Carl, the most practical of the group, appeared the most frayed by the incident. He stomped around the sand muttering to himself. "This place is damn near ready to drive me nuts. First we get our water tank blown to hell, then we run into a bunch of killer skunks. Then the lights go out all of a sudden in the middle of the mutha fuckin' kiss-my-ass day. Ain't no wonder why Orion Industries sent us out here in the first place. We're the only ones stupid enough to get caught up in something like this!"

Samantha cringed. "Speak for yourself, Carl. Nobody asked you to take the ride."

Zaz let them argue, running their own gauntlet. This time he had no intention to interrupt or make peace. Whatever had just happened had not been written in the manual – Sidus had just thrown another mystery into their laps. It seemed that the natural laws of science and nature did not apply to this strange new world. It insisted on remaining an enigma.

He had no answers for the crew, or the slightest clue about what they were up against.

CHAPTER TEN

THE MYSTERY CREATURE REVEALED

Sidus Log, Rotation 18.

"The heat is oppressive - unrelenting. This afternoon it topped 126 degrees. All crewmembers are now wearing what they laughingly call 'full battle dress.' I wonder if the persistent cussing and damnations I am hearing are directed at me for imposing the rule. I'm sure they resent me, though not openly. Even Dendy has been short with me lately. She putters around in her garden and has thrown a number of fits directed at Carybell for what I would deem minor infractions.

Three of the automechs have lost servo power and keeled over on the desert floor. Their internal coolers quit and the electronics have melted causing surge failures. We can't move the rest of them back into the hull area for fear of a premature detonation. They are wearing bomb packs, but they have not been armed yet. Carl and Samantha have all of the automechs wired into their remote portables, so either one can operate them as a group or independently. Even the machines can't take the stress in this hellish place.

Galoot is recovering nicely. He seems to be the least affected by the hardships. With antibiotic supplements and Dendy's care, his attitude and outlook have been on the rise. I'm elated to see improvement in him.

I can only laugh at Carl's attempts to transform our buggy and vehicle fleet into makeshift war chariots. They remind me of the old 20th Century fighting demolition robots, only not as extreme. I hardly think they can be used effectively against the Jacks, but I have been proven wrong in the past by some of Carl's innovations. I pray he does not get it in his head to drive out in this wasteland and do any safari-type hunting.

Our water supply is holding nicely, given the strict rationing I've imposed. No one has abused the rules. This fact has been the highpoint of our cooperation, when I first thought it might have proven to be our worst violation.

An old telescope has been fitted to the top of the ship near the emergency hatch, since our main gun scope was damaged upon impact. It is mounted on a makeshift railing. I call it the crow's nest, and have spent many hours up there. It affords a view of the desert floor over the tops of the barrier fence. I've seen nothing moving out there, save for some of the armadillo creatures, which are intent on chasing the small locusts.

It is late in the evening. The chill is coming on. I will make one last on-foot patrol outside before we rally and close ourselves up in the ship for the night."

Captain Zachary Crowe, PJ.

ZAZ KNEW WHERE Dendy would be. Arriving at the garden, he stopped to admire the small plot. He had to admit that he liked the little garden, with its shade canopy, the struggling little seedlings trying to push up through the soil, and the sight of her in that chopped-down suit. It gave him some brief, but welcomed amusement. She looked like a miniature gladiator – all armored up with no games to attend. Carybell looked equally comical and weighted down, since it took great effort for her to crouch to push seeds in the dirt.

Zaz was just about to comment on the garden when he heard a deafening explosion.

Dendy dropped her water can. Carybell spun around. Zaz looked out across the compound. He could see a rising plume of dust at the southwest corner.

Samantha's voice came over his wrist-com loud and clear. "We've got movement in the southwestern quadrant. They just jumped the fence and set off a trip wire!"

Zaz brought the scope to his eye in the dimming light. Behind him, rigged on the top of the ship, the high-intensity flood lamps popped on, pouring a swath of light over the compound and out onto the desert floor. He steadied the scope; he could see a segment of collapsed wall in the southwest corner. A cloud of volcanic ash began to rise up into a blunt mushroom shape. He saw bits and pieces of things on the ground but couldn't tell if they were wall fragments or animal bodies. They might have been both.

Samantha trotted across the sand to where Zaz stood. She adjusted her portable view screen, focusing the image. "It's no good," she said. "They must have knocked the automech down before I saw anything. Carl's motion sensor never tripped. All I'm getting is a close-up camera view of the sand. I'll bring the snoop in there – it's in another grid, so it will take some time. I'm sorry, I was preoccupied and not watching the screen."

Moments later, Carl and Galoot appeared, dragging tripods and heavy weapons across the sand. They'd heard the explosion from inside the ship and knew it meant trouble. Carl had brought his portable screen under his suit vest and brought up a visual grid showing the placement of the pole bombs. Zaz didn't know if there was another tripwire this side of the southwest corner. They didn't have much in the way of explosives in that area to begin with. They had barely covered eighteen miles of fence line with fifty percent of their explosives inventory. The rest was held in reserve for the percussion weapons.

Zaz cursed himself. *Naturally, I didn't have anybody operating the telescope on the ship's roof. We could have had an early warning!*

Paddy and Lyle appeared in a huff. Paddy had a tank strapped to his back that led to a nozzle attached to a portable beam welder. He looked like a WWII infantryman ready to torch a cave full of hostiles. Lyle resembled a medieval warrior, complete with crossbow and bolt-filled quiver. There was a crank arrangement fashioned on the crossbow spine, designed to pull back tautly on a thin, strong wire. When Zaz looked at Dendy, he found that she'd taped a bird feather to the front of her helmet. She told him it was the way braves always went into battle.

This is what I've got for warriors, he thought bleakly. They were junkyard marines who'd never been in a battle in their lives, save for Carl Stromboli.

Zaz, with the scope to his eye again, was unsure of what he was seeing. "They've hesitated about coming through for now. Maybe we've given them something to think about. Carl, send about seven automechs out there in a wedge formation. Make it about one fifty yards wide. They might get over the shock and decide to push through. Arm the automechs when they're far enough out."

"Okay, but I still think we kicked their ass."

"Don't think," said Samantha. "That's how we land in trouble. Just send those automechs out there like you were told."

Zaz did not want to see anything come through the fence into the compound. He had no idea how many creatures were out there, nor did he want to find out. He wished they would all go away – wiped from his sight and memory. That was never the way things really worked, though – not for Planet Janitor. They had always been dealt the black marble; nothing had ever been normal or easy for them.

It looked almost like a mirage when Zaz spotted movement through the broken fence line. The enemy was on the move. The sooner they got it over with the better.

At first, it looked like shadows, a creeping river of indistinct dark shapes. As it increased in mass, it took on the likeness of a pyroclastic flow – a lahars that surged across the desert floor, flowing like one enormous body. Looking like a large twisting thread, it began to fan out, and that is when Zaz truly saw their numbers.

As the sun dipped completely behind the horizon, the darkness crept over them like a shroud. The floodlights were effective out to three thousand yards. He still had the Silver automechs in sight, moving at a rapid walk in the distance. No other tripwires or mines had gone off.

"Carl, set off the pole bombs now!"

Carl consulted his screen. He ran his finger over the keypad, arming and detonating everything in that grid. Sudden starbursts flashed, accompanied by fiery tails that shot up like small comets. A second later, numerous *pop-pop-pop* concussions shook the ground with small tremors. The tent poles shivered, threatening to topple.

"I've got the snoop over them now," said Samantha. "I'm picking up hundreds of images at the corner – they're bottlenecked in a large mass, trying to push through the opening. Strike that – they number in the thousands!"

Of all the things to forget was a good pair of infrared binoculars, thought Zaz, which he knew was stowed in a cabinet up on the bridge. If he had them he could time the automech's advance on the Jacks then set off the charges precisely.

An eerie caterwauling came from across the desert sand. It rose in a crescendo of barks and growls – a frenzied cacophony. There was also the noise of howling animals mixed in, an indication that their bombs had maimed several, if not dozens of advancing Jacks.

Zaz told Carl to halt the mobile automechs at the fringe of the floodlight's range. Carl did so and awaited the next command.

They came leaping out of the dark, swarming over the desert floor. Creatures unaffected by the first blasts now advanced in a second wave. They trampled over the automechs, knocking them down like tin toys. Zaz waited for the main surge to pass over the downed machines, allowing the rear horde to catch up. He could see them more clearly now. The largest mass was now in position.

He gave the order.

Seven explosions went off simultaneously. A wall of earth erupted in a vivid light show. Bodies and chunks of flesh launched into the air like so much flotsam, becoming small missiles. The P-wave and resulting windblast hit the crew's faces, bringing several of them to a crouch lest they lose their balance. Bits and pieces of bone, skull and teeth rained down on the camp not twenty feet from where they stood.

Zaz un-slung his rifle and brought it to his shoulder. Carl pulled his pistol. Paddy and Lyle raised their weapons. Galoot wrestled a tripod-mounted cannon into position, then set another one up for Samantha.

They listened for more commotion, waiting to see if anything emerged from under the gray umbrella of smoke-laden ash.

"Paddy," said Zaz, "are we doing the right thing?"

"Yes, they must be discouraged from approaching. It they have any memory at all they must learn from their mistakes and know that to come near us is a very bad thing. It is akin to swatting a puppy with a rolled paper. They *must* be conditioned so they learn."

It would have been so easy to swat puppies. They ran when frightened. This menace came head-on.

Samantha put her screen down in the sand and took up a station behind one of the homemade cannons. "My snoop must have caught some shrapnel – it's down and out."

Zaz watched as five figures emerged from the dust cloud. Several more appeared out of the smoke; one of them dragging a half-severed leg. One Jack jumped blindly around in circles. Another one pulled its rear over the sand, both legs and tail blown off.

Zaz sighted down the barrel, wishing he had fixed the broken stock since it was difficult to hold the rifle steady. When the Jacks were within 50 yards, he gave the command to fire.

Zaz put three shots into the abdomen of the nearest animal, then re-sighted and did the same thing to the next, not waiting for them to fall. Carl's shots were less accurate, but Zaz could see that when the other man hit one, it would buck up in the air or spin wildly with the heavier bullet impact. Bullets that missed penetrated to the back of the group and hit others.

Galoot pressed a remote firing mechanism. His small cannon went off with a thunderous crack. There was a whistling sound as shredded metal flew through the air, followed by the *plap-plap-plap* of contact. Chunks of Jack flesh vaporized into misty sprays of purplish blood. Lyle fired his crossbow, the bolt flying in a great arc and disappearing amongst the rushing shapes. It took him several seconds to reload the contraption, but he remained undaunted.

Dendy and Samantha set off a cannon and were instantly knocked to the sand by the recoil. The charge, obviously too strong, had blown the end of the barrel into a flower shape.

Paddy covered the left flank, peering into the dusty light. Two Jacks had somehow come up on his left, closing the distance. He spun, wielding the nozzle in their direction and fingered a valve. As soon as he hit the welder ignition, a scorching flame erupted, sending out a billowing fireball. The Jacks jumped directly into the inferno, their fur igniting instantly. They staggered, barking and snapped at the bright orange flames that engulfed them, until finally they flopped to the sand, smoldering. Lyle gave out a victory yell.

Zaz took the time to reload during a lull in the attack. He dropped half his bullets in the sand and had to kneel to pick them up, his hands shaking. When he rose, he caught sight of a blur in midair heading directly for him. He crouched, looking up in time to see the top half of the Jack's body disappear in an explosion. Galoot stood over him with a mini cannon in his arms, the barrel smoking. He helped Zaz to his feet.

"Couldn't let 'em jump you like that, boss." The giant man backpedaled in the sand to find his bomb charges for a reload.

Zaz braced, took aim, and though he could not see any more advancing Jacks, ticked off fifteen more shots in a spray pattern. All he could see in the distance were hundreds of sprawled corpses; several of the prone forms were still squirming in the last moments of life.

He ordered a cease-fire and called his crewmembers into a close ring around him. Though none of their eyes left the scene out in front, they kept their weapons poised and ready. A few more tripwire explosions went off. Zaz imagined that some wounded or dazed animals had wandered into another grid, tripping additional charges. After a few minutes, the noise abated, except for some howls and the sound of clacking jaws. There were a few angry barks that smacked of rage, too. Many of the maimed animals tried to rise defiantly, even though they had no legs to stand on.

Dendy wiped a soot mark on her cheek. "They don't learn so well, do they?"

"Got more guts than brains," said Carl.

"Kinda like you," snapped Samantha.

Zaz told everyone to assemble the camp chairs in a semicircle. Carl went off in the opposite direction and had to be ordered back into line. Right now, no one would be allowed to leave.

"I say we take some buggies and go out there and finish them off," Carl announced. "I don't want to sit here all night listening to them bitching and screaming."

"You're staying right here," said Zaz, "because we don't know what's out there. They have to come straight across the floodlights to get us. That's our advantage. It's their turf out there. If they have half a brain they'll be waiting to jump us. We're not surrendering the upper hand because we *think* we licked them."

"Crap!" Carl sat in the sand and set his pistol in his lap.

Zaz arranged for half the crew to nod off while the others kept watch. Dendy decided to stay awake on the first watch with him. Carl and Galoot volunteered to be the third and fourth pairs of eyes. Samantha wanted to put another snoop in the air, but Zaz nixed the idea, preferring that she opt for some sleep instead. They could send one out in the morning, and besides, he didn't want her to walk to the ship alone to retrieve another. He wanted everyone close and accounted for in one fighting group. If they disconnected from each other they weakened their firepower.

Zaz stared out into the night, scanning the desert compound almost like a machine. He was so hyped he wondered if he'd ever fall asleep once his turn came. He felt Dendy's eyes on him. He turned to her with a weak, apologetic smile. She returned it, seeming to draw on some inner courage to speak.

"I'm kind of glad that we're wearing these suits. It's not so bad once you get used to it. That's what I like most about you – you're more right than wrong."

"And I like the fact that you don't have trouble expressing yourself," he answered. "Although your compliment might be premature; I forgot about the temperature drop out here at night. The insulation is great on the torso, but my arms and lower legs are beginning to feel the bite. I didn't think of everything."

She laughed. "I never said you walked on water." She lowered her voice. "You're not all bent and macho like Carl. You keep your strength all bottled up and hidden away. You don't advertise. I think that pulls much more respect."

"Who, me? The mysterious captain type? Look, if I wanted to blow my stack I would. But it's not going to get us anywhere if I start thinking irrationally. People can get killed on account of a few bad calls. It was PJ that brought us here. I can at least provide some type of survival plan. We all deserve to get out of this."

She looked up forlornly into the sky, picking out stars with her eyes. "Do you really think they will come?"

By "they" he knew she wasn't talking about the Jacks. She was wondering if Orion Industries were going to send construction battalions and follow up with their settlement plans within a year. That question nagged at him as well. He gave it some thought before he answered. "The way I figure it, with the hefty advance they gave us and the fact that they believe they have ownership of Sidus, there's no reason to believe they'll drop their interest or investment. I'd say they score high on the greedy side, so the chance that they'll be here before a year or sooner is a good one. That's the only way I can look at it. Are you missing old blue already?"

"Kind of. Just for your information, none of us really went off to visit our families or relatives. I don't think anybody said their goodbyes except you. I haven't spoken to my mother since I left home… I don't even know if my dad is still alive. I do miss grandma in Texas, but I didn't want anyone to know where they could find me. I think we've all been running from something. All you have to do is single each one of us out and you can find a cartload of flaws. Me miss Earth? Since when did Earth ever miss me?"

"It's not all that bad."

"Oh, yeah? I've been branded a slut; Galoot feels like a carnival freak, Carl is an asshole, and – "

"I heard that!" said Carl.

Dendy said, "The professors are insufferable eccentrics; Samantha thinks she looks like a toad, and Carybell has a short circuit in her wiring . So what do we have?"

"Each other," said Zaz

"I don't hate any of you," said Galoot. "I just think you all are just a bunch of funny little midgets." He laughed at his own joke, but had to hold his stomach lest he tear the staples.

Dendy's expression changed. Her features softened, like a puppy that had just been stroked. The "each other" remark was good enough for now.

Zaz looked up just in time to see Carl holding the pistol over his raised knee to fire into an oncoming Jack. The bullet passed through its midsection and exited the other side, severing the spine. It dropped face down without a twitch. A moment later, another one popped out of the dark. Zaz easily dropped it, but it took four shots. The smaller caliber weapon was not as effective as the .45 in the trauma department.

Zaz spent the rest of his shift dividing his attention between small talk and keeping a wary eye on the compound. Three other Jacks found their way into his sights and were quickly dispatched. Galoot ran to the ship to bring back a portable heater and some blankets, which he passed around to the crew. After six hours, the other team members were awakened to stand their shifts; although they'd found it hard to sleep from the noise of the gunshots, they did not complain. Zaz fell asleep under a thick blanket while the others watched the compound and spoke in hushed tones.

*   *   *

Someone roused him with a gentle tug. For a moment, Zaz had no idea where he was. That was, until someone pulled the blanket from him. A weak late-morning light filled the compound. When he looked at his watch he saw that he'd been asleep for nearly ten hours. He took a breath of air. The air smelled of gunpowder residue, mixed with the sickly sweet smell of dead Jacks.

The first thing that caught his eye in the distance was scores of black and white lumps scattered in the compound. Some were very close to where they had positioned their chairs. It was strange, but he didn't remember killing any Jacks so near. It must have happened while he slept, having had no recollection of waking during those close encounters.

Samantha confirmed his suspicions a moment later when she handed him a hot cup of tea. He felt for his rifle and noticed it was missing. The tall redhead had it slung over her shoulder. "You missed the excitement," she said. "Six of the bastards charged us, but we cut 'em down. Paddy flamed that one right there. Carybell and I shot the other five. The main group just disappeared."

Zaz could see Carybell standing ten feet away, grinning under her helmet. She had Carl's .45 tucked in her waist belt. She looked like something out of an old celluloid western, where the deputy had just finished cleansing the town of the outlaws.

Carl woke up, glanced at his side. "Where's my damn hog-leg?" He looked around. "All right now, little missy, hand that over before you shoot your foot off."

Samantha opened her mouth to throw a barb at Carl but Zaz beat him to it. "She probably just saved your meatballs. Have a little respect, Carl."

Carybell handed the .45 over to Carl under the watchful eye of Galoot, who'd just arisen and stretched his arms to the sky.

"Mrs. Samantha said that I shoot like Annie Oakley," Carybell said proudly. To which Carl gave her a quizzical double take then shoved the .45 in his waist belt. It was doubtful that Carybell had gotten off anything more than a lucky shot.

Zaz noticed that everyone was awake, but he still couldn't keep his eyes off the carnage out in the compound. Something would have to be done about it, like redirecting the front loaders into the area to carry off the corpses before the heat of the day did its damage. He would not tolerate a stink fest of decay in proximity to their camp. It was also morally unacceptable to leave such death out in the open as an assault to the senses. Another matter nagged at him: the whines of dying Jacks in the distance. As much as he hated the creatures, he was not about to let any of them suffer.

He ordered all hands into the six-wheeler, armed with whatever they could carry. They started off with a slow roll, carefully steering around the bodies so as not to catch them in the undercarriage. They followed the stream of bodies out to the fence corner to survey the damage to the wall; Carl guided them on a course that would take the six-wheeler between the unexploded trip wires on the south and west walls. They would use a grid pattern to search the Jack corpses, checking them for signs of life.

The first live Jack was lying on was side, shivering in spasms. Zaz pulled up close enough to it for Carl to put several bullets into its lower chest. They nearly passed one that was showing signs of life, its chest heaving in raspy breaths. Zaz backed up and rolled a wheel over it, snapping its neck.

"Damn it," said Carl, fidgetin. "We've got to walk a line out here so we don't miss anything. This is gonna take forever!"

"I don't want anybody to step foot out here unless it's safe. How would you like one of them to suddenly rear up and take a chunk out of you? Stay in the vehicle."

They continued on, crisscrossing over the maimed bodies. Zaz ran over the ones that looked unscathed, but unconscious. Soon they came to the spot where the automechs had exploded, leaving crater holes in the soil. Here the Jacks had been exposed to titanic forces; most of them were torn to pieces, with sinew, bone and great tufts of fur scattered about. Bits of the Silver automechs caught the reflection of the early morning sun glittered like jewels.

They arrived in the area of the pole charges. The ground was torn open in star-spiked patterns. Even the buried bones of the giant Paddymous creatures had been blasted from under the surface, acting as lethal projectiles. It seemed fitting that the Jacks occupied the same graveyard as their victims, dying just as horribly. Truly one massacre had been answered by another.

Paddy leaned over the seat. "Most of the intact Jack Lions are in extraordinary physical condition. There is not one undernourished specimen in this count that I can see. Fat layers are well pronounced and their coats glisten with a vitality that I would not have expected from any animal in this environment. I should like to know what their diet consists of. It is unlikely that they can be finding such sustenance in this area."

"Then why don't you scoop up some of their poop," said Carl. "Because we sure as hell blew the shit out of them."

Paddy turned on Carl, trying to steady himself in the rocking vehicle. "Would you like to know something? I find you highly offensive. You're completely ignorant of the pursuit of science. You care about nothing more than wreaking havoc by bringing destruction down upon everything you encounter. I'm simply saying that these animals are too fit to have subsisted on the meager protein sources that inhabit this desert. I doubt very much if they could even open up one of the armadillo creatures. Nor could they likely catch the Microraptors on the wing. I am only curious to know what they are consuming and where it might come from."

"What is it that you need?" Zaz asked. "I thought that you already checked them out for that."

"Those were poor specimens – probably scouts. I would like a sample from the digestive tract of one of these soldier animals – a bolus sample from the gut. Lyle and I can analyze it to determine the chemical makeup."

Zaz slowed the vehicle down. He picked out a lone animal that looked to be intact and parked next to it. Paddy pulled a small bag from a waist pouch and, brandishing a knife, approached the creature. Carl stood over him, providing cover. After retrieving his sample, Paddy insisted on another stop a moment later. After collecting a few more samples, Zaz power throttled over some heaped up corpses as he neared the fence corner. Here the devastation was more obvious. Twenty yards of the wall was gone. Dead creatures lay on top of one another stacked three bodies high. He couldn't tell if the creatures had knocked down the wall or if the explosions had caused the destruction.

"I'll send the dozers over here to clear the area," said Carl. "We'll just bury the sons-a-bitches in the same trenches with the rest."

Lyle had been silent, muttering to himself throughout the ride. "Sir," he said, looking up from his notebook, "I counted approximately four hundred and fifty individuals from the camp to here, give or take since many of them are in pieces."

Zaz stopped just before the ragged opening; the six-wheeler balanced awkwardly on a pile of corpses. He could see very few dead animals on the other side of the fence. If some had survived, they had hightailed out of the area, retracing their tracks to their origin, wherever that was.

Zaz turned in his seat to address Paddy. "Do you think we've dealt with all of them?"

"That is difficult to answer. On the one hand, this is a sizable crowd – a large breeding group. I would say yes, it is quite possible that this could be the main group. But there is still a problem with that. How is it likely that four hundred, or possibly five hundred of these animals wiped out a population as large as the Paddymous on a continent of this size? I have not begun to estimate the dead Paddymous population out here, but I would conservatively say that it numbers in the hundreds of thousands. Perhaps millions."

Lyle waved his hand for attention. "You forget, my dear colleague that the behavior of the Paddymous giants seems to have been of a docile nature."

"That's speculation so far," said Zaz.

"Perhaps, but we found no weapons associated with them," said Paddy. "In accordance with what we've just seen, these beasts are ferocious and unrelenting. I believe they kill for the sure instinct or pleasure of it, much like the African lion does on occasion. I can remember a scientific documentary in which three hundred giant Japanese hornets wiped out a hive of thirty thousand honey bees. Anything is possible."

Galoot was having trouble with the analogies. "Now, I'm not saying that being big is a real good thing in a fight – I know that I got beat up pretty bad – but these big Paddy-such fellows looked pretty strong to me. I was wondering how they couldn't fight them off. Those giants were even bigger than me, and I'm not much of a pushover in a one-on-one tussle."

Galoot only mentioned the size issue because he somehow thought it relevant; it was one of the very few times he had expressed the notion that bigger could somehow be better, or an advantage. He failed to realize that he nearly lost his life in his confrontation. If it were not for the assistance of the others, he would have succumbed. The Paddymous might have been big and strong, but they were not equipped with killing claws and teeth. Though a walrus could outweigh a polar bear, it is still no match for it. Paddy explained the analogy to Galoot as delicately as possible, without insulting his stature.

"Galoot is the strongest man in the world," said Carybell with a flourish of her arms. No one argued the point. Though Zaz could see that the sun had brought some pink to Galoot's cheeks, he still noticed what looked like a blush race across the big man's face.

"I say we killed 'em all," said Carl. "And if we didn't, then we damn well bloodied their nose enough so they'll think twice about trying that again."

Zaz backed the vehicle up and turned around, heading back to the jobsite. He heard raised voices in the back, knowing full well that Carl and the professors were trading verbal blows. The personality clash could have only been expected; the academics against the demolition expert – it wasn't a fair fight. Carl happened to be on the losing end, but espoused his Neanderthal-like thoughts as though they were the end-all of the argument.

By the time they got back to the jobsite, a full-scale shouting riot had materialized, prompting the scientists to storm off toward the ship, throwing their shredded notes to the sand. Samantha had to be restrained from slapping Carl, who jumped from the vehicle and marched off in his own wounded fashion. Galoot went after him in an attempt to cool him down, but Carl shrugged off the gesture.

Heat. Tension. Aggravation. Fear.

Zaz stepped out of the vehicle and headed for the bridge. He felt as low as a snake's belly in a wagon rut when he entered the ship. During his stuporous march, he kicked out angrily at pieces of debris on the deck, swearing loudly. Arriving at the bridge, he sat on the edge of his command chair. Dendy stuck her head around the hatch door and rapped on the bulkhead.

"Sure," he said without looking up.

She approached tentatively, taking the seat next to him. "I don't think you're going to find a simple answer to this. You're expecting too much of yourself. Or you're trying to be something for all of us, which is impossible."

"We've got a long ways to go," he said. "We haven't even scratched the surface so far as teamwork. How in the hell are we ever going to get through this without some patience and perseverance?"

"By taking it one day at a time," she offered.

"I'm not worried about the immediate concerns, like I am about the long haul. We're in it for the long haul – make no mistake about that. If it happens that we *are* stranded – marooned – what kind of mental condition are we going to be in to handle the situation, especially if we're unraveling this early in the game?"

"That's a pretty bleak outlook."

"It's one that I have to consider. Complete isolation. I'm not a psychiatrist, but that doesn't mean I'm not aware of the consequences. I can manage with the deck stacked against us. But if we have no cards at all we don't have a chance."

"Then we'll bluff with an empty hand. Look," she said supportively, "we've never had to face these types of problems before. No one could have predicted how we were all going to react. So it's not right that you have to beat yourself up over it. You'll make it right and safe for us. You always do – that's why I'm here now."

She couldn't have known how much he depended upon her support. Trivial as it seemed, her assurances would be sorely missed if she were to keep them from him. She had thrown the "we have each other" remark right back in his face.

"I can fix you some breakfast," she said.

"I'm not hungry right now." He reclined in the chair, holding her in his arms. They rocked together for a long while. She fell asleep on his chest just as he began to doze off.

*　　*　　*

Zaz woke with a start and checked his watch. He had been asleep for five hours! Dendy came alive in his arms. "What, no end of the world?" she said. "What are we missing?"

"Nothing, I guess. I can't believe we weren't interrupted."

"Would you interrupt us if you found us like this?" She scratched his cheek playfully. "Now will you have something to eat?"

"Not just yet. There's something I want to check on first."

Zaz got to his feet, shook his legs out. He checked in with his personnel, making sure everything was normal – or at least stable. He took Dendy on a walk down the A-Deck corridor to the science lab. He nearly broke his hand throwing the latch lever back – the door was locked. He tapped the barrel of his rifle on the bulkhead metal. A crashing sound came from within, followed by the words: "Go away!"

"I'm not going anywhere until you open this door."

"I am not in the mood for company." That was Paddy.

"This is your Captain, Zachary Crowe, and I come in peace."

"Then would you mind leaving in peace?"

Zaz heard some more shouting, then the squeak of the latch handle. The door pulled inward. Hot, putrid air gushed out; it smelled like a mortuary on a hot day. Zaz waved a hand in front of his face as he entered.

Paddy had his hands on his hips, eyeing the two suspiciously.

Zaz pulled up a stool then pinched his nose. "Look, I apologize for Carl. He's not the brightest gem in the rock collection. I'm very much interested in your research and what you and Lyle have to say. I have some questions that are in desperate need of answers."

Paddy considered Zaz's comment. Lyle looked up from a microscope, nodding in an affirmative gesture. "At least that is a refreshing admission," he said. "Is this a scheduled routine visitation, or perhaps something more?"

"Don't get all defensive. This is an off-the-record powwow. I know that you've both been busy and are concerned about the animal life, the biology, and the geology of Sidus. I also know that you wouldn't go out of your way to examine something unless it was important. Anything that is of importance to you concerns me because it concerns us all. I trust your evaluations. I'd like to know what you're working on and why."

"There's no need to pander," said Paddy, taking a seat. He looked at some beakers under a small flame, then stood up suddenly and rolled up a long scroll, stashing it below the table. Zaz had seen what it was before they could hide it away: a photo mosaic documenting the wall inside the Paddymous cave, including all of the pictographs and etchings. A large notebook with strange symbols was also on the table. Paddy brushed it off the table onto the floor. Clearly it was part of his research and not meant for laymen's eyes.

Zaz let go of his nose, breathing deeply through his mouth. "Not pandering – just surrendering. You mentioned that these Jacks were incredibly fit and seemed out of place. You also wanted gut specimens. That means you've got some kind of a working hypothesis. This is off the record – I won't cast any secret pearls."

"Would you like the abstract or the full spiel?" asked Lyle.

"I wouldn't mind a little of both."

Paddy still looked defensive. It was not just because Zaz sat in the room with them. It felt deeper than that. Dendy leaned forward, biting a knuckle in anticipation.

"Very well." Paddy tossed his dirty yellow tam on the table. "But just one cheeky barb and this meeting is over. As of late, we've done an extensive DNA workup on both the Paddymous and the Jack creatures. The Jack's, at least two of them, contain slight traces of DNA profiles found in the Paddymous. The trace is so minuscule that it is nearly impossible to link the two species. Hold that thought. Now, we've done thin sections, mineral and chemical analysis of the Jack's digestive tract. The contents contain a high-protein meat meal that has no similarity to any biological substance associated with any indigenous creature living on this planet. These are not scant samples from undernourished animals – they were all well-fed. Actually, overfed."

Zaz nodded. "You're saying these animals had plenty to eat. Where did they get it from?"

"I'm coming to that. Not only did we find prodigious amounts in the guts, but we found it to contain every vitamin from A-Z and some we were not familiar with. They contain vitamins, hormones, steroidal traces, and even synthetic chemicals that I cannot identify. This super slurry of ingredients is similar to what cattle ranchers might provide for their prize market herd. The meal food is enriched, free of bones, gristle, fat and substandard filler. It is the most high intensity meal I have ever seen."

"Could they have found this food substance in nature?"

"With all our technology, and as top food chain consumers, *we* do not even eat this well. I let two grams of the substance dissolve between my gums. Too my surprise, twenty minutes later I experienced a stimulant effect. It was almost a feeling of euphoria."

"You ate that stuff?" Dendy was aghast.

"I sampled it, Ms. Dendy. It was an experiment performed in the name of science, not lunacy, as the look upon your face would suggest."

"That explains their energy and adaptation to this environment," said Lyle. "They are virtually athletes, in such a state of physical superiority that they are nearly indestructible. If not for our percussion weapons and bombs, we would have been hard pressed to dispatch them in any other fashion."

"Good God," said Zaz. "That's why they keep coming, even when they've been hit."

"Oh, it gets better than that!" Paddy leaned toward Zaz, squinting. "We first thought that the Jacks had some type of primitive central nervous system, owed to the fact they were hardly aware of their own traumatic injuries. Not so. Their blood also contains synthetic coagulants and numerous antibiotics, along with a plethora of painkillers, least of which is a superior version of our own Demerol 6, only more specific in application. Now, to beat the band, as some might say, we managed to run a few primitive CAT scans on some of the skulls. I found this object." Paddy picked up a small, pea-sized sphere with a pair of forceps.

Zaz leaned over the table to look at the object. It appeared to be a metal BB that had a small barb-like shaft protruding from one end.

"This tiny device," continued Paddy, "was retrieved from the base of the lower skull, just above the cerebral cortex area. It gives off a very weak electromagnetic signal that I believe can be controlled or amplified. It came out of one of the largest alpha males. In short, we believe it to be a tracking device, or some type of recall receiver or motivator. It just might perform all of those functions. We haven't determined the frequency level yet, but we do know that it has one."

Zaz sat down on the stool, stupefied. "Do you believe these things are genetically engineered?" he asked, unsure of what else to say.

"With all of this evidence?" answered Paddy. "I would wager the riches of Orion Industries on it. The animals appear to be a crossbreed among many species. All of their traits dictate an intelligent design. They are synthetically equipped with the best immune systems, meal, and health accelerators – a master race of animals. No proverbial stone has gone unturned to guarantee their superiority. They are designed for one purpose only. We believe it is to kill *on command*."

"Do you remember the ferocity of the African killer bee before it was exterminated?" asked Lyle.

"I do," said Dendy. "Once roused they would follow you for half a mile and die in the hundreds trying to kill you."

"You do not have to rouse the Jacks," said Paddy. "They seek you out, free of charge. Only they can be motivated for the time and place of the encounter. I would call it 'directional homing,' if you can perceive of such a thing."

Zaz cleared his throat. "Then we're up against true assassins."

Paddy gave a helpless chuckle. "More like pets, the way they are cared for and groomed. It would not surprise me if they were mentally superior as far as learned memory response. They might even benefit from their mistakes through no outside help. It means that they would not likely repeat an error. That is why the main rush stopped, except for a few diehards. I believe all the alpha males are implanted. The rest of the horde follows their direction."

Dendy shifted on her stool, her eyes riveted on Paddy. "Then if these animals don't belong here, where did they come from?"

Paddy picked up his soiled tam and put it back on his head. "You might have to ask their masters that question, Ms. Dendy."

"*Masters?*" Zaz said to himself, his eyes dropping to his lap. He looked up. "Then not only do we have a genetically engineered killer species on this planet that's got our ticket punched, but now we're talking about their owners, who might damn well be on this rock with them. Did you ever consider that who, or whatever made them, drop-shipped them here to get rid of them? Maybe they became a nuisance so they had to quarantine or maroon them." Zaz knew that digging for excuses hardly followed any logical trail, but he did not want to believe it was as elaborate as the scientists suggested.

Lyle looked at him, perturbed. "Do you believe that any alien race capable of engineering these creatures and possessing the technology to transport them here would be incapable of eradicating or controlling them if they became too much of a pest? I hardly think so. Tell me, what is to be gained by destroying something so magnificent that is already under your complete control?"

"They would keep the creatures so they could continue to manipulate them," said Dendy.

Zaz wanted to ask a loaded question, not sure if he was ready for the answer, "Are these Jacks a recent arrival?"

"Most assuredly," answered Paddy. "Now whether it was timed with our arrival is not clear. That might never be answered. It could be a coincidence. Don't ask me to speculate."

"Okay, I know that neither of you are military tacticians, but is there any way we can protect ourselves from these things in a physical sense? I mean, if it looks like we might end up on the losing end."

"We've given that some thought," answered Lyle. "The Jacks have a peculiar rat-like foot. Short of climbing a tree, or scaling a steep incline, there would not be any way to escape them. They are not designed for climbing. I would think that a high-up fortress would keep you from harm's reach. Unless, of course, they are afraid of water, and from the appearance of them, I doubt that. They look like they could be great dog paddlers. Their fat is very buoyant. So your answer would undoubtedly be to go high."

"We are not wanted here," said Paddy, mysticism edging his voice. "That seems very obvious."

Now the plot thickened, thought Zaz. "But why?"

"Are you asking me to be philosophical?" asked Paddy. "I can no more know or anticipate the motivation of an alien race than you can. Allow me the speculation of saying that we might be an experiment. They undoubtedly know of our presence. They certainly know we are different from the Paddymous giants. Maybe they are testing their mettle, or ours. We are guinea pigs."

"So we could kill every Jack out there," said Dendy, "even if there were a hundred thousand more, and still have to face off with something more powerful – their owners. We didn't come in a military Sky Galleon – there's no way we can defend ourselves against such superior technology. So where does that leave us?"

Dendy's questions had the contemplative effect of silencing the room for an uncomfortable five minutes without so much as a cough.

Finally, Paddy threw up his hands. "It leaves us bloody well doomed! If our extermination is their sole mission, then they will obviously finish the task. We know they have no compunction. You cannot bargain with something that you cannot see. I am terribly sorry, but as the Yanks say, 'check and mate.' Game over, wot?"

Lyle blinked tired, haunted eyes. "Sir, do you recall the day when we experienced the blackout and the electromagnetic disturbance? We do not believe that it was a force of nature that came over us. That could only have been a reconnaissance pass from a solid object. I believe it was a ship that passed over us. A very big ship that could disrupt an electromagnetic field. You can draw your own conclusions from there."

Zaz stood up, taking Dendy's hand. He felt a tremble in her grip and spoke under his breath: "I would appreciate it if you kept these revelations to yourselves. I can't think of a reason for letting any of this out – best to play it stupid. I think I now understand your obsessions. I don't know what to say, other than to try and keep up a positive outlook. We have more than a lot to think about."

Zaz left with Dendy in tow. He marched with long purposeful strides down the corridor.

Dendy stumbled, trying to keep pace with his ceaseless pull. "Where are we going?" she asked.

"To the raspberry bushes!"

CHAPTER ELEVEN

PRECIOUS RUNAWAYS

Sidus Log, Rotation 25.

We suffered a massive attack by the Jack creatures six days ago. We killed about 500 of them. It has taken us several days to redirect the earth moving equipment in order to pile the corpses for removal, then another two days after that to gather and bury them outside the south fence, with the Paddymous remains. We had to remove the smaller, fleshy pieces with garden tools. It was, a grizzly and arduous duty. We called it the Death Detail. The creatures looked ferocious, even in death.

Our normal duties have remained a constant reminder of why we came here in the first place. We continue to level and prep the compound. The fences have been mended; we occasionally ride out to check the grids. There's nothing else to do but watch and wait.

Dendy and I have escalated the status of our relationship. I proposed to her that we officially become a couple. She accepted, of course. We openly announced it to the crew - it was a great excuse to throw a party. The party lasted the night, with liberal amounts of the captain's whiskey thrown into the mix to officiate a proper Planet Janitor occasion.

Galoot popped a few staples from laughter as Carybell performed her rendition of the "Seven Veils" dance and messed up the whole act. It was a reprieve in the turmoil that has become our lives.

Paddy and Lyle refused to answer the summons, preferring to remain locked in the lab. Their attendance was missed by all. I worry about the professors - they have grown increasingly agitated and distant. They are damning their health in the name of research.

I harbor a terrible secret. It has to do with the opposition we face. I regret that I cannot even reveal what this mystery is, since it would cause unrest to the crew. We need our optimism to perform our duties and interact with one another. So I won't record it here for fear that it might be discovered.

Though we are not out of water yet, the need will come soon. I wonder if it is better to leave in this lull of activity. Paddy and Lyle have assured me that the Jacks are not done with us yet. I believe them and we know that the beasts are out there, regrouping somewhere in the south. I say, bring on the fight and let's put an end to this. Let the winner take all. I don't have it in my blood to run, regardless of what happens.

Captain Zachary Crowe, PJ.

AFTER AN EARLIER routine check of the *Shenandoah's* systems had proven satisfactory, Zaz found himself drawn in the direction of Dendy's garden. Though the sun had been up for only two hours, he thought to steal some time with her.

He found her in the garden, reclining in a chair under a relieving gush of air provided by a small portable cooling unit. Nearby, Galoot and Carybell toweled a new row to prepare for the planting of some new seedlings. The automechs stood guard out in the compound.

Dendy looked up as Zaz stepped under the canopy. She managed a bright smile, but there was a listlessness to her face that he couldn't help noticing. Her smile switched off like a toggle had been thrown.

"Hey, there, little one," he said. "What, no energy today?" It was hardly a topic of contention when it was already 115 degrees – the promise of another scorcher. He saw her helmet at her side, but said nothing.

"Hi, gorgeous," she said. "I don't know, I just don't think there's any sense to it anymore. The plants will probably die."

Zaz jerked his head toward Galoot and Carybell. "Don't you think we should at least keep up appearances, if you catch my meaning?" He walked over to the small watering can and picked it up. He set it gently in her lap, then playfully ran his fingers over her scalp.

"I suppose so," she said, taking the can.

Zaz answered the sudden buzz on his wrist-com. It was Samantha.

"Zaz, this is the second time I've called on Lyle and Paddy for breakfast. They're not answering the two-way and the door to the science lab is auto-latched from the inside. What do you want me to do?"

"Nothing right now, I'll take care of it." Zaz called to Galoot.

Together they walked to A-Deck, where they found Samantha standing at the science lab door holding two plastic breakfast plates. Zaz rapped hard on the door with the rifle barrel, just as he had done before. He listened for 10 seconds before trying again. Nothing stirred from within – not even the voices of the two professors. He tried a two-way call, threatening everything from hard labor to drawing and quartering. Silence. They'd locked the door with a delay timer and an access code.

"Galoot, get a beam torch," said Zaz.

The large man ran off and returned moments later with the torch. Zaz ordered him to sear a hole though the latch mechanism. Amid the smell of scorched slag, the door popped open with an audible hiss; a flush of putrid air assailed them.

"Bleggk," groaned Samantha.

Zaz checked behind the heavy drapes – the anterooms were empty. The lab was in a state of disarray, but that was normal. No open flames burned under beakers; the centrifuge was off; the CAT scan was unplugged, its connector ribbon lying on the floor; the overhead lighting had been turned off. The only thing that drew Zaz's eye came from a dripping water faucet over the lab sink. He could just make out the faint outline of wet boot prints on the deck.

"Have you seen the professors at all this morning?" Zaz asked the two crewmembers.

They shook their heads. Galoot looked especially worried since he had been the first early morning riser. With a shrug, he said, "Not this morning. Just saw them last evening when they came for their dinners at the bridge. But they took off without a word."

Zaz spoke into his wrist-com. "Carl, we're looking for Lyle and Paddy. Have you seen anything of them this morning?"

"I haven't seen those idiots for two days, which is fine with me."

"Do a vehicle check and get back to me. No questions – just do it."

He couldn't believe they would just disappear without calling in or leaving a note. He knew they felt disrespected. They'd always had a penchant for wandering off to quench their curiosity with some damn fool project in mind, but they'd never wandered too far off the radar, save for the recent gorge incident. They would always show up at the last minute and explain how sorry they were for wandering off. This felt different.

Zaz paused with another thought: what if they'd become frightened at the prospect of their own revelations? Could they be hiding from what they believed to be a mass invasion? Or was it some other brainstorm that prompted them to run off in the heat of discovery? The list of possible reasons for their departure made Zaz's head spin. He realized, in some deep well where his thoughts lay mired, that it was conceivable he'd had something to do with their departure – to *wherever* the hell they'd gone.

Zaz opened their personal lockers. The lab smocks were filthy, but hung neatly from their hooks. On closer inspection, an extra change of clothes and footwear seemed to be missing. They were last seen wearing their cut-down suits. He could not see any field canteens either.

He shut the lockers and looked at the long table. Four paperweights sat at the ends of the table, two on each side. There was a long section of clean space surrounded by trash, bones, instruments and other objects. The clean space had the perfect dimensions of the long scroll – the photo matrix containing the interior cave shots.

Carl's voice came over the two-way. "Everything's here, except somebody must have moved my scout buggy."

Zaz paused for a beat. "I was out there earlier this morning and I never saw it."

"Those no good sons of bitches!"

"Hook up the water trailer to the six-wheeler and prep the truck. Have everything ready to go." Zaz shut his com off, not wanting to hear Carl's rants. Samantha and Galoot were close on his heels when he left the lab, headed down the corridor.

"They just up and skedaddled?" asked Galoot.

"What in the heck could they be up to?" Samantha added. "Where would they go? We've made them break out in hives before but they've never stomped off to parts unknown."

They wouldn't need water for another week. It was just as well they go early to fill the trailer tank. There could have only been one place for the scientists to go that made any sense. Zaz would bet his Orion's advance that they were out at the gorge, dinking around with their hammers and scrapers.

The captain stepped out into the sunshine; the six-wheeler and truck were parked close by. Carl was checking the container straps for tautness. After hearing the news, all Dendy could do was shake her head disgustedly. It took them an hour to pack enough supplies for a three-day expedition. There was no reason to believe they'd need any longer to find two scientists. Zaz had some misgivings about leaving their jobsite unattended, so he made sure that the main hatch was secure and the construction equipment had been shut down.

From the moment he took off in the six-wheeler, Zaz knew that he was hot on their trail. He followed a squiggly pattern of tire marks – the hesitant wandering of a person who was not skilled at driving the swift little scout. Neither one of the scientists had logged any driving time with any of the vehicles; they'd always been ferried to and from all jobsites. It would be a disaster to find them flipped over in a ditch somewhere.

Galoot and Carybell followed close behind, the large truck jostling over the terrain.

The trail might have been easy to follow, but the heat still proved to be a persistent aggravation. Zaz tried some music to curb the monotony. Having no canopy, except for a roll cage bar, the sun beat down on them with an unmerciful intensity. Sweat gathered under his goggles in small puddles, and once the lenses were wiped they smeared. The half-uniforms became exceedingly hot, chaffing at the stomach and neck.

After the halfway point, they stopped to remove their suits and pat water on their skin. After a quick leg stretch, they dressed and started off again. One of the four-winged Microraptors followed them overhead, acting as their escort.

As Zaz entered the foothill region, he slowed the vehicle, negotiating the arroyo-like depressions. He still had a bead on the wavering buggy tracks – they led straight to the gorge. It hadn't occurred to him what he would do when he finally caught up with the scientists. He felt more pity for them than anger. He could understand their sudden plight, but owed it to the stress, the self-inflicted pressure, and the belief that they were hopelessly doomed. Maybe he could have stopped them if he'd recognized the symptoms of paranoia. That affliction, coupled with the approach of a nervous breakdown, would have thrown anybody over the edge. He realized that they were as vulnerable as children, in a symptomatic respect. Rather than talk to anyone about their concerns, they had simply run away like petulant teenagers.

The tire tracks narrowed into single-track lines where the scientists had slowed down, driving with greater care. Zaz followed them up the gorge, happy to see the gurgling creek once again. Even the trees proved to be a welcome sight, though their branches sprouted such peculiar blue and gray leaves. Soon they fell under the shadow of the lofty cliff face. A few Microraptors leapt from their perches, annoyed at the large vehicles blundering through their quiet domain.

Zaz stopped the vehicle where he had parked before in the large sandy clearing. The trail ended here, yet there was no sign of Paddy and Lyle's vehicle.

They unloaded their gear and set up all three tents in anticipation of finding the scientists. They wouldn't need their helmets, which would only inhibit their vision, so they stowed them in the tents.

Zaz walked over to the slide area and knelt down. He still saw no evidence of tread disturbance, and the limestone spill would have shown signs of passing. He told the others to double back on foot and look for any disturbance in the brush or between the trees, indicating that the missing vehicle might have taken another route.

He checked the pond area for recent evidence, finding nothing newly disturbed. He was positive that they'd followed their tracks to this point, but saw nothing to indicate that the scientists had come through. He hollered several times at the top of his voice, the echo rebounding off the cliff face.

It was disturbing to think that the professors might have deliberately hid or camouflaged their trail in order to evade discovery. What did they have to gain by hiding? Though they really wouldn't have had to pack water and food, since there were fruits and nuts and a fresh water creek, it still begged the question of why they would want to leave the ship to take their chances in the open. All in the name of science?

Galoot stumbled back into the clearing, shadowed by Carybell. "Boss, there ain't no way they went off the main path – I couldn't find so much as a bent twig. There was no backtracking, either."

Carl appeared a moment later, soaked from the waist down – he'd crossed the creek to check the other side. He looked especially agitated, having nothing new to report. Zaz wondered if he was more worried about the missing scout buggy than the people who were in it.

Samantha and Dendy came from another direction with similar news – no trace of the professors.

Zaz told them to pack up some light gear, including the mini-lanterns. Samantha had brought a fully fueled snoop. He instructed her to remain behind and run it up and down the gorge, keeping an eye glued to the monitor. He left her with his rifle and instructions to fire off a warning shot if anything happened.

"Dendy and I will take the west cliff face on this side of the creek. Galoot, Carl, Carybell, you take the other side. It's a long walk, so take your time. We'll meet back here at 9:00 PM – that's three hours from now. Make sure your lanterns work. Take a meal pack with you if you want. You know what we're looking for – try and find the buggy or the tracks. That will be the most obvious sign that they're in the area. Look for broken or disturbed twigs or grass – especially footprints, since no one has been to the east side of the gorge."

"What do you want us to do with those stinking cowards?" asked Carl. "They should be tied to a tree so the birds can peck their eyes out for what they've done!"

Samantha took fast strides across the sand – hands in a claw-like pose. Zaz intercepted her before she dove at Carl. The momentum of her charge almost brought them both down.

He held her shoulders as her chest heaved. "There's no reason for that," he said calmly. He let go of her and marched over to Carl. Zaz feinted with a front snap kick then brought his fist around in a right cross, connecting with Carl's jaw. The blow sent him backwards onto his tailbone in the sand.

Carl sat there with his legs splayed, running his tongue around the inside of his cheek. "Whud you do that for?" he asked, spitting blood as he talked.

"Because you're way out of line. Again! You're talking about our friends out there. We don't know what's happened to them or why they left, but I think that your attitude is probably what drove them off. You better start showing a little consideration for people around here or it's going to be you who is tied to a tree waiting for the birds. That means respect, Carl. You hear me?"

"I was just kidding."

"I wasn't. Now get up and help find our friends. It's going to be dark soon."

"Do I have time to bleed?

Zaz glowered at him.

Okay, okay, I'm on it!"

Zaz took Dendy by the hand. They trudged up the shale and then slid down the opposite bank. He decided to check the first cave they visited upon their last visit.

The interior felt spookier than it had been before. They saw the same implements, beds and toys, the dusty floor showing where they had walked last time. Zaz fondly remembered Paddy and Lyle's excitement when they showed him the interior, their eyes sparkling in the dim light. A deep melancholy overcame him; he knew the cave's true occupants would never return. But now the biggest fans of the caves were lost and unaccounted for. *His* people.

"I guess we keep going," Dendy sighed. "They've already been here. I think they're off spelunking."

"Yep, next address."

They found another cave opening further down the gorge. It contained most of the same contents as the first one; the wall carvings and paintings were slightly different, evidence of another hand's work. Here the beds were laid out in neater rows, but woven from the same type of fibrous grass material. The craftsmanship was identical. He expected to see more of the same as they continued to search.

They hiked on, making a side trip to the creek. Zaz thought it best to cover as much area as the sunlight would allow. He checked the creek bank for any type of human passing; he'd been a fairly good tracker in his younger days as a Boy Scout, so there wasn't too much that could get past him. Just the right broken twig or disturbance in the grass would be enough of a tip-off.

Galoot would do the same on the other side of the gorge. The large man had once remarked that his mother had taught him some of the old ways. He had a keen eye for things out of place on the ship. It wasn't too much different when it came to studying the Georgian Sidus environment – human interaction on this world showed notable disturbances.

Though Dendy had American Indian blood, she had never expressed a lot of knowledge about the culture of her tribe. She had always identified with the message and plight of the Indian, but had never experienced the lifestyle firsthand. She'd once told Zaz that her mother was an alcoholic, consuming only the most potent liquors – there couldn't have been much time for cultural education in her youth. In spite of her past, Dendy had become someone he could trust.

They hiked back to the cliff face and entered two more cave dwellings, the last of which was very revealing. Its back wall was crowded with portraits rendered in a fresco style. Zaz moved his lantern light over the artwork, seeing individual faces starring back at him. The material used to bring out the colors must have come from the vicinity; the minerals or plant dyes showed blues, browns, reds, with smatterings of yellow. There were 10 adult faces, all of them very similar. They had a cow-like face, with a flattened muzzle and a wide lower jaw filled with huge rock-like teeth. The ears looked like they could have belonged to a goat. The eyes were large and dark, close-set under a crested skull. The nose looked like a blunt flap of meat. The skin tone was bluish, with gray highlights. All of the faces seemed to be smiling in pose, as though they had been told to say, "Cheese." The representations were uncanny, almost surreal; it could easily have been a human photoshoot.

Dendy stood very still while gazing at the artwork. "I just can't believe it." Her words had a hollow ring to them. "Look at them. They seemed so sweet, so happy to be alive."

Zaz stepped further down the wall, examining a lined calendar, which appeared to be a detailed archive of their day-to-day existence. Somehow he knew the secret of what happened here might lie in the calendar etchings. He also knew the professors had photographed similar etchings, which revealed something important to them. It might have been what prompted them to return so suddenly without notice. They might have known even more than what they had told him. He hoped that was the case instead of the alternative: *they hate us.*

They continued down the gorge, checking the crannies. They scanned the terrain with the scope, hoping to spot any upright figures.

"What was it that piqued their interest so much?" Zaz wondered aloud. "What drove them out here? I wonder if it has something to do with the Paddymous calendar. I can't make heads or tails out of the script."

"Maybe it had something to do with being afraid of what they found," said Dendy. "You know, beyond what they told us. If that's even possible."

Zaz helped her over a boulder. "They approach things academically. If something frightens them, they're prone to chase it down out of curiosity. I've never known a scientist that didn't have some form of dumb bravado. Those types get themselves into jams and lose their lives. Volcanologists have a terrible record of traipsing down into active calderas. They know the risks better than anyone, yet they persist on spitting in the face of danger. All of it in the name of science?"

"I miss them already." Dendy's voice shook. "Paddy and that dirty little hat of his; the way he's always scratching at his head. Lyle, with all those dumb lenses and filters, blind as a bat and *so* helpless. The two of them together – they're a whole bunch of conundrum with some riot thrown in. I just hope they don't have any ill feelings toward us. I *do* love them."

"They know that, Dendy. I'm hoping it's nothing we did or said that drove them away. Carl is the exception, of course."

She stopped for a moment, giving him a profound look. "Yeah, that reminds me. Since when did you ever resort to fisticuffs? I always took you for the mellow type. I don't know why I'm surprised, but I am. Actually, what you did was not uncalled for. It kind of shows how much you love your people, albeit in a gorilla type of way."

He found the compliment curious. There were more layers to him she hadn't seen. He felt content that he had surprised her in some fashion.

He kept her hand tightly grasped as they continued on, scaling some rocks to the next cave entrance. As he approached the entrance, Zaz held Dendy back from entering. He waved his light over the floor, noticing a thick layer of dust, just as he had seen in the last caves.

He pointed. "See how it's undisturbed? There would be obvious footprints in the dust if somebody had passed over it. We can speed things up by skipping the caves that show no signs of entry."

They quickened their pace, searching multiple cave dwellings and looking for the telltale signs of human prints. The remaining light diminished with the approaching gray shroud of darkness. They went as far north as they could before checking the time. They would have to turn around and head back now if they were going to meet up with the others by the deadline. Rather than retrace their footsteps, he decided to cross the gorge to find the creek and follow it back to their camp.

He shined the light out in front of them as they hiked. They beat through a heavy island of grass then ran into a tangle of brush that they were forced to circle around. They could hear the happy giggle of water just up ahead. They made it to the creek, which was actually a large, swift moving stream at this point. He'd forgotten they had trekked some miles north where the snowmelt had produced more of a torrent.

They walked swiftly, reading the ground for any signs of disturbance. Dendy held onto a pinch of his suit, keeping in perfect step. He stopped to yell once, starting up again when his echo came back to him, like a distant reply. He continued on, feeling his way over the terrain and making sure Dendy didn't become detached from him in the advancing darkness.

At one point he heard the snoop overhead and stopped to look up. His lantern beam found the tiny flier hovering forty feet over his head. He gave an excited wave. The snoop did a little aerial curtsy then buzzed off to the south.

After another 30 minutes of swift marching, they found the camp. Samantha had a small welcome fire blazing within a ring of large creek stones. She stood up from her camp chair, cradling her screen.

"I've been doing sweeps up the gorge," she said. "I just now located Galoot's bunch. They're about three hundred yards out, heading our way. There's nothing to report on this end. The only other heat signatures I picked up were from armadillos and birds. Sorry."

Zaz and Dendy took seats in the small camp chairs. Samantha fetched them some field jackets, since the temperature was dropping rapidly with every minute that passed. Cooling collars and britches were removed.

Zaz stretched his legs toward the fire, working his ankles around in circles. "We hit about twenty caves," he told Samantha. "Not a trace of them. We doubled back, following the creek course just to make sure they hadn't wandered out toward the middle of the valley. I thought for sure we'd pick them up right away. I hope Galoot's found some evidence."

Samantha looked up in the air, guiding the snoop in for a landing next to her. "That's my little birdie," she cooed. "I don't understand what Paddy and Lyle knew, or *thought* they knew, that would make them leave like that."

Dendy fingered a twig then looked knowingly at Zaz. She snapped the twig. It sounded like a gunshot. "Oh, you know those two, Sammy. There isn't a crack or crevice they won't climb into. What makes you think they knew something we didn't? They pretty much gave us the rundown on everything."

Zaz admired Dendy's fishing technique. He didn't think Samantha knew anything for certain. At least not the dreaded news they were privy to.

"Hell, you know what I mean." said Samantha. "They knew more about those Jack Lions than we did. In fact, they were obsessed with the giants and the Jacks. I'm thinking they scared their own pants off. I'm the first one to admit that those Jacks made me wet my britches too, but I also know that we've got the *Shenandoah*. As busted up as she is, she's still a fortress. Like right now, I don't feel so damn good about being out here in the open. Paddy said those Jacks could sniff us out like vultures. That's more than enough to creep me out."

Galoot and his people slogged into camp. They shook with cold, having just crossed the creek. Samantha threw another pile of wood on the fire, bringing the flames up to a full roar. More jackets and blankets were passed around.

Zaz took one look at Galoot and knew the news was not good. Carl sat down, wiggling a swollen jaw. Carybell just looked tired. She had two seashell necklaces dangling from her neck, no doubt finds of her recent excursion.

"Boss, as far as we got, we didn't find anything out there that even looked human," said Galoot. "There were no tire marks, no footprints, not even the trace of anything going through the bush except some of those little dinosaurs that roll up into a ball. Those caves got the same things in all of them. Some have pretty pictures on the walls. I put a stick in the sand in front of cave number fourteen – that's the last one we checked."

Zaz stared hypnotically at the flames. "It was the same with us. All you have to do is check the entrance. It isn't necessary to go into each one. I put a small pyramid of stones in front of our last cave – that was about cave number twenty."

"Yeah," said Galoot. "We figured that out, too. Carl, the dumb bastard, wanted to fire his gun off as a calling card, but I put a stop to it seeing as how you might get the wrong idea and think that Sammy was in trouble."

"What?" Carl looked perplexed. "I thought if we put a couple shots in the air they might hear it and come running. Anyway, what are we supposed to do now? I mean, what's the next step we're looking at to find them?"

"Sleep," said Zaz. "Then more searching tomorrow. We'll switch sides. That way we might cover something you missed. No stone goes unturned."

No one argued with Zaz that night. They hit their sleeping bags early.

Sidus Log, Rotation 27.
I'm awake in the middle of night writing this. I can't sleep. We're in the gorge, after learning that Paddy and Lyle took a scout buggy and abandoned the compound. Some of the crewmembers believe I've made a hasty decision to come out here, neglecting our safety. I share the apprehension, knowing that we're largely unprotected from an attack. I have nightmares about those infernal Jack demons and how they might be ripping up our jobsite again. Or worse, that they've caught our scent to the gorge and are on their way en masse to root us out. I could never forgive myself if something like that happened. Samantha said that she would try to get a signal from the sentry automechs on

her monitor. Up until now it's been impossible - the reception is bad in this canyon. Funny thing, if Lyle were here he might tell me the exact mineral in the cliffs that was causing the interference.

I believe that I'm doing the right thing. I would like to believe if I disappeared one day that someone, anyone, would put a leg forward in an attempt to find me.

Mom and dad - I send you a hello across the light-years in hopes that you are happy and that I have not brought you any undue sorrow.

Zachary Crowe, PJ.

They woke early and started out again. This time they had packed large meals in anticipation of a full day's expedition. Carl was shouted down for his suggestion: setting off explosives in the valley to attract the scientist's attention.

Zaz and Dendy walked downstream to a shallow section of the creek where they could cross with ease. It took them a half hour of swift marching to reach the other side of the gorge. They walked on, counting caves until they came to the telltale stick in the sand that Galoot had planted. From then on it would be new territory.

They searched all morning and into the afternoon before Zaz called for a meal break. They sat in front of a large cave opening that lead to an enormous interior cavern, the entrance sheltered from the sun by a natural overhang of limestone. The interior was laden with stones and shelves, looking like accommodations for a large group. Dendy picked some wild berries from a thick shrub, which she used to sprinkle over her bean and sauce plate.

Zaz spoke around a mouthful while he pointed a cautionary finger. "Do you think that's wise? Those haven't passed inspection yet."

"Oh yes they have. I saw the birds eating them, so I used my toxin analyzer on them. They passed. You ought to try some. They're scrumpchalicious."

"No thanks. My digestive system is seriously compacted and I would like to keep it that way. Don't come crying to me tonight when you have a stomach ache." He cocked a thumb over his shoulder. "What do you make of that arrangement in there? That's the first time I've seen a cavern with that type of layout."

"I was wondering about that, too. Those forty or fifty flat stones arranged around that huge fire ring looks familiar in an ancient sort of way. Some American Indians used to have very large council teepees or longhouses. They were designed to be tribal headquarters, where neighboring chiefs met to hash out hunting, trading and marriage matters. They would even resolve disputes. It was like their City Hall. Something similar is going on in there."

"It does look like an arena of sorts. Even the slab stones, or chairs, have individual markings on them. It's like they're reserved seating or something. Kind of reminds me of the Senate floor."

"Definitely tribal. They must have had a primitive social structure – almost a cooperative. That means organizational skills, including communication and negotiation. It's the hallmark of a primitive society on the slow road to a democracy. I think democracy is the right word, since they probably valued freedom and peaceful coexistence. You see it in their artwork. The Inuits of the great north and even the plains Indians had such government-based societies."

Zaz tried to imagine the huge cow-faced Paddymous creatures, with their large flabby noses, involved in some political discussion with raised voices and pointing fingers. He had to dispel the notion that it was a ridiculous idea. Their artwork showed a remarkable sense of detail and sophistication. Assuming they were subordinates, he envisioned the wives, children, and commoners standing outside the circle, scratching their great crowned heads, getting their first taste of bureaucratic buffoonery in the round.

He laughed out loud. "I wonder what they discussed. At worst, I would think they might have to prosecute nut and berry thieves. Or sort out infractions for committing artwork to the walls without a talent license?"

Dendy elbowed him in the ribs. "Don't make fun of those dears. They're the sweetest things I've never seen alive." She suddenly realized what she'd said and put her plate down in the sand. "I'm not hungry anymore."

Her sudden loss of appetite said it all. She felt that inner pain and suffering again. What could one say about a population of primitives who'd probably never hurt a living thing, who were catastrophically wiped from the face of the planet they loved? Dendy harbored such sensitivities about living things; she was defenseless when it came to concealing them.

They packed up and marched on, checking the caves as they struggled to get to each one. Sometimes it was difficult to see them as a passerby, requiring that they double back. Zaz went as far north as he dared, then cut overland across the valley floor. When they found the watercourse, it was a raging river driven by powerful currents. Sand beaches were in abundance as far as the eye could see. Small tributaries led to numerous ponds.

Here, farther north, the birds flew in increased numbers, gliding from branch to branch. Their purple and blue wings painted surrealistic colors in the sky as they swooped and dived. The rope-like twisted trunks of the largest conifers stood like giant sentinels, reaching up to staggering heights. Some of the pond grasses grew to over six-feet high, waving with the slightest breeze, a cool breath coming from the north where the giant snowcapped mountains stood guard.

The landscape reminded Zaz of panoramas he had seen in Wyoming and Montana. He could remember river rafting down ice-cold rapids that showed as much grandeur as what he was now marveling at. It was enough to lift anyone's spirits. If he had paint and a brush, he knew it would be the ideal landscape to capture. He could see himself sitting serenely, breathing in the fragrant air, making colorful dabs across a large canvas. This part of Sidus made up for the desolation of the desert plain.

They trudged on, every so often splashing in the cool water to find relief from the heat. They took a break after a few miles and sat up against a large fallen tree trunk. It was mid-afternoon. Zaz felt determined to cover as much ground as possible, hopefully arriving back at the camp before nightfall.

They had only a few minutes to catch their breath when the great north decided to disturb the solitude. It began with a low rumble, followed by the sound of rocks raining down in the distance behind them. The birds squawked, lifting from their perches and flying madly down the valley, toward the south. The huge trees began to sigh and weave, their branches trembling; needles and twigs came loose, showering the ground. It sounded like heavy raindrops hitting plastic.

Zaz rose to his feet, pulling Dendy up with him. Looking to the north, he could see the ground rushing toward him in a ripple. The ripple quickly became a wave, rolling the earth up like a carpet and coming straight at him with a thunderous rush. The valley floor suddenly rose up in a tsunami-like wave, a tower of earth and twisted vegetation.

"Brace!" he yelled, throwing Dendy to the ground.

The shockwave hit, throwing them up in the air. They came down sprawled in a tangle of arms and legs, while the ground beneath them shook. The earth swayed to and fro, as if a giant had taken hold of the corners of the continent and wrung it. All they could do was slide and roll about, helpless against the heaves and uplifts. The lofty cliffs shed slabs of rock like unwanted skin, sending it tumbling to the valley floor with great thuds and clacks. Trees cracked at their bases, toppling over in jackstraw disarray.

The earthquake gradually calmed, and after awhile they felt only a gentle sway under their prone bodies, like a boat caressed by gentle swells.

Zaz got to his feet, dizzy. Dendy climbed up his pant leg and stood next to him. She'd bitten her tongue, but it wasn't bad enough to keep her from speaking.

"What the hell was that? A nine-five?"

Zaz blew out the breath he had been holding. "I wouldn't doubt it. I think we're standing right over a fracture zone." He looked to the north. He could see a white haze spreading out over several of the mountaintops. Snow slides. Lots of them. One of the mountain peaks to the northeast looked like it had fractured in half, starting its own avalanche. He used his pocket scope to inspect the range. A thin, black stream of ejecta curled up from one of the highest peaks, where it was just beginning to catch the high-altitude winds to form a sheet-like anvil. Volcano.

"We're on double-time now," he said. "Can you keep up with me?"

"Just try and stop me!"

He started with a swift jog and held it. Although her legs were much shorter, Dendy had no problem matching his pace. They cornered around trees and hopped over boulders, expertly negotiating the rough terrain. Zaz ran until his legs felt like stumps dragging through quicksand.

They made it back to camp in an hour, bent over and heaving. Samantha and Galoot's crew were there, on their feet and waiting. Acting on a stroke of premonition, they had packed the camping gear and managed to fill the water trailer and extra cans. One look to the north showed the mountain range lying under a black plume from the east to the west, the prevailing winds scattering the pyroclastic ash, putting half the valley in darkness under the suffocating cloud. The ground under their feet continued to shimmy with aftershocks. Great cracking sounds echoed down the valley, evidence that the faces of the cliffs were being torn asunder.

Samantha reached up with one hand while working the remote on her screen with the other. The snoop swooped in one great arc then landed gently in her palm. "You don't have to say anything," she said. "We might be looking at a debris flow coming down into this valley. That's why I ordered everything packed and ready to go."

"You did the right thing," said Zaz, having barely caught his breath. "We're not taking any chances. The earthquake started that volcano. The way it's belching, we can't risk being caught in a lava flow or lahars.

Zaz took the driver's seat of the six-wheeler and punched the throttle. Dendy sat opposite him, holding firmly to the roll cage. Behind them, Galoot swung the large truck around in a great arc, pushing the heavier vehicle hard, running recklessly over a large fence of shrubbery.

As he drove south, Zaz felt guilt creeping over him like something cold and slithering. Knowing that he'd possibly left the scientists behind to face a natural calamity did not sit right with him. Yet there had been no other recourse other than to get to safety, whether or not he knew the valley was at risk of a massive flood. He could only hope that such a disaster was not in the making. On the other hand, if the valley was flooded, he knew that he'd made the right decision. That left little hope for Lyle and Paddy if they were caught in the havoc. There would be no rescue for them – they would be buried under tons of debris and mud.

He didn't order Samantha to send a snoop back to the valley. Somehow he didn't want to know the outcome. No news was good news. It was too late to change his mind, anyway. In his mind's eye, he could see the two scientists running for their lives from a massive lahars in an attempt to find higher ground. A titanic wave would barrel over them, burying them under hundreds of feet of Sidus real estate.

Samantha spoke above the whine of the vehicle. "I just got a readout on the compound. It's clear from all vantage points. From what I can see from the ground up, it appears okay. I'm sorry to say that – "

"No need to be sorry," said Zaz. "You don't have to tell me that all the automechs are on their keesters in the dirt. I wonder if the big machines have upended. That was the mother of all quakes."

He had a wishful, but fleeting thought that the Jacks had ended up being crushed or killed in the hundreds by the same quake, but realized that he was asking for fairytale wishes. Ah, but the sadistic glee that would fill his heart if such a thing had happened!

After six hours and two large aftershocks that nearly flipped the vehicles, Zaz and the others made it back to the compound. A mile and a half past the northern fence opening, he could see that the large gun truck and the fence driver had been knocked over on their sides. Several sections of the fence line leaned. The *Shenandoah* looked sound, but different in some way. At first, he couldn't understand the discrepancy.

"Goddamn it!" exclaimed Carl. "Look at that shit. We're going to have to use some A-frames and block and tackle to hoist those hogs back up on their rims. Some of our retaining walls are down."

As soon as Zaz pulled up to the jobsite tent, he disembarked to survey the damage.

A few of the automechs were on their feet. The rest of them lay sprawled, attempting to self-right their clumsy metal physiques. The automechs self-righting feature only worked well when they could propel themselves back up into a standing position from a hard surface. As it was, they had been gouging into the soft soil, furrowing small ditches that only dug them in deeper. It seemed more comical than tragic to see their spastic attempts to get up, looking more like broken robotic toys than the high tech pieces of equipment that they were.

Samantha glanced at her monitor, then at the gyrating automechs near the ship hatch. "We sure have our work cut out for us."

Dendy cursed when she saw that the garden tarp had blown away. The soil had vomited up her precious seedlings and bulbs. All of the larger plants were keeled over and had dehydrated.

"It isn't going to fix itself," said Zaz. "Galoot, you and Carl take the six-wheeler and set up our perimeter sentries. Bury the damn things up to their knees to keep them stable. We might have to ride out some more aftershocks." He told Samantha and Carybell to right all the other automechs near the job site. "If anybody needs me, I'll be in the ship with Dendy checking for damage."

Before Zaz could unlatch the small hatch door, he backed up and looked at the *Shenandoah's* profile. He didn't remember it cantering so much to one side.

He knew for certain it was off kilter when he entered the ship. The deck listed 10 degrees to starboard. Not only that, but when he walked across B-Deck, he saw that the C-deck elevator hatch had buckled; he could look through the opening down into the crushed cargo area. He suspected that the other cargo and elevator hatches were similarly damaged.

Dendy peered down into the gaping crack. "Man, the earthquake did us in."

"Looks like it. The seismic wave came down the valley across the desert floor, lifted the ol' gal straight up and slammed her back down. Looks like it opened up her underbelly."

Dendy suddenly looked over her head. "Oh, no. The aquarium. My fish!" She sprinted to the elevator.

Zaz caught up with her, jumping in the cage just as it began to move. The lift squeaked with protest, rising slower than usual. *Quake damage – misalignment.*

When they got to A-Deck, Zaz tried the corridor foot tram, but it was dead. They might have miles of shorts in the wiring looms. The overhead lights were still on, which meant the primary line was getting juice from the hydrogen generators. At least the main power supply was still putting out.

When they entered the hydroponics lab it was a relief to find that the aquarium cover had only misaligned. A good deal of water had sloshed over the tank, but the fish were alive, swimming in the remaining shallow water.

"Thank goodness they're okay," she said. "I've grown attached to them. *All life is precious*, Zaz."

All life is precious, thought Zaz. He thought about Paddy and Lyle and how life was precious to them, too.

They spent the next hour touring the ship, looking for damage, shorted circuits, and system failures. The generators were functioning properly. They repaired a few burst waterlines and reset some breakers. One air conditioning unit was down, although the two backups were still humming. Most of the structural damage had been sustained on the underside of the *Shenandoah*, where several bulkheads had split apart.

Once outside, Zaz walked an inspection tour of the grounds. Tau Ceti was setting in the west like a giant ruby. The last of the mirage-like shimmers of Sidus could be seen in the thick atmosphere just above the desert floor. The armadillos began to tuck themselves into their protective shells to guard against the approaching cold. With their metabolisms slowed, the locusts settled into the cracks to wait out the night.

Zaz felt every tortured muscle in his body. Legs that were now lead weights pulled on him, making every step through the sand a Herculean effort. Exhausted beyond any measure of normal fatigue, he could only move in slow motion, stumbling to the jobsite tent. He found Samantha sitting in the sand, her back up against a tent pole. She had the screen in her lap, one eye closed and the other on the device.

He gave her a nod then spoke into his wrist-com, ordering everyone in from the compound to seal up in the ship for the night. He noticed a small trail of dust heading in their direction through the failing light. It was Galoot and Carl, who had been wrestling a front loader into an upright position outside the south fence.

Carybell and Dendy walked away from the garden plot. Their faces sagged with the pain of fatigue that even Zaz could see from a distance.

A few minutes later the horde came. Their sound was like a whirlwind.

CHAPTER TWELVE

THE SWARM

SAMANTHA BOLTED to her feet and rubbed her eyes, staring at the hand-held comp screen that defined the compound's perimeter. "Drop my britches and count my stitches!" she boomed into her wrist-com for all to hear. She looked out into the desert, then back at the screen, changing the output to night vision mode. "We've got multiple bogies showing up in the south, west and the east. They're coming in fast. I make them one mile out past the fence line in all directions. I repeat, it's not one group – they're surrounding the compound."

Zaz made it to her in two strides. He peered at the screen in disbelief. A bright neon ring of hot targets had formed a thick bracelet around the outside of the perimeter fence. "Galoot," he said into his wrist-com, "put your foot on it – we've got Jacks on the way."

"Okay, Boss, we just heard it on the com. What – "

"Just move it!"

Dendy and Carybell, who had heard the transmission from fifty yards, broke into a run. They joined Zaz at the jobsite tent.

Dendy looked flustered. "Then it's true – they're on us again."

Zaz nodded. "Okay, we're going to assemble in front of the ship's hatch. Sammy, arm and position the automechs in a wide semicircle around our position. Put them two hundred yards out. Dendy, I need you on the flamethrower. Carybell, I sure hope you know how to operate that crossbow. Hold on a sec...."

Zaz produced a small vial of stim tabs, to be used only for emergencies and extreme fatigue. The pill-form supplements used a synthetic adrenalin to elevate the body's vital signs. He had no qualms about using them now. Zaz passed them out, instructing Samantha to give some to Galoot and Carl when they arrived.

He ran for the ship's hatch and ducked just inside the door, hauling out the crossbow and a huge cannon barrel. Dendy picked up the flamethrower. He set the cannon barrel up on the tripod, while Dendy strapped the tank on her back, ignited the torch and adjusted the nozzle. Carybell wound the crossbow and loaded it with a steal bolt.

Galoot and Carl arrived in a swirl of dust. They jumped out of the truck and hurried to Zaz's position, both chewing on stim tabs. One look at the expression on their captain's face put them in emergency mode.

Carl ducked inside the door and brought out a large bag of charges for the barrel cannon, with an additional count of handheld charges that could be detonated with a timer. He dragged out the second tripod-mounted barrel cannon and set it up.

Galoot opened the larger hatch and drove the truck into the cargo bay, parking it next to the six-wheeler. He shut the hatch on the way out. The only way into the ship now was through the small access door.

Samantha took up a station behind the second barrel cannon, keeping an eye on her handheld screen. "We've got a thick mass converging at all points of the fence," she said urgently. "It's definitely a surrounding maneuver. But they haven't broken through yet. I'm starting to lose transmission signals – they're knocking our sentries over."

"You're going to need extra bullets for those guns," said Dendy. "I know you have some under your command chair in the bridge. I'm heading there now while the gettin's easy."

Zaz felt his pockets – she was right. "Go quick. Get Carl's too!"

Dendy hefted the flamethrower off her shoulders then dashed through the door.

A minute later, a light-sensitive timer inside the ship clicked. The floodlights popped on, washing over the compound. The automechs that had reached their position were just under the illumination.

"Look, people," said Zaz, "if push comes to shove, we go indoors fast. I don't want to be overrun. We can always lock them out."

Samantha frowned. "I don't know why we don't do that now. It's a whole lot safer in there. They'd never get through this hull."

"Because that's what they want us to do. We bloodied their noses before. Maybe if we put up a similar fight it will have the same effect. If they get a chance to box us inside, all they have to do is wait us out while they shred our camp again."

"Okay," said Samantha, her eyes on the screen. "They're closing in on the fence – taking down the rest of the sentries. Want Carl to blow their packs?"

Zaz nodded, wiping a river of sweat from his face. "Let em' eat shrapnel." He knew this meant knocking multiple holes in their walls. *Screw the fence line*. Numerous flashes of light ignited in the distance. A moment later they heard seven loud *pops*. The perimeter sentries had exploded, including three behind the ship and to the east. Zaz knew the count was wrong. One of them had miss-fired, failing to blow.

"Damn it all to hell," Carl swore. "A Silver hang-fired."

"Too late to worry about it now," said Zaz.

"Well, we won't need this for awhile." Samantha dropped the screen to the sand. "Carl can detonate our first line, then it's all close quarters from there on out."

Carl spat in the sand. "I prefer it straight up and in my face. Let 'em bring it on with all they've got. They're going the way of the Dodo as far as I'm concerned." He readied his fingers on the remote detonator.

Zaz might have had some reservations about Carl, but cowardice was not one of them. He knew that with his military training, the Italian would stand his ground. Then again, Zaz was feeling the effects of the two stim tabs and noticed that his own courage index was climbing. *Steady boy, calm that inner machismo.*

Dendy returned with the two heavy ammo pouches. Zaz and Carl tore open the bags for easy access and filled their pockets.

Zaz readied himself, hoping that the rifle would not jam or malfunction. So far it had worked perfectly, even if it was an antique. "People, we have a one hundred eighty-degree flank to protect. Keep your eyes along the side of the ship. I think their tactic is to overwhelm us. Carl, detonate the first line of automechs – but let them cross the line by fifty feet so we take out the forward and middle mass."

They didn't have long to wait. The Jacks surged over the fence in massive attack waves, pouring across the sand like a plague controlled by one collective brain. Shapes materialized at the fringe of the powerful floodlights. The white stripes on their pelts danced in a blur. Their collective barks and snarls rose in pitch until it seemed that the whole planet was alive with their racket.

Nearly 200 yards out, the Jacks ran straight into the bomb-laden automechs, knocking them onto the sand.

Carl watched them, biting his lip. His timing had to be perfect for the most destructive results. He tripped the ignition switch a second later.

"Duck!" Zaz yelled, almost too late. The ground rocked with the explosion-induced quake. A wall of earth rose straight up into the air in a wide horseshoe-shaped curtain, taking with it everything caught in the powerful upsurge. For a moment, the entire compound became engulfed in a blinding flash. Like a freeze-frame picture, Zaz saw Jack bodies spiraling, launching up into the heavens; some of them had been torn in two, while others had their heads ripped from their bodies. He could see teeth and glistening light-reflected eyes flying through the night air.

Pieces of bone and sinew rained down upon them, some of the larger chunks hitting the sand near their feet. Shredded bones and skulls clanged off the ship's hull.

For a moment, Zaz thought he'd lost his hearing until he shook his head clear. He raised his rifle, waiting for something to come out of the vast brown storm. It came. He began firing at individual targets – three shots per torso.

Carl took careful aim. The large caliber gun bucked in his hand.

Carybell, though unskilled with the crossbow, fired a slow but steady stream of bolts into the approaching mass. The bolts that flew higher than intended managed to hit several targets in the rear.

Samantha swiveled her cannon directly into a large knot of advancing Jacks, then clicked the detonator. The barrel spat out sharp metal, the projectiles whistling through the air and striking dozens of targets. She unscrewed the cap, placed another charge and shot again. Another spray of hot metal fragments screamed through the air.

Dendy took the extreme left flank near the ship. She aimed at a batch of Jacks that were coming in single-file along the bulkhead. She cranked the tank valve and pressed the trigger. A tight, orange stream erupted from the nozzle with such force it instantly ignited the Jacks. Others came from behind those, leaping over the flames. She burned them down before they hit the ground running. She swept the nozzle in a wide arc to the right, igniting another advancing line of Jacks. Their pelts caught on fire and they tripped over one another as they burned. Those still alive staggered up, hairless and looking like roasted chickens on a spit. Another line of Jacks charged Dendy's position, but they ran headlong into the incinerating spout of her flame.

Carl marched the last remaining automechs out into the compound. The suicide robots reached their targets and exploded, ripping great chunks out of the advancing line. It rained blood and bone for a full 10 seconds.

Galoot quickly packed charges, firing them off at twice Samantha's speed. His cannon barrel wreaked the most devastation of all the weapons, his shots drove gaping corridors through the creatures, like a torpedo piercing a mass of jelly. The cannon barrel glowed an eerie pink in the night air.

Temporarily out of ammo, Carl stuck the gun in his suit vest and began hurling hand charges that exploded after a three-second delay. He pitched them as fast as he could from a crouched position. He didn't have time to aim, tossing them recklessly as though he were fighting the entire horde single-handed. Some of the charges landed dangerously close, opening up small craters in the sand and spewing pebbles that stung the crew's skin.

Zaz reloaded hastily. He fired from the hip in a spray pattern – aiming was useless. Everywhere he looked, the Jacks were there. For every animal that fell, three more leaped over it, fighting through the barrage of firepower thrown at them.

At 50 yards away, the Jacks became a solid wall. They rushed the compound even faster, but due to the mass of corpses, they tripped and tumbled to the ground. Those that got up became targets for the projectiles and were blown backward into the onrush.

As he tried to reload, his shaking hands fumbling the ammunition, Zaz had a bleak thought flash through his mind. He suddenly felt like a Spartan under King Leonidas, trying desperately to defend the pass at Thermopylae. His people were those valiant warriors, fighting shoulder to shoulder with him. He realized then that the Spartans and the other Greeks had at least a decided advantage, for they had clashed in a bottleneck, which evened the odds man to man. Zaz and his crew's flank was so wide open that they now faced the very real possibility of overwhelming defeat.

The advancing Jack line pressed in on all sides within 20 yards of their position. There could have been ten thousand of them in the compound; there was no way of knowing their total number. Zaz had to call it. Retreat did not mean a loss of honor, it meant saving their lives.

"Break and get back into the ship!" he yelled, his voice hoarse.

Samantha and Carybell, being the least effective with firepower, began dragging the equipment through the open hatch door while the others provided cover fire.

Zaz waited for them to pull everything in before he waved the others toward the opening. He had to yell twice at Carl, who continued to chuck bombs at anything that rushed forward. Carl finally broke off the attack, and together with Galoot, they rushed through the door with the remaining ammo and weapons.

Dendy, laying a covering jet of flame, spun and ran for the ship while Zaz backed up, making sure everybody was inside. He emptied the last bullets in his clip into the swarming Jacks then dove through the opening. As the door slammed shut, he heard the barks coming closer. Heavy objects hit the door hatch, nearly springing it open. Galoot drove his full weight against it while Carl threw the heavy latch.

They stood there for a while, chests heaving, staring at the massive bulkhead and listening to the frantic snarls and nails tearing at the fortified door. A moment later, the unnerving sound of thousands of Jacks hitting the outside of the ship echoed like the beating of kettledrums. The bulkhead struts rattled with each impact. It sounded as if the entire ship was threatening to come apart at the seams.

Dendy pulled off her flamethrower. "I can't believe that just happened."

Carl stomped around the deck flailing his arms. It was hard to tell whether it was his temper or the stim tabs that had a hold on him. He stopped and kicked the hatch door. "We just got our asses kicked. What do you think about that? Now we're crammed up in here like a bunch of sheep ready for the slaughter!"

"We didn't have much of a choice in the matter," said Samantha. "If you want to go out there, I'll be happy to open the door for you."

"Yeah, shut up," said Galoot. "I'm getting plum tired of your crap. We did the right thing by coming in here. We got swarmed."

Zaz noticed the noise outside had changed in pitch – the Jacks were howling and whining. *They can smell us just on the other side of the hull.* "We're moving up to the bridge to formulate a plan," he announced.

The elevator cage squealed in protest with the added weight and misalignment. Zaz stepped off with the two men while the women continued up to the bridge. Zaz and the other two crossed the deck to the bulkhead and climbed up the utility catwalk. It was a tiring trek, even with the stimulants in their systems. When they made it to the top they took a short rest then continued down the corridor.

Zaz walked into the bridge, noticing that the women had reclined in the command chairs with their helmets off. The looks on their dirt-smudged faces was one of utter defeat. No one had to tell them that they were now prisoners within the ship.

Dendy pointed to the blacked-out nose windows. "They're trying to get in everywhere. I taped up some star charts so we don't have to look at their ugly mugs."

Zaz set his rifle on his chair. He could hear sharp nails skittering on the thick observation glass. "The problem we have now is options," he said. "I'm not willing to remain bottled up here and do nothing about it. We know we're surrounded. With the temperament of those things, it's a sure bet they'll stay here unless we do something to drive them off. We can't kill them all. We can only hope to thin them out."

Carl spat on the deck. "If we run them off again, they'll just be back. That's their MO. They ain't never going to let up until they get us."

"Then we have to wait it out or abandon the site," said Zaz. "One or the other."

Galoot cuffed soot marks from his face. "A break for where, boss?"

"We know we have to refill our water supply every two weeks or so. If the Jacks stick around, we'll eventually have to deal with them to get out of here. I see no difference between an early or late departure. Paddy and Lyle seemed to think that these creatures are incapable of climbing – they aren't built for it. When we were searching in the gorge, I saw a steep side canyon that led straight up to the top of the west cliff face. I'll bet there's a plateau or mesa at the top. It's not easily accessible. Do you remember the story of Masada and how the zealots held out in their fortress because the Romans couldn't get to them? Well, that's the idea I have in mind. We have the creek and the edible plant life in the area, plus everything we can carry in the two vehicles. I thought I'd never say this, but it looks like the ship is forfeit."

"You mean abandoning the ship?" Samantha said, surprised. "Everything we have is here. It's our electricity source, with our portable coolers, our pumps, lab equipment, hydroponics, hydrogen fuel, all of our tech support and gear. Do you intend to rough it out there until those land grabbers show up?"

Dendy looked adamant. "I sure am glad you didn't say anything about our construction project, Sammy. Because we know it's a big fat bust right now. To hell with the contract, electricity and shipboard life. We're in a fight for our lives. Everything's changed now."

"It's a sure bet those creatures won't leave us alone for one minute," said Galoot as he made a chopping motion with his hand. "Maybe they will go away during the heat of the day, but you better believe they'll come out again in the nighttime. Boss is right – it's our move now."

Carl walked around in a dizzying circle, but he had little else to add to the conversation except the obvious: "Then we've got to blow these bastards to hell."

"We have to be outside to do it," said Samantha. "We can't throw bombs through walls."

"But we can throw them from the top of the ship," said Zaz.

Thoughts flashed from one mind to another, fighting back the inner turmoil to arrive at a collective eureka."

A twisted grin broke out on Carl's face, a sign he knew his pyrotechnics expertise was going to be a major player. "We can rain hell fire down on them. I don't know to what point I'll have to lessen the charges so they won't crack the hull, but I can come close."

"I doubt you'd be able to breach an Ultrinium hull unless it's one of those cutting charges," said Zaz, considering Carl's suggestion. "That's not the problem. If they've surrounded the entire ship, it means a hell of a long walk down the *Shenandoah's* roofline just to take care of all of them. You'll have to wear some magnaboots to keep you planted when those charges go off. Boots and a safety line are the best insurance."

Carl did a little dance. "I could stand on the end of an imperial in a tornado and chuck bombs."

As they spoke, Zaz could feel a slight vibration radiating up through the deck floor. There had to be thousands of Jacks stacked up against the hull, trying to claw and shove their way in. The closer the better, he thought. With any luck, all they would have to do is roll the charges down the hull.

The stim tabs wouldn't last long enough for them to accomplish anything without exhausting vast energy stores. Any more speed in their systems would lead to an overdose that would hamper sound thinking and coordination. They needed rest, especially after the day they'd just gone through. There was no way the Jacks could reach them. They were safe for now.

Zaz ordered everyone to sleep, knowing that the next day would test their mettle.

Sidus Log, Rotation 27.
We've been attacked and completely surrounded. We are
locked up in the *Shenandoah* and can only move freely
within the confines of the ship. I am too tired right
now to record any other details. I have proposed that
we abandon the ship permanently if we cannot drive
the Jacks off for good. That means a desperate escape
attempt. I wonder if it is the heat and the stress
that has driven me to this insane decision.

Zachary Crowe, PJ.

*　　*　　*

Zaz started up the emergency hatch ladder with a line tied around his waist. It was high noon. He was checking to see what numbers they would be up against during the day, seeing how strong the opposition was. It would also help with the bomb placements. He couldn't deny that he wanted to see the animals blown to smithereens.

When he reached the top under the closed hatch, he tugged the line up hand over hand. On the other end of the line was a large bag of explosive charges. Carl followed him up, his magnaboots clanging on the ladder rungs. He had a heavy pack on his back filled with the pyrotechnic hardware and more charges.

Zaz popped the hatch; the familiar blast of desert air rushed over him like a furnace wave. He climbed out with his pack and crouched beside the opening. The air wafting up from below was filled with the stink of urine and feces. One glance around the ship filled him with dread – he made sure to not show that face to Carl as he squeezed out of the opening. They steadied themselves on the safety cage as they surveyed their surroundings.

A full third of the compound was alive with the snarling Jack Lions. A headcount was impossible unless one counted them by acres. They had pressed themselves up against the ship so tightly they appeared as a large, unbroken mass. The ones nearest the bulkhead used their sickle-like claws to tear at the glass-metal surface. It was a miracle they hadn't trampled each other. On second thought, when Zaz examined them more carefully, he could swear that they were snapping at one another as they stood on heaps of their crushed comrades. Clearly, they were growing more hostile with each passing hour. The collective snarls, howls, and barks sounded like a berserk crowd's roar.

Carl reached around to undo his backpack. He took some of the charges out. He thumbed a small button on one of the small charges then heaved it. The bomb arced in the air, flying out past the edge of the hull and landing in a solid mass of Jack Lions. The explosion blew a circular pocket of flesh and dirt up into the air. The remaining live animals pushed forward to fill the cavity.

"Concentrate it in one area," said Zaz, pointing downward.

Carl pitched two more charges in the same vicinity. They had the same result: the detonations obliterated a circular mass of animals, which was quickly replaced by more that surged forward. Carl taped three charges together and heaved them into the mass of Jack Lions. The explosion rocked the ship, momentarily knocking Zaz to his knees. The triple charge only managed to make a larger crater, taking out a greater number. The empty pocket once again filled with more of the aggressive creatures, their numbers seemingly unaffected by the blasts.

Zaz recovered slowly, gripping the crow's nest cage. Looking down, he could see the creatures swivel their heads up, making eye contact with the tiny humans atop the ship. Incensed, they leaped on the hull, scrambling with legs that could not make it up the slick surface. Some climbed on top of the construction equipment and jumped at the ship, only to hit it and skitter down.

Zaz wondered if their numbers would grow as the sun fell, drawing more of them out. It was astounding that a population of such animals could concentrate so exclusively on one main objective. Hadn't Paddy and Lyle proposed such a theory?

Carl walked down the length of the ship, carrying his pack of charges. Zaz fed out the safety line, one end of it secured to the ship and the other tied firmly around Carl. Every so often Carl tossed a charge down then followed it up by heaving one to the other side.

The new tactic had no effect – there were too many of them to wipe out at once. It was a wasted effort.

Zaz spoke into his wrist-com. "Carl, head back. It's useless. There's too many to deal with."

"If I can just keep it up we – "

"It ain't happening! You could be out here all day and not even take a chip out of them. This is not what I had in mind. We've got to come up with another plan."

Zaz watched him return, reeling in the line slowly so Carl wouldn't tangle in it.

Zaz knew that back down on A-Deck, they were surrounded by anxious crewmembers who'd gathered there waiting to hear the results.

Zaz stowed the bomb packs and slack line at the bottom of the ladder. He looked at the expectant faces at the base of the ladder and shrugged. "It's no good."

Dendy's face collapsed. "What is it going to take to drive them off?"

"We have the right idea," Carl said as he wiped the sweat from his face. "We need something with a little more razzmatazz. They look like a swarm of locusts – must be millions of 'em out there."

They walked back single file toward the bridge. Zaz could hear them speaking amongst themselves, but he was busy thinking of another way of dealing with the enemy. Nothing short of an apocalypse would annihilate such an immense number of foes. Where was Satan's hellfire when he needed it?

"What do you mean 'razzmatazz'?" Samantha asked. "Is that anything like oomphah?"

Carl scowled. "I didn't see you up there chucking bombs, Ms. Perfect thirty-eights."

"I'm a thirty-six-double D, and you're the one who called me perfect."

Zaz couldn't imagine those two locked up in the same room together. They'd cat-scratch each other to death before they came up with a survival plan.

When they got to the bridge, Samantha busied herself by preparing a quick standup meal. The captain sat on the edge of his chair, trying to clear his fatigued mind. They needed something to dissuade the creatures, some type of overwhelming weapon. They couldn't kill them all. They would have to scare them off with something so terrible it would force them to run – or at least addle them long enough for the crew to escape. Hellfire. *Satan's hellfire.*

The ship creaked and groaned. They heard thumping noises that seemed to come from above. Was it possible the creatures had gained the roof?

Zaz snapped his fingers. "Carl, I know we don't have any Napalm onboard, but I thought we had some surplus diesel fuel.

"Yeah, we've got about a dozen five-gallon cans. But that stuff is old, not as flammable as you think. I thought about making firebombs earlier, but dropped the idea."

Samantha began passing around flash-cooked meals. She looked menacingly at Carl. "Well, you weren't thinking much before you dropped it," she said, tossing a meal into his lap. "I have about twenty gallons of high-octane snoop gas. All you would have to do is add some to each can. That would make it highly combustible. Detonate that with one of your hand-thrown charges and you have a nice firebomb. If you splash those Jacks, their pelts will go up like dried straw, especially in this heat; those fat reserves they're carrying will act like candle wax. Poof!" Samantha went back to the galley and began mixing a chilled fruit drink. She spoke over her shoulder. "But it means that we wouldn't have any fuel for the snoops. It's a tradeoff."

"Sammy, you're a showoff," said Dendy.

"And she's got a brain in that beautiful head," said Zaz. "I wasn't thinking about the snoop gas. I've got another idea that will use fire. In fact, it will consume everything around the ship. All we have to do is…"

He let the words trail off, remaining perfectly still. Carl Stromboli was pointing his .45 directly at Zaz's forehead. It had happened so fast. One minute Zaz was scooping hungrily out of his meal plate about to say something – the next minute he was staring down the length of a pistol barrel. Right now that gun barrel looked as large as a stovepipe.

Carl got to his feet slowly. Between his teeth he said, "When I tell you to, duck."

If Carl was intent on blowing Zaz's brains out why was he ordering him to duck? Was he going to shoot one of the other crewmembers? He couldn't – he wouldn't shoot Sammy for a couple of insults!

Zaz felt like he was stuck in a barrel of molasses. He turned his head in a slow clockwise direction. From the corner of his eye, he saw Samantha turning around in response to Carl's command. The next instant brought their attention to the open hatchway door, catching sight of something that did not belong there.

Zaz ducked low, grabbing the sides of his command chair. He heard a series of rapid *click-clacks* instead of a loud gunshot.

He turned toward the doorway again. A large Jack lion filled the opening. It was stooped in a crouch, its head just inside the opening. Its eyes were fixed on Samantha.

Zaz threw his arm backwards to grab his rifle.

Carl repeatedly pulled the trigger of the .45, slapping it once with his hand, but the gun did not fire. He pitched the gun at the open doorway, grabbed for the sword under his chair cushion and pumped his legs across the floor. "Luggout, Sammy!"

Zaz flung the rifle up to his chin and tried to steady the barrel but Carl had crossed the distance in two seconds, blocking his shot.

Samantha shrieked; a juice container fumbled out of her hands and splashed on the deck. As she recoiled, the Jack stepped in and clawed at her, hooking a talon in her suit and yanking her within reach. It reared up on one leg, ready to disembowel her with a kick.

Carl dived, bringing the crude sword down with a vicious hacking motion. The blade caught the rat-like claw with an audible crack. The Jack howled, jerking its hand away and shredding Samantha's uniform down the middle.

Carl swung again, hitting the creature's shoulder. A spray of hot blood shot across the deck. Indifferent to the pain, the Jack darted forward once and clamped its jaws down on Carl's shoulder. It shook him back and forth like a dog with a rag. One of its hind legs came up in a blur. Carl went down on his back, throwing a hand up in defense.

Galoot thumped across the deck, cocking his fists. "Not this time!" he bellowed, bringing both fists into the creature's chest and knocking it back toward the door.

Zaz still couldn't get a steady bead on the animal, fearing he might hit one of his crewmembers.

Dendy threw her dinner plate at the Jack, hitting it squarely in the face and temporarily blinding it. Carybell rushed forward and pitched her own plate, but it slapped harmlessly against the bulkhead.

Finding an opening, Zaz got off four quick shots. He had to lower the rifle when Galoot blocked his view again.

Galoot drove the wounded creature backward, throwing powerful punches into its midriff. The Jack's ribs cracked with each blow; it stumbled, trying to bring its tail around though it was confined in the doorway, thumping harmlessly on the jam. Galoot threw one final right cross that sent the animal reeling backward, tripping over its own legs. It fell to the deck outside the bridge. Galoot slammed the hatch door.

Zaz got to Carl at the same time Samantha did. They turned him over to check his injuries. Zaz had to pry Carl's hands away from his left thigh, and that's when he saw the blood spurting from an artery. Carl's leg had been opened up like a side of beef from his knee to his pelvis. He had a few teeth marks in his shoulder, but the uniform fabric had held.

Dendy retrieved the med kit and broke it open on the floor. She found a clamp and, with slippery fingers, pinched the artery off. Zaz and Galoot had to restrain Carl, holding his hands. Samantha found some quick-shot painkillers and poked two of them into his bicep. After a few moments, Carl's muscles relaxed and his eyes rolled back. He tried to speak, but Samantha put a finger over his lips.

They lifted the injured man onto a fully reclined command chair, affording Dendy easier access to the wound. She wasted no time applying antiseptic, then probing further into the cut to determine its depth.

Zaz held a cool pack to Carl's forehead. He watched as Dendy strapped a lighted pull down magnifier to her head. She clamped the wound closed in three places and began the delicate task of using the tiny auto-feed suturing tool.

"I'm not trained in microsurgery," she said, concentrating on the work. "But I do know the difference between a ligament and a tendon. I don't want you to hold it against me."

Zaz couldn't believe she was apologizing. "For God's sake, Dendy, you're all we have. No one is going to hold anything against you. You do what you have to do. We'll hope for the best."

"Will he walk again?" Carybell asked through the trembling hand she held to her mouth.

Dendy nodded, sweat dripping from her chin. "I'll do one better and make sure he can run," she said, though her expression showed otherwise.

Zaz left the cool pack on Carl's forehead and stepped back. The patient was asleep. It was just as well – better he was immobile, letting Dendy work without difficulty. Samantha remained close, bending over and assisting Dendy. He could see a large red welt on Samantha's breastbone and asked her if she was seriously injured.

"No, it's just a flesh thing," she said. "The suit protected me."

Zaz looked at the closed bridge hatch. He could hear snarls coming from the other side. It sounded like more than one creature had found its way to A-Deck. Galoot also stared at the hatch. The big man expressed what Zaz had been thinking for the past five minutes.

"How in the hell did them critters get in the ship, boss?"

"I know we didn't crack the hull with those charges. They were too weak. I'm wondering if they took the temporary door off its hinges. I can't figure how they applied that much pressure to it."

"That door was solid – two feet thick with two-inch diameter pins. There ain't no way, boss. What the hell are we missing here?"

What we're missing is a way to get off the bridge and take care of this new threat. Never mind protecting the exterior of the ship now, the question was how to get out of yet another corner they'd painted themselves into. Instead of being confined to the ship, they were confined to the bridge. Now they had a real mobility problem, not to mention a weapon's shortage – all of the heavy firepower was stacked on B-Deck next to the exit door.

Zaz picked up the .45 pistol and jacked the hammer slide back. It was empty.

He found extra shells in one of Carl's pockets – counted out fifteen rounds. He had about thirty rounds for his own weapon. He rustled through the cabinets, not knowing what he was looking for – anything to help with an assault. Then he found something. He held the bomb pack up to his face and read the designation number on it.

SILVER TWO.

Galoot slapped his thigh. "Hey, that was the squirrelly automech that I had to manhandle back into its cradle."

"Yeah, the berserker," said Zaz. "If we can arm this for a delayed ignition we could pitch it out the door. It would clear a pathway."

Zaz looked at Carl, knowing that he was the only one who could set the timer perfectly. But Carl was gone to the world of painkillers and unconsciousness.

Galoot licked his slab-like lips and held out a hesitant hand. "I think I know how to do it. I've seen him make the packs hot and put them on a timer."

Zaz handed the pack to him. Galoot opened it up and pulled out the fist-sized charge. His big fingers worked on a small access latch, popping it open. Inside was a tiny dial with clock increments on it. Galoot showed the tiny control panel to Zaz. "I set this here dial to seconds or minutes. Then I push these three toggles to the red side. After that, you give it a heave."

"Okay, we'll have to time this just right. Let's say a ten second delay; you unlatch and spring the door open a crack and then I pitch it through. You'll have to hold the door with all your strength if they rush it. Then we slam it shut."

"He can hold any door in the world," said Carybell. "I can help – I can shoot like Annie Oakley. I want to go, too!"

"It's true," said Samantha. "Carybell's a deadly shot. Don't ask me how to explain it, but she's got the eye and the reflexes. I've never seen anything like it."

"I was second place in the Las Vegas Cyber Shooting Championship," Carybell explained. "I used to enter every year, even had sponsors. I used to shoot at old-time iron silhouettes with live ammo on the Antique Firearms Road Show."

"God, I hope you're right." Zaz handed her the .45 and the shells. The pistol looked like a locomotive in her hand. She loaded it quickly, jacked the slide back and then spun the gun around her index finger. After three twirls, she snapped the grip back into her palm. She crouched, waving the gun to and fro with a two-handed combat stance. Standing up to her full height of five-two, she announced, "Yeppers, I can do this."

Zaz and Galoot exchanged two blinks and four raised eyebrows between them. They knew she had performed well with the primitive crossbow, and even capped a few Jacks with the gun. But, hell, who would have known that she was a professional pistol-packing mama?

Zaz told Dendy to cover Carl with a few blankets to shield him from the blast, then to duck down behind the chairs at his signal. He made sure his rifle was fully loaded. Everyone donned their helmets – protection from flying debris.

Galoot braced against the door with a single massive forearm ready to throw the latch. Zaz underhanded the bomb package and sidled up against Galoot, who set the dial, then flicked the three toggle switches.

"Now!" Zaz told him.

Galoot unlatched the handle and cracked the door open against his planted foot. Zaz bent down then tossed the bomb pack through the opening. A giant rat foot kicked it through the crack back into the bridge. Zaz scooped it up and pitched it hard through the narrow gap of the door, just as another hairy rat foot clawed at the opening.

Galoot slammed the heavy door shut, driving all his weight behind it. He couldn't latch it, since the Jack's foot protruded through the opening. Zaz dived at the door's base, butting his shoulder against its surface. The animal tore at the door, trying to widen the opening.

Zaz got a hand to one ear before the bomb detonated. The hatch door blew open, knocking the two men to the floor. A tornado of shredded flesh flew though the opening and splattered against the bulkhead walls.

Carybell was the first one on her feet. She raced out the door commando-style, brandishing the gun.

Galoot pressed through the door, sword in hand. Zaz followed close behind, checking both directions. Bloody smears and animal parts lie at his feet, evidence that at least three animals had met their end. He wheeled around to reseal the door, but Samantha already had her hands on it, pulling it shut.

"Lock it," Zaz told her. "If we need back in we'll holler."

The door slammed. He wheeled around to rejoin the others. There was movement to his right. A Jack came around the portside corridor, sniffing the deck.

Carybell shot it low in the guts. It pinned eyes on her then wobbled once before it fell over. Heart shot. She ran up to it and delivered a hefty kick to the head to make sure it was dead.

More scuffing noises came from around the corner. Zaz instantly knew how they had gained A-Deck. "They're coming up the catwalk. We'll head them off there. Watch yourselves."

Now it made sense. They should have cut the catwalk loose with a beam torch to restrict access. The Jacks surely couldn't operate the elevator cages. But that was crazy! How in the hell could they have guessed that the creatures were going to get into the ship?!

The weapons. They were one deck lower, still out of reach.

Zaz pushed ahead of Galoot to keep him out of his line of fire. He walked abreast of Carybell, who had eyes alert for any movement. She crept on spongy legs, ready for any surprise that might come at them.

Galoot hushed his voice. "I thought these critters couldn't climb up things."

"I wouldn't consider walking up a wide staircase climbing, Galoot."

"It still doesn't make sense to me."

Zaz shushed him to silence, proceeding cautiously. He was just about to turn left into the corridor when the ship's lights went out.

CHAPTER THIRTEEN

A ROCK AND A HARD PLACE

THE GENERATORS!

Zaz fumbled in his pocket and brought out a mini-light. He switched it on, illuminating the corridor ahead. The creatures could be heard, but not seen. The Jacks had excellent visual acuity in the dark – at least, that's what the professors had said.

"We've only got one light," said Galoot. "I'm going back to the bridge for more. Stay put. I'll be right back."

"Okay, I'll give you some light," said Zaz after two hesitant seconds. "Make it quick." He backed slowly away from the corridor and shined the light toward the bridge hatch. Galoot took hefty strides to the door and banged on it, shouting for the others to let him in. He disappeared inside for a few moments then reemerged with a lantern for Carybell and another for himself.

The captain spoke softly as he led the way: "Galoot, watch our six. I'll keep focused ahead of us. Carybell, you watch our sides – I don't want to be out-flanked."

The Jacks had managed to disable the hydrogen generators, meaning they would have to get to that station and repair them. They couldn't take the elevator to B-Deck – the catwalk needed clearing first.

Where were the beasts entering the ship?

Zaz got to the top of the catwalk near the bulkhead. He shined his light down the stairway. Two black-white forms were struggling up the steps toward them. They froze momentarily when hit in the eyes with the light beam. Zaz and Carybell dropped down a dozen steps before they stopped to raise their weapons.

Zaz took time to aim precisely and pulled the trigger four times. Carybell's pistol bucked in her hand, her shots going through the creatures and ricocheting off the bulkhead walls. When they ceased fire, Zaz could see one of the Jacks had toppled backward and lay still on the stairwell. The other had died, its limp body flopping over the handrail.

Galoot preceded them down the stairs and, hooking a large arm under the groin of the dead Jack, heaved it off the rail. It landed with a thump thirty feet below.

The rest of the stairwell was clear. They hurried down the catwalk, leaping three stairs at a time. When they reached the bottom landing the coast was clear – no movement. They rushed to the exit hatch and gathered up the weapons: Galoot donned the flamethrower then tied the crossbow over his back; Carybell picked up a bomb pack and both bags of cartridges; Zaz managed to heft one of the smaller cannon barrels over his shoulder.

They headed down the cavernous expanse of B-Deck. Everything seemed quiet, save for the persistent caterwauling noise outside the ship. They heard a snarling ruckus just up ahead. At the end of Galoot's lantern beam, Zaz saw a creature wriggling like a hooked fish, prying itself up from a crack in the deck. It thrashed wildly, tearing great tufts of fur from its hide on the jagged opening. The creature was stuck in a hole made in the elevator hatch that led down to C-Deck. A corner of the hatch had been twisted up like a dog-eared page.

But that would mean…

"Boss, those sons-a-bitches dug up cunder the ship, right through the dirt." Galoot marched over to the squirming Jack. It gave a snarl then whipped a claw at him. Galoot triggered the flamethrower and the animal burst aflame with a crackling hiss.

Zaz coughed from the stench. "Quick," he said, "get the tow truck. Run a wheel over that metal lip to crush it down."

Galoot jumped into the truck's cab and activated the engine. He rolled across the deck, driving over the jagged opening and bringing the wheel to rest over the tear. He left it there then waited for Zaz and Carybell.

The generators occupied the starboard side of the ship toward the aft end. It would be a long haul on foot, but they had no other choice. Then Zaz remembered something: the six-wheeler was also in the cargo bay.

He headed for the six-wheeler, feeling a sudden burst of elation. They climbed aboard and stowed their weapons. He fired up the motor and turned on the powerful headlights before spinning the vehicle in a 90-degree turn and heading down the cargo bay at full-throttle.

A Jack froze in front of the headlights, caught in the glare. The animal bowed its head then charged at the vehicle. There was a loud *thwack* – legs and arms cart-wheeled over the roll cage and disappeared behind. Another Jack came out of the dark and struck the six-wheeler broadside, smashing a door panel inward and knocking itself unconscious.

Carybell stood up in a half-crouch, holding on to the roll bar for dear life. "That's the way to put the slap down on them beasties, captain!" She waved the gun back and forth, eager to shoot something. Zaz couldn't decide if she was full of bravado, bloodlust, or kooked out. It had to be all three, he decided, since it was a part of her personality he'd never seen before.

They reached the generators in two minutes, nearly sideswiping the huge motors. Zaz did not immediately disembark. He looked between the two huge hydrogen tanks for any sign of the animals. Seeing nothing, he jumped out and inspected the wire loom connected to the massive armatures – the main power feed for all the ship's electricity. Something caught his eye – the power control panel box. It had been bashed in. He studied the manual control levers next to the primary breaker switch. His boots ground over something on the floor. He bent down, picked up two white objects.

Teeth.

That part of the equation made sense; attracted by the low vibrating hum of the giant motors, a Jack had bitten the control panel thinking that it was alive. It shorted out and broke the animal's jaw in the process.

Galoot shoved up to Zaz. "It ain't a problem, boss. Let me in there and I'll splice her back together. Just keep my back covered."

Zaz stepped aside, giving Galoot room to work. "Stay frosty, Carybell," he called out. Galoot went to work on the panel.

"Aye aye, sir. They won't get through."

Zaz felt more than a little nervous. The only thing he knew about electricity happened to be of the static kind. He listened as Galoot mumbled to himself, thrusting his hand inside the control box.

"Not to worry, boss – she ain't hot to ground, just knocked a lead off the connector."

Whatever that meant. He could feel himself aging a year for every minute he had to stand there, wondering how much longer it was going to take before they could restore power to the ship.

"Just about got it crimped, boss."

And I've just about got my balls caught in a nasty crimp. For God's sake, hurry it up, Mr. Master Technician.

Zaz saw a lightning flicker overhead, then heard the hum of the hydrogen generators snap in and out with electronic seizures. Galoot cursed. There was a loud *snap* and the ozone suddenly smelled like burnt insulation. A steady whine grew from the bowels of the ship. The overhead lights brightened. The big armatures spun to maximum revs.

"That should do it," said Galoot, sucking on a burned thumb.

"Pile in." Zaz was in no mood to stick around. They jumped into the vehicle. Just as he backed up to turn around, he heard a thud from on top of the roll cage. His foot came down on the accelerator. He craned his neck back to look up, catching a face full of bitter drool. Trying to wipe the sting from his eyes and handle the wheel at the same time, Zaz caught the blurry image of a Jack's face snapping at the cage mesh.

Galoot hurried to duck as sharp claws poked between the metal crosshatch. He drew back a bleeding scalp. Carybell stood braced in the front seat where there was roof of bars and cage. When she turned around to face the rear of the vehicle, the Jack took a vicious swipe at her, catching her helmet. The helmet toppled off her head and landed on the floorboard. She brought the pistol up over the end of the cage and pulled the trigger three times. The Jack swiped at her again, catching the knuckles on her gun hand and forcing her to drop the weapon. Galoot rammed the sword up through the cage, impaling the beast through the belly. It shook violently then collapsed on top of the cage. It lay stuck there, its tongue hanging limp through the grate like a slab of raw liver.

Distracted, Zaz nearly ran straight into the tow truck. He whipped the wheel around hard. The Jack rolled off the cage, hitting the deck. Zaz slammed on the brakes skidding to a stop next to the freight elevator. They dragged the weapons and ammo bags to the lift. Zaz worked the controls, his fingers slipping over the buttons. The lift rattled once then began a creaking climb upwards.

No one had the breath or ventured to speak until they were 15 feet above the deck's surface. Zaz was hyperventilating; he bent over and grabbed his knees. "There's eight cargo hatches to C-Deck," he gasped. "If any are cracked open they'll find their way up again."

Zaz glanced at Carybell; the fingers on her injured hand had begun to swell. "How bad is that?" he asked.

"I'm okay," she said with a grimace. "It just nicked me."

Galoot, who had a bleeding flesh wound on his head, gently took her hand and examined it. He picked her up in his arms, cradling her. "Her little hand's broken, boss. I'll get her in right away." The giant gazed down into Carybell's eyes. She looked up adoringly into his. It was the kind of love caught in a moment that transcended all normalcy – like the big ogre in love with the little princess, a page torn out of Beauty and the Beast. But Zaz knew that's why it was so special.

The elevator stopped. Galoot waited with Carybell, tight in his arms. Zaz grabbed the ammo bags then led the way down the corridor to the bridge hatch. He pounded for entry. The door snapped open. Galoot laid Carybell on a command chair, asking Dendy to check her hand before leaving to retrieve the rest of the weapons.

Samantha stood over Carl, tissues and antiseptic in her hands. "Thank Jupiter you guys made it back in one piece. You were gone a long time in the dark. What blew the electricity?"

Zaz gave her a recap of the run-ins, including the problems with the generators. She nodded, but kept her eyes on her work, cleaning up Carl's leg, where Dendy had just finished stapling the wound shut. She was blood-smeared from her wrists to her elbows, having insisted on serving as Dendy's assistant. "You mean to tell me," she said, "they got in from the bottom? Who would've known those suckers could dig like prairie dogs?"

Lyle and Paddy knew the animals could dig like prairie dogs, Zaz painfully reminded himself. He missed those two more now than ever. Besides the extra firepower they could have provided, the scientists understood the habits of the creatures, and quite possibly might have predicted their behavior.

Dendy finished splinting Carybell's hand. She quickly dressed Galoot's head wound, then sat down on the edge of Carl's command chair. She looked exhausted, near collapse. Zaz told her to get some rest. She made no effort to lie down, but continued her protective hover over Carl.

The Italian stirred, moaned. His eyes cracked open to see Samantha standing over him. He tried to talk but his tongue floundered.

"You are one crazy idiot," Samantha said to him, "you know that? And you've got the greasiest hair I've ever seen."

Carl smiled, looking up at her with what could only have been a little schoolboy glow. For the first time in Planet Janitor history, Carl's eyes favored Samantha with a softness that had been lacking ever since they'd met. Surprisingly, Samantha returned the gaze. She placed a palm to his cheek. Zaz wondered if there might be a trip to the raspberry bushes in their future. He turned away – it was their moment.

"Boss, before we got interrupted you said you had another idea about getting out of here alive. We sure do need a game plan before we get picked off. It ain't looking so good. Those nasty skunk lions are going to dig their way in here again, sure as shittin'."

Galoot's words got everyone's attention: Dendy stiffened on the edge of her chair; even Carl turned his head, focusing expectant eyes on the captain. Carybell gave him a curt nod.

"Yeah, right." Zaz tried to shake off the fatigue. "We already know we can make a high-octane cocktail out of the old diesel gas, thanks to Sammy's suggestion. I think we should launch those cans from the ship's roof in strategic locations. Then we can detonate the cans, causing a firestorm. Hopefully we can kill enough of them to run the rest off. Fire is still an animal's worst enemy. I don't think it's any different with these Jacks."

"What if that doesn't get them to clear out?" Carl managed to croak. "We only have so much of that fuel. Then we're back to hand-chucking bombs, and you've already seen that won't work."

"That's true," said Zaz. "It's a one shot deal, but let's say we could add to that inferno and keep it going for a long time. Something that wouldn't burn off after a while. Something that would make it so hot they wouldn't have any choice but to back off."

Samantha wiped her arms off with a damp towel. "Now wait a minute, you're not thinking of firing the hydrogen retro jets, are you?"

Zaz gave a telling glance.

Galoot said, "There's twenty-six attitude nozzles on the *Shenandoah*. Eight of them are positioned under the ship. The ship's underbelly is crushed, buried in thirty feet of desert soil. The feed lines to those jets are crimped or split. And if they're not, with all that back-pressure and load, you might cause an explosion. Boss, we've got electrical shorts in the secondary systems all over this ship."

"I only want to shut down the hydrogen feed lines that lead to her keel, firing the port and starboard attitude jets. We've got the big aft thruster engines that we can light up, too. I think the ship will hold together against the force. We've done it before with a dry-dock engine test."

"Yeah," said Dendy, "but we were anchored in a port cradle to withstand the strain. You could rattle the whole ship to pieces, maybe even break her in two."

"Not if I take the thrusters up gradually and find a safe equilibrium. I'm telling you, the *Shenandoah* can take the strain."

Zaz looked at Galoot. "What do you think, big guy? You know this ship better than the Russians who built her."

Galoot looked confused for a moment. "Well, it could work if we fire the main rears and all the midline jets, seeing as how they are above the sand. We'd have to program the nozzles for the correct aim. But that means some of them might exhaust against the sand. As long as the backpressure isn't dangerous, I think it would work. Hell, exhaust flare just might blow out some big glass craters – so maybe no back-pressure at all."

Zaz looked at Samantha. "Sammy, can we do it?"

"Logistically, I guess it would work. We're not in the vacuum of space so I don't know how the ship will react. Worst case scenario? Too much aft thrust, the ship could break loose and fold over on itself. But you're right, we can control the thrust. In atmosphere with full power, those midline thrusters have a flare cone of fifty yards, so we'll cook anything within that radius. The aft engine flare won't dissipate until a quarter mile out."

"Nothing could live through that," Dendy said. "At least the main force of those varmints surrounding the ship will get barbecued real good."

Zaz leveled his eyes on Carybell. "What do you think, darling? Do you think we stand a chance?"

Carybell dithered. Then she pointed at Galoot. "I think what he thinks."

Zaz shook his head. "You don't understand. You're are part of this crew. You're also a damn good soldier. Whatever you think is important to us all. Do you think we should fire up these rockets and burn the Jacks? It's risky."

She looked around from face to face then burst into tears. Galoot put a hulking arm around her. "I'm sorry," she coughed. "It's the first time anybody ever asked me what I thought. Okay, then I think we should light them all on fire so it will make us safe. I just want to go home with papa bear." Carybell had never belonged to anyone or anything. Now she was Planet Janitor stock. Nobody would ever argue with that commission.

"Okay, then it's unanimous. That's the way I want it – no regrets. The next order of business is an escape plan. Once we have the distraction we need, we have to hit the ground running if we're going to get the hell out of here. We need to pack up everything that's essential: meds, food, weapons, tools, bedding, clothes and shelter. I want the big binocular telescope, the Sat dish, radar gun and the remote devices. Those are on the priority list. If you can think of anything else I want you to make a list of it."

Dendy wrung her hands. "I hope we can find room for some seedlings and sprouts. I'll take responsibility for them – they shouldn't take up too much room... I suppose my fishes aren't going to make the cut."

"Seedlings, fine. Fishes, sorry. We'll take the marine life and plant it in the ship as bait before we leave. It should make a nice stink and draw some attention, provided some of those things come back after we've torched them."

Carl grimaced and rose up on an elbow. "I know you want to take the vehicles, but how are we getting out the door? You want to blow it or open it?"

"I thought about that. It wouldn't make sense to blow it. It might not fragment enough and it could block the exit. It's designed to swivel up, so I figure we can torch the latch until it's weakened, hook up a towline to the top of the brace beams. By backing a vehicle up, pull the door open and take off. Then we drive right through the opening. Our momentum should snap the line loose."

"When are we going to do all of this?" Samantha asked.

"We'll spend one more night here, maybe two. It will take us some time to pack up."

He could have heard a feather drop. There it was: he'd actually said they had one, maybe two more days left. He couldn't believe it himself. For the short time that he'd owned her, the *Shenandoah* had been all he knew. She'd given him a new lease on life, opening up new vistas, letting him explore the universe. He'd always felt the comfort of her secure embrace and provided him with a home. Now she would be discarded like some piece of space junk.

"Carl, you're staying here," ordered Zaz. "The rest of us – full armor and weapons. We've got to go over this ship inch by inch to make sure we've got the rest of the Jacks. Any cracks or breaches get sealed up. We have to keep those things out of here at all costs."

They suited up and filed out of the bridge. They spent the next six hours searching every crevice of the ship, making sure it was secure, that no other animals had found their way in. Anything that looked like a crack in the deck was sealed. The dead Jacks were left where they were to serve as bait.

They arrived back at the bridge, too tired to talk, bathe, or strip off their uniforms. Barely coherent, Zaz refused a cold meal. With what little strength he had left, he could only think about writing in his log. He thought it might be his last entry.

```
Sidus Log, Rotation 28.
It's late. I'm functioning on nerves as I write this
- truly the "walking dead." We've been on Sidus for
less than a month and it has become a complete hell.
The Jack Lions got into the ship, nearly killing
us in the process. Carl has sustained a potentially
life-threatening injury. I'm doubtful he'll ever walk
without a limp. I wonder which one of us is next.

    I have an escape plan. If the plan fails and you
find this log, know that this was my last entry and we
fought to the end to save each other. Yet there's a
good chance we will make it out - I have a brave and
resourceful crew.

    Since the beginning, I have been assaulted by a
never-ending shroud of guilt for having set foot on
this wretched planet. I could have vetoed and refused
the mission, but I didn't. They say that hope springs
eternal, but I find nothing but hardship and finality here.

    Above all, I miss our resident scientists, Lyle and
Paddy. I'm beside myself with grief, knowing that we
might have driven them off. I find it impossible that
they could have survived out there alone. I only hope
they went swiftly and without suffering.

                            Zachary Crowe, PJ.
```

* * *

There was much to do; Zaz was spread thin over multiple tasks. Galoot and Samantha had prepared and transported 12 cans of spiked fuel to the emergency hatch on A-Deck. The heavy cans would have to be lifted one by one up a pulley system and then secured to the roof. Dendy made numerous trips to the science lab and hydroponics, packing everything she could from a prescribed list. Carybell had gathered most of the med supplies and taken them to the elevator to pack with the other gear stacked there, all of it waiting to be transported to the deck below. Carl had been moved to his quarters to recuperate.

Zaz finished loading the radar gun, telescope, and Sat dish in the six-wheeler. He made sure the items were wrapped to prevent buffeting. The high-tech instruments were the most important items of cargo, especially for what he had in mind. He took the freight elevator to A-Deck. Instead of taking another load down, he checked the corridors to make sure he was alone, then went straight to the bridge and locked the door.

Zaz walked to the front console and brought up a schematic of the *Shenandoah* – a giant skeletal framework of the ship and all of its component locations. This was so he could pace off the locations of each nozzle then drop the fuel cans directly under them

A display showed the angular rotation axis of the jets, so he adjusted them manually to the correct angle for a downward blast.

His wrist-com buzzed. He ignored it.

Sitting at the navigator's control panel, he nervously rapped his knuckles on a small glass bubble, exposing the printed words above a small bank of switches. A digital warning stared back at him: NUCLEAR DETONATION TIMER OVERRIDE. He twisted the red lever to the "HOT-ON" position, then dialed in a specific radio frequency and locked the calibration in against tampering. He flipped ten toggle switches to the "ARMED" position and looked up at the large view screen. The image of the ship's aft filled the view, along with the Bang Drive compartment, showing several blank circles that represented the nuclear pods. After a few seconds, all ten circles turned blood red. Another moment and the circles began to blink in a steady pulse.

A message in yellow block letters appeared at the top of the screen: IS THIS INPUT CORRECT?

He typed: AFFIRM.

The next block letter message read: ENTER IDENT NAME AND PRIORITY CODE.

ZACHARY CROWE, 5-9-5

ACCEPTED. ARMED FOR REMOTE FREQUENCY DETONATION.

Zaz taped some paper over the access hole he'd just broken. He leaned back in the small chair, his heart hammering in his chest. The cool bridge air did nothing to relieve the heat upon his face. There was no moral justification for what he'd just done; he was now the choreographer of their own new disaster.

There came a frantic tapping at the bridge hatch. He stuffed the small notebook in his vest pocket and turned the view screen off. "Be right there," he said, backhanding the sweat from his face before opening the door.

Dendy stood at the open hatch with hands on hips, head cocked. "I've been looking all over for you," she said. "You didn't answer your com." She looked around his shoulder. "How come you locked yourself up in here?"

"I was just going over some final calculations. I needed to be alone with a clear head." He gave her a quick kiss, ushering her back into the corridor. "How's the packing going?"

"Carybell and I are just about finished. We have the foodstuffs to load yet. But I came to ask you about, well… where do you need the fish?"

"On either side of the hatch opening where they can be sniffed out. I'm really sorry, honey, I know how you feel about them."

Her lip quivered. "I won't say that it's not going to hurt. You know how I am with animals." She paused. "Zaz, I'm not going to lay them out to suffocate. I'll poison the tank then haul them down."

"That's probably best." They headed for Carl's room together, holding hands. He hoped she couldn't read the tension in his grip.

I'm a fine mess. Chalk this up as the first major breach of trust with the woman I love.

When Zaz entered Carl's quarters, he found him sitting up in bed with his leg elevated. He had his nose in a graphic magazine titled *Women of the Great White North*. The cover featured a nude woman making snow angels on the side of a glacier bank.

"Well, I can see that you're feeling better." Zaz narrowed an eye.

Carl ditched the magazine and gave him one of those 'I was just reading the articles' looks. "Actually," he said "I was just about to hobble down to see if I could help out. I feel about as useless as tits on a walrus."

Dendy eyed the corner of the magazine sticking out from under the mattress. "Tits, eh?"

Zaz looked at his leg. "We're going to move you out and get you settled in the six-wheeler. I thought you might need a little help getting down."

"I can walk a little, just poorly. Besides, Sammy is going to help me get down to the vehicle."

Zaz smiled. "You're in good hands then."

Carl managed a sly wink. "Now, who's going to walk the hull and set off the charges? I can be there, you know, to serve as the tech advisor. By the way, tell the shrimp she can keep the pistol. I hear she's a better shot than I am."

"Not necessary. I want you to rehab, starting now. Galoot and I will handle everything. You've done a hell of a lot already. I'm going to need you later.

Zaz left the room and continued down the corridor. Dendy shadowed his steps. When he got to the freight elevator, he stopped. Only three large bundles remained to be loaded. He looked past the bundles down the other corridor – the one that led to the emergency roof hatch.

Dendy could read his mind. "I can get these down. It's nearly time for you to go up. Galoot fixed an electrical short in the roof top camera eye, so we'll be watching you from the bridge." She shivered for an instant then hugged his neck. "I don't think I could bear it if something happened to you. Please, please be careful."

"I'm not going anywhere, Tiny Dancer, unless it's with you." He tried to think if he had missed anything in the plan – something left out that could foil their escape. One mistake and they would all pay for it. Then it came to him: once again, the distant voices of Paddy and Lyle spoke in his mind and he remembered what they had said about the Jack Lions.

"Dendy, you know that these creatures have got a real good sense of smell. They could eventually track us down if we don't throw them off somehow. Can we use something from the science lab or hydro to cover our trail?"

"My great grandmother used to say, if you want to throw a bloodhound off the scent you have to give him a nasty nose. I've got about thirty pounds of ground up cayenne and chili peppers in the galley. Heck, I've been using it to season your food for the past two years. All we have to do is sprinkle it behind our trailing vehicle – that will have to be the six-wheeler. I don't care how super-special those things are, there isn't an animal alive that would follow a scent like that."

"That's perfect. You're a lot smarter than Sammy."

"Aw, get off it. Sammy's got boobs *and* brains. I've got neither."

He gave her a passionate kiss then held her at arm's length. "You've got the whole package, plus heart." He left her standing there, looking over his shoulder once before hurrying his pace.

When he got to the emergency hatch, Samantha was guiding the last of the five-gallon cans up the ladder. Galoot pulled them up to the roof on a zip line. A hot draft of outside air funneled down through the opening. Samantha rained sweat from every pore of her body; she turned to Zaz as he stepped closer, gazing up the ladder shaft.

"That's the last can, Cap'n," she said. "Galoot has them stacked up there. All you have to do is shoulder a bag of charges and head on up. I'm going to help Carl get to a vehicle then head straight to the bridge. You just need to give me a call when you want me to start the engines. Is there anything else?"

"Just take care of Carl. Make sure he's tucked in with a lot of padding. Once we bust out of here it's going to be a rough, full-throttle ride with no slowing down. There won't be any need for me to revisit the bridge, so I'll meet you all at the vehicles. Make sure you're lined up and ready to go."

She gave him a bone-crushing hug. "Good luck, Zaz. See you below."

He felt for the remote detonator in his pocket, making sure he hadn't forgotten it. He slung a charge pack over his shoulder, stepped into a pair of magna-boots and headed up the ladder. Galoot's anxious face gazed down at him; a dribble of sweat plopped on Zaz's forehead.

"Sorry, boss!"

Zaz pulled himself up through the opening, catching his hip on a protruding piece of metal, where Galoot had widened the opening. Up top, the area around the makeshift crows' nest was crowded with fuel cans. They were loosely tied together so they wouldn't plummet off the hull. Once again, the stifling heat and stink of Sidus hit him full force. He realized with some dread that very soon he and his crew would have to acclimate to the intense heat or perish from it. That meant they had to make it to the gorge alive.

Galoot stood still like a stone pillar, hanging on to a support bar with one hand. The sweat poured down his face, his skin doubly burned by the sun. He had worked incredibly hard to get them ready for the assault. It hadn't been easy, what with his additional bulk and the injuries he'd sustained. Zaz gave him a look of admiration, telling him how proud he was of his behavior. Galoot smiled timidly.

Far below, the Jack Lions sounded their fury. A new vigor came over them once they spotted the two humans moving about on top of the ship.

Galoot waved his hands over the fuel cans. "They're all ready and topped off, boss. We just have to place them." Like Zaz, the giant had donned magna-boots; he was ready to go.

Zaz lifted two cans then headed toward the aft part of the ship, taking careful, measured steps. Galoot ran a long bar through the handle straps of four cans and, balancing them on his shoulder, followed Zaz down the roofline. Zaz stopped at the approximate location of the first placement and took the paper map out of his pocket. He stared at the sketch, counting the seams in the hull. The slight protruding lump on the port side indicated the location of the jet nozzle. He placed one can on its side and gave it a shove. It slid down the hull and landed amongst a mass of snarling Jacks. He noted with glee as it smacked one of the creatures in the face, knocking it senseless.

And there's a lot more where that came from, Zaz cursed silently, tossing a charge down after the fuel can. He did the same on the starboard side of the hull. They trekked on, the small map clenched between Zaz's teeth, until they arrived at the next drop-off spot – two cans, which Galoot supplied.

It took them an hour to reach the stern of the ship, where they placed the last of the cans and charges. Samantha and Dendy spoke to them over the com, watching their progress.

"Now watch your pace," Dendy kept saying. "Don't get too close to the edge."

It was a long trudge back, even without the load of the fuel cans. Zaz's thighs burned with a persistent ache – the magna-boots pulled hard, making it difficult to disengage his feet from the hull. The cooling devices had lost their effectiveness; he felt as if he'd lost two quarts of water with just that one trip.

When they arrived at the crow's-nest, they loaded up again, this time headed for the prow. Zaz's com buzzed again.

"You need to take a break, said Samantha. "You don't look so good."

"Nonsense. It's a stroll in the park. Just sit tight – six more to go."

"Slow yourself, then." She cleared her voice nervously. "Did you know that the override panel to the Bang Drive was – "

"I know all about it."

"Zaz, are you out of your mind? Do you realize what you've done?"

"I'm not out of my mind, yet. That's why I did it."

"Did what, for gawd's sakes?" asked Carl, listening in.

"This isn't Zaz. This is Captain Crowe. Shut up and keep this channel clear."

"Awe, shit," Samantha swore.

Zaz ignored it. Dendy was on the bridge – she probably knew what was going on. He had no mind to confess to anything right now. It was his ship – his decision. Thankfully, Galoot had kept quiet, whether he understood the subtlety of the message or not.

Before they reached the nose of the ship to drop the last two cans, Zaz dismissed Galoot.

"Make sure you hitch up that pull wire to the hatch and the front bumper of the six-wheeler, just like we rehearsed, big fella. Remember, the truck is the lead vehicle. I'll call when it's time to brace for the shock."

Galoot gave him a snappy salute. The giant walked back to the emergency hatch, wavering from side to side as he moved.

Zaz pressed on with the last two cans, the weight pulling his shoulders down into his chest. He stopped several times to unburden the load, then resumed. He felt faint and decided to pop a stim tab – a final burst of energy was needed for the last drop.

Keeping his vision concentrated on his every step, he could see the Jacks from the corners of his eyes, jumping wildly against the hull and scratching to get at him. He made the last two drops and turned around, but found it hard to stay balanced. Everything swam around him in a dizzying blur. His guts churned – he felt like throwing up. Heatstroke.

"Have a swig of water *now!*" Samantha coached him over the com. "Just take it nice and easy-does-it, We're in no hurry."

Water. He obeyed, pulling the small clip-on canteen from his belt. He took several large gulps. It cleared his mind and he continued on, throwing one foot out in front of the other until he reached the hatch.

Zaz kicked off the heavy magna-boots, preferring to descend the ladder in his socks. When he reached the ladder base, he stepped into deck shoes and took several deep breaths. He did not need to pass out now!

"Brace for impact," he said into his wrist-com. He held his thumb over the remote detonator button. "Five...four...three... two...one – ignition!"

The ship rocked as multiple explosions shook the ground around them. He swayed with each violent jolt, his grip on the ladder rung keeping him on his feet. Thunder claps rang the hull like a giant bronze bell.

"Sammy, hit the jets and bring up the thrust."

"I've got ignition – raising thrust now."

There was a steady vibration under his feet. The bulkhead walls shivered. He could hear the faint sounds of loose gear and objects falling from their perches, bouncing and clattering on the deck.

A heavier vibration followed – more of a shaking, like a small earthquake. The bulkhead struts groaned; the *Shenandoah* cried out.

"Steady, girl," he said to the ship, patting the hull.

Samantha said, "I'm advancing to eighty-five percent thrust pressure, Zaz, but I'm reading a high temp climb. Okay, it's leveling off now, but we're still in the high orange zone."

"Take it up another five percent; keep it just under critical."

"Let her go there, babe," said Galoot, breaking in on the conversation. "She'll take it."

Zaz felt the ship rock under him, then lift up momentarily before slamming back down.

"Peg it – lock it down there!" Zaz yelled. "Acknowledge."

"That's affirm – she's maxed. See you below."

Zaz broke away from the ladder, wobbling on unsteady feet. The ship heaved under him with the sound of shearing metal. It felt as if the old gal wanted to lift off, but a giant was holding her firmly in its hands – two forces locked together in a power struggle. The hope was that neither of them would win out – the ship had to remain stable.

He trotted wearily to the freight elevator, hopping in and pressing the down button. The cage shuddered for a second then started to move. It jammed suddenly, screeching to a halt. He punched the button several times, but only managed to produce a sickening buzz. Something snapped with an electronic flash. The ship's massive superstructure bucked again.

"Damn you – not now!" He looked over the rail. It was a 15-foot drop to the deck. He pitched his helmet over the side then threw his legs over the rail. Lowering himself hand over hand, he hung onto the bottom of the elavator floor and let go. He hit hard but managed to roll. He grabbed his helmet and hobbled to the six-wheeler. The crew was already on board, braced and ready.

Licks of fire and smoke streamed through the gaping seams of the hatch door. The tortured howls of the burning Jack Lions came through the cracks.

He took the controls of the six-wheeler. "Helmets on – heads down." He watched Galoot back the big truck up with a hard lurch. The bumper line grew taught. The large hatch swung open from the bottom and revealed a scene straight out of hell – a column of black smoke swirled up inside; with it came a rush of super-heated air and a violent stench of death.

Looking through the dust, smoke and fire, Zaz saw a stack of flaming corpses piled five-high at the hatch entrance. Dozens of animals, charred to the bone and blistered, hobbled over the carnage. They moved like zombies, unaware that their nervous systems were gone – that they were dead on their feet.

Zaz shouted into his com: "Make us a hole, Galoot!"

CHAPTER FOURTEEN

A NEW BEGINNING

THE HUGE TOW TRUCK lurched forward, picking up speed as it moved. The towline snapped. The lead truck rammed through the fiery mass, its huge bumper blades cutting a swath through a dozen advancing Jacks, clipping them at the knees. Bones cracked under the ponderous weight of the vehicle as it slammed through the mass of flesh and sinew.

Zaz stomped on the accelerator, aiming straight for the hatch opening. He hit a curtain of smoke as thick as a concrete wall. The front of the six-wheeler struck a pile of corpses and heaved upward. Carl yelped as it slammed down again. Zaz fought the wheel as the vehicle bucked wildly. The wheels spun over the flesh-smeared ramp until gaining traction on the solid earth.

He could barely see past the choking soot-smog, the heat searing the back of his exposed neck. The truck bounced wildly, the six-wheeler crushing everything in its path. Galoot swerved hard to the right as the smoke began to dissipate in wispy patches. Zaz followed close behind, tracking the truck's path, nearly on its rear bumper. Galoot continued running interference, mowing down anything in their way. Jacks were flattened under the heavy onrush of the truck, some struck so hard they flew up and over the cab.

Thousands of the Jack Lions had retreated from the intense heat, gathering in a secondary line away from the ship. It was impossible to avoid hitting the dead and dying creatures that occupied the compound. They could only hope that the massive horde would hold back in fear.

Samantha spread her body over Carl, sheltering him. He gasped for air from a small breathing hole in the blankets that covered him. Hitting some of the charging creatures proved unavoidable; Zaz hoped that Carl's wound would not tear open with the impacts.

Dendy fired the rifle from the passenger seat. She tried to pick off the Jack Lions in pursuit of the vehicle. Many of her shots went wild due to the roughness of their trek. She quickly emptied the gun, finding it impossible to reload with all the radical swerving. She picked up a blade, prepared to hack at anything that got too close. A huge sack of pepper mulch was at her feet.

They headed north, toward a broken down section of the compound's wall. The Jacks were spread thinly; some rallied in groups, while others ran around aimlessly. Galoot pushed into the lead, swerving occasionally to run down any animals that happened to be too close to the convoy's path.

They slowed down as they approached the crumbled breach in the wall, searching for an easy way around the mess. Galoot lined the truck up and then ploughed through the least crowded section, clearing a path. A corner of the retaining wall toppled in foam chunks at the sudden impact, leaving a ragged hole through which to pass.

"This bottleneck is the best place to spread the hot stuff," said Zaz. "Lay it down from here on out."

Dendy donned a pair of gloves and started tossing handfuls of the pepper mulch into the air, making sure it spread out in a large fan behind them. Nothing followed them out past the wall. Zaz chanced a look back but could not make out the ship through the rolling mass of dust and smoke. It looked like a war zone – even the stench of it had trailed in their wake. He hoped that nothing alive would gain its senses and come after them.

"How's Carl?" Zaz yelled over his shoulder.

Samantha sat up. "I gave him extra painkillers. Thankfully, he's out of it. She twisted in her seat. "Dendy, pass me some of that trail killer and the gloves – I can throw some off the back."

Dendy passed a small bag over the seat. Samantha began flinging the ground pepper over her shoulder. With no wind on the desert plain, the granules would remain where they were thrown. What irony, thought Zaz. If he ever got back to civilization, how would he explain that he had escaped the clutches of the most vicious creatures he'd ever known by throwing seasoning at them? It almost made him laugh out loud.

Galoot's voice came over the com. "It looks like we gave 'em the slip. Are you okay back there, boss?"

"Yeah, we're tight and right behind. Any closer and I'd scrape your rear. Let it out a little more."

"Gotcha, taking it up to seventy."

Zaz noticed Dendy rubbing her eyes, hissing through her teeth. He unhooked his canteen and passed it to her. "Don't rub it – you'll make it worse. Flush it out with water."

"I should have known better!" she gasped "Never throw hot pepper against the wind." She tilted her head back, splashing copious amounts of water in her face. She blinked several times, biting down hard against the pain. It took awhile for her to recover. "That's better," she said at last, gazing back at him with red-rimmed eyes.

The glint of metal off to the left caught Zaz's attention. As he got closer to the object, he could clearly see it was one of their automechs, treading across the sand.

"Galoot, we've got a stray machine at our eleven o'clock," said Zaz.

"Yeah, just saw it now. Want me to pull over?"

"Affirmative."

Galoot did one better and pulled ahead of the automech, blocking its path. Zaz pulled up next to it and looked the automech over. Its body was dented and scratched, splashed with what looked like dried blood. It had a flap of a bloody Jack Lion pelt on its head that looked like a bad toupee. Most shockingly, he recognized the call numbers on it. *Silver Two* – one of the original perimeter sentries that had failed to detonate.

Finding its way blocked, but in the presence of humans, the Silver automech inquired, "How may I be of service, sir?"

"How did you get out here, Silver Two," asked Zaz.

The machine swiveled around. "I have no memory of it. I have been displaced from my work station."

Zaz shook his head. "Leave it – it's defective. Remove the bomb pack and deactivate him, Galoot."

"Aye, Cap'n."

"Oh, you can't leave him out here!" Dendy protested. "He's circuit board-shocked. If we fix him, he might come in handy."

"For what" asked Zaz, "as a waffle iron?" He looked at Dendy's imploring eyes and his heart softened. "Okay. Galoot, stuff him in our rear compartment, quickly."

Galoot stripped the bomb pack off of the automech and tossed it into his truck. Then he carried Silver Two to the back of Zaz's vehicle and poked him headfirst down between the rear seat and floorboard next to Samantha. The automech's legs protruded vertically out of the vehicle. "My attitude gyro indicates an inverted position," said Silver Two. "A one-hundred and eighty degree rotation will remedy the situation."

Miffed, Zaz said, "Shut him off Sammy," and stepped on the accelerator pedal.

As the miles disappeared behind them, Zaz stressed over three things: first, he had no idea what condition the gorge was in – whether it had flooded from the ice melt, contaminating the water supply and laying waste to the nut and fruit trees. There was a small water treatment system onboard, so they could make due with even the filthiest water if necessary. They had at least six to eight months of preserved foodstuffs packed in the vehicles; it would remain edible unless spoiled from some unknown bacterial attack.

His second thought concerned his ship, which had been left behind. He would never see her again, of that he was certain of. They'd abandoned he as a trashed hulk, left to rot in the hellish desert environment of Georgian Sidus.

The third concern was something he'd pushed even further from his mind – the loss of Lyle and Paddy. Truly, the memory of them negated any thoughts he had about abandoned ships, bad water, or having nothing to eat. He wished he could turn back the clock – just to see their silly, dirty faces again, to hear their eccentric rants, to listen to their boring dissertations.

After five hours of nonstop travel, Dendy grew restless in her seat. She'd been watching Zaz' face for the past hour. He knew she had something on her mind, something she was yet to come to terms with, or struggled to find the courage to express. That wasn't at all like her. He also felt Samantha's eyes searing through the back of his head; even more than Samantha's stare, Dendy's gave him the jitters. He knew their thoughts, and would have to deal with them eventually. Now seemed as good a time as any.

He made sure his wrist-com was off before speaking. "I know what you're both thinking. I gave the matter a lot of thought before I committed to it. I don't have to tell you that the decision was final – it can't be undone. It's the only way to keep us from harm. I'm sorry if you have any reservations about it."

Dendy spoke above the hum and the rush of wind. "I thought that you might have at least discussed it with us, Zaz. I want them wiped off this planet just like anybody else, but do you know what the environmental consequences might be for what you're preparing to do?"

"To fry some eggs you have to bust a couple of shells," he said.

Samantha leaned over the seat. "We're not talking about eggs, Zachary Crowe. We're talking about a nuclear detonation on a young planet that might not recover from it. The radioactive afterlife is what concerns me – we're talking about a dead zone, for God knows how long. Forty or fifty years? With no wind or rain erosion, not a speck of weather out there to dissipate the radioactivity?"

"That's precisely why I did it. It will be localized – no wind currents to carry it. I doubt if there's a water table under that desert to soak anything up." He didn't know that for certain.

"The indigenous wildlife," Dendy began, "especially the birds that wander into that area, will be compromised. Their reproductive functions will be altered. They'll carry those mutations back to their cubbyholes and roosts, transmitting the deformed genes. It could start a chain reaction that could get completely out of control."

"I think you're selling this planet short," he said. "It's a lot more resilient than you think. Do you have any idea how many devices were set off on Earth in the Twentieth Century? Those creatures are killers. They are never going to go away. If they figure it out and get wind of us, they'll give chase. I want to strike while the iron is hot. There won't be another chance to take them out. Ever."

Samantha slapped the seat top. "Have you even tabulated a blast radius? Will we be in a safe zone? Will we suffer the fallout? Damn it, Zaz, how much thought did you give this?"

Dendy seemed equally galvanized in protest. "I love you with all my heart, Zachary, but I want to go on record as protesting this decision. Why can't we just climb away from them like you said?"

"Because I'm not going to get chased up a tree like some helpless pest. I won't give these things one inch – one centimeter – to make any gains on me. That's the end of it!"

Zaz might have seemed harsh. He might have seemed sadistic. But it was his ship and his decision to make. Damn the environment and the consequences; he'd already lost two souls – he wasn't about to lose six more to some idiotic, compassionate requiem for a planet that had every intention of wiping him and his crew from existence. He flicked his com back on.

They slowed the vehicles upon reaching the lowlands as they had done before. Dendy and Samantha threw out more of the trail killer as the path narrowed into the vast valley floor. Zaz drove perpendicular to the opening several times, covering as much of their escape route as possible and allowing Dendy ample opportunity to spread more of the pepper.

As they drove in through the valley mouth, Zaz was surprised to see that the landscape had been unaffected by any flood-like cataclysm. The small trees were upright; grasses waved in a mild breeze. In the distance, a lone volcano spewed a thin ribbon of black smoke into the air and curled off to the east. A few of the armadillo creatures skittered about. Some of the four-winged birds even circled overhead, seemingly oblivious to any past calamity.

They soon came upon the wetland fan, with its tiny trickle of water. Nothing had changed. If there had been a flood, it must have happened further up north. Either that or the flood had been channeled off by some unseen side canyons. It was a relief to see that nothing had been killed or destroyed.

Dendy and Samantha sat rigid in their seats, inconsolable. Carl was lost to painkiller-fueled dreams. For all the companionship around him, Zaz could have been alone in the vehicle. He suspected the icy treatment would continue for some time. *My ship, my decision, our lives – to hell with it!*

Galoot easily found the worn path and fought to keep the heavily laden truck from getting bogged down. Zaz kept the six-wheeler as close to the truck's rear bumper as he could, trying to keep the tires in line and following the packed soil.

When they reached their old campsite next to the rock slide, they parked the vehicles on the south side of the perimeter, leaving the open ground for the supply tents. The area was just as they had left it – pristine and tranquil. Even their footprints remained visible on the ground.

Fatigue had claimed the crew; they went about their chores of unpacking and rigging the shelters with a dazed, zombie-like countenance. The stim tabs had worn off, and Zaz dragged his body around with elephantine steps. He felt like he had been awake for a week, then clobbered over the head with an ore freighter.

Galoot looked especially unsteady on his feet; he lumbered more than he walked, his hand clutching the lower part of his stomach. He managed to set up two tripod-mounted cannons pointing down the gorge toward the entrance. Zaz made a mental note to have Dendy check his wound. Galoot finally collapsed on the sand with an arm over his eyes. Zaz didn't have the heart to rouse him, especially when he saw Carybell curl up next to him, like a kitten snuggling up against its mother.

Dendy and Samantha took up residence in one of the tents and pulled the flap down. It was only yesterday that he held the title of the esteemed Captain Zachary Crowe of the Planet Janitor Corporation. Today he was a *planet killer.*

Oh, fuck 'em all, he thought, taking another stim tab and wondering if he could stay awake for a guard shift. He unhooked the water trailer then slumped to the sand. He didn't have the energy to program the Silver for sentry duty – especially since its operational program was defective. The shadows of the cliff face crawled over him as the first stars appeared over the horizon. They were unusually bright. He put the rifle on his lap and glanced down into the gorge, his vision beginning to blur. The countless days of fatigue and stress finally jumped him like a strong-armed robber. He fell back on the sand in a dead sleep.

```
Sidus Log, Rotation 29.
I woke up this morning with a terrible headache, not
knowing where I was. Then I remembered that I was
in the gorge - we had come here after escaping the
ship. I found myself outside, shivering in the sand.
At least someone had the courtesy to cover me with a
blanket. I hope it was Dendy.

   It's become obvious that my ultimate decision to
bring about the total destruction of my ship and those
accursed creatures has been met with resistance. The
only two crewmembers that know about my plan are
not speaking to me. I don't think Carl caught the
conversation, having been unconscious on the ride out
here. They claim that I possess a doomsday weapon that
could upset the balance of the entire planet. I can't
predict what will happen if I should carry out my plan.
No, I did not give preemptive thought or concern to the
matter. I acted on survival instinct. Ours. If that's
selfish, well, let 'em get the hanging rope.

   I wonder if I have been a failure in everything I've
tried to accomplish. My fear is that I've lost the
companionship and trust of my crew. Maybe even the
love and trust of Dendy. If we should go our separate
ways, then we will surely perish one by one. We can
only succeed if we hold out together, since that is
where our true strength lies.

                              Zachary Crowe, PJ.
```

Zaz tucked his log back into his pocket and stood up, brushing the sand from his pants. The morning sun had already cast shadows in the deep gorge. Two of the Microraptors fought over a seed bundle nearby. The camp was quiet and very cold, much like the way Zaz was feeling, only with a dollop of loneliness thrown in to make matters worse.

He walked over the land spill in the rear of the camp – taking a hike would get his engines fired up. When he reached the bottom of the other side, he turned and headed in the direction of the creek. It was funny, but he hadn't really appreciated the grass, plants and trees of the valley before. Everything around him seemed precious now, knowing full well that his life might depend upon the resources. He came upon the gurgle of water. He decided to walk north, following the creek bed. He reached out to touch some of the petals and leaves, gently caressing them. He felt like such an idiot. *Planet killer.*

He stopped at a plant that looked like a giant clump of broccoli and snapped a piece off, studying it. He wondered if the Paddymous giants had eaten these plants and others like them. It was likely the whole valley had safe things to eat, given the many varieties of plants and shrubs that were about. Certainly the Paddymous had survived on the pickings. Even the soil looked fertile, likely capable of nurturing the seeds they brought with them. Maybe the Paddymous had eaten the algae and lichen on the creek rocks. The resources were vast if one knew where to look and how to use them. As he walked, he thought back fondly to his days as a boy scout.

He recalled an age-old ritual from the Boy Scouts called "The Order of the Arrow," and how initiates were stripped to a loincloth and given a knife to survive for three days out in the wilderness. It was another rank of privilege that he desperately sought, to prove to himself; that he had the stamina and wits to survive in the wild. He remembered shivering half to death the first night, then waking hungry and thirsty the next morning. He found dewdrops to lick, but his main concern was something to eat. He'd tried to set traps with twigs, but caught nothing other than more hunger and desperation. The second day went like the first: he found a sluggish creek, caught a dozen minnows and some tadpoles that made him gag when he ate them. Later on, he tried some roots and bark, but broke a tooth on a piece. He threw a fit that day, cursing every plant he came across as if unable to understand why the forest wasn't just some big supermarket.

At the beginning of his third and final day in the wilderness, Zaz resorted to covering himself with leaves to ward off the chill of night. When he woke, he was reduced to eating some potato bugs and one small king snake. He filled the empty cavern of his belly with water and then slept to ward off the pain. They finally came for him, using a locator device that he wore around his wrist to track him down. He wasn't any worse for wear other than having dropped five pounds in body weight, but he had acquired a new respect for living in the wild. Though he'd made the Order of the Arrow, he still felt like he was a terrible survivalist.

He followed the creek bed with no particular destination in mind. He had a sudden urge to urinate and turned away from the creek to find a bald spot on the sand. He finished quickly then stepped around a large brambly bush, freezing as he caught sight of movement. He could hear the sound of a stone hitting a piece of tin. Advancing further with silent footfalls, he discovered what had made the sound.

Squatting on the bank of the creek and filling up a small metal jug was a human. As Zaz stood perfectly still, watching the being, he realized it was not just any human. Paddy. The scientist was shirtless, wearing only a tattered pair of Kaki shorts. But the dirty yellow tam on his head was unmistakable.

Zaz stepped out from behind his cover and moved into view. Preoccupied, Paddy did not notice him until he stood up and turned around. Their eyes met. The silence was thick between them. Paddy neither had a look of surprise nor shock upon his face – if anything, his eyes showed the slightest amount of irritation. An initial flush of relief at seeing Paddy alive and breathing was quickly replaced by another emotion: anger. Zaz had no intention of breaking the silence, feeling more than a little outraged at the sight of his crewmember and friend. He had never wanted to punch somebody as much as he did this man – this runaway, who had given him nothing but nightmarish grief. And in the name of all that was holy and decent, what was the professor doing in this area – the area they'd searched from one end of the canyon to the other?

Paddy slipped the lid back on the jug and wiped a few sand grains from around the rim. "So, you've found us," he said. "Now what? I suppose you will drag us back to the ship then give us a spot on thrashing about how bloody awful we were to abandon you."

Zaz felt his blood pounding in his temple. He didn't know quite what to say. "You said 'we' – am I to assume that Lyle is alive?"

"He is."

Zaz fought to calm himself. Under the circumstances, it was like trying to understand a Jack Lion – impossible. He stepped a few feet closer. "Where have you been?"

Paddy's gaze fell to the ground, then up again to look Zaz right the eyes. "Right here."

"You mean you've been here all this time? Were you aware that we were in this area, combing the countryside for the both of you? And you didn't answer our calls? Is that what you are saying, Paddy?"

"We heard you. You were here for two days before leaving abruptly. We assumed the earthquake panicked you."

Zaz looked around, turning in a slow circle before bringing his eyes back to Paddy. "I don't see a campsite, supplies, or even the vehicle that you, to put it mildly, 'commandeered'. What were you expecting to do, Paddy? Live off the land like a couple of eccentric hermits and kiss off humanity? Which is us, by the way, since there are no other souls on this God forsaken planet that got so unceremoniously dumped."

Paddy cocked his head. "What kind of humanity are we talking about? The one that you and your shipboard mates provide? We *had* to answer to a higher calling. One that had no fine lines or protocols to restrict us."

"That's right, I'm a real heartless case. I only care about the welfare and survival of my crew – the people who signed on with me and agreed to a contract with certain bylaws and conditions. I have no conscious empathy for my fellow man, either. I don't fret or become heartbroken over the disappearance or possible death of my friends. No, none of that affects me. Nor does it, Galoot, Dendy, Sammy, Carybell, and Carl. You know what gets me, Paddy? I catch you out here red-handed, tucked away in this brush, deliberately hiding from us. You let us go through the agony of your loss, and you have no legitimate excuse for it."

"Then I can only offer our most heartfelt regrets. We did not mean to cause you any pain."

"I think you're incapable of feeling regret. You and your academic lust just about got us killed back there. We could have used you in the struggle. But I don't suppose that matters much."

"I knew nothing about a struggle." Paddy shuffled uneasily, his facade cracking in increments.

"You're not sorry about anything. I'm tempted to let you rot out here."

"Then why don't you go back to the ship and leave us in peace?"

"There is no ship. We were overrun and had to leave her. Where is Lyle, anyway? I don't care so much that you're speaking for him. I'd rather he talked to me face to face about this whole matter."

"I can assure you that he feels like-minded, primarily on account of Carl's insults. We have no ill feelings about the rest of you. But none of that prompted the reason for our departure. Do you plan on staying for long?"

Zaz folded his arms across his chest. "Last time I checked there was no emperor of this valley to draw lines or enforce boundaries. Unless, of course, you plan on staking a claim here and keeping us out by force."

Paddy's expression softened further. "Then I believe that we are to become neighbors, if you'll have us. And there are no landowners or emperors here, as you declared."

"Why, Paddy? What drove you to this?"

"Like I said, you wouldn't understand. I haven't the time to give you an explanation."

Zaz looked around again quickly. "I'm not going to stand here and argue with you. What have you done with the scout car? I want it back."

Paddy wiped his face with the tam. "You'll find it sunk in the large watering hole next to your camp. I don't know if it will be salvageable."

"You ditched the scout in the pool?" That's why they couldn't find it, though it had been right under their noses. "Then you had no intention of ever coming back. I see. I don't know what it was that we did to earn your disapproval. For now, I would appreciate it if you would call out to Lyle or take me to him."

"I will take you to where we live. Our home is a bit crowded, so I hope you won't mind."

Zaz didn't know whether to believe him or not. "All right. I have to get back to the others. They might have wondered what happened to me. You may not play by those rules, but I do. I'll be right back. Where will you be?"

Paddy placed the jug on the ground. He sat down next to it. "Right here."

"No tricks – no ghostly vanishings?"

"You have my word."

Zaz turned on his heels and strode toward the campsite. *You have my word. Higher callings. I wouldn't understand.* It was damned nonsense. Paddy and Lyle had received a bout of sunstroke or lost their minds; or they'd been daft from the very beginning. Why hadn't he screened them more thoroughly when they applied to Planet Janitor? Had it started there? Or had it been something progressive and neurological that affected them?

It was only 500 feet back to the land spill. By the time he hobbled over it, his thoughts were so dazed he couldn't decide how he was going to explain any of it to his crew. Would they understand?

When he reached camp, he went straight for the six-wheeler and pulled a pack out of the rear compartment. He pulled out and uncapped a bottle of aspirin, taking several tablets, hoping it would numb the headache.

Galoot, who was busy unloading supplies from the truck, stopped what he was doing and walked to where Zaz stood. "What's up, boss? Where you been? I was just about to go – "

Zaz shook his head, chopping off the words. He walked into the pool, all the way up to his chest. He reached down, waving his hands underwater.

"Boss?"

Dendy and Samantha popped out of their tent, looking in Galoot's direction. Carybell burst out of her tent, brandishing the pistol in her good hand.

Zaz struck something hard underwater with his hand – it was the framework of the scout car. He marched back up onto the bank, soaking wet and looking like a wild man.

He took a deep breath and spat it out for all to hear: "I found Paddy and Lyle. They're about fifty yards up the draw."

Dendy looked at him. Her eyes began to mist over. "Oh, dear, God. No!"

Samantha burst into tears and fell to her knees in the sand.

"Aw crap!" said Galoot. "Those poor little bastards."

"They're *alive*, damn it!" shouted Zaz. "I was just talking to Paddy. If you could call it talking."

He took a few minutes to explain his meeting with Paddy and why he'd searched the pool.

"Those little sons of bitches!" said Galoot.

"What's going on out there?" Carl shouted, followed by a crash coming from his tent.

When everyone had settled down, Zaz called them into a tight circle. "We've been invited to visit their home, or camp, or whatever it is. Paddy spoke about some kind of a higher calling. So I think it's best if we humor them and try to understand." He looked at the women. "I think a female touch is needed here. Any volunteers?"

Samantha nodded. "I'll give it go. I'll have to tell Carl what's going on – he can't make the trip."

"Do that now."

"I think I can pull the scout car from the water and dry it out," said Galoot. "Most of the systems are sealed, so I might be able to get her running again."

"What I don't understand," said Dendy, "is Paddy's attitude. Why would he be so indifferent? I mean, seriously, what have we done to hurt them? What kind of an insane tangent are they on this time? Are they dangerous?"

Zaz thought about that for a moment. "If eccentricity and babbling means danger, well, then, yeah. I mean, no. I mean… I don't know anymore about this than you do. We're about to find out."

"I want to go too!" said Carybell.

Zaz gave the small girl a nod.

When Samantha returned, Zaz took off heading for the last place he saw Paddy. Galoot, Samantha, Carybell, and Dendy walked in silence, not knowing what to say to one another. Dendy held on to Zaz's hand, glancing at him with softer eyes than she had the day before. At least he hadn't cornered the market for hatred. There was a moment when he had had his doubts. He hoped Samantha had also forgiven him in some small measure – he could use the positve reinforcement.

They found Paddy sitting in the sand with his knees drawn up and head down, nearly dozing off. The scientist gave a spastic jerk upon their arrival. He favored them with a halfhearted smile as he got to his feet.

Acting as the spokesperson for the crew, Samantha took a step forward. She refrained from hugging Paddy, although Zaz could clearly see that she wanted to embrace him.

"Hello, Paddy. I hope you're well. We missed you very much. Dendy and I cried for days, wondering what had happened. I want you to know that you are very much loved."

Paddy gave her a curt bow and doffed his hat. "I thank you for your profound concern. Lyle and I want for nothing other than our investigation. I imagine you are eager to meet with the more congenial of the two of us?"

Samantha smiled. "That would be wonderful."

"This way." Paddy picked up his jug then walked south, retracing the steps that Zaz had taken to find him.

But that was all wrong. How could he be walking back toward the camp? How could they have been that close to them without knowing it?

Paddy walked toward the cliff, slinging the water jug over his back. He reached a slide area in a boulder field and hefted himself up onto one of the giant rocks. From there he hopped to another rounded boulder, then another, until arriving at the cliff face. He then turned his back against the wall and sidestepped over a narrow rock ledge.

It was at that point that Zaz looked up at the cliff face. He could see a dark cleft in the rock. It was not unlike a typical cave opening, similar to what he had explored before, only 75 feet off the ground and nearly inaccessible. One had to look at just the right angle to see the opening. He estimated it couldn't have been anymore than 400 feet from their camp.

Zaz followed the route up. When he got to the narrow ledge, he slid his back against the wall, holding hands with Dendy and Galoot. Samantha brought up the rear. Galoot had a hard time with the maneuver, owed to the narrowness of the ledge. They soon found themselves sidestepping around a bend, where a small promontory afforded them a platform to stand on. A pyramidal crack in the rock that had been widened served as the opening to an interior expanse.

Paddy halted just before the black chasm and turned around. He looked at each member of the crew with a grave expression. "I don't expect you all to understand. However, be forewarned. Do not make any sudden moves and do exactly as I tell you. Any transgression and I will ask you to vacate our home. Are we agreed?"

Zaz had to cap his temper again. *Who is giving the orders now?*

Samantha nudged her captain and said, "Agreed, lead the way, dear."

Paddy un-slung his water jug then stepped into the darkness. The crewmembers followed, Zaz taking up the rear, holding Dendy out in front of him by the tops of her shoulders. It was insufferably dark, save some glowing red balls of light that turned out to be a large stack of volcanic rocks and burning wood in a fire ring. Zaz blinked against the darkness, waiting for his eyes to adjust. He nudged up against a wall of human flesh, realizing that his crewmembers had bunched up in front of him.

"Oh, dear Lord," said a female voice. It sounded like Samantha.

Zaz pushed through the knot of people, looking to the back of the cave. He saw a modern lantern flicker on, illuminating the interior. The person who'd turned the lantern on stood up. It was Lyle, looking tattered and worn, though his eyes appeared bright and full of wonder. He looked genuinely pleased to see his companions again. But it was not the sight of Lyle that drew the attention of the crew.

Dozens of Paddymous giants were huddled against the back of the cave, gazing nervously at the human intruders.

"Oh, my," Samantha mumbled under her breath. "I count thirty-five of them, including infants and youngsters."

Dendy clasped hold of Zaz's hand again. He could feel it shaking.

Lyle waved his hand in an introductory sweep. "Ladies and gentlemen, these are the Maximus Paddymous, the true native species of Georgian Sidus. As far as we know, they are the last of their kind. Don't be frightened. They are more frightened of you than you are of them. Trust must be earned. Do not come any further into the cave until I tell you to."

If the Jack Lions were unique, thought Zaz, then the Paddymous giants were extraordinary. The adults were as tall, if not taller than Galoot, but more heavily built. They had a face not unlike that of a cow; only it lacked the extended muzzle. A flabby nose, something resembling an elephant's trunk but only four inches long, hung from the brow of the wide face. The eyes were every bit as large as the Jack Lions, but they were equipped with enormous lashes. The ears drooped, like those of a hound dog. Each hand had four fingers with a very small opposing thumb. The feet were equipped with four toes, each the size of potatoes. They were naked, hairless. Their skin color was like that of a mottled robin's egg. Being mammalian-like, the males were clearly defined from the females – the females possessed multiple teats.

The Paddymous made chortling noises in a range of frequencies. Sometimes their vocalizations were nothing more than garbled coughs and sneezes, occasionally a low-pitched gargling. At one point, Zaz could have sworn he heard a bovine "moo," but he might have been mistaken.

The adult Paddymous had formed a ring around the juveniles, who peeked around rumps and between legs, showing an obvious curiosity toward the humans. One of the females caressed a smaller one with reassuring strokes on her crowned head. The Paddymous did not do anything worrisome upon seeing the new arrivals; there were no barks, growls, snarls or quick movements. The noises they made were somehow soothing – almost singsong in fashion.

"They are so pretty," said Carybell.

Dendy agreed. "What fabulous, exquisite animals. I mean, beings."

Zaz didn't know what to say. He found it hard to believe what he was seeing. Up until now he had only seen their bones. He remembered the portraits he had seen in the very large cavern and some of the other caves – the portraits were accurate representations of the creatures in front of him.

Galoot tried to talk but could only croak. The expression on his face spoke volumes – he no doubt found it hard to believe that there was anything larger than himself that walked upright. The Paddymous seemed especially drawn to him with their curious eyes.

"I don't know why you are all standing around with your mouths agape," said Paddy. "The proper thing to do is to introduce yourselves. It is safe to do so."

Zaz raised an eyebrow. "What are we supposed to do, shake their hands?"

"Don't be a bloody dolt," said Paddy. "Walk up one by one and extend your arm so they may touch it. These beings identify with high skin temperature. It shows you are warm-blooded like they are. They will also sniff you. If they sneeze, it is an approval."

"How do you know all of this?" Samantha asked.

"They taught us," said Lyle. "Oh, and remove those helmets. They need to see your faces; you are out of proportion to Paddy and me."

"Do not go near the younger ones," warned Paddy. "Only the adults."

Samantha bit her lip, stepped forward, extending a hand to a large male. It stood there for a minute and then twisted its wrist to lay the top of its forearm across hers. Then it leaned toward her and sniffed, blowing exhaust out of its nose flap. Instantly the others began chortling in melodious notes.

The crewmembers each took a turn. By the time it came to Zaz's introduction, the Paddymous had relaxed somewhat. When he held his hand out, a female grabbed it and pulled him in closer. In the next moment her large hands were clumsily fingering his hair and pulling strands of it out, which made him grimace. She passed the hairs around for inspection, releasing him after an appreciable sneeze.

As Zaz backed away from the female, her eyes followed him, eyes that seemed soulful and full of inquiry. He sensed a deep tranquil peace in her face, one that was hard to ignore. The emotion of the moment sucked Zaz in, leaving him with a strange calm. It was as though a god had touched him.

Still amazed by the incident, Zaz walked calmly to where Paddy and Lyle had taken seats on a grass mat. The other crewmembers joined him in stunned silence, but they could not refrain from staring over their shoulders at the Paddymous creatures, who had started to break from their defensive knot and wander about the cave's interior. A few of the juvenile Paddymous began playing with toys they'd left on the floor.

Zaz had a dozen questions that screamed for answers. He began with the most obvious. "What are they doing here?" he asked.

"They are surviving," answered Paddy. "Life is resilient. Consider it their due."

Zaz persisted. "We all believed that they had been massacred. How did this group manage to survive?"

"It has everything to do with the physiology of their attackers. I do remember telling you that the Jack Lions were probably incapable of climbing. Well, now that fact has been proven. The ledge that you came up to gain access into this cave proved more than a deterrent to those hellish killers. Apparently, the Jack Lions leave if they cannot catch something. How long their persistence lasts is anyone's guess. It could be days or even weeks. I presume the Paddymous remained here to wait out the siege. Normally their hovels are the caves on the lower levels. In this case, owed to a housing shortage, this group had to take up higher ground. It certainly worked in their favor. Lyle and

I believe they might be the sole survivors, though several mountain ranges in the distance could hold similar dwellings."

It made sense. The Jack Lions were not built to shimmy up rock faces, or climb anything steep. With the proliferation of wooden containers and bowls in the cave, it was likely that the Paddymous had stored enough water and food to wait out the siege. A definitive amount of luck had played out to ensure this group's survival.

"Did you know they were here all along?" asked Samantha, her voice etched with curiosity. "If so, why didn't you tell us?"

Paddy frowned. "When we read the pictographs, especially one in particular, we discovered that their last entry indicated some type of catastrophe. The markings showed their population represented in great numbers, then what appeared to be large storm clouds above them, accompanied by sheets of rain – a downpour. The more we studied the picture, the more we believed that the downpour was actually a horde descending upon them from a high altitude. It could only have meant that the Jack Lions were dropped on them like rain. I will not elaborate any more. Some things are better left unsaid."

"What do you mean, better to be left unsaid?" Samantha asked, losing a bit of her pleasant edge. "Spill your guts, Paddy. There are no secrets amongst us."

"I'm afraid that's my fault," said Zaz, "I'm sorry that I kept it from the rest of you. It concerned Paddy and Lyle's belief that these Jack Lions were deliberately planted here by an intelligent force, with the express purpose of wiping out our large friends here. I know it sounds hard to believe, but the Jack Lions don't belong here. Paddy can explain it with more detail than I can."

Paddy did just that. He told them about the DNA chains of native animals and how they should reflect their planetary environment. He used examples of phosphorous, calcium and carbon, and how they related to human life forms. He finished by describing the Jack Lions as genetically engineered frauds – trespassers that had been installed on the planet by a much higher but more dangerous intelligence. In summation, he used the word "pets" to describe the intruders.

Paddy produced the long scroll of photographic documentation containing the pictographs. He pointed to the last entry. Lyle held the lantern high so everyone could see the details.

"This represents the Paddymous," Paddy said, pointing to the pictograph with a twig. "These dozens of stick-like figures on the planet's surface. Above them, you see the downpour of these crude figures. Farther above that, what looks like two ventricular clouds represent the source of the downpour. Except they are not clouds, even though they look like it. They are – "

"Ships," said Dendy, cutting in. "I'm afraid I was in on the secret, but wasn't totally convinced until now."

Samantha slapped Zaz's shoulder. "Damn you for that. What kind of reaction did you expect, anyway?"

Galoot looked hurt, crestfallen. "I am not that dumb, boss. I could have understood it. Why leave me out of the loop?"

The whole discussion went over Carybell's head – she had spun around to play a clumsy patty-cake with a small Paddymous.

"I'm sorry for breaking that trust," said Zaz. "But I had my reasons. I didn't want to add any more panic to an already panic-stricken situation." He directed his attention to Lyle. "Why didn't you tell us this, or at least pass on your suspicions about these survivors?"

"Because you would not have let us come here," said Lyle. "Not on that hypothesis. We had to find out for ourselves."

"You're right about that," said Zaz. "But it didn't mean that I wouldn't have eventually given you permission."

"Eventually was not good enough," said Paddy. "The preservation of these beings was paramount in our decision to leave with such haste. After arriving, we performed a cursory walkabout. It was then we had the distinct feeling of being watched. We looked up and caught one of the Paddymous spying upon us. We endeavored to seek them out in person. It was not easy at first; when we confronted them, they urinated upon themselves in fear – much like a beaten puppy. After that, we slowly gained their trust. We then decided to ditch the scout vehicle and stay. Frankly, we have come to adore them without reservation. If you are going to fault us for that, then so be it."

"Well I'm glad you don't hate us," said Galoot.

Lyle put a hand on Galoot's big shoulder. "Hate had nothing to do with it, kind sir. We were driven by universal laws of survival, and the balance of nature. They are concepts that might seem secondary to you. Nevertheless, they were supreme in our decision to intercede. The prime universal law is the sanctity of life. That is the highest calling. Should you be deaf to it, then you are damned."

Zaz noticed that Dendy had slid away from the group to retrieve a reed-woven ball that had rolled across the floor. She rolled the ball back to a small Paddymous, who sat crouched, studying her. They began a game of roll and catch while the youth's parents looked on.

Samantha's wild red hair attracted the attention of yet another juvenile, who began fingering it from behind. Samantha tried to remain still while being probed and pinched. "Are they aware of what has happened to them?" she asked.

"It is not likely, but perhaps to some degree," said Paddy. "They show no inherent violent qualities. I highly doubt they have ever struck one another. The siege was most likely swift, the main inhabitants running away from the gorge. In the panic, this group was left behind. They never witnessed the violence brought to bear on their fellows. However, I believe they are capable of mourning the dead because we have found evidence that they bury their own – we discovered a small grave on the valley floor. It's been decorated with hand-made baubles. They are *aware*."

"You have to remember," began Lyle, "that there has never been a carnivorous predator on this planet, aside from these recent Jack Lions. What was there to fear? The armadillos or Microraptors? Hardly. This must be the first hardship they have ever endured. Still, I believe they are ignorant to the scale of the disaster. It happened so many years ago. Perhaps they have forgotten the tragedy, or adopted a type of 'life goes on' mentality.'"

A few of the Paddymous beings retired to woven beds, while some of the other adults began mashing up a vegetable-like meal in wooden bowls. Others began to partake of the water that Paddy brought back in the jug, only they were having trouble opening the lid. Paddy excused himself and attended to the chore, pouring the contents into a large community bowl. This produced a cacophony of happy snorts and chortling.

Paddy rejoined the group. "They are really quite intelligent, only they do have trouble unsnapping a lid. That will be the second time I have done it for them. I suspect that they will catch on next time. It's that short thumb that gives them problems manipulating things. Of course, they can render like artists, in a Picasso sort of way." He gave a small laugh.

Zaz chanced a look at a feasting Paddymous. It looked just like a cow chewing its cud; the jaws rolled sideways and moved around loosely. He leaned closer to Paddy, as though the creatures might overhear him. "What exactly do they do all day?"

Paddy shrugged. "You mean besides eating, defecating and sleeping? They render their art and play with toys – even the adults play with toys. They only go to the creek for water and the gathering of fruits, grasses and nuts. I have not seen them wander the valley floor. Perhaps it is a tribal or social thing. They stick together. There is a patriarch, the large one there with the black spot on his cheek. He leaves the cave on a regular basis and treks the length of the valley. I haven't deduced the meaning of this foray. Possibly he is a tribal elder who had the distinction of meeting with the other leaders. Whatever they discussed is a mystery."

Zaz remembered seeing the large cave that looked like a council chambers. He wondered if the patriarchs were the representatives of a particular group. Sadly, there would be no more council meetings. The surviving patriarch could only puzzle over the disappearance of his fellow clan leaders. It might have been the reason for his aimless pacing in the valley.

The captain felt the back of his hair being examined. There was a sudden tug and a tuft of hair disappeared from his scalp. He cleared his throat, suffering the laughs of his crewmembers.

"Very funny," he said with a snicker. "As long as they don't intend to weave a blanket with it." He got back on track. "All right, I appreciate the fact that you two felt the need to study these beings. Does this mean you've signed us off as associates?"

Lyle, being the more diplomatic of the two, answered, "We have no reservations. But we are determined to stay right here. We have to document everything – it is imperative with a species such as this. We will not deny you visitations. But we also reserve the right to privacy with our studies."

"Let 'em write in their notebooks," said Galoot. "There ain't any harm in it. Just tell us if there is anything we can do for you."

"Thank you for the gesture, my prodigious friend," said Lyle. "Where is Carl, by the way?"

Zaz explained what happened to him. Paddy and Lyle seemed genuinely concerned. They offered to assist with the healing process, especially if they discovered any medicinal plants.

"Might I ask what your plans are?" asked Lyle.

Zaz paused for a beat. *Plans? Oh, nothing much, guys. Just some living and loving, with a subplot of trying to stay alive. Oh, yeah, and by the way, did I mention I want to nuke the compound? Nothing out of the ordinary. Nothing to worry about.*

CHAPTER FIFTEEN

CLOUD'S REST

Sidus Log, Rotation 36.

We've found our long lost scientists, hunkered down in the gorge, living with a family of Paddymous creatures. I have mixed feelings about the reunion, but I will say that I am thankful that they survived, and for the discovery of what are possibly the last Paddymous giants on this planet. Lyle and Paddy have taught us a lot about our new friends, and we discover new thrills, and sometimes spills, every day. They are an adorable, gentle life form, nothing that comes close to what I might have imagined. They are so much more. Such sublime innocence has taught us all about humility, with a respect for even the lowliest of God's creations. Instead of case studies, they have become friends. And no, I'm not crazy.

It's been a week since we arrived in the gorge or the "beautiful valley" as we've taken to calling it. All is as well as can be expected. We are gradually learning about this strange environment and how to exploit its resources without permanent damage. Dendy wasted no time in staking out a garden plot and poking seeds into the earth. My fondness and love for her is beyond measure. She is particularly endeared to our large friends. They have taken a liking to her as well.

It took us two days to hoist the large binocular telescope up to a place we call "Cloud's Rest." We used the refurbished scout vehicle, which Galoot repaired with the help of Silver Two, to travel two miles north up the gorge to a side canyon that led up the cliff face to an altitude of 3,000 feet. From there it is another two-mile hike to the precipice. This vantage point allows us an unobstructed view of the desert floor and the area surrounding the *Shenandoah*.

The compound is a disaster area. There is nothing left but smoldering wreckage. I've watched the activity for over four days now and have not seen any living Jack Lions. There is nothing alive down there, save for bacteria that will eventually devour the corpses. I don't know where the remaining enemy creatures have fled to. I hope they are gone for good, but we will remain on a constant vigil.

Carl has managed to take his first steps since the attack that nearly took his life. Dendy has fitted him with a bubble cast that has aided in his mobility. He insists that he be allowed to visit Cloud's Rest. Nothing short of being carried upon Galoot's back would get him up here. I think he's just feeling bored and useless.

Dendy is tugging at my arm. I think it's time for another look through the telescope. Until next time…

Zachary Crowe, PJ.

ZAZ POCKETED the journal cland took a drink of water.

Dendy gave Zaz a slit-eyed look. "What are you writing in that book? Is it personal things about you and me?"

He gave her a playful shove. "It's about all of us." He rose to his knees to look through the scope. The large binocular cylinders were locked in position on a tripod, trained to the outline of the ship. The powerful resolution brought images into fine focus, with a sensitivity dial that negated the heat waves.

He could distinguish individual corpses at a distance of over 400 miles. The compound looked still, devoid of any movement save for some very thin wisps of smoke that he surmised came from the fatty tissues in the corpses. He pulled away from the scope.

They hadn't killed all the Jacks. He was certain of it. He knew what he saw when he'd dropped the cans and charges. There had been tens of thousands of living Jack Lions in the compound. They couldn't have killed them all, but he couldn't account for them now. They could have run off to the south again where they had first come from.

Dendy patted his shoulder. "There, you see? There's nothing there anymore. They're all dead or they've run off. So now you don't have to destroy everything. We might even be able to go back to the ship again for more supplies."

"Visits, maybe. We'll never live there again; our power source is depleted, there's no hydrogen to run the generators. I doubt if there's anything more we need to salvage except raw materials. The construction vehicles are useless, and it's a graveyard of stinking corpses."

A cool breeze played upon his cheeks. He liked it up here. He could see for a thousand miles in any direction. The only things alive on the plateau were the Microraptors that spiraled overhead, carried upward by the mild thermals. Every now and then a locust jumped in his lap, but that was it. He could see the moons overhead with crystal clarity. He named the two white moons, which looked like they had small cloud atmospheres, Ah and Bay. The smaller moon that was cracked in half, he called Cay. Cay was a haunting sight, especially at the terminator, where he could see immense gorges, spires, and craters. Every fifth day, the three moons would rotate in sequence, appearing together as if they were chasing each other across the horizon – the two sisters, Ah and Bay, endlessly pursued by their tiny, broken bother, Cay.

His wrist-com buzzed. "If you're finished fooling around up there," said Samantha over the com, "I have dinner ready. Take a break."

If I'm finished fooling around, take a break? And if I keep taking breaks who is going to monitor the situation down below? Who's going to give a damn by making sure we're safe and secure in our little valley?

"I repeat," said Samantha. "You need to quit. You've been up there for eight hours again."

"Okay, okay. I copy that. On our way down."

Zaz lens-capped the telescope and pulled a cover over it, tying it down. The mount wouldn't go anywhere – it was staked to the rock.

They began the long hike back. The trek was all downhill; it didn't take them long before they reached the small scout buggy at the base of the side canyon. Once strapped in, Zaz drove over the small trail he had blazed days before. When they arrived at camp, Zaz parked the vehicle on the north side of the huge land spill. They walked into the clearing as the sun was setting, a fire blazing in the central ring.

Zaz and Dendy joined the others, collapsing into camp chairs. Samantha presented each of them with a precooked meal of beans, peas and syntho beef.

Carl kicked back in a portable recliner. The injured man hadn't ventured away from his shelter much, relaxing within the plastic womb of his tent while enjoying the constant attention of Samantha King. She's kept a watchful eye on him, jumping at his every command.

"Glad to see you're out and about," said Zaz. "How's the leg progressing?"

Carl took a swig from a container Zaz suspected held whiskey. "On the ol' mend. I wish I could hurry it up, but it's taking its own sweet time. See anything up on the cliff?"

"Same as last time: nothing. It doesn't mean that it won't happen again." He threw in the last part as if wanting to justify his time spent up there – they were all getting a bit too complacent, as if there wasn't anything to worry about. Yesterday they had refused to wear their helmets or keep their weapons at the ready. What would tomorrow bring?

Carl raised his mug in a toast. "I think we put a fire under their asses. They won't be back. Between the flames and the hot pepper, they're all burned out. It gives me a whole lot of pleasure to know that we crisped those critters. I bet we've seen the last of them."

Dendy looked up from her dinner plate, waiting for Zaz's rebuttal.

"I hope you're right, Carl," said Zaz. "But I'm not going to let my guard down because I *think* the problem has gone away. I'm not convinced yet – I don't see any proof that they've hightailed it for parts unknown."

Zaz tore into his meal, hoping the subject was dead – or at least on hold. Hoping he was wrong about the Jack Lions.

"I think we deserve a well-earned break," said Samantha. "You're just going to wear yourself to tatters in your constant state of being on-guard. Have you seen your eyes lately, Zaz? They look like two holes in a Paddymous dung pile. I also know you've been tossing stim tabs down your throat as if they were candy. I admire your vigilance, but I'm concerned about your health; you've dropped at least fifteen pounds in the last month. It's all going to catch up with you, whether you like it or not."

He had heard the same argument for the past week, and he was bound to hear it again. "I'm glad you've all decided that my health is at risk, or I might be over-reacting to the situation. I'll state for the record that I don't think we've seen the last of it. Call it a guess, or a hunch, whatever you like. If we don't stay frosty when the threat comes, we won't have the chance to meet it head on. We'll be caught napping."

"You're speaking in riddles again," said Carl. "Just what the hell are you looking for?"

Dendy gave Zaz a knowing glance then shook her head in the negative. She wanted that part of the riddle kept under wraps from Carl just as much as he did. Zaz looked at his dinner plate, suddenly seeing the irony in it. Did he have to spill the beans again to the only member who'd been left out of the loop? What surprised him was that Samantha, with her newfound intimacy toward Carl, hadn't divulged the potential threat of an alien presence.

No more secrets. Wasn't that what he'd told them before? But why should he tell Carl something that would send him into frenzy? It would serve no purpose. Besides that, they had reached a fragile status quo right now, something he had no mind to upset.

"Let's just say I want to be ready for any contingency. We can leave it at that."

"The way I see it," said Galoot, "if they are still out there, then they'll have to come up the gorge to get us. That's if they get through all that bad smellin' stuff. Then we beat them off again. Or if they get the upper hand, we go to high ground and figure it out from there."

"I agree," said Carybell.

Zaz heard the sound of pebbles falling behind them and turned around to see Paddy and Lyle making awkward progress down the rockslide. They approached the camp, grinning.

Paddy stepped up to their fire ring and warmed his hands. "Would you mind," he asked, "if a couple of old potentates joined you in repose?"

Samantha favored them with a gracious smile. "We could certainly stand some elevated company. Can I get you anything? I'm serving."

They politely declined and took seat in the sand, landing hard. *Fatigue.* Zaz got a whiff of the scientists – they smelled as if they had just finished frolicking in a manure pile. No doubt their proximity to the Paddymous had included an odiferous relationship.

Carl raised his mug in salute. "It's good to see you two. We were just talking about those critters coming up the gorge and what we were going to do if they got here."

"I would not fret too much over those creatures," Lyle said, eyeing the fire. "I would be more concerned about the – "

Dendy coughed loudly and kicked sand toward Lyle. Lyle looked at her and then lowered his head. "I was just wondering professor," she said, "have you witnessed the mating habits of the Paddymous?"

"In all honesty," answered Paddy, "I have not yet seen a coupling. I can only suspect that the female's readiness runs in a cycle; she might have to be in heat during a particular season.

What season that is can only be estimated. I am not quite sure what passes for spring on Georgian Sidus – I haven't given it much thought. I would assume it is not unlike our own biological ritual. If they are true mammals, the result might produce live births."

"Do they kiss?" asked Carybell.

"No," said Paddy. "They hug and stroke continually, though. It is a physical reassurance behavior where touch is very important. Primates display this same type of interaction. Physical manipulation and touch creates a mental stimuli response – good nervous system development."

"You can say that again," said Carl, blatantly eyeing Samantha.

"As I was saying..." Paddy gave Carl a rude look. "The young need this gratification in the very early stages of development. It assists in their motor skills, mind, and nervous system development. Not to mention, it keeps peace within the family group. They are not as monogamous as you would think. The matriarchs trade off with the sitting duties, leading me to believe that any one of the males could be the father. I can only try to pair the offspring with the parents by making note of coloration and physical traits...and even then it is difficult. I have refrained from drawing blood for any type of analysis – it is too intrusive."

"We have our work cut out for us," agreed Lyle, his eyes glassy under heavy lids.

Who was it, Zaz asked himself, that studied and lived with the great apes? Jane Goodall came to mind; Dian Fossey also shared habitats with the creatures, but her life came to a tragic end, possibly as a result of her passion. Swap the gender and there you had it – Paddy and Lyle were Jane and Dian.

Three large figures crept out of the shadows and approached the campsite: one male Paddymous and two females. The large male made cautious steps into the camp. When he saw Paddy and Lyle on the sand, he gave a happy snort and joined them at the fire, sitting down between Lyle and Carl with his legs splayed. The two females exhibited what passed for smiles and then took up positions behind Samantha, fingering the woman's wild explosion of hair.

Samantha grimaced. "Here they go again."

At Carl's order, Silver Two had brought a collection of stones and dropped them at his side. Carl repeatedly tossed small rocks into the fire, causing the embers to burst. The large male Paddymous watched the little missiles of light as they arced through the air. Carl, seeing that he was confusing the creature, picked up larger stones to throw. The Paddymous watched Carl's every move. At one point, the big male caught a stone in midair then duplicated what he had seen by pitching the stone into the fire, which created a shower of sparks and ashes.

The creature chortled and slapped the sand, obviously pleased with what he'd done. Carl laughed oafishly and threw a bigger rock. The Paddymous giant caught it then flung it hard into the fire, breaking a charred log into a burst of embers.

Carl gazed at his new friend. "That's the way to do it!"

Dendy stood up and stomped her foot in the sand. "Stop teaching him to do that, you dumb barbarian!"

"It's only monkey see, monkey do," said Carl. "It ain't hurting anything."

"I'm afraid lady Dendy is right," scolded Paddy. "Stay your hand and refrain from such displays. He should not be allowed to mimic the antics of a human, and I use that term loosely. He is the patriarch of the group, and as such is liable to pass on that behavior to the others. It could result in an injury, especially to one of the minors."

Carl threw one last large stone out of spite. The big male caught the stone and pitched it, sending the object sailing over the fire and landing outside the campsite.

"What's happening? I can't see." Samantha had her head down nearly between her legs as the two females pushed her down, plucking out strands of her hair.

"If you ask me," said Carl, "these big pushovers could stand to learn a little bit about bad behavior. They didn't know how to put up a fight against those critters. Laying around and playing with toys all day – no wonder they got their asses whipped. I'll bet you if they knew how to fight they wouldn't have gone down so damn easy."

Paddy pushed to his feet. "That is not your determination to make. You can only foul their character by introducing them to acts of violence. It's contrary to their normal behavior. You are an outside agency dealing with something you know nothing about."

Lyle nodded. "They are herbivores. Vegetarians. If they were carnivores and competing with others, they would likely have developed additional survival skills: weapon making, hunting, stalking, all of it requiring cunning behavior. Meat eating results in a larger and more complex brain, which intensifies further hunting behavior and, granted, all-around intelligence. However, there is nothing here for them to kill, unless you would suggest making the armadillo one of their dietary sources. They are not destined to follow the same evolutionary line as Homo Sapiens. Their path is fixed."

"We started off eating roots," said Carl. "Then we started bashing things over the head. We got smart. We didn't turn out too bad."

Paddy shivered, shaking his head in disgust. "Bollocks. I suppose next you would give them the wheel. Then they could build a crude vehicle and end up barreling down hills, killing themselves in a crash. The Paddymous are a young species, perhaps only a million or two years old. They must evolve with time, unhampered and uncontaminated. Perhaps a few million years from now they will be able to send their first radio messages to another civilization. Until that time, they should remain on Darwin's slow ride until they earn those natural transitions."

"Hunting and gathering *did* go together," Zaz remarked. "What would you call the great K-T extinction? Was that chance-chaos, or was that an orderly and natural event? We mammals evolved to dominate our planet because of that catastrophe. It could have gone the other way just as easily. We could be speaking reptilian today if not for a six-mile wide asteroid."

"Yeah," said Carl, "we're in the cards with these dumb bastards."

Samantha broke free and crawled across the sand to snatch the mug from Carl's hand.

"Hey, that was my whiskey!" Carl said, feigning hurt.

"You've had enough for tonight," she said. She took her seat again and the hair pulling continued. "Ugh, they're snatching me bald."

"You know," Zaz began, "Carl might have hit on something there. I'm not saying that we should let them pick up our habits; it just seems to me that it's normal to teach them by example. If they had been trained in self-defense beforehand, I bet the conflict wouldn't have been so one-sided."

Carl nodded. "Yeah, that's all I'm saying. Give 'em a fighting chance. Show 'em how to defend themselves. You know, put 'em up?"

"Would you like to know something?" Paddy pointed a finger at Carl. "You do not permanently reside on this planet, nor did you come from here, so – "

"We do *now*," said Carl. "Any way you look at it, this place is going to be crawling with colonists. So there's going to be even more people teaching them much worse things than throwing rocks."

"Not exactly," said Paddy. "It is against galactic law to colonize a planet that has a viable population of native residents defined as having a primitive Stone Age developmental culture. They cannot be disinterred, interacted with, harmed or removed from their rightful residence. These Paddymous beings are the rightful residents and owners of Georgian Sidus. We have here a viable breeding group – if not that, a truly endangered species that screams out for protection. Orion Industries has no further claim to this real estate."

Zaz was intrigued. "We're not talking about upsetting the balance, Paddy. We're talking about giving them a little shove."

"And a little shove quickly turns into a big shove," said Paddy. "Would you take responsibility for the consequences of your interaction with them should something disastrous happen?"

Zaz cocked an eyebrow. "Did you say disastrous, Paddy? If I'm not mistaken, we have been the witnesses of a felonious disaster that has already occurred. I don't care what brush you stroke it with, we are now residents of this system."

"It was not in the cards of fate to bring us to this…" Paddy trailed off. A look of anguish came to his face as though he'd realized that the interaction had already taken place, whether destiny had played a part in it or not. The scientist trembled visibly, fighting against what should have been, with what was *now*. He couldn't come to grips with the fact that the Planet Janitor crew had already changed the course of Georgian Sidus history. They'd done so the second they crash-landed on the surface. From early on there had been no expectation that the Paddymous had survived. It was by chance that they were discovered alive. If humans had not been in the gorge to find them, then the colonists would have eventually found them and impacted their evolution, possibly in more dramatic ways.

God and science were using the professor's minds for a battleground. Science and logic wanted to win so badly.

Paddy shook his head. "But...we...we have no right. We are interlopers."

"It was an accident, professor," said Galoot.

Zaz couldn't have agreed more. "You are living with them, Paddy. It's too late. You've impacted."

Paddy was flustered. "I don't believe it. I can't believe a word of it!" He marched across the sand, his mind short-circuiting. Lyle hurried after him, followed like a mother duck by the three Paddymous beings.

Paddy's voice echoed against the cliff face as he trudged up the landslide. "You should all know that your theories are unfounded."

"Don't look now," said Carl. "But your non-interaction directive is following you."

"Damn and curse you all!"

The Planet Janitor crew sat in stunned silence.

Samantha fingered her tender scalp, exhaling hard. "That went well, don't you think?"

Zaz threw Carl a hot stare. "There's no need to rub it in, Stromboli. They're committed to something they love."

Carl held up his hands. "Hey, don't shoot – I was only trying to let them see the other side of the imperial. They got huffy when they knew they'd been proven wrong."

Zaz blew a sigh. "In a perfect world they would have been right."

Galoot pointed a pudgy finger to his temple. "I think they've got something wrong up here, boss."

"No, I think they have too much passion. That's what's wrong with them. Too much of it can have adverse affects. It's not for us to judge – we've got to show them some patience."

"This is an impatient planet," Dendy said, staring at the fire.

That summed it up pretty well, thought Zaz. They'd hardly landed and settled in on Sidus before all hell broke loose. He couldn't think of a more unforgiving place. However, it wasn't the planet, but the circumstances brought about by other difficulties beyond their control – namely the unprovoked attack of a vicious species. If Sidus had such a thing as a natural balance, it was the Jack Lions who had obliterated it, not the arrival of Planet Janitor.

Samantha looked thoughtful. "Granted that we've all received an advance payment for our contract, and a nice one at that, but if what he says is true, then Orion Industries has no rightful claim to this real estate. Their initial probes missed these surviving Paddymous. Everything's changed now. It's all been for nothing – unless they ignore galactic law."

Zaz put his plate down. "With so many billions invested, I'm wondering if they're prepared to simply write it off or ignore it altogether. Somehow, I doubt it."

"That's where we come in," said Dendy. "It's our duty to inform them when they arrive. There's a thought – what if they are unable to send the crews? What if they have a change in their plans? I don't feel like being marooned here, especially when I can't spend all of that advance money. So we would lose, too. Only our beneficiaries would profit, which is okay, I guess."

Galoot shifted uneasily in his little camp chair. His massive weight won out over the flimsy construction – the chair snapped, dropping his ass to the sand. He got up, unperturbed, and pitched the wreckage into the fire. "Boss, as much as I like this place, except for them critters, I don't want to spend the rest of my life here. Of course, I've got my baby." He stroked Carybell's head affectionately. She hugged his waist.

"I sent a sub-space message the minute we hit the ground," said Samantha. "But a lot of good that will do – they'll receive it twelve years down the road. We're counting on them to keep their contractual promise – they said less than a year, unless they find the contractors sooner."

"Yeah, but what if they never find the contractors?" asked Carl.

Zaz got up and marched for his tent. "I don't *know*," was the last thing he said before turning in.

```
Sidus Log, Rotation 39.
They say that I'm spending too much time on Cloud's
Rest. I don't know exactly what I'm looking for. I'm
not at ease on Sidus. I'll never be. Something tells
me we haven't seen the last of the Jack Lions. But
it's the prospect of there being something worse out
there that gives me the chills. I'm not raving mad.
I'm not paranoid. I feel it. Somehow, I know that
presence feels me too.
   The bright spot in my life is Dendy. Her instincts
about me are always right. She seems to know what
I'm thinking from one minute to the next. I would be
lost without her. Still, I'm depressed. The others are
asking difficult questions. I can't answer all of them.
                              Zachary Crowe, PJ.
```

The wind blustered as he tried to keep the telescope steady, targeting the valley below. He tightened the mount then refocused again. It broke his heart every time he looked at her: the *Shenandoah* sat crumpled like some giant, spineless slug – hardly a dignified repose for what was once such a magnificent ship. His eyes were sore from the constant strain of trying to discern objects at a distance.

He pulled back from the scope and glanced at Dendy. She sat Indian style on the hard ground, running bits of broken rock through her fingers. The wind, especially strong on this day, ruffled her hair. Her face gleamed with a golden tan under the glare of the sun. She almost looked whimsical. His heart gave a tug, knowing that she had followed him up to the plateau every day without complaint.

He gave her thigh an affectionate stroke. "Sweetie, you don't have be up here, you know. I think you'd much rather be tending your garden. It's starting to look pretty good."

She brushed some strands of hair from her face. "I don't really mind. I love being with you. I know that what you're doing is important, and if it's important to you, then it's important to me. I wouldn't worry about what the others think."

"I'm not worried too much about what they think. Just worried about them. I can't help thinking I got us into this mess. If I hadn't met with Orion at the bar none of this would have happened. We'd be out carving up some asteroid somewhere. Or maybe screwing up the environment while trying to save it." He thought about his plans for a refueling station and amusement park on Titan that would probably never happen – another dream shot down a swirling black hole.

She laughed. "You can say that again. Why were we always dealt the black marble? I believed in this mission. Why did it have to come crashing down on top of us? Is our universal karma all bolloxed up?"

"Just mine it seems."

"You didn't hijack us. It was a democratic vote. Even if you had vetoed the trip, we would have won by majority then forced the issue. We were all dead-set on going, Zaz. It was the first decision we passed. So don't go telling me it was all your fault."

He studied her face again, admiring the profile, the succulent lips. Her hot-blooded personality was showing again, giving him that irresistible tug. He couldn't help himself. *I'm the moth – she's the flame.* He took her in his arms and laid her down, kissing her passionately. He moved to unbuckle her suit top, but she stayed his hand, telling him that she could do it easier. The sun shined on her bare skin, as he ran his hand over the flat of her stomach.

He knew this stolen moment would give them with another passionate memory. They were on a hostile planet with no hope but the comfort of each other's embrace. It seemed so out of place, but that's also why it was so meaningful and full of magic. Two tiny souls lost in an all encompassing universe.

He remembered being smitten with such feelings in his youth. He had been the pursuer of a girl once, enraptured every time he came within shadow distance of her. He couldn't eat, sleep, or work for days. Ultimately, it had ended when she grew weary of his attraction for her, but it lasted a fruitful two years. With Dendy, however, he knew the perfect match had been made. She had been the pursuer, using her intuition to forge a lasting relationship that would stand against time. She had known they were meant for each other from the very beginning, casting a spell on him that he was helpless to fend off. He would like to think he would have eventually dogged after her. She was just too patently charming and beautiful to have ignored.

"How do you know you love me, Zaz?" she asked with a timid voice.

He paused, looking down upon her with soft eyes. "It's a question of love?"

"Yeah."

He felt a lump in his throat as he considered the question. "Well," he began, "true love comes when a man's needs are outweighed by those of another. It arrives when the first thoughts you have upon waking concern the welfare of someone else. It's the reflection of joy you see in a pair of eyes that don't belong to you; the discovery of commitment and sharing, the willingness to sacrifice all that you have, even if you have next to nothing to give. Understanding is the manifestation of true affection, and you realize that understanding softens the heart. You have to be willing to compromise, even when you know you're right. You have to know that to keep something beautiful, you're honor-bound to protect and defend it against all enemies and harm, suddenly realizing one day that you'd be willing to give up your life for the other, with no hesitation or regrets."

He watched as her eyes opened. She drew in a long breath, blinking back tears. "Oh, that was so *beautiful*, Zaz."

"We're going to get off this rock and start a life, Dendy. I promise you that. But if we don't make it, my feelings won't change. I couldn't be more happy to be marooned on a place like this, knowing that I've got you with me."

She smiled lovingly. "I can't wait to get you back down to camp and inside our tent. Let's just take one last look…" She knelt next to the scope, bringing her eyes to the oculars for a quick glance. She pulled away. Her jaw dropped.

"What is it, Dendy?"

She went to the scope again and yanked back in wide-eyed shock. She tried to talk, but could only point.

Zaz scooted to the scope, peered through the double lens. What he saw took his breath away. He began to shake, jostling the scope out of alignment. He still couldn't believe his eyes as he brought the image back into view.

It was a ship.

He tried to repress the sudden onslaught of emotions triggered by what he saw through the scope. The problem was he didn't know *what* it was he was looking at. The *Shenandoah* appeared minnow-sized in the scope; by comparison, this new ship was a leviathan. He changed the lens setting and pulled back until he could see it more clearly, hovering about 500 feet off the desert floor, a hundred yards out from his ship.

The new arrival looked like an enormous manta ray, complete with a stubbed tail and two hook-like projections on the front; it had a bilateral spine from nose to tail that resembled a dorsal airfoil. There was no disturbance under the craft that he could see, only a wavering bluish haze – an anti-gravity amplifier of some sort. It cast a monstrous shadow over the compound.

He rubbed his eyes hard and looked again. He felt Dendy's knee brush up against his shoulder as she pulled the small portable scope from his pocket.

From a distance it was hard to make out the color of the craft or any discernable markings. Zaz pulled away from the eyepiece, speaking to himself as much as he was to Dendy. "That sucker has to be a mile long and another mile wide at least. Jesus!" He chanced another look – it was still hovering over the compound like a giant leaf that refused to fall to the ground. He snatched the small scope away from Dendy.

"Hey!"

"Yep, it's still there," he said. He spoke into his wrist-com, but the words came out in stammers. A little self-control helped with the next transmission.

"Come in, Sam, I need you. Sam, come back!"

"I heard you the first time. What's the matter?"

"Listen, we've got company. I can't leave the perch, so I want you to – "

"Not them again!"

"No, it's not Jacks." He fumbled to get the words right. "It's a ship, and it's down in the compound right now. It just got here."

"Wait a minute – what kind of a ship?"

"That's the problem – I don't know. I need you to double-time it up here with some things. First, make sure the small satellite gun is in the six-wheeler. I hope you last-minute-packed our bridge charts and books. I need the International Ship Registry with the structural profile data."

"I have all of that. What does the ship look like?"

"Well, it's a pancake design with triangular wings, except it's notched in the nose and has a double stabilizer on top running the length of it. It's queer-looking, absolutely enormous."

"It sounds Chinese, or even – "

"Sam! Pack that gear, take the six-wheeler over the slide area and beat it up here. You know the way. Have Galoot pack the Sat, you bag the rest. Pace yourself on the way up – it's a hard climb. I'll be waiting for you."

"Copy. We'll get there as soon as we can. I'll leave Silver Two in camp, as gorge lookout."

Zaz dropped to his knees and looked through the big scope again. The ship remained in a hover pattern exactly where he'd last seen it.

Dendy twined her hands together nervously. "I can't believe it. I can't believe we're going home!"

He glanced at her. "Not so fast. We don't know *who* we're going home with. Don't you think it's a little early for the follow-up team?"

"What of it? They said they'd make it when they could. Who else knows our coordinates besides Orion Industries? Our ride just came!"

"Maybe so… They're checking out our handiwork right now. I can imagine what they're thinking; 'What the hell happened here' has got to be high on their priority list. We're not going to get any points for housekeeping. We're also better than four hundred miles out in the wilderness."

Dendy laughed. "We should have left a note on the door."

"That's why I told Sammy to bring the Sat dish – we can pop 'em a message. It'll be a lot faster than driving out there."

"Too bad we don't have a flare rocket."

"That's not enough – they'd have to be outside the ship to see it, or at least scoping in our direction. I think they're more concerned with the damage that's right under them. They're probably running biohazard and toxicity analysis on the ship. That could take a while. What would *you* think if you came across a horde of dead animals and a burnt-out ship?"

"Yeah, I guess you'd investigate the scene first." Dendy sobered somewhat. "I just hope it doesn't scare them away before we can contact them."

He pulled her into his lap. They had at least a two-hour wait, but he couldn't refrain from looking in the scope every 30 seconds. It was maddening having a ship so close, yet unable to communicate with it. The thought that Orion had arrived spurred a dollop of hope in him. He began to think of rehearsed lines he could use to explain what had happened. Surely they couldn't blame him for the gravity accident. And there was no way they could hold him accountable for the Jack lion's attack. He had not altered or destroyed the environment – the environment had nearly killed *him*.

Two and a half hours later, Zaz saw several figures trudging single file up the incline. He stood up, waved his hands. Samantha was in the lead with a pack slung over her shoulder. Galoot trailed behind her with a very big parcel on his back. Carybell brought up the rear, hefting her own burden.

When they got close enough Zaz could see that Carl was strapped to Galoot's back, riding him like some two-legged horse.

"Stromboli, if this was your idea, I'm pitching you off the cliff!"

Samantha arrived in a sweaty heap, dropping her pack. She didn't waste any time going straight to the scope and tweaking the dials. Zaz rifled through the pack and brought out some large bound books. He flipped the pages rapidly until he found the constructional blueprints he was looking for.

Galoot, with a few quick grappling moves, unhitched Carl from his back and placed the injured man on the ground. Carybell set the portable satellite gun down, taking a seat next to it.

"Couldn't resist the damn mystery," said Carl. "I hear we have a ship."

"Galoot's not a damn mule," said Zaz without looking up from the registry. "Don't do that again."

Galoot wiped the sweat from his brow. "I don't mind, boss. I need to lose a little weight."

Samantha turned around. "She's a big one all right. Looks Chinese, with some French design flairs. My recollection is pretty good, but that exact design escapes me. I heard some scuttlebutt before we left that Orion had a new flagship design under construction – this could be it."

Everyone took a long look through the scope. Even Carybell wanted a turn to look at the mighty ship. Carl whistled upon seeing it. Galoot stepped back, rubbing his chin thoughtfully.

"I can't find anything in here that approaches that size," said Zaz, slapping the book shut. "Some of the designs are close. There's no hull identification markings either – that's suspicious."

Galoot knelt down again, twisting the dials on the zoom. He growled under his breath. Looking up he said, "I know a little bit about structural mass and load, boss. I used the scope's survey crosshairs to calibrate the size of that thing – she's darn near a mile long, four thousand feet wide. Now, we don't have an Ultrinium hull that will stretch to that size without caving in on itself in a gravity atmosphere. I should know – I apprenticed on the really big freighters, ships bigger than *Shenandoah*."

Zaz looked encouraged but perplexed. "What are you telling me?"

Galoot turned his head and looked down upon the desert plain. "Just that we don't know how to keep a mass that big together without it bustin' up under its own weight. Most of our Earth-based ships are tubular in design, like the old submarines. It's the best profile for withstanding high pressures. I don't like the looks of it, boss. Nope. Not one bit."

"What did he just say?" asked Carl.

"He said, the design of that ship is too fragile-looking – too big to be anything we could have produced," Zaz explained. "Galoot was born in a shipyard. If anybody knows about structural integrity, it's him. The Reticulian Grays have the market cornered on the saucer and cigar-shaped designs, but those snots have never let us study their technology. However, even they don't have anything that comes close to these dimensions."

"Sure," said Samantha, "but what's to say there isn't some new technology on Earth? It could be something we haven't heard of before. Maybe it's a new prototype they launched just after we left."

Zaz looked through the scope again then gave it back to Galoot. He whispered, "What do you make of that repulser plasma? Have you ever seen anything like that before?"

Galoot pulled away. "It looks funny to me. It's got a different discharge corona – the color is off, unless we're getting some distortion on this end."

"I say we beam them a message and hang tight for a reply," said Carl. "How else are we going to find out? Besides, who the hell else would be dicking around this rock anyway? Orion are the only one's who know about it."

Zaz gave Dendy a hushed look, remembering what Paddy and Lyle had said about the masters likely in charge of the Jack Lions. He had to admit that it was a stretch to accept that conclusion, but the scientists had so far been right much more than they'd been wrong.

Zaz looked at each one of his crewmembers in turn. "No," he said. "I'm not buying this. Something's wrong."

"Yeah, and it's you," said Carl. "If you had your way you'd blow our ticket for a chance out of here."

Samantha stuck a finger at him. "Shut up, Carl. Nobody is cutting our ride loose. Zaz just wants to explore the other side of the issue."

"I'm just saying that it doesn't have the configuration of a freighter," Zaz reasoned. "We were expecting freighters with large cargo holds – construction battalions."

"Hell," said Carl. "It's big enough to be anything."

Zaz looked at Carl, wondering if he'd been guzzling whiskey again. "I'll say it again: that ship looks like some type of a war galleon, or at the very least a transport yacht."

"All right," said Samantha. "Zaz doesn't like the looks of it. Who else agrees?"

"I don't like it," said Galoot. "That ship didn't come from any Earth port."

Carybell hesitated. "I think it looks wicked," she said, without staring directly at Galoot. "It scares me." She went to the scope again.

Dendy looked at Zaz. "I'm sorry, honey. I'm willing to take the chance. Even with what you and I know."

"Know what?" Carl tried to stand up.

Zaz sighed. He decided to tell him about Paddy and Lyle's warning that the Jack Lions were not true residents of Georgian Sidus, explaining all the scientific evidence as best he could. He finished by saying he believed the Jack Lions were deliberately transported to the planet by a higher intelligence. The reaction to the news was disbelief mixed with total denial.

Carl scowled. "Those two again! For gawd's sakes, we already know those two are off their camp chairs. They would say anything to throw a wrench in the gears. They even slipped off like a couple of thieves in the night so they could run away and do what they wanted. Those two would do anything to stay here."

Samantha sighed. "That would explain a lot, but it still doesn't make sense. Why would aliens show themselves now? Why didn't they confront us from the start?"

Once again, Zaz had no answer. He only had a feeling, a gut instinct he wanted the others to rely upon. It was clear that wasn't enough.

"That's three pros to three cons," said Samantha, counting off on her fingers. "Now what do we do?"

"We wait," Zaz said. "We watch that ship – see what it decides to do. If it's one of ours, it'll stick around and investigate. They wouldn't leave us behind or abandon their project."

"Oh, my goodness," said Carybell, still peering through the scope. "There's another ship – they're landing!"

CHAPTER SIXTEEN

THE WELL LAID PLANS
OF MICE AND MEN

ZAZ DROPPED to the scope, skinning his knees on the rock. He gently nudged Carybell aside and gazed through the eyepiece. A second ship had appeared next to the first one. The two ships descended, wingtip to wingtip. Their mass displaced nearly a quarter of the compound. The underbelly of each ship was equipped with spider-like landing pods; there were four joints in each pod. The two ships settled on the west side of the *Shenandoah*, near the hatch opening. The construction equipment that had been abandoned in the compound looked like specks under their immense shadows.

"That checks out," said Carl. "The corporate ship and a construction ship. What's so strange about this?"

Zaz was nudged aside by Dendy. The others formed a line behind her, anxious to see the ships for themselves.

Carl pulled the .45 from Carybell's waistband and fired several shots in the air. "We're over here!" he shouted.

Zaz took two quick strides and kicked the pistol out of Carl's hand. "What the hell's the matter with you?" he snapped. "They aren't going to hear that!"

Carl sucked his bruised thumb. "You didn't have to do that."

Zaz pulled his rifle off his back, holding it at hip-level – everyone's attention turned to him at once. "So help me," he said, "the next idiot who pulls something like that is going to get shot. We don't know what we're dealing with here. If this is trouble, now it's double trouble. It's obvious that whoever, or whatever is in those ships is going to come out and do some reconnaissance. I say we wait it out until that happens. They don't know we're here. We have a vantage point – we can see them. They can't see us. We hold on to that advantage. Everything clear?"

No one argued the matter. Zaz's cheeks had flamed up – they could plainly see that he was in no mood for objections.

Galoot backed him up, planting his hands on his hips.

Zaz went back to the scope, watching for any signs of movement. Having never seen a ship of such size and construction, he wondered where the ramps or lifts would appear.

The two ships were like giant flounders on an ocean sand bar, actually quite beautiful in appearance. Appearances, however, were often deceiving. Great evil could come from the most innocuous looking things. It brought to mind a high school girl Zaz had once known – she was such a Siren that boys would go out of their way just to get near her. She had a despicable habit of leading hopeful boys off the end of love lorn cliffs, and that was before she'd plucked their hearts out. Her name was Saritam, and Zachary Crowe had fallen victim to her wiles in his youth. He wondered if either of those ships down there was a Saritam.

The crew grew restless behind him.

"What's happening?" Samantha asked.

"Nothing yet. Oh, wait. Okay, something's going on now. It's a..." Zaz shut up. He saw a large cylinder drop from the bottom of one of the ships. It extended down to the desert floor. He dialed the magnification up, zeroing in on the large white tube. According to the survey crosshairs on the scope, it was 225 feet in diameter and stretched 100 feet down to the desert floor. It looked like a loading dock. A massive panel slid open a moment later, revealing a dark interior.

Zaz expected to see scout vehicles or shuttles emerge. Instead, he found himself watching a dark ribbon of movement exiting the chasm. The strange mass spread across the desert floor like a river of water. He dialed for max magnification.

Jack Lions. Thousands of them.

The animals poured out of the ship in a ceaseless stream, cavorting over the construction site, running over the charred corpses. Hundreds of them overran the construction equipment, snapping and gnawing at the steel. Another line made haste for the ship's open hatch, charging inside the cargo hold. Still other groups raced around either side of ship, surrounding it. They looked like drunken pirates boarding a treasure ship.

Zaz felt sick to his stomach. He couldn't bring himself to watch any more. He got up from the scope and backed away. The other crewmembers, who'd been watching his reaction, stormed the scope to see what had addled him.

One by one, the crewmembers turned away from the scope in disgust. Carl, the last to look, fell back on his rump. He tried to talk but couldn't. Galoot crossed himself while Carybell clung to him. Samantha sat down in a daze. She began pulling at her fingers. All she could say was, "I'm really sorry."

Dendy stepped up to him, tears streaming from her eyes. Her face flashed red for a moment. "Kill them, Zaz. Kill every goddamned one of them. Blow them into the next galaxy!"

"With what?" asked Carl. "His mean eyes and foul language? Shit, girl, it's game over. Did you see what we're up against? Why don't we just fuckin' surrender and get it over with. We might come out of this with our lives. You know those damn things are going to find us again. Either that or those aliens will do a survey and pick our asses up by some probe. They came here to wipe everything clean. That means us."

Galoot fingered the scar on his stomach. "I don't know how anyone expects us to fight them off again. Maybe if we stay good and tucked in they'll pass us over."

Zaz felt for the remote device in his pocket. He addressed his crew in a steady voice. "It's about time I squared with you all.

A few of you guessed my intentions – Sammy, and Dendy, I'm talking about you. The rest of you don't know, but I've rigged the *Shenandoah* for a nuclear detonation."

Carl stared at him. "What the flak are you talking about?"

"I armed the Bang Drive pods to detonate simultaneously via the Sat and this remote. I locked in a frequency on the bridge. That's why I wanted to bring the Sat dish, just in case. I have to know who's with me on this."

"Whoa, just a second," said Carl. "I'm the doctor of pyrotechnics around here. How many pods did you arm and what bank of toggles?"

"It was ten – the extreme left bank."

"That's over a hundred megatons, but only ten toggles. It might set the rest of the pods off through chain reaction. How far downrange are we?"

"Over four hundred and fifty miles."

Carl sighed. "Lucky for that. We might feel a shock wave, but it'll probably be more like a hot wind. I couldn't tell you what would happen if every pod ignited. Hell, I say go for it."

"If we can take them out," said Galoot, "then we have to do it."

The women nodded. Dendy swallowed dryly. "We don't have a choice. You were right all along. I'll push the button if you want me to."

"Oh, no you don't," said Carl. "I'm the one that blows shit up around here. I've been aching to light that old girl up ever since I stepped aboard. No offense, Zaz. If we goof, you can blame it on me."

Zaz grinned. "Then you have the honor. Understand one thing – once we do this, it's done – there's no taking it back. The landscape out there will be unrecognizable. It's possible that our real rescuers will think that we died in a freak explosion and avoid the area. We'll set up our emergency hardware to try and draw attention to ourselves, but there are no guarantees from here on out. Everyone understand?"

They all nodded.

"Good, we have to make this quick. Sammy, rig the Sat dish, then train it on the *Shenandoah*. We'll calibrate just before ignition."

Zaz went to the scope and watched the ships, trying to determine if anything had changed. They hadn't moved, or even retracted the elevator cylinder. As long as they weren't wise to the ship being hot-wired for a nuclear detonation they had little time before discovery. He didn't want the Sat dish turned on until the very last moment – the aliens might be able to trace the signal.

Something else appeared in the view of his scope. Zaz saw stilt-like, gangly creatures emerged from the cylinder. They were as tall as the Jack Lions, and moved about them with ease. Zaz could swear he even saw one of the stick aliens stroking the back of a Jack Lion. He cursed the fuzzy optics, trying to resolve their facial features, but it was no use. All he knew was that they were tall, spindly, and not wearing any type of suit or garments. There was something disproportionate about the size of their large heads. By Earth standards, they were hideous, looking like upright roaches that walked with a stiff, ungainly posture.

"Jesus, what next?" Zaz swore. He checked Samantha's progress. She had another minute to go before the set-up would be complete. He pulled the remote out of his suit pocket then turned to the others. "Helmets on, everybody. Put on your sun goggles, pull down your visors. Nobody looks at the flash."

"What about Paddy and Lyle?" asked Dendy.

"They have more protection than we do in that cave. They'll be fine."

The captain looked through the scope again. He could see dozens of stick-like aliens in the compound, clustered around the construction equipment. A few of them found paths between the dead Jack Lions and began to enter the *Shenandoah's* hold.

Zaz fought the urge to tell the others what he was seeing. This menace had to go *now*. These aliens were responsible for the mass extinction of the Paddymous giants. Whatever their reasons, they had committed genocide on an unfathomable scale.

A sudden, sadistic glee grew inside Zaz. *They would pay for what they'd done.* Soon there would be a smoking black hole in place of the great alien ships, a desert plain littered with slag and molten glass. An eye for an eye – balance would be restored.

In his mind he saw millions of gentle Paddymous beings in a not-so-distant past. In those days there was a peaceful and loving coexistence. He could see the children playing with straw-woven toys; hear the happy chortling noises from the contented parents. Flash forward: he saw them screaming in fear, running for their lives from the Jack lion horde, only to be stalked and cut down like cattle. They had been torn limb from limb, not one of them able to escape the vicious attack that must have gone on for days, possibly even weeks. Like Christians in a coliseum, or Jews in a gulag, they had been forced to simply wait for their deaths. How apropos that one annihilation should be answered by another.

Zaz handed the remote to Carl, never taking his eyes away from the scope.

"I'm ready," said Samantha. "The signal is live."

Zaz had just started the countdown when something shot out from the top of the nearest ship: a small dot screaming upward into the air. He unlocked the scope and tried to follow the object by the white contrail left in its wake, but lost it in the sun's glare. It startled him. Was it a missile launch?

"Five…four…three…two…one…let them have it Carl!"

"Givin' it to 'em now!" Dendy hollored.

Zaz backed away from the scope and pulled his goggles on. Carl clicked the detonator button. A white-hot bulb of light replaced the area where the ships had been. Through his heavy goggles, Zaz watched as a fiery mass expanded outward at the speed of light, like a sun going nova. He fell to the ground, pulling his hands up over his eyes, fearful that such radiant light would tear through every part of his body. The others had already fallen to the ground, shielding their eyes from the sight. Zaz thought he could see through his eyelids down into his hands, past that into the rock beneath him. It was like some ghostly x-ray, where he could see straight through the very atoms themselves.

"Stay down for a fifteen count," Zaz ordered, shouting above the chaos.

They stayed down longer just to be sure. Zaz began to move. Dendy clung to him like a tapeworm. He pulled her into his arms and stood up. In the distance, he could see a turbulent cloud of fire and smoke vomiting upward in a vertical column. Like a tree, it grew outward in branches of orange and yellow, the gases rising higher into the atmosphere. Another dizzying array of colors, from deep purples to bright reds and greens, were backlit by streaks of lightning that snapped within the blossoming mass.

"Yeah! Eat that!" Samantha shouted, taking a victory punch at the air.

The others joined in, jumping, dancing about. Carl slapped the rock at his side. "You assholes weren't counting on that, were you?"

Zaz could see other pinpricks of light bursting at the base of the mushroom-like cloud. The million-degree surge set off the rest of the ship's combustibles, including, he assumed, any delayed explosions resulting from the alien ships. The *Shenandoah's* Ultrinium hull and the heavy construction equipment had become instant shrapnel, vaporizing anything in the vicinity. Nothing could have survived the massive detonation.

They watched the pyrotechnic conflagration for a long time, marveling at the atmosphere that had become a collage of colorful swirls. More than a half hour later after the blast, there came a series of snaps and pops, then a sustained noise like rolling thunder. For a brief moment it sounded like a centennial fireworks display that Zaz had once attended in Washington D.C. The ground rattled under their feet – a seismic shock. The sound wave concussion had finally caught up with them. The huge slab of rock underneath their feet shimmied drunkenly, threatening to bowl them over.

"Hit the deck!" Zaz yelled.

The crew hugged the rock, Dendy shivering in Zaz's arms. Seven minutes later, a series of heated blasts swept over them – secondary waves. Static electricity snapped in the air, bringing the smell of burnt insulation and ozone. It resembled the odor of a hot weld from a torch – a smell that could be tasted. Zaz thought that they might have absorbed a lethal dose of radiation. Samantha put his mind to rest when she pulled a radiation detector from her pack and declared that fallout was present, but not lethal.

When the wind had died down, Zaz called out, "All clear!"

Dendy walked with cautious steps to the cliff edge and looked out at the devastation on the desert floor. She turned to Zaz, her cheeks tear-stained. "You don't have to feel bad about this – we did the right thing. Those things will never hurt another living creature again."

Zaz took some solace in the comfort she offered. There wouldn't be any more secrets. "I saw something leave the ship," Zaz began in a loud voice. "Just before the detonation. It went straight up into the atmosphere, where I lost its trail. I didn't have eyes on it long enough to know what it was. It might have been a hallucination or distortion of the lens. I also managed to get a look at the aliens: they're ghastly looking things, tall and insect like. No other discernable features – nothing resembling a human."

"I wish I would have seen those goons," said Samantha, giving a chuckle. "Maybe you could sketch one for us and include it in your little diary. It should make for interesting reading. Contact with anotheer species and we blow them to hell. Not much of a plot after that."

"So they were just skinny stick men, eh?" Galoot wondered aloud. "Rotten bastards made those critters do all the dirty work for them."

"You would think that with ships and technology like that," said Dendy, "they would have come straight for us without wasting any time. I'll bet they could have blown us right off the continent."

Zaz looked to the south again. The funnel shaped cloud with an anvil on top had reached 100,000 feet and was still climbing. "That's the mystery," he said. "They had complete control over the Jack Lions. I wonder why they went to all this trouble to keep their hands clean. They were smart enough to have super high-tech ships, yet too dumb to use the right tactic for their objective."

"Objective?" Carl rubbed his leg. "What the hell did they want? I mean, besides killing everything in sight – including us."

"Maybe they were just plumb mean," said Galoot.

Zaz couldn't figure it out. "You would think that, along with superior intelligence, mercy and compassion might also be present. How could they be so advanced, yet so ruthless? None of it makes sense."

"Doctor Jekyll and Mr. Hyde," said Dendy. "Isn't it always the mild-mannered bookworm, married, with a steady job, that ends up being the serial killer? Wasn't Hitler an artist?" Who knows what evil lurks in the six-chambered hearts of pirate aliens?"

Samantha did not try to hide her uneasiness. "I just hope we got them all. It would be a real bummer if there were more of them where those came from. We're fresh out of ships to blow up. I don't think the rest of their kin would take too kindly to what we just did."

The implications of what Samantha had just said were staggering. Was it possible that they had just initiated a galactic war? Had Planet Janitor's blind idiocy just gotten them out of a jam, but forced the hand of a superior race to seek revenge? Those were a lot of nasty 'what ifs' to consider.

Zaz chalked it up to needless speculation – they could contemplate the end of the world tomorrow. "Let's pack it up," he said. "Put the Sat on a rotation scan then key it in to your screen, Sammy. Set up a security-coded distress beacon. It's the only calling card we have to attract our people."

They started down the long incline. Zaz heard what sounded like a hissing noise and a few more snaps. He didn't bother looking over his shoulder to gaze at the nuclear cloud – he knew it would be there for hours, maybe days.

*　*　*

They parked both vehicles in the campsite, having managed to groove a nice path over the slide area. It was now much easier to travel over when making expeditions to the north.

Lyle and Paddy were sitting in camp chairs. The two scientists rose quickly at the sight of the others. Paddy looked genuinely upset. Lyle appeared more subdued, but still agitated.

"Forgive our impertinence," said Paddy. "We were concerned about the peculiar quake and wind gusts. We thought that we would check on you. I'm glad to see that you are all safe."

Zaz took his helmet off, dropped it to the sand. He took a long pull from his canteen. "Well, we might have had something to do with that quake. You can rest easy though, there won't be another."

"Whatever do you mean, sir?" Lyle asked, concerned by the news. "How did you have something to do with a tremor?"

Zaz collapsed into a camp chair. "Would you like the full spiel or the pithy abstract?"

"Either rendition will do," said Lyle.

Zaz swapped stares at the two. "That assumption you had about a master race in charge of the Jack Lions? Well it panned out. Two ships landed in the compound while I was monitoring the site. Both species disembarked together. I knew they weren't going to stop. I had no choice – I lit up the desert. That's what you felt. There are no more masters on this planet intent on harming anything ever again."

Galoot ground his fist into his palm. "Boss saw those aliens chumming it up with those Jack creatures, like they were pets!"

Paddy chewed his lips. "But how did you, I mean…" He didn't have the words to convey his astonishment.

Zaz smiled, gazing at the two as if they were children. It was just like a geologist and a zoologist to seldom look to the skies. Even from Zaz's vantage point, he could look straight down the gorge and see the enormity of the explosion – the soot-filled cloud snapping with residual lightning that stretched up into the upper reaches of the stratosphere.

Zaz pointed a finger over their shoulders.

They turned around. Their heads cocked upward in unison.

Lyle put a hand to his chest then sat down on the sand.

Paddy clapped a hand to his forehead. "Oh, my… what have we done?"

Samantha walked to them, offering water. "Here, have a drink. Everything will be all right in a minute."

Galoot carried Carl to a spot with a blanket arranged for him on the sand. The Italian groped under a corner of the coverlet and pulled out a hidden whiskey flask. He wasted no time in taking a long swig.

Out of his peripheral vision, Zaz could see several Paddymous giants creeping out from the shadows of the trees. They moved just inside the perimeter, watching the motions of their favorite humans – the scientists. Silver Two rounded a bush and stumbled in their direction, drawing all eyes: its entire frame was covered with locusts; the head case was marked with a runny splotch of bird droppings that had dripped onto its shoulder and ran down its arm. The automech stopped in the midst of the humans and relayed his report:

"The gorge area is free of hostile life forms," said Silver Two. "We have no unauthorized entries. There are several free-roaming species in the vicinity – a Dasypodida variant, and an unknown avian creature. I am distressed to report that my frame is inundated with a profusion of Acrididae insect members. They could be attracted to the electrical hum within my chassis because – "

"That's enough, Silver Two," said Zaz. "Stand down."

"Somebody should gag that walking scrap heap," said Carl.

Dendy made a face. "Leave him alone. He's only trying to perform his sub-routines. He can help me prepare dinner. Can't you, Silver Two?"

He stepped toward her, gave a curt bow. "I would be delighted to be of service, Miss Dendy."

"There. You see?" she said.

Zaz frowned. "Clean him up before he handles food."

Dendy ignited a pile of wood in the fire ring. Then, hand-in-hand, she walked to the mess tent with Silver Two to prepare an early dinner.

Zaz shifted his mind back to the topic at hand: there was no reason for another ecological or humanitarian debate – if anything of any worth had died, he thought, it had been the *Shenandoah*. If not for the warnings of the scientists, he wouldn't have moved to the gorge, or rigged the ship for destruction. The fact that the aliens were caught in the crossfire was a lucky break.

"Then it is over," said Paddy, finally offering a word on the matter. "Those foul hellions have met their end. Those who wield the sword in violence shall fall by it. What is most important is the survival of Maximus Paddymous."

"Don't forget us," said Samantha. "If it weren't for us, these giants would have faced total obliteration. I think we deserve some of the credit."

"We are dedicated scientists," said Paddy. "I believe it is our duty to restore the Natural Order – to preserve what was nearly lost."

"First and foremost," said Zaz, "our job is to preserve ourselves. That means cooperation in all things. We have to tend to our gardens, cleanse our water, keep ourselves clothed, clean and free of disease and injury. We need to uphold our moral attitudes. That means no quarreling or vindictiveness. We have to monitor our food rations or find a way to provide alternatives. The Sat dish and the emergency beacons have to be maintained and operable at all times. We should have a disaster contingency plan for earthquakes, bad weather, floods. Least of all, the mechanical equipment we've brought with us has to be preserved. *Those* are the duties we must carry out."

"It's like *Robinson Crusoe*, only we don't have a Thursday," said Carybell.

Samantha tousled the small girl's head. "That's right, sweetie. We're stranded just like he was. Only he had a beautiful island, and his helper was named Friday."

Robinson Crusoe? That story was tame in comparison. This was The Island of Doctor Moreau.

Carl heaved a rock at a tree. The Patriarch Paddymous, standing at his side, did likewise. Zaz sighed disgustedly, wondering if all the killing that Carl had seen in the fourth Global Conflict had anything to do with his persistent displays of machismo. True to form, the man aired his less than sympathetic views a moment later.

"We come first because we're the alpha species," said Carl. "We have to watch out for number one before we help the dummies along."

Paddy scowled. "By alpha species, you must mean the superior race that just set off a nuclear device in a pristine ecosystem. Indeed, that shows a great deal of intelligence."

"What should we have done?" Zaz narrowed his eyes at Paddy, unappreciative of the sarcasm.

Paddy kicked at a small sand pile, showing his displeasure. "Nothing. You seem to have all the answers." He strode from the campsite, not once looking back.

"Dinner is served!" Dendy announced. She exited the mess tent with an armload of flash cooked meals. She frowned when she noticed Paddy's departure. Silver Two walked behind her, cradling a small load of utensils – Dendy had cleaned him up and tied an apron around his middle.

"It is a pleasure to be of service," said Silver Two. The automech's foot caught on a root snag. The machine pitched forward and hit the ground with a calamitous thump, spilling the dinnerware.

The crewmembers passed each other dumbfounded looks.

Lyle lingered for a moment, distracted by the mishap. He regained his thought process and said, "You must forgive Paddy. He does not see things as cut and dried as you do. His disciplines are derived from science and nature. Unfortunately, I am predisposed to act along that same mindset." He gave a curt bow. "I bid you goodnight and good tidings." He left to catch up with his colleague.

A few of the Paddymous hesitated at first then decided to stay. A young female locked eyes on Samantha's flaming red hair.

"Uh, oh," said Samantha, hurrying to her tent and yanking the flap down.

Sidus Log, Rotation 43.
I've brought a holocaust upon the planet. The alien threat that we had been worried about showed up. There was a connection between the non-indigenous Jack Lions and these creatures - they were their keepers. We took them out, destroying two large alien ships in the process They could not have survived the blast. From our cliff-

top observations, we can see streaks and melted slag where the three large ships once stood. We are alone again, save for the 35 remaining Paddymous survivors.

I feel that if I was a resident of this system, I would be arraigned and court marshaled by some galactic council, then sentenced to a million executions for what I've done. Such is the way we do things on Earth. How strange is it to feel that, though I performed a necessary evil. I alone was the evil in it? I'll carry these damning feelings forever, I suppose.

Paddy and Lyle are incorrigible. They insist on isolating themselves from the rest of us. I don't think they like the company of humans anymore. The Paddymous have replaced us for them. I understand their preoccupation and the thrill of discovery. I think, as time passes, they'll adopt an even more cynical view of us then break off contact completely.

Carl's wound is beginning to heal. He is out of bed, hobbling around the camp. He shows sadistic pleasure in demonstrating childlike behavior in front of the gentle giants. Just yesterday he instigated a fight between two juvenile Paddymous that Galoot and I had to break up. We've taken Carl's whiskey away from him, hoping to curtail some of his more bizarre antics. Samantha admits that she is at a loss for looking past his behavior. She has accepted his wild side and renewed her search within him for that softer, kinder Carl she once glimpsed. I believe she is in love with him, though he makes it difficult for her. Still, I wish them happiness.

We've only been here for a little over a month. It seems like it's been a million years and a billion parsecs away. I yearn for Earth, wondering if I'll ever see her again. I miss her bright greens and blues. Colors and shades here are washed out, faded, almost like our hopes and dreams.

Zachary Crowe, PJ.

Zaz awoke to a numbing cold, despite Dendy's warmth beside him. His wristcom thermometer read 34 degrees. There had been colder mornings, but somehow the constant near freezing temperatures were arousing a persistent ache in his bones. It wasn't anything like the southern California winters he had gotten used to.

He kicked out of his blanket then tucked it firmly around his partner. Dendy moaned, mouthing silent words, but did not wake. He slipped on his boots and pulled a heavy jacket over his shoulders, creeping silently from the tent. He stretched for a moment, feeling a persistent pressure in his bladder. He cursed himself for not building an enclosed latrine within walking distance. *One more project for the Sidus day-planner.*

He started off walking south at a leisurely pace, admiring the scenery and listening to the babble of the creek. He picked a few banana-like fruits off one of the trees and ate them both, enjoying their sweet tang. He found a spot to relieve himself and toed a small furrow. Once finished, he kicked some sand over it, his inner voice reminding him to keep his environment clean. It was funny, but in a very small way he was still a janitor. Perhaps "planetary caretaker" would have better described his station on Sidus.

Zaz walked for what he estimated to be a mile. The hike gave him a renewed feeling of vigor, fully awakening his senses. As he walked, he made it a point to keep within the old tire trails where the ground was solid – it made for easier strolling. It was the first real road blazed on Sidus. *Note to self: name this road.*

Gravel crunched, followed by the snap of a twig behind him. Startled he whirled around to discover a large male Paddymous standing in the path, his big arms swinging like massive pendulums. It was the one Paddy called the patriarch – the leader. He stood there loitering, a big stuporous grin plastered on his cow-like face.

"Oh, all right," said Zaz. "You don't have to sneak around. C'mon." Zaz held out his arm. The big lug gave a happy snort and followed. He quickly caught up to Zaz, watching the human closely. They walked together like old college chums. Whenever Zaz looked at something interesting the big male would also look at it.

"I guess we're just as much a curiosity to you as you are to us." Zaz plucked a twig off a tree and put it between his teeth. The big male followed the example.

Zaz welcomed the company, as he did when Dendy accompanied him. Between his Boy Scout past and Dendy's tireless energy, they were seldom idle, hiking up and down the valley floor or climbing to Cloud's Rest every day.

"I'll bet you're a pretty good Boy Scout, too," said Zaz. "Only it would be a hell of a thing to fit you into a uniform."

Zaz laced his fingers behind his back and looked to see if his big walking companion would do the same. The Paddymous tried, but he couldn't clasp his hands behind him – he was too broad in the shoulders. He just stuck them back there.

"Maybe it isn't such a bad thing that you try to be like us. We just have to be careful of what we show you. It must be fun for you to have all the girls, without the hassle of marriage. Or maybe you're married to all of them. Now there's a thought… You must be pretty busy at anniversary time!" Zaz cackled loudly, startling a few birds.

The big guy chortled, a spray of snot ejecting from his floppy nose. He seemed to be listening – not to the words, but to the volume and tone. It was possible they communicated by a series of frequencies, Zaz thought, like elephants or dolphins. Amazingly, the Paddymous had not found anything in the normal human tone or speech that frightened or disagreed with them. Of course, none of the crew had given them provocation by yelling at them. Could it have been that they were not as different as once thought?

"Hah! Then you'll tell us that you were just faking it and we're all mental cases – a bunch of violent little midgets. Carl would really like that one. Speaking about…"

Zaz stopped in a small clearing. His hiking companion had lagged behind; the Paddymous was licking the leaves of some stunted gray plant. He turned around, suddenly feeling an unmistakable foreign presence. It was not much more than a twinge – a nuisance – but he could feel it. The silence made the feeling all the more pronounced. It reminding him of the times he went hunting in the wilderness, trying to flush out a wounded animal. But the creature or beast, whatever it was, was hunkered down, controlling its breaths and watching him silently.

A whisper in his mind reached out with a tendril of thought: something menacing was stalking him – something all-powerful.

Zaz took a tentative step forward then remained still again. He held his breath, carefully studying the trees, shrubs, and brambles. The menacing feeling came over him again. Something was definitely out there. His eyes traveled to a stunted tree with slim, spindly branches. It was a dozen feet tall, covered with sharp thorns.

His eyes picked out something inside of the tree, camouflaged.

It was a stick-thin creature, resembling a tall humanoid crossed with the worst parts of a praying mantis. It had a multi-jointed exoskeleton, something akin to the carapace of a lobster. A triangular head sat on top of a stalk-like neck. Long, articulated arms ended with spidery hands, six fingers on each – three opposing three, like claspers. The feet were small skis, giving the appearance that the legs could scissor upwards while leaving the toe spikes on the ground.

The insect-like creature had frozen in a stealth pose, its head pointing away from Zaz. He would have looked right past it if not for the contrast in color against the tree it had become part of, a barely perceptible shade of green against the gray stunted branches.

It dawned on him – this was one of the alien creatures he'd seen in the compound, the same type that had exited the alien ship.

Zaz reached for his shoulder, discovering that he'd left his rifle behind. He damned his luck, stepped back and froze. The frontal lobe of his head began to throb – a skull full of hot lead.

The Mantis alien turned its head a full 90 degrees around, fixing on him with bulbous, yellow eyes. The orbs mesmerized him with a strange, invisible lure. His legs refused to move, having become mired in the ground, as if they had gained roots. His body was now cardboard, slave to an increasing paralysis. He tried to call out, but his throat had closed.

CHAPTER SEVENTEEN

VISIONS OF ANNIHILATION

THE ALIEN DISENGAGED itself from the interior of the tree and stepped out on its stilt-like legs, its eyes trained on Zaz as it made awkward, hinge-like steps towards him. The creature's head swiveled from side to side as it moved; its mouth, an ugly maw with two scissor-like mandibles, made strange, rapid, nibbling movements. A line of drool hung threadlike from the lower jaw.

It stopped in front of Zaz in a bent-over crouch, and still it towered over him. The alien's fingers clacked together in an agitated state.

Zaz couldn't fight the alien's hold on his mind. He feared his head would burst from the swelling pressure – it was as if his head were trapped in a vice. The thing was trying to get in there – trying to tear it open! He struggled against the force. He could hear *clicks* and *snaps* in his head, like some type of alien Morse code.

The noise became more intense – the intrusion full of hooks and barbs. Fleeting images passed behind his eyes: images of Mantis aliens; of eggs; of their hives. He saw vast tunnel complexes that resembled birthing chambers, filled with nests and tiny Mantis bugs slithering out of egg sacks. The Mantis infants were attended to by dwarfish mammals that resembled stout monkeys; small hominids, covered with matted hair. Ghastly smells reached his senses, putrid odors, sucking-noises coming from the birthing chambers. Visions of their hierarchy came to him: the dwarves were the labor force of their society, the ones who fed the infants, built the structures, and maintained the mighty ships. He saw piles of flesh and bone chopped up into pieces – the mangled corpses of the small dwarves, cast aside into other chambers. Gathered around these piles, he could see the Mantis aliens crouched low, using their mandibles to strip off chunks of the mangled body parts, consuming them with reckless abandon. Zaz's guts churned.

More images came forth: a scene of the Jack Lions, their ultimate pets. They emptied from the ships in the thousands, swarming over a medieval-like village and tearing its inhabitants limb from limb. Those who escaped the onslaught were run down and dispatched. The Mantis aliens looked down on the destruction, like the directors of a well-acted stage play. Soon there was nothing left but bloodied rags and discarded corpses.

More scenes of death and destruction on other alien worlds continued to flash in his mind like the passing frames of an old celluloid film. In those scenes the Jack Lions set upon countless aliens in many different star systems, to mete out annihilation until there was nothing left. The aggressive attacks played out over and over again in Zaz's mind, from one world to the next.

Zaz screamed, Weakness overtook his body, his energy drained. He dropped toward the sand, an unknown force crushing him. Spittle ran from his mouth and down his chest. The psychokinetic force that held him in place finally managed to force some recognizable words through the veil; they were fragmented, like his mind:

"NOT HAVE YOU...OURS IS THIS...GO AND WILL YOU DIE... OURS IS THIS...OURS IS THIS."

"Nothing is yours," Zaz managed to croak out. "You go and die!"

"PLACE IS YOURS NOT...PLACE IS YOURS NOT...KILLER OF THE HORDE."

Zaz gasped. He tried to move his head but it wouldn't turn – his eyes were frozen in place. The pain traveled down his spine – he felt as if his bowels would let loose at any moment.

As he fought against total collapse and unconsciousness, he saw something peculiar through his peripheral vision. The giant

Paddymous had been standing there the whole time, a witness to the confrontation. Whether he knew or felt the pain and fear that had gripped Zaz was unknown, but still he acted on instinct: the Paddymous picked up a huge rock and hurled it with such force that it nearly took the alien's head off. The Mantis creature flipped backward, sprawling on the ground like a batch of broken sticks.

Zaz felt the pressure lift from inside his head, like steam escaping from a kettle. Everything was spinning around him as if he were drunk.

"Thanks, my big friend," he said, finally capable of speaking again. "Good on you for knowing that was a bad thing!"

Zaz stumbled over to the alien's body. It looked dead; he couldn't see any signs of respiration – he was not even sure if it had lungs. The eyes were wide open, glassy. A milky white substance leaked from its mouth. The side of the alien's skull had been caved in.

The male Paddymous approached it cautiously, reaching out to touch it. He picked up a spindly arm then let it flop back to the sand. The Paddymous made a whining sound, a sort of sympathetic vocalization. The Paddymous had realized what he had done – he understood what the stillness of death meant. He knew that the act was connected to him: throwing the rock meant stillness. Death.

Zaz stroked his big shoulder. "It's all right for you to feel that way. But you saved my life. You fought back. There's nothing wrong with that." He reached down to grab what looked like the alien's ankle and pulled. The thin stick-like body scraped across the sand for a few feet. It weighed almost nothing. Zaz pulled again. "Here," he said, pointing to the other ankle. "You grab this one, see?"

The Paddymous, shown by example, grabbed one of the alien's legs and tugged. They trudged together through the sand, dragging the Mantis alien over the path toward the campsite. Zaz felt a peculiar feeling of victory; he had in his possession one of the monsters responsible for all the killing on Sidus. It had to be seen to be believed – he *had* to show the others that he had not been mistaken.

One major concern nagged at him: how many more of these aliens were out there?

They dragged the alien into camp and dropped it next to the fire ring. Dendy had just exited the tent, wiping sleep from her eyes, when she looked over in their direction.

"There you are," she said, pointing a playful finger at Zaz. "I keep losing track of you in the mornings. Is it because I snore?" She stopped near the fire ring, staring at the stick-like body sprawled there.

"What the hell!" She yelped.

Zaz held up a hand. "Shush! Don't wake the others."

Too late. The remaining crewmembers crawled from their tents. Galoot tromped across the sand with Carybell tucked under his arm. Wrapped in a blanket, she made muffled cries, trying to extricate herself from his grip.

Dendy knelt next to the Mantis alien. She jabbed a finger at it. "What's that? Where did you find such a thing?"

Carl popped his head out of his tent and began to crawl across the sand with frog-like hops. "What's going on around here? Silver Two, get your ass over here and help me!" Samantha followed Carl, rubbing her eyes.

Zaz waited for them to assemble around the creature before he explained. He told Galoot to go fetch the scientists. Galoot dropped Carybell in a heap and ran over the rockslide.

Carybell peeked out of her blanket. "Oh, a bug!" she said.

Samantha froze when she saw the large insect. She backed a few feet away.

"I was walking down the gorge when I ran into it," said Zaz. "It was camouflaged inside a tree. It put some kind of a whammy on me. It's hard to explain, but I think it was trying to communicate through some kind of mind transference. Whatever it was doing, it nearly killed me."

Paddy and Lyle arrived nearly 10 minutes later, dropping to their knees in the sand next to the Mantis alien. Lyle adjusted a lens on his optipak and peered down at the thing. "Goodness me. Wherever did you find it, sir?"

Zaz described his encounter a second time for the benefit of the professors. He recalled everything he could remember up until the point he began to lose consciousness. He told them about the thought transference – what the alien had said, including the anger it directed at him. He told them about the images he saw of the egg nests, the dwarves, the feedings, and the planet conquests.

"You say it communicated with you, Zaz?" Paddy asked, kneeling next to the alien. He poked a stick in its mouth, wiggled it around. "Inexplicable. It is a bipedal mantid, having lost a pair of legs in its evolution. You say it talked to you in your mind? *Most extraordinary.*"

A six-figured hand thrust up and grabbed Paddy by the neck. The scientist flailed his hands. "Help! I'm done for!"

Samantha screamed.

Galoot dived, landing hard on the alien. It kicked out from underneath him, standing up and holding Paddy in a death grip. Galoot sprang to his feet, wrapping his hand around the alien's neck. He gave a hard yank – the alien's head snapped off and dropped to the sand. The torso, still standing, released its grip on Paddy and then ran across the clearing with long loping strides. It disappeared in the foliage. They could hear its crunching footsteps on the gravel, heading south down the gorge.

Samantha held her cheeks. "Of all that is unholy!" she exclaimed. "Did you *see* that?" She stared down at the triangular alien head, its tiny mouth still moving, contorting, its mandibles clicking. A milky white substance leaked from the broken neck and pooled on the sand, producing a bitter stink.

Carl, having been dragged to the spot by the automech, stared pop-eyed at the severed head. "What in the hell just happened?"

Galoot brought a size-18 boot down on the head, cracking it like an eggshell. A puss-like liquid frothed out of the mouth. The eyes burst open.

"Obviously insectoid," said Paddy as he rubbed his neck, more frightened than harmed, "It had a secondary nervous system – a backup defense mechanism that allowed it to flee."

"*What do we do now?*" Samantha asked in a shrill tone.

Zaz looked at the professors. "How far can it get like that?"

Lyle stared trancelike at the cracked head. "I'm not familiar with its physiology, but it might be able to survive for days, much like a cockroach without its head. Yet, how could you know such a thing, with a creature that is functioning on pure nerves?"

"That's about all I'm functioning on right now," said Dendy with a shudder. She looked around to see if anyone else felt the same. "What's next?"

Galoot spat in the sand. "Like a chicken with its head cut off. Maybe it ran off to find its friends."

Zaz massaged his aching temples. "All right, pack up the scout and the six-wheeler. Load the weapons."

"What for?" asked Dendy.

"We're going after it. There's no way I'm letting that thing get away alive."

They packed up the vehicles. Zaz jumped in the driver's seat of the six-wheeler. The male Paddymous, who'd watched the commotion with interest, jumped up on the roll cage, prepared to go with the humans. When Zaz hit the accelerator, the giant fell off the roll cage and landed in the sand.

"Oh, the poor dear," said Dendy. "Stop, he might be hurt."

Proving Dendy wrong, the giant male once again climbed onto the cage, this time grabbing the frame securely.

Zaz smiled. "He's okay; trust me – he learns by doing things." He took off again but kept it to a comfortable speed. He leaned his head over the doorframe, trying to spot the telltale white mucus dribbles left by the escaping alien. Every so often he would come across the macabre trail and slow the vehicle, making sure he was following in the right direction.

Two miles out he lost the trail. He slowed the vehicle to a crawl, watching for anything out of the ordinary on either side. Three miles down the gorge, they found the alien – supine, half in and half out of a very strange looking object.

The crew disembarked to investigate. They could see the alien body twitching with a deathly spasm.

It looked as if the creature had attempted to re-enter its craft. The device itself was a large tear-shaped object, smooth in profile; it was five meters long, two meters in diameter. Filament-type wire hung from the sharp end of the teardrop, leading to a tattered parachute of thin, reflective foil. The chute had settled downwind of the craft, half of it snagged in the branches of one of the spiral-trunk conifers.

Zaz frowned. "They didn't have time to inspect the ship and see the threat. I can only guess that this one picked up on our remote detonation signal just before we keyed in the final sequence and beat it for the escape pod. The first one on a submarine to detect an incoming torpedo is always the sonar operator. This guy could have been at their nav console – he only cared about getting away, not about what would happen to the others."

"Looks like it," said Dendy. "He was probably the smartest bulb in the batch, while the others were standing around twiddling their stupid little claspers. They had no idea what hit 'em."

Galoot stepped up to the Mantis alien, grabbed a spindly ankle and pulled it from the hatch opening. He dragged it to a small clearing and raised a ponderous leg, with the intention of crushing the corpse.

"Hold off on that," yelled Zaz. "We've got an unknown species here that might come in handy later. I think our Earth compatriots would like to be apprised of its biological makeup." He felt a far more reaching need in his guts, to retrieve the creature – proof that they were attacked – evidence that an intelligent, lethal species was on the loose, with the dangerous implications of a future confrontation.

Zaz walked up to the craft and peered in. The inside did not look large enough to seat the alien, though it had obviously arrived in it. There were several straps inside that hung limp over a recumbent seat – a harness arrangement. There was no dash panel, only a number of long levers in front of a large black crystalline ball that might have been a flight control panel or holographic projector. He could see no markings or alien graffiti denoting control gauges or instrumentation.

Zaz walked around to the bulbous part of the teardrop, noticing a rainbow spectrum of color that denoted extreme temperatures. Black soot marks spiked outward from a central point.

"It's an ejection pod," he told the others. "An explosive launch tube blew this pod out of the mother ship. When it reached high atmosphere, the chutes opened. It drifted on the high altitude currents to land here. It was just a stroke of dumb luck it ended up in the gorge. It wasn't a controlled flight – it's a non-propelled emergency escape vehicle." That was the best explanation Zaz could offer.

Galoot nodded. "Might have been a high-ranking dude that got away, but he was the last big man, or queen."

"Are you certain of that?" Samantha looked around between the trees.

"I only saw one launch – one contrail," said Zaz

Paddy knelt down next to the broken alien. He fingered a red welt on his neck. "I find it nearly impossible that a creature with this body arrangement could possess a marked intelligence or even consciousness. An insectoid life form that can think, process information, create and use mental telepathy staggers the mind. What kind of evolutionary path did it take to arrive at this stage of development? How many billions of years were required to perfect this species?"

Lyle sat down, studying broken pieces of the alien's shell under one of his optipak lenses. "Somehow, on their home world, this taxon evolved to dominate the other groups. It must have spawned an early intelligence, allowing it to manipulate its environment. If there were such a thing as reptiles, mammals, and avian life forms, they took back seats to this species. We already know that the marsupial lions were under their dominion. Now I'm wondering if the aliens are in fact biologically connected with the Jack Lions. I believe a complete autopsy is in order."

"You can haul him back to camp then," said Zaz. "Wrap up the corpse and submerge it in the stream water. That should keep it fresh. Remove it when you have to perform the examination."

"Excellent suggestion, sir," said Paddy.

"Boss, it doesn't have a suit or stitch of clothing on either," said Galoot. "Not even a weapon."

"No sexual organs to cover up," said Paddy. "Perhaps they had a developmental notion of the Geneva Convention, in a twisted sort of way, by allowing lesser species to fight their battles for them. Perhaps they had some form of religion that forbade them to carry instruments of war. I admit it is far-fetched, but from what we know of their technology, they *are* highly evolved."

"That makes a lot of sense," said Carl, balancing upright on his good leg. "They make somebody else do all their killing. Where are the morals in that?"

"I'm not saying that I understand their motives," said Paddy, speculatively, "only that it is possible. Religions and cultures from another star system could have evolved in a dissimilar fashion to our own. Just because we are familiar with our own rules and standards, doesn't mean it could not be contrariwise with a foreign entity."

"The Trojans despised the use of arrows," said Zaz, "believing them to be the instruments of women, unfit for a manly war. But the Trojans were not averse to showing incredible violence by other weapons and means. It's just different principles and applications. Maybe they're not so different from us after all."

Samantha spoke up. "Maybe they have rules that say they can't wipe out a race with sophisticated weaponry, but have to use underlings to do their dirty work. Maybe they follow some galactic council like we do – a non-interference policy – only they bend the rules for the sole purpose of disposing of unwanted species. Now that would be as narcissistic as you can get."

Zaz thought about what Samantha had proposed. "It did say that this planet belonged to them. Like they were claiming ownership. Only they found it occupied by a primitive race, so they let their hounds loose to eradicate the natives. Genocide, plain and simple."

"That just makes them cowards – galactic pirates," said Carl.

"I'm not disagreeing with you, Carl. What they did was unconscionable. Perhaps they answered to a hive queen, like Paddy suggested, or possibly a deity of some sort. Maybe their home world was dying out and they needed real estate. Who knows? Why, if they could navigate the stars, did they pick this planet? Why didn't they find an alternative? Could it have been the atmosphere? The resources?"

Lyle took several photographs of the dead alien. "All of the above, sir. Their need for a planet, combined with their conquering mentality, could only have meant that Georgian

Sidus picked them. When the right criteria were met, they acted swiftly. They arrived here fourteen years ago. They cleansed the planet then left, only to return to what they thought was a sterile environment. Then they ran into us – another equation – another problem to be solved. Only it did not go quite as expected. *We* knew how to fight back."

"Maybe they were amateurs," proposed Dendy. "Maybe this was the first time they tried anything like this. Who's to say they've been barbarians all their lives?"

"I saw terrible images within the mind of that thing," said Zaz. "This was not the first time for them. They're professional assassins."

Carl sneered. "Don't start making excuses for them, Dendy. I don't care how you paint it or who did what to whom. They're a bunch of natural born killers. They deserved to get their asses blown to dust. How would you like them coming into our solar system and claiming this and that?"

They stood in silence, absorbing the philosophical issues. The downside was now evident, considering how ruthless some of their neighbors could be. There was no room in the galaxy for conquerors bent on annihilation. Every planet that had taken its first baby steps in evolution was at risk of being wiped from the slate if species like the Mantis aliens were allowed to have free reign. Such aggression would call for a galactic response from all peaceful planetary civilizations – all out war.

"I wonder where they're from," said Dendy. "It couldn't be too far away from here. Anything fewer than fourteen light-years would be a good candidate. Unless there's a closer base, or they have some type of hyper-light drive."

"Well, Sammy's got our star charts," said Zaz. "She'll have months, with lots of time on her hands to grapple with that question. They seem to like G-type stars with oxygen-nitrogen atmospheres, so that should help narrow it down somewhat." He looked around. "For now, I think a few words over the deceased are in order."

Lyle looked confused. "You mean a eulogy, sir?"

"Just parting words."

Carl guffawed. "I say we burn the whole mess to hell fire, kick some sand on the bastard and call it a day. I'll take the honors of pissing on him."

"That's exactly what we're talking about here, Carl," said Zaz. "Dignity and human compassion are what separates us from that thing. It doesn't mean we have to enjoy killing them – dishonoring them. They had no intention of doing right by us. I doubt they would have said any words over us, either. But that's not how we operate."

Carl scowled. "There ain't a kind word coming out of my mouth for that piece of shit. Not doing it!"

Zaz looked at Galoot, expecting a response.

"I don't mind doing things for the crew, boss," said the giant. "But not for the likes of that bug who tried to punch our ticket."

The girls looked pensive, while the scientists appeared undecided. Zaz thought that the moral collision was in respect to what the creature was entitled to. He'd suggested a human ritual for an inhuman monster.

"Okay," Zaz said, "You can turn your back if you want."

Zaz bowed his head. The others were hesitant at first, but followed suit except for Carl, who turned away. Zaz had no idea how many Jack Lions or aliens he'd killed. He'd destroyed countless lives, even if it had been in the name of self-preservation. He could not harden his heart to the incredible loss, enemy or not. He would also speak for the Paddymous.

"Though we are compelled to damn this enemy," Zaz began, "I would ask that each of us find it in our hearts to forgive them, and wish them fond journey in life's end – wherever that may be. I can only hope that there will never be a repeat of such aggression and destruction in our lifetimes. We want for nothing, except for solidarity and mutual understanding among all races, be they near or extending to the farthest reaches of the universe. We mourn the passing of the Paddymous beings, who lost their lives in incalculable numbers through no fault of their own. To live in peace, and to let live in harmony, is our most profound desire in a space and time that was meant for all. Captain Zachary Crowe, Planet Janitor and crew – ashes to ashes, dust to dust."

Heads raised. "Can we transport the creature back to camp in the vehicle?" asked Paddy.

Zaz nodded. "Do so. Wrap the chute line up in the back tow-hitch so we can drag the capsule back. We might salvage something out of it."

Carl spit in sand. "I'm not riding back with that stink bug sitting next to me!"

Zaz whirled on him. "Then you've got a hell of a long walk back to camp."

Dendy turned to face Zaz. He saw a soft expression in her moistened eyes. Her voice was thick with emotion when she spoke. "You're a good man, Zachary."

CHAPTER EIGHTEEN

SURVIVAL – SIDUS STYLE

ZAZ ADJUSTED his grass-woven hat to keep the glare from the sun out of his eyes. His unruly hair stuck to the sweat on his cheeks, annoying him whenever he turned his head. It felt as if his face had been wrapped in a mat of hot seaweed. He tried to twist a lock of hair into a ponytail, but didn't have anything to tie it off with. He cursed then flailed his hands, one of which hit the binocular scope, knocking it off its trajectory. What he had said about crew hygiene had now come back to bite him in the briskets.

"Come here," said Dendy. "Let me help." She expertly twisted some braids into his hair then knotted it behind his head. "There," she said. "All better now? You ought to shave that beard off. You look worse than Paddy. And in case I haven't told you…" She put a hand to her bulbous stomach and furrowed her brows. "Whoa, now *that* was a kick! I guess he doesn't like me scolding you." She laughed.

"That's my boy," he said. "Or girl. I guess we'll find out soon enough."

"The way he's riding me, I think he's a boy. It will be a few more months. Oh, Zaz, I hope we're picked up soon. Nothing against Sidus, but I don't want our baby born here. Just think of all the nationality jokes."

Zaz nodded, readjusting the scope again. He moved it gently on its axis, scanning a southern quadrant of the desert plain near the tree line.

"Do you see anything interesting?"

That was the same line she had been using for six and a half months, every time they'd climbed Cloud's Rest. She hadn't missed a day or complained, even though the advancement of her pregnancy had made it a more arduous climb for her. There would come a day when he would have to leave her behind – they couldn't risk a slip and fall. A miscarriage could have dire consequences in a place that had no real doctors or hospital facilities.

He stared at the emergency beacon for a moment. It emitted a steady *bleep…bleep…bleep* with every pulse of a tiny blue indicator light. The charge was still good; the battery pack would last another year if necessary. The Sat dish battery pack was equally strong; the dish was set for wide sweep scan. The only thing left that had to hold a charge were the humans.

Zaz looked off into the northwest. He could see a solid haze in the distance, a dust storm near the great sea where the weather was less temperate. Just above the horizon, the small fractured moon, Cay, hung in the sky, making its lone orbital journey. He began to reminisce over the last few months, over the countless log entries describing the antics of the giant Paddymous, birthdays, holidays (some they had made up), fights, council meetings, campsite songs and love-making sessions. One particular incident stuck out in his mind from rotation 75:

He had woken early on a frigid morning to the groans of his mate. Having had a nightmare, she'd mumbled about babies, death and danger. The day before she'd suffered a bout of morning sickness and lashed out at him. Seeing as there was little he could do to stave off such pains, he decided to venture out that day and bring her back a bouquet of flowers. When he got to the creek, he found a patch of bright pink, triangular-petal flowers. No sooner had he bent over to pluck some when he noticed Galoot doing the same thing several yards down the creek bank. The giant had picked a large bushel of yellow flowers, turning to hand some off to

Carl, who was sitting close by. The two whispered to one another. Zaz moved closer to hear the exchange, remaining concealed.

"I know she likes these ones because I saw her sniffing them the other day," said Galoot.

"Go back and get some of the blue ones."

"I'm not going to tear the whole valley floor up. You have enough. Besides, we better scoot. If Carybell wakes up, she'll come running after me to see what I'm doing."

"That don't even compare to my situation. I get it all the time. Sam told me it was bad enough she had to look at me every day. But now she has to carry me around inside her for nine months!"

"Hush up!"

Zaz stepped out from his concealment. He cleared his throat, the flowers dangling from his grip.

Upon seeing him, Galoot started, dropping the precious blooms. "Damn, boss, you puckered my pooper. Uh, it's a good morning, eh?"

Zaz looked down his nose at them. "Looks like some extra seed planting going on around here. Or am I wrong about that?"

Galoot clapped the dirt from his hands. "Uh, what?" He looked back at the flowers by the creek. "Oh, yeah, except these are wild flowers."

"I'm not talking about that type of seed, you big lug. It's not a holiday. It's nobody's birthday. Neither one of you are daisy sniffers. So what's the occasion?"

Galoot faltered, "I don't think there's any occasion here, boss"

"Oh, the hell with it," said Carl. "Samantha's got a bun in the flash cooker. She's all cranked up and looking for trouble."

"You mean she's pregnant?"

"That's what I mean." Carl hunched his shoulders. His looks said, *it wasn't my fault.*

Dear God, thought Zaz. How could it be possible? The odds of it were staggering – there had obviously been multiple trips to the raspberry bushes. He couldn't decide whether it was impeccable timing or unfortunate circumstances. *All of a sudden you say "boo" and two women are plugged and splitting cells!* Was there something in the air on Sidus, or had the Paddymous performed some fertility ritual that had snagged the humans by accident?

Zaz couldn't suppress a chuckle. "It looks like we're pregnant, too." He held up the flowers like a badge of honor. The other two laughed.

There was another time worth noting, four months ago, when Samantha King exited her tent to serve breakfast. She was completely bald. The double takes went fast and hard. Nobody spoke up at first: it was Zaz who finally broke the silence:

"That's a new look for you, Sammy. Beautiful, but bold. Any reason?"

She looked askance. "Nothing special. It's more comfortable, convenient. I've been thinking about doing it for a long time." Then she scowled. "Aren't those good enough reasons?"

Zaz shrugged. "They are, if those reasons include a couple of female Paddymous named 'comfortable' and 'convenient.'"

"Okay, fine," she said, giving in. "I just thought I would lessen the opportunities for them to filch my hair. They have a bizarre preoccupation with it."

Dendy fingered her locks. "Hey, that's not a bad idea," she said.

Zaz whirled on her with dagger eyes.

"Okay, maybe it's not."

Then there was the time Carl decided he was going to coach the first-ever football league on Sidus. It took him three days to teach the Paddymous giants the basics of the game's strategy – the fundamental idea of carrying a grass-woven object from one goal post to another without being tackled. During the first game the ball was hiked to a young Paddymous quarterback, who snatched it and ran through the opposing line, past the goal post, only to disappear south down the gorge. It was a great maneuver, inducing much snorting and jumping up and down – a definite "hoorah" for the home team. The trouble was, the quarterback didn't return for twenty four hours. He'd ran all the way to the desert plain, never realizing he hadn't been followed. More than a few photos were taken that day.

The antics of the Paddymous beings when dealing with the automech had caused more than a few fits of hilarity. It seemed they'd never taken a liking to the metal man, often pushing him over or hitting him over the head with sticks. Zaz suspected that the hairless and cold-blooded automaton never registered as a living animal to the Paddymous, so he wasn't entitled to any dignity or respect. Often times, the younger Paddymous beings had made sport out of Silver Two by dragging him across the ground, sometimes for hundreds of yards, along with plaintiff inquiries of "May I be of assistance, sir?" It was a wonder they hadn't completely dismantled or destroyed him.

Zaz sighed. It hadn't been all bad on Sidus. Though they hadn't run out of hydrogen fuel for the vehicles yet, and though some of their battery packs were weakening, they could still get around by rationing their travel time. They'd miscalculated upon packing before they'd left – they hadn't brought enough hydrogen canisters to last a year. The threat was that they would eventually end up on foot if their rescuers were delayed any longer than the proposed year.

"Whatcha thinking about?" Dendy asked as she ran a finger over his arm.

"Just some fond memories. Sometimes I think we've gone over the edge of sanity."

It brought a smile to her face. She couldn't resist offering up some of her own recollections: "Remember the time we held the Miss Georgian Sidus Beauty Contest and I made grass-woven bikinis for the swimsuit competition? Who would have known that they would keep tearing them off during the posing routine? I laughed so hard I thought I was going to pass out."

"You did pass out. Then you changed the name to the Miss Nude Galaxy Contest. But when you made trophy banners for all of them they tore those off, too."

They broke into a fit of laughter that brought tears to his eyes. Dendy got a case of the hiccups.

The Sat dish alarm went off.

Zaz jerked around. He stared at the units and then at Dendy – she was tense, wide-eyed. Both sprang to their feet. Zaz took note of the Sat dish's aim. He read the coordinates on the small screen then looked up, following its line-of-sight. He broke out the portable scope and brought it to his face, his hands trembling.

"My god," Dendy whispered. "Do we have a object in atmosphere?"

Zaz wanted so much to believe that Orion Industries had finally arrived. He steadied his hand, trying to spot any small incoming speck. After a minute, he saw a tiny blur arcing across the sky. He followed its track as the object made a slight course correction, then its lateral movement ceased. It began to increase in size – it was coming toward them!

Zaz dropped the scope. He could plainly see a craft approaching. It was football-shaped, possessing two stabilizer airfoils on its underbelly.

Dendy hugged him hard. "Oh, let it be *friendlies,*" she cried.

He gulped, easing the rifle off his shoulder. He spoke hurriedly into his wrist-com before remembering that it no longer functioned. He brought Dendy's arm up to his face and used hers: "Sammy, come in. Repeat, Sammy come in. Emergency here!"

Samantha's voice came through the tiny speaker. "I copy. Go ahead, Zaz."

"We've got company – some type of shuttle on descent right now. Lay low. If you don't hear from me, take evasive action and tuck yourselves in. Read it back."

"Oh, lord, no!"

"Acknowledge, Sam!"

Her voice came out as a squeak. "I'm sorry – I copy. Out!"

Zaz watched as the vehicle approached. It came into a low orbit hover 500 feet above their heads. It held the pattern for what felt like an incredibly long time, though in reality it was only a minute or two. He raised the hand scope to his face again, looking for hull markings – there were no insignias or numbers on the nose.

The ship flipped around in a tight maneuver then began to descend, its repulser field clearly visible, sending static prickles through the air.

The hair on Zaz's arms stiffened with the electrical discharge. He gasped when he read the starboard bulkhead markings.

ORION INDUSTRIES 002 ASTRODYNAMICS PRIVATE SHUTTLE

Zaz drew in a sharp, excited breath. "You can look now, honey."

Dendy turned her face from his chest. When she saw the craft, she clutched him harder and made a whining sound.

Zaz backed them away from the energy field as the craft settled on six landing skis. The shuttle was as large as his tow truck, sporting an aerodynamic profile and looking a little bit like a fat penguin on its belly.

A side hatch swung upward with a *hiss* and a ramp descended. A three-person squad of armed men dressed in white coverall uniforms walked down the ramp. They wore Orion Industries insignia patches on their left breasts – a Viking Norseman holding a raised sword. The first one to step off the ramp and walk toward them stopped in his tracks a few yards from the ship, keeping his distance from Zaz and Dendy. He had a pair of hash marks on his collar, which Zaz interpreted to mean that he carried a high security rank. The man wore a skullcap that barely hid a shock of gray hair. His goggles were reflective gold. The only facial expression evident was a set of thin lips that stretched in a straight, neutral line across his face.

Zaz dropped his rifle – it clattered on the hard stone. He offered his hand for a shake. The security officer made no motion to come any closer.

Samantha's tinny voice came over the com: "Zaz, what's your status? For God's sake you have to – "

"Shut up!" said Zaz.

"What did you say?" asked the security officer.

"I wasn't talking to you," Zaz said, holding Dendy in a crushing embrace.

"What's wrong with the little gal?"

"Nothing's wrong with her. She's happy.

"Let's see your identification."

Zaz searched through his pockets – they were empty. All his identification was down below in the camp. He suddenly felt very self-conscious of his appearance; he imagined he looked like a bedraggled ore miner on leave from Triton after a six-month shift without soap and water. Still, he did not like their line of questioning, nor their attitude.

"I'm Captain Zackary Crowe. Who else do you think would be on this goddamned planet besides me?"

The security officer raised his weapon. "Easy there, fella. Just following regulations. Do you have any crew left, or did they vaporize in the explosion?"

"No, no. We're all here. The others are below in the gorge. We have a settlement – a small community. I know we must look a sight, but we've been through hell. I can't explain it to you all at once – I have it all written down in this log." Zaz removed the small notebook from his vest pocket. He tossed it across the ground. He watched as the man picked it up and scanned a few pages, but then he threw it back.

"You'll need to be examined – checked for contaminants by our techs before you're allowed to board," said the security officer. "Then you'll be transported to the *Majestic Sun*. Do you agree to those terms?"

I sure don't have any choice, you insolent lackey. "Of course," said Zaz. "We'll agree." He motioned to the side. "This is my girlfriend, Dendy."

Samantha's voice blared from Dendy's wrist-com. "What's happening, Zaz?"

Zaz had to slap Dendy's wrist to his chin. "Just shush. Clean yourselves up and pack. Orion is here. And Sammy..." He turned away from the security men and lowered his voice. "This is important – tell Carl to pack a charge, proximity breaker with programmable frequency, and a timer. Read that back."

"Okay, clean, pack, bring a charge, proximity breaker, and timer. Got it. Oh dear lord, what else?"

"Get ready to go home."

"Yippee!"

Zaz walked down the incline, holding Dendy against his hip. At the top of his mind was the disposition of the Paddymous giants. He had a mountain of legal issues to thrash over with Orion Industries concerning the welfare of the creatures. Thrilled with the prospect of going home, he still refused to leave this planet in anything less than pristine condition. He had an approaching fight on his hands, and it would be a knock-down, drag-out match.

The security officer called out to Zaz: "Where are you going?

We'll take you down in the shuttle."

Zaz changed his mind about the trek. So close to going home now, he didn't want Dendy risking a fall. He would never forgive himself if something happened to her.

They turned around and headed for the shuttle. A man stepped forward, wielding a scanning wand. His eyes fell upon Dendy's stomach. "Are you pregnant, ma'am?"

"Yes, I am. Nearly seven months."

The man yelled into the shuttle cabin. "Blake, get me a groin shield! Got a preggie here!"

"We didn't bring any scanner shields with us. I think double O-three' got 'em all and they're down on the plain."

"What the hell am I supposed to do?" asked Blake. "I've got to board her."

"Do a visual on her. You wand her, you'll end up with a lawsuit."

Dendy was not scanned. He let her pass with a brief visual inspection and a pat-down. The scanner they attempted to use on her was an older model that Zaz was familiar with. It had no high-tech innovations or improvements. This gave him a reckless, but marvelous idea. It had everything to do with finding the proper "mule."

CHAPTER NINETEEN

HOOK LINE AND STINKERS

Zaz paced in the Paddymous cave, trying to think up some new tactic to quell the argument. He was losing his patience. The other crewmembers, seated around the fire ring, anxiously looked to their captain.

At the mouth of the cave, darkened in silhouettes, stood three Orion security guards. One of the guards tapped his foot impatiently. They had no desire to enter the cave after finding out that it was inhabited by dozens of giant aliens.

Most of the Paddymous had gathered at the back of the cave. They remained quiet. It was evident from their postures that something was wrong, and they had no intention of interfering with the new arrivals. For the moment, playtime with the humans was over.

Zaz spun, facing the two scientists. "This is ludicrous!" he said, throwing his hands in the air. "I'm your captain. I order you to board that shuttle."

"Would you like to know something?" asked Paddy. "You have no ship; you have been *grounded*. Therefore, you have no authority to impose such an order. We are not leaving. There is nothing you can say or do to change our minds. If you choose to resort to violence and attempt to forcefully remove us, I shall put up a bloody good row."

Zaz felt like tearing his shoulder-length lion's mane of hair out. "No one can guarantee that there will ever be a ship here again," he said. "I don't know what Orion's plans are, but I know that we're entitled to a return trip home. They have a vessel specifically for us. Please, listen to reason."

"They have no right to take up residence here," said Paddy, "due to the galactic bylaws that protect any primitive Stone Age culture, which this planet, Georgian Sidus, certainly has. Lyle and I will serve as environmental stewards to uphold that standard. We stay."

Zaz persisted. "What if they abide by the laws, pulling out all ships and returning to Earth? Then will you come with us?"

"No," said Paddy. "We've decided to make it our life's work. Like I have told you before, we answer to a higher calling. We have been given the opportunity to study and document a primitive alien species, which will add to our knowledge bank. This chance will never come again for us."

"Who's going to benefit from this?" asked Zaz. "How are you going to deliver your papers? By carrier pigeon?"

"No, by sub-space Sat relay, if you would be so gracious to leave the apparatus and a small charger behind. In the meantime..." Paddy handed him a notebook. "This has a preliminary report, complete with artwork and photos. I think it should whet the appetites of Earth's academics. Please make sure it reaches the Museum of Natural History, or the Anderson-Smithsonian."

Zaz took the report from Paddy, staring at him for several seconds. Paddy reciprocated with a sincere, gentle smile. It was then that Zaz realized that the scientists had not made a rash decision, but had probably debated the idea shortly after discovering the Paddymous creatures. Zaz had one last warning for the two scientists:

"Paddy, Lyle; you remember what I did to the Mantis aliens? If they return, they'll root out you and your giant friends. I don't have to tell you what they might do to you. It wouldn't be pretty."

Paddy puffed his chest out, looking like an old soldier from a bygone era. "I am reminded, sir, of what one of my countrymen was overheard to say when he was aboard a White Star Liner that struck an iceberg. He said, 'I'm afraid that is the way of it sometimes. We are dressed in our finest and prepared to go down like gentlemen.'"

Zaz gave Paddy a full arm-wrapping body hug. "I've always loved you, Paddy," he said softly, his voice cracking. "I'm going to miss you terribly. It looks like you've chosen your home. May you find joy in your discoveries. You'll forever be in our thoughts."

Paddy swallowed hard. "Would you like to know something, sir? That is the kindest thing you have ever said to me. Thank you for understanding. You have always been an upright and proper mate, and I shall miss you with equal fervor."

Zaz turned to Lyle, walking over to the scientist with one eyebrow cocked.

Lyle smiled then sucked in a breath. "Sir, Paddy has been like a brother to me. We don't always agree. However, we are unanimous about where our paths lie. This will be our life's work. We're happy here; we are amongst creatures, and they do not regard us as eccentrics or crackpots. Maybe one day you will completely understand. I am extraordinarily blessed to be here on this planet, and my heart calls out in celebration every time I am reminded of it. Although this task is monumental in scale, I consider it a privilege to spend the rest of my days here with such wonderful companions. Now, you take care, my friend. You really should be off – they'll not wait forever."

Zaz hugged him then backed away. The other crewmembers waited in line to say their goodbyes. The women gave the two scientists affectionate kisses and hugs, but not without dropping a few tears. The Paddymous giants sensed that it was a sad occasion and pressed forward to pet the tiny humans. Samantha, whose hair had partially grown out, allowed one of the female Paddymous a final souvenir.

Carl limped over to his favorite friend among the giants, the patriarch of the group. He gave him a hearty handshake. "Now you keep your mitts up, you big dope. Don't let anything happen to the rest of your folk, or to the little professors. Aim straight and true." The giant gave him a sad chortle, followed by what passed for a nod.

Zaz's eyes misted up. Just like he'd done with his parents, he turned his back on the scientists, trying to fight down a disturbing feeling in his gut – one of abandonment.

The six crewmembers assembled at the cave entrance, where they picked up their tote bags. They would carry only essentials back with them, mostly memorabilia and keepsakes from their time on Sidus – mementos of living with the Paddymous giants. They headed to the shuttlecraft parked on the valley floor on the other side of the creek.

As they passed through their tattered campsite, Zaz stalled momentarily to take a final look, gazing fondly at the tent he and Dendy had occupied for so many months. He looked at the fire ring, where they had spent many joyful nights huddled together against the cold. He looked up one last time at the Paddymous cave; the professors and several of the giants looked down upon them. He waved. They waved back.

"I hope you don't mind," said Dendy, "but I had Silver Two transported onboard the Orion ship. I told them to take him to maintenance for repairs. I couldn't leave him behind to go offline and rust to death out here."

"I suppose it's all right. He does carry a record of our activities in memory."

They crossed the creek at the shallows. The security team led the group, forcing the pace and observing the strange vegetation they passed. When a Microraptor flew near, one of the guards raised his plasma rifle. Samantha slapped his shoulder. "Don't do that. Not here."

When they reached the Shuttlecraft, a technician holding a scanning wand stepped forward. He pointed to Zaz and Dendy. "Not you two, you've passed – just the others."

Zaz and Dendy held back while the crewmembers were systematically checked for contaminants and foreign substances. Carybell took a few hand strokes over her small torso before she was cleared. They took longer with Samantha, spending a little too much time patting her down, but they were not alerted to anything, which gave Zaz a moment of profound relief."

"That's enough, buster," Samantha told the technician.

They filed in one by one, Zaz and Dendy taking up the rear.

Twelve accelerator couches were placed mid-deck, separated by a pilot's cabin. Two private sleeper booths and a commode occupied the aft section. Zaz looked around, trying to mask his disgust. The executive shuttle smacked of opulence – luxury beyond functionality. They were almost afraid to sit on the furnishings, convinced they might crease or smudge the material.

Zaz strapped himself in along with the others. The craft lifted noiselessly, banked and flew over the gorge, gaining altitude as it headed to the Orion flagship in orbit. The security officers asked Zaz numerous questions about their ordeal. He offered them a less than detailed account of their experiences – citing some of the severe hardships, but leaving out most of the more personal accounts. Their interrogation made him uneasy; after a while, he refused to answer any more questions.

They gained orbit in 20 minutes and rendezvoused with the elegant Orion flagship. The shuttle cut its engine directly under one of the large ship's hulls. Then it was drawn into its interior through a docking hatch. They disembarked and boarded a foot tram that wound through a maze of pristine white corridors; niches with glass covers were molded into the walls at precise intervals, which held what appeared to be precious antiques. They took a lift carriage to the bridge.

The first room they passed through was an immense flight service lounge, complete with an entertainment area, deck sofas, and concave wide-screen viewers. Smartly dressed uniformed staff rushed about, involved in various activities. The next section housed a typical half-moon shaped bridge at the ship's nose; the location was inundated with high tech navigational instruments and holograph maps. Large composite glass panels provided a 180-degree view of the universe outside. A long boomerang-shaped conference table took up space in the middle of the deck, where 10 corporate officers were seated, awaiting the arrival of the Planet Janitor crew. Bureaucracy and opulence infested the ship.

Henry Gable, the vice president of Orion Industries, sat squarely at the middle of the table. Behind him was a very old man in a float chair; he was an invalid – nearly comatose, aside from the slight movement of his head and a bit of drool on his chin.

Gable, who looked as impeccable as ever and dressed in an expensive black suit, stabbed a half-dozen console buttons: six visitor chairs with sleek contour bucket seats and black syntho-leather rose up from underneath the deck with a soft pneumatic hiss. The remaining executives and corporate officers looked up from their work and eyed the motley group.

A ship's steward appeared from a nearby alcove, almost gliding across the deck. He gave the crew a curt bow. "I'm Steward Atkinson, at your service, sir. May I take your baggage?"

"Thank you, no," said Zaz. "These are our only possessions – personal property."

Gable held his hands out. "Please be seated," said Gabel. "You look fatigued. Is there any additional comfort that I might extend to the ladies?" Their pregnancies were quite obvious.

"I don't think that's necessary," Zaz remarked. "They're quite healthy and fit." The women nodded in affirmation.

The atmosphere on the bridge was difficult to read. Obviously the Planet Janitor crew had been expected to make an appearance, but the comfort level and attitudes were unexpectedly polite. Zaz found that amazing, chiefly due to the fact that future settlement operations on Sidus were now impossible, at least from his contractual end of it. The investment was a colossal bust. He expected at least a plasma shot to the knees or a severe dressing down.

Gable laced his fingers. "I'm very glad to see that you all made it. As I recall, there were seven of you. A fatality?"

Zaz knew that Gable was baiting him. The vice president would have been apprised that two crewmembers had stayed behind – the shuttle crew would have passed that news on to him. Orion Industries was too regimented to let that information slip through the cracks. Unless Gable was digging for something more.

"Our ship's scientists preferred to stay behind," said Zaz. "It did not go without my severe objections. Let's just say they have a dedication to another calling, one that I now highly approve of. At the last minute, before leaving Earth, we accepted the services of Carybell, our assistant botanist."

A gleam of pride showed on Carybell's face when she heard the words "assistant botanist." There was no reason to reveal that the young girl had stowed away – it was none of Orion's business.

Zaz glanced at the very old man behind the table again. "Is that your father?"

"Ah, forgive me." Gable stood up. "Permit me to introduce the esteemed Reginald Harold Gable, president and founder of Orion Industries. Although he has suffered some disabling cerebral blockages, he does remain coherent. As you know, I have taken over the more ardent responsibilities of Orion Industries. Let it be known that I speak for my father. He is quite cognizant of all proceedings and decisions made here, I can assure you." Gable sat down again.

It was all a lie.

Zaz doubted that Reginald Gable was capable of knowing whether or not there was a feeding spoon in his mouth. He bowed out of respect. In response, the elder Gable blew a saliva bubble that popped over his chin. Carybell emitted a small chirp-like laugh at the sight.

Zaz sat down, trying to read the intense stares of the 10 seated executives.

"Captain Crowe," Gable began, "I am not one to mince words. I'm well aware that you have experienced a tragic event here. It was obvious from our orbital survey that a nuclear detonation destroyed your ship. We thought all hands were lost until we picked up your beacon. I've received a few scattered reports from the shuttle officers who told me that you set off this device as a defensive measure. It's also come to my attention that you discovered a supposedly native animal on the planet. What exactly happened down there?"

Zaz walked to the desk and handed Gable his small log notebook along with Paddy's binder. "It's all here. You can scan this – examine it at your leisure. It's an accurate account of the events we endured while on the planet's surface. I have digital and hard-copy photographs of the native animals in question, along with some that depict the horde of attacking marsupial lions. I also have proof of the master race that arrived on the planet and released this horde. You'll have to make copies of the documents – I want the originals back today. I promised to deliver our scientist's material to confidential sources on Earth."

Gable skimmed through the pages then snapped his fingers for assistance. He gave the steward the materials with instructions to scan the text and enter it into the main computer database.

Zaz took his seat, waiting for Gable to lead the conversation. The vice president rose from his seat, pulled on his ponytail. "Mr. Crowe, where are the lions now? Where is this master alien race?"

Carybell bounced to her feet. "We killed a sticky bug because he tried to choke us."

Gable narrowed his eyes at the young girl. "I see. And where is this dead *sticky bug*?"

Zaz took the question. "The remains of the Mantis alien are preserved in our camp on Sidus. Our scientists performed a full autopsy on the creature. The escape pod the alien arrived in is wrapped in tarp in the campsite, as well. That should be proof enough."

"As for the rest of them, we blew them to flaming fuck," said Carl, unable to contain himself any longer. "Those Jack Lions attacked our ship and surrounded us. We killed as many as we could until they got inside. Then we broke out and headed north to the gorge. Zaz, I mean, Captain Crowe, rigged the ship to blow the Bang pods. When the time was right, I hit the button. The two alien vessels were caught in the explosion. They were giant ships, maybe war galleons – nothing like you've ever seen before. We smoked 'em good."

"And you are?" asked Gable.

"Carl Stromboli, doctor of pyrotechnics, Planet Janitor."

"I think I've read accounts of you, Mr. Stromboli. I seem to remember seeing your name in the contract – you're a sapper. That said, where are these ships? Where is this horde? Where are the aliens? Certainly there must be some residual evidence of this catastrophe. Our snoop surveys found nothing but a glazed crater in the middle of the desert plain. That's exactly where you were contracted to construct a settlement compound."

"There were enough megatons in the blast to vaporize all of it," said Zaz. "Everything went up, including the ordinance, if they had any, and the drives on the alien vessels. Ironically, your contract called for a twenty-mile square clearing – you now have a hundred square miles cleared."

"Yes," said Gable, "and a radioactive hot zone unfit for settlement. It begs the question: what drove you to such extremes?"

Zaz leaned forward in his chair. "Look, we were more than provoked; we were attacked en masse. We fought back and destroyed the attackers. If your initial survey had been thorough in the beginning, you would have found a living population of Paddymous giants still residing on the planet. Granted you sent us to bury an entire civilization of skeletons, but you failed to discover that this planet contained survivors."

"Aren't you talking about a herd of animals? My shuttle officers told me they were beasts, with no more intelligence than a cow or a horse."

Zaz knew where this was going. "Your shuttle officers are not zoologists. They have no education in the core sciences. They are unqualified when it comes to making such a determination."

"If I'm not mistaken," said Gable, "your shipboard zoologist was never accredited. He received his degree through a cyber course – hardly a recognized seat of believable or vetted accomplishment in the academic world. On the other hand, your geologist checked out with a bona fide degree, but he is hardly an expert on biology and living species. I have real biologists and zoologists on board this ship who can perform a proper study."

Galoot rose a few inches from his seat. "You're not calling the boss a liar, are you, Mr. Fable?"

"The name is *Gable*. No, I am merely questioning the authenticity of his claim. You are suggesting that this planet is occupied by a sentient race with a technology and intelligence that borders on human capabilities."

"Yes," said Zaz, "as provided by the stipulations in the Stockholm Treaty of 2065. I'm well aware of what constitutes a sentient race, and I'm telling you that there is one down there – a believable society-culture."

Gable cocked his head. "Did these animals tell you this? Have they written you a full account of their history on parchment?"

"Not on parchment, but on the stone walls in their caves – pictographs and renderings that plainly demonstrate the knowledge of their own history in archival form. Their records are accurate – logical. Not just scribblings. They are accomplished artists, intuitively aware of scale and dimension. They are carvers of wood, skilled weavers, and are advanced enough to distinguish between functional items and toys. They fit the criteria of an advanced Stone Age culture, as defined by the law."

Gable gave Zaz a hollow, sympathetic smile. "I understand that you lived with these animals for over six months. Perhaps you taught them by example. Maybe the artifacts that presently reside in the cave were produced by you. Even an ape can mimic the motions of a human; given enough time, they can even appear to duplicate human behavior. We call these actions 'trained responses.' Six months would be adequate enough for them to recycle what you have taught them."

"I get it," said Zaz. "You're turning a blind eye to this. You've decided to dispute the fact that such beings exist. That's so you don't have to write off this project with all those billions already invested, and then go right on with your original settlement plans. I suppose you have several ships parked in orbit, with contractors just itching to get down there. Every minute you're delayed costs you untold fortunes in investment, so you'll do anything to poke a stick in the galactic eye that you know is watching. But this is one quick moat you will be unable to get out of. The evidence has been documented, along with the testimony of eight living witnesses. Your conclusion that this planet is legally uninhabited will not hold up in a supreme court of law."

Gable held up the books. "These are written by your hands. You say you have photographic proof, but it's possible that you had a digital photo lab onboard your ship to concoct such material. You have no solid proof – no debris, wreckage, lion bodies, or aliens. You ask us to take your word for it. You ask us to believe that you blew up your ship intentionally, when in fact, you might have suffered an accident by ruining your construction equipment, thereby throwing off the job you were contracted to finish. Then you deliberately nuked the site to hide the subterfuge. That would be a breach of contractual law. Where are the perimeter walls that you were instructed to fashion? Not one foam speck was detected from our survey."

Zaz felt his temper boiling to the surface. "I told you, the alien and craft are in the campsite. Recover them and perform your own examinations."

Samantha King stood up. "I. Don't believe this. Are you space happy? You, sir, are a liar and a fraud!"

Gable waggled his head sadly. "Taking your condition under consideration, I'll ignore that comment."

"Her hormones are just fine," said Carl, a vein appearing on his forehead.

The executives seated at the table stirred. Zaz knew they were pondering the possibility that his crew might be telling the truth. Gable acted the diehard; the vice president took a lot for granted, speaking for the rest of the board. Zaz knew he'd opened up a few chinks in their corporate armor. He decided to press the issue.

"Of course you think this is all some elaborate hoax, since we've had so much free time to concoct such a story, but how do you intend to disprove it?"

Gabel answered easily. "I'll send down my own team of experts to recover this so called evidence. It will be turned over to my experts for analysis. I'll peruse your paperwork. Then I'll retire with my board, and we will give you a decision tomorrow evening. Is that fair enough?"

"That's reasonable, as long as your prejudice is not involved. I suggest you confer with our scientists while you are down there. Regardless of your opinion, they do have viable firsthand experience with the matter."

Gable clasped his hands. "Then it's settled. I have arranged private accommodations for you aboard this vessel. We have three luxury suites available. I think they might be quite the treat for you, considering the basic inconveniences you've gone without."

Zaz glanced at his crewmembers. "Just the same, we'd like one large room with some sleeping mats, if that's possible. Equip it with a small conference table, a mini-computer with wafer inscription, and a single lavatory. We're used to each other's company."

Gable looked at the two pregnant women. "I can see how close," he said. "Very well. I'll arrange for the mini-lounge to be made available. If you'll accompany my stewards?"

The Planet Janitor crew was escorted to their one-room accommodation. Outside the entrance, the young steward informed them he would return with the necessary bedding and arrange for their meals. Once the crewmembers had stepped inside, Zaz shut the door and tried to lock it. It had no such security. He put a hushed finger to his lips and walked across the room to the lavatory. He waved them inside and then shut the door.

Carl was the first to speak. "I wanted to bust that white space trash bum in the nose!"

"I'm glad you all *tried* to keep your tongues in check," Zaz said, keeping his voice low. "As for my request, I figured they would have every room on this ship wired for visuals and sound. We have to be careful what we say – best to keep up normal appearances and general chat. I don't want to rouse their suspicions. I think we're safe in here, but just to be sure…"

Zaz and Galoot checked every inch of the large lavatory, looking for micro spy components. Finding nothing, Zaz continued. "It looks to me like they want to continue with their settlement plans regardless of what type of evidence we have. I have no idea how they're going to justify their end of the debate. Obviously they have their own scientific panel, bought and paid for. The outcome will likely be in their favor. The problem is we're scheduled to return carrying contrary information. If we return at all."

Samantha shivered. "They wouldn't dare keep us here. What could they do, make settlers out of us against our will?"

"I don't think boss was thinking along those lines," said Galoot.

"They wouldn't get rid of us to hide their plans, would they?" asked Dendy. She looked from face to face, frowning. "Yeppers, they would do something like that for the almighty imperial. Maybe we should just play along until we're out of here."

"I've thought of that," said Zaz. "We can use that tactic later if we fail to convince them. The fact remains, a lot of accidents can happen in space. It could be a shuttle accident, toxic gas through an air vent in a mini-lounge, or maybe a freak on-deck explosion. Or even a – "

"Cryo pod accident," finished Carl. "If I was going to take out six potential witnesses, I'd fuck the sleep chambers over. Permanent snoozers."

Samantha sighed. "There's eight lives here, you idiot." She held her belly, nodding her head toward Dendy.

Carl dithered. "Yeah, sorry, six and the bambinos."

"Dead men tell no tales," said Dendy.

"You catch on," said Zaz. "What we have to do is play along until we get to the transport ship and they ready us for the jump. We need leverage and a plan. Provided we get to the sleep chambers, my idea will work. We'll have to keep up the guise that we disagree with them, not give in too easily. Caving in would arouse suspicion." Zaz looked at Carl, then at Samantha. "Did you pack that equipment where I told you to?"

"Got it right there." Carl pointed to Samantha's belly. "The C-6, timer, and proximity breaker."

Samantha smoothed a hand over her protruding stomach. "He had to break it down in pieces, but it's all here."

"Great. Later tonight, Carl, you and I are going to build a small device in here. I'll tell you what my idea is – I want you to perfect it."

"Anything that goes boom is up my alley."

"Good. Now tomorrow, before we meet with the Orion board, I need everybody to split up and wander around the ship, just like a tourist would do, except I want you to be more intrusive. Trespass into restricted areas and potential blind spots wherever you can. We need to violate as much secure space as possible. If you're caught, explain you were only marveling at such a great ship and wanted to see the *Majestic Sun* in all her glory. Play the awe-struck curiosity angle. Take your tote bags with you – don't let them out of your sight for one minute. Keep their noses out of the contents."

The captain could see that Carl was loving every minute of the plan – his services were needed again. He kept his voice low. "You want me to plant a timer charge on this ship – and you want me to rig it to blow sometime after we're already in transit, on our way home."

Zaz nodded. "That's our bargaining chip. We need to put it where nobody would ever suspect it. C-6 is undetectable. They could sweep this ship from stem to stern for a year and never find it. However, the proximity breaker could be found with an intensified probe. I have just the place to hide the package, but we'll need a major distraction."

Zaz explained the details of his plan, electing individual actors to play their parts. It had to go off with perfect timing. He went over the plan a second time just to make sure everyone understood their role. When he was finished, he unlocked the lavatory door. They filed out into the mini-lounge. At that precise moment, the young steward returned, guiding an electronic luggage cart into the room, complete with bedding and ready-cooked meals.

The steward staggered for a moment, then looked completely flustered as the crew had exited the lavatory in a group. He had the good grace to blush. "My word. When you said you did everything together, you weren't fibbing!"

"We're just one big happy family," Zaz said. "We're used to each other."

The steward gave them an admiring look bordering on envy. "I think it's positively delicious! Oh, I have something for you." He reached into the cart and pulled out the Sidus log, along with Lyle and Paddy's report binder. He handed them to the captain.

Zaz looked at the papers and notebook, recognizing that they were copies. Gable had kept the originals. He didn't want to show any reaction or say anything in the presence of the steward, but he felt like cursing his throat raw and putting his fist through the bulkhead. After showing Gable his trust and taking his word for a fair hearing and trial concerning the evidence, this was the final betrayal – the last straw.

*   *   *

Sidus Log, Rotation 202.
After nearly seven months our rescuers have arrived. Though we have mixed emotions about the true intentions of Orion Industries, we are relieved to be finally on our way home. Leaving Sidus has not come without its regrets. Paddy and Lyle will be sorely missed and I already feel the vacuum of their absence. I'll remember a proper little zoologist with an insufferable scalp itch, and a meek geologist, who could never quite decide on the proper filter or focus on life.

It is likely the Orion executives will place us aboard a jump ship for our journey home. I hope we will meet one last time to discuss matters in a more congenial fashion, and that our survival accounts are believed. An important decision relies on our testimony and the welfare of the Paddymous survival. It will be a true David and Goliath moment. Whatever the outcome, we want to go home and put all this behind us. I say goodbye and farewell to Sidus in the hopes that the next visitors here have a pleasant and peaceful stay - whoever they may be.

Mom and dad: Your son is coming home a tad more disheveled and worn. You don't know how hard I've wished to see you again. I hope you can forgive me for the many mistakes I've made.

Zachary Crowe, PJ. end of log.

The Planet Janitor crew left their quarters early the next day, dispersing in different directions. Zaz found his way to the aft drive engines and entered several restricted areas before he was caught and escorted to a "safe zone." The minute they'd turned their backs, he was off wandering again. He'd managed to trespass into every accessible and inaccessible crevice he could find. At one point a tour director was called to intercept Zaz and offer his services, but Zaz declined. The director became so frustrated he slapped a bulkhead wall in disgust, threatening to call security as he departed.

The *Majestic Sun* was immense – truly the proud flagship of Orion Industries. It was also brand new, judging from all the fresh paint and hardware – more than a substantial investment and reflecting the narcissistic tendencies of its owners. That was a plus as far as he was concerned; they would be entirely put-off at the prospect of losing the shining gem of the company fleet.

The others spent their time getting lost in her bowels, sneaking off onto the multiple decks, opening hatches, asking useless questions and making a general nuisance of themselves. The disruptions went on all day, stopping only for a quick lunch break and then they were back at it again. Several loudspeaker messages hailed them to return to their quarters, but none of the crewmembers obeyed, feigning ignorance. Finally, security was dispatched to round them up. They were quarantined in the mini-lounge "for their own safety."

Zaz and his crew were called to the bridge during an evening break. The board members were all there, occupying seats at the long table, with Henry Gable seated squarely in the center. Zaz noticed the addition of two lab-coated individuals, who had taken up seats to the extreme left, near a portable viewing screen; he presumed they were the vice president's handpicked scientists. Old man Gable was immobile in his glide chair, seated behind the long table next to the viewing windows. The illness-stricken man hadn't moved an inch from his previous placement the day before.

Before Zaz sat down, he chanced a look at Carl. The explosives expert had changed into a baggy shirt top that concealed any signs of what lay underneath. Athough Carl could easily palm the device, it was much safer to keep it out of sight.

"Please be seated," said Henry Gable. "I'm sorry that we had to resort to confining you to quarters today, but several of you inadvertently ended up in high hazard and restricted areas. I'm afraid we don't tolerate free-roaming personnel in our more sensitive zones. In the future, please refrain from wandering about."

Zaz hadn't noticed it before, but when he looked carefully at Henry Gable, he could see that one of the man's eyes glowed with a purple hue. A lump protruded from his brow; it looked as if he'd been punched.

"Looks like a recent injury," said Zaz. "I hope you're okay."

"Oh, this?" Gable fingered his cheek. "I accompanied our science officers down to the surface to evaluate these so-called natives. I walked into the path of a missile."

"Ha!" said Carl. "Wait until you play football with them."

Gable rolled his eyes. "I'm *sure*. Look, I am still not convinced. On the one hand, they demonstrate an instinctive but undefined awareness of their environment. But they show no outward signs of intelligence reaching past the point of mimicry."

The lights dimmed and the viewing screen brightened. The film contained a short documentary of the Orion scientists going through a series of experiments which challenged the dexterity, memory, spatial relations, and other attributes of a few of the Paddymous beings that they had singled out for the tests. It showed nothing other than what the scientists were trying to prove with their one-sided theories – that the Paddymous were not on par with the development of an Earthbound Stone Age hominid. Paddy and Lyle were not in the film. The whole thing was a fix; Zaz knew it proved nothing. As the film ended, Zaz cued Samantha: act one, scene one.

Samantha unseated and took a couple of steps toward the scientists just as the lights brightened. "What does that prove? You only spent two hours with them. We lived with them for months at close quarters. You saw only what you wanted to see."

"I can assure you," said one of the company scientists, "that they had nothing to offer apart from some basic animal behaviorisms. They have only mimicked human behavior. They were taught how to weave, draw, carve and make bedding – because that is *what humans do*. And for your information, the so-called alien life form turned out to be a simple insect, probably a resident of this planet. Your escape pod was space junk. In fact, the pod could have been yours, launched at the time of your crash landing. Nothing unusual with either."

Zaz looked at the scientist in disbelief. "An insect that large with bipedal capability? Anyone can see that the pod is of alien design. Are you crazy? No, wait... I think I just answered my own question."

Carl casually strode across the deck with his hands in his pockets, his eyes on the bridge window. He rounded the table, placing his hand on the elder Gable's glide chair. "Just because this old man can't move or talk doesn't mean he isn't human. It's just like the big giants – they don't do what you expect them to do, so you think they're dumb."

"He's right," said Dendy, pointing at the blank screen. "You only saw what you wanted to see. You tried to study them in a controlled environment. You haven't seen them like we have. We didn't have to interact with them. All of their accomplishments were their own before we ever met them. You just want to cover up this whole thing."

"That's right," Carybell added. "They are very sweet and very smart. They wouldn't hurt a June bug in July!"

"They are nothing but brainless herbivores," said one of the scientists. "They live in caves like bears. They cannot converse – they only make grunting sounds. They are no more culturally enlightened than a domesticated dog."

"Now *that* is selling them short!" Samantha said, red-faced. "And I happen to like dogs. We are dealing with a completely new species here. A species that has evolved over millions of years. They are the alpha, the top of the food chain on this planet. The microraptors, armadillos, and locusts do not know how to manipulate their environment."

"Spoken for truth," said Dendy. She marched to the long table to plant her palms on it. She looked defiantly at the executives. "There is not one of you here that is qualified to make a decision on this."

"Young lady," said Henry Gable, "you seem emotionally wrought. I hardly think that *you* are in any condition to express logic on this matter."

"That's right, you hardly think," Samantha cut in. "And further more…"

Zaz couldn't have been more proud of the three women. The proceedings were fast approaching an emotional crescendo, complete with timpani drums and cymbals. It was only a matter of time before the payoff.

When Samantha finished her tongue-lashing, Dendy took over. "This is not a serious evaluation panel – this is a pig sty!" Dendy clapped one hand to her forehead, the other to her belly. "Oh..." She staggered, trying to maintain her balance.

Zaz bolted to his feet. "Dendy!" He ran to her side and fanned her cheeks. "Someone get her a glass of water."

Samantha squared off at the long table, glaring at the executives. "Now see what you've done!" She wavered for a moment, eyes crossed, then dropped one knee to the deck.

"Oh my gawd," said Carl and started out for his mate, but he tripped and went down next to the float chair, thrashing on the floor.

Carybell burst into tears, yelling, "Something's happened! She's probably losing her baby."

Galoot let out a primordial roar and launched from his chair. "Now that just plum tears it!"

The executives were on their feet by now, mouths open, head-scratching. One of them grabbed a water pitcher and headed for the women, but he collided with Galoot and went down to the floor. A few minutes later, a medical team arrived to offer emergency assistance.

It took several minutes to regain order. The women were given mild sedatives, but they refused to be transported to sickbay. They asked to be returned to their quarters. Two air gurneys were rushed to the bridge. The women were taken to the mini-lounge, accompanied by an attentive physician. Zaz remained behind on the bridge. Henry Gable ordered his executives back to their seats. Zaz apologized for the heated display, explaining that the women had been suffering from bouts of stress lately.

Henry Gable loosened his collar then blew an exasperated sigh of relief. "I must say that you all subscribe to convictions that are inconceivable to me. I don't think I've ever seen such fervor. Nevertheless, we'll take your views into consideration. I can assure you that a fair and balanced decision will be reached that will satisfy both interests in this matter."

Zaz nodded; he hadn't gained any ground, nor had he expected to. "Given the fact that this matter might cause more stress, and considering the condition of the women, I think it would be better for us to drop this subject. You can arrange for our immediate transportation home."

Gable brightened. "Now that is the first sensible thing I've heard! We'll arrange for your immediate transport – that was our mission plan from the beginning. When would you like to leave?"

"Tomorrow won't be soon enough. Just for the record, I would like to ask your forgiveness for the outburst. Furthermore, I think an agreement is in order. My crew and I will abide by a secrecy pact if you arrange to get us home safe and sound. I don't care what you do on the planet's surface. It's none of my business. I think your advance was sufficient compensation for our troubles."

"Done – accepted," said Gable, swallowing dryly.

"Good luck with the project. Again, I'm sorry for all of this." Zaz watched the vice president lean back in his chair and gaze up at the overhead. A smile came to his face.

Third act – cut and print. Credits – fade to black.

*   *   *

Henry Gable waited until the rest of the Planet Janitor crew had vacated the bridge before he called his chief of security on a private line. "Chief," he said, speaking as clearly as he could, "I want you to halt the termination directive immediately. We'll not have any trouble from this group. I repeat, this will be a live fly home. Understood?"

"That's affirmative, Mr. Gable. How should I handle this?"

"Be innovative, but swift. Get over to the Achilles tonight and take care of it at the source. Cover your tracks."

"Will do. I'm on it now."

But the security chief did not feel like making a trip to the Achilles jump ship that night. He had a date with a company records officer that couldn't wait. Instead, he used his com to contact a subordinate onboard the *Majestic Sun* and told him to handle it.

CHAPTER TWENTY

TREACHERY AND THE JUMP FOR HOME

THE PLANET JANITOR crew were each given physical exams early the next morning. All passed with stellar results. Zaz felt particularly good, discovering he'd lost 15 pounds during the seven months he'd spent on Sidus. The exams of the two pregnant women had taken twice as long, involving more rigorous tests; the fetuses would have to survive the stresses of a long jump sleep, thus requiring more precaution.

They dressed in the Planet Janitor jumpsuits that they had brought with them. The Orion staff whisked them to a transfer shuttle, which flew them to the small company jump ship, Achilles. Two doctors and three stewards escorted them to the pod chamber, where the crew disrobed and prepared to enter the capsules.

Dendy insisted on prepping her crew, showing no trust to the strangers. "I want to make sure the hookups are properly administered," she told the Orion employees. She began the task of placing each person in a capsule, then installing the hardware.

Zaz was second to last. While he waited, he traded small talk with the doctors. They began by telling him what to expect during and after the journey.

"It's an autonomous flight," said one doctor. "The jump will commence after you're secured in the pods. We have a dozen automechs on board to monitor the systems, including your own, which we've locked down for transit. The trip should be routine. We've made arrangements for the storage of the Achilles at Pier K, so just bring her down and sign for her at Port Administration – they'll take care of the rest. We've sent an arrival message ahead; they'll be expecting you. Do you have any questions?"

"Not really," said Zaz, as he stepped out of his jumpsuit. He removed his dead wrist-com and put it in the pocket of his jumpsuit, which he handed to the doctor. At the last minute, he reached into another pocket of the jumpsuit and pulled out a small business wafer. He handed it to the doctor. "Make sure that Henry Gable gets this. He's expecting it, and said that the courier who fails to get it to him on time gets fired. If the message is delivered post haste, there's a bonus involved. In addition, a formal apology is included, along with a nice little surprise contained within that concerns precious minerals on the planet's surface."

Zaz knew that the jump sequence could not be tampered with. Once the programming was set, the Achilles could not be stopped in flight or recalled. They would be on their way in a few minutes – free and clear.

Dendy shouldered the doctor aside. "Let a nurse do her thing." She stepped up to Zaz.

He kissed her and stroked her hair. "How appropriate that the last thing I see for twelve years will be your beautiful face. Sleep tight, Tiny Dancer. See you on the other side of the constellation."

"You too, gorgeous." She helped him settle into the pod and hooked him up. "See you on the other side."

The bubble canopy came down over him. He watched her through the glass as she slid into the next unit beside him. There was a familiar rush of liquid about his feet, the fluid beginning to rise. When it reached his neck, he took one last breath then shut his eyes. The bang pod ignited – the ship launched. He heard a small voice in his head – it seemed so far off.

Godspeed, my son.

*   *   *

When Doctor Shamus got back to the *Majestic Sun* he took a fast tram to the bridge. He found Henry Gable busy with his executives, going over geological survey data.

Gable had a liter of Russian brandy at his elbow, well on his way to being a happy drunk. He looked up when Shamus approached the table and handed him a wafer. Gable looked at the wafer and set it down, preoccupied with his studies. He was currently trying to decide on a new name for Georgian Sidus.

Doctor Shamus cleared his throat. "Sir, I think you should read that wafer. Crowe said it was important, and that if I got it to you in time, there would be a bonus in it for me. Not only did he say it contained a formal apology, but that there was some type of surprise in it for you. Something to do with valuable minerals, I think."

"Oh, really?" Gable looked up, slightly perturbed with the interruption. "That's got to mean we're finally rid of them. And you should know I do not award bonuses for regular work assignments."

"My apologies, sir. It appears I've been misled. Anyway, they were away as of…" Shamus checked his watch, "nine minutes ago."

Gable clucked his tongue. "Well! That calls for a…" Gable took a hefty swig from the bottle. "Yes, a celebration! Now what's this about a surprise? The apology is expected." He guffawed. The executives joined in, making several sarcastic comments about the Planet Janitor crew. A vintage bottle of champagne was uncorked.

Henry Gable inserted the wafer into a small input drive and hit the play feature. "It's probably best to get this over with," he said. "I don't want the image of Crowe hanging over my head." This brought another round of laughter and toasts.

The screen brightened. Gable turned the visual feature off, opting for the audio message only. That last thing he wanted to see as they celebrated was Zaz's face.

"Solicitations to the eminent Vice President, Henry Gable, and to the esteemed executive officers aboard the *Majestic Sun*. Allow me to extend my heartfelt apology to all who were offended by our discordant behavior.

"Secondly, let me apologize for ever believing that you had a speck of human decency in you. Thirdly, let me apologize for believing that you would do the right thing by Georgian Sidus and pull your ownership flag, knowing full well that it is an inhabited planet and that you are in direct violation of the Stockholm Treaty. Finally, let me apologize for never suspecting you of chicanery and false pretenses upon our first meeting. You can take these apologies six-fold, including our scientists, Lyle and Paddy, whom you also humiliated.

"Be advised that we have taken steps to preserve our lives just in case you're inclined to see that we meet with an unfortunate accident while in jump. At the same time, we hope to discourage your plans for a permanent settlement on Georgian Sidus.

"We have placed a one-half kiloton charge of C-6 explosive within the confines of your flagship, along with a proximity breaker that is set to go off the minute the frequency is too weak between the receiver and the transmitter. You have the transmitter on your ship. One of us has the receiver, which controls the detonation device. The charge and the proximity breaker are nearly undetectable, as you may well know. You would never find it in time, even with a complete ship scan, using all of your resources. You will remember that we put boot prints to every sector and deck of your ship?

"You have about twenty-eight minutes after our departure, to follow this jump ship with the *Majestic Sun*. If our receiver gets too far out from your transmitter, the frequency signal breaks. Then, well, let's just say your *Majestic Sun* goes nova. It would be a shame to waste such a grand flagship. You might get most of your high-ranking officers off in time, but not the whole complement. Of course, then you could continue with your ill-gotten gains, but we will still beat you back to Earth.

"Once we are Earth-side, we'll be sure to expose your planet-theft to the International Space Authority, with all of the humanitarian violations that accompany it. You have one logical choice – that's to shadow us to Long Beach and make sure that we arrive safely.

"You now have about twenty-seven minutes to make your decision. And by the way, Carl says that you can crawl up his blast chute to get the receiver."

"Captiain Zachary Crowe, Planet Janitor and crew."

Henry Gable had a glass of champagne to his mouth but hadn't taken a sip during the entire message. He was stuck in a freeze-frame of idiocy. He put the glass down. "Can they do that?" he asked to no one in particular. "Can they wire us like that then threaten us with a connection break?"

One of the executive officers, who had a background in high-tech military ordinance said, "I'm afraid they can do that quite easily. I've seen it used before. The proximity breaker is the only component that gives off a detectable signal. Find that, and you'll find the package."

Doctor Shamus closed his eyes, looking ill. "They couldn't have scanned the pregnant women, sir – it's against regulations. I would wager that's how they got the device onboard."

The senior Gable, who somehow began to come to life with much saliva spitting, drew the attention of the others. He attempted to rock in his chair, but only managed to keel over, striking his head on the armrest.

Doctor Shamus went to him, readjusting the old man in his seat. "What are you trying to say, sir?"

Reginald Harold Gable, president of Orion Industries, could only pop bubbles over his lips and waggle his eyes.

"Nonsense!" Henry Gable declared. "He probably has to take a crap."

Doctor Shamus let the old man's head flop. "What are we going to do?"

Henry Gable gulped his champagne. He threw the glass across the bridge, shattering it against a bulkhead. "We've been duped! Prepare to make the jump – we'll scan the ship en route. If we find it, we'll jettison it out the airlock and turn around. If we don't find the damn thing, send an immediate message to Long Beach, requesting a return flight priority for the *Majestic Sun*. Follow that ship!"

*　　*　　*

Someone called him Peter. The voice sounded very near to him. Peter Pan? Is that what she said? He'd had the sensation of flying for a very long time. He was so very high up that when he looked down he could barely make out the city lights below. Only those were not city lights, he realized after a while: they were stars, tiny little specks in an inky black. Then he heard his name again – "Wake up Peter, we're home." It was Wendy Darling. She was so close he could feel her warm breath on his cheek. *Wendy? I'm so glad you found me.*

"It's Dendy!"

There was a sharp slap to his face.

That was not any way to treat Peter Pan. You shouldn't show disrespect to the boy who'd saved everyone from Captain Hook. He paddled his hands at the foe who'd struck him. This got him another slap.

Zaz opened a sticky eyelid. "Guh. Wendy?"

"Dendy."

Zaz opened the other eye. The room spun. Warm hands lifted him up and wrestled him into a standing position. He felt as if he weighed a ton. Somebody walked him around, holding him up like a small puppet. He recognized a deep raspy voice.

"C'mon now, boss, it's just like walking off a bad hangover."

After 10 minutes of shark walking, Zaz could finally stand by himself. He looked around him, recognizing familiar faces. He went to grab Dendy in his arms but missed her, nearly falling down. He got her on the second try. "Tiny Dancer! I had such a dream. Is everyone all right?"

He looked down into her face. Her eyes seemed to clack together like two marbles. She rubbed his hands vigorously and said, "We're alive and well. Happy sixty-fifth birthday. I had to zap you twice; you weren't coming out of the cryo sleep."

"Yeah, well if you were Peter Pan flying around for twelve years, you wouldn't find it so easy to land all of a sudden. Damn, has it been another twelve years? Never mind. Where's Sammy?"

Carl rubbed his eyes. "She's on the bridge getting ready for dock. We're in the ionosphere over the Southern California coast."

Zaz struggled into his company jumpsuit, trying to throw his legs into the fabric without falling over. Athough he had a nasty cryo headache, he felt an overwhelming thrill to be back home. And damn if they hadn't come out right over their destination! But then another important matter slowly took shape in his mind.

Orion Industries. Had they followed him out?

He made his way to the bridge and found Samantha. She was nude, having not taken the time to dress before hurrying to the controls. He sat down beside her. "Brief me, Sammy."

"We're awaiting clearance to land at Pier-K, slip one-twenty-one."

"Hey, that's our old slip." He licked his lips. "Mind if I take her down?"

"I don't see why not – you're the captain.

Samantha eased out of her seat, accepting a jumper suit from Carl. The crewmembers strapped into the accelerator couches.

"This is Port Traffic Control to Achilles 27JS, Orion Industries, you are positioned for a vertical descent to slip one-twenty-one, Long Beach. State your captain's name."

"Yes, this is Captain Zachary Crowe of the Achilles 27JS, Orion Industries. Thanks Control. It's nice to see you again."

"Control here – acknowledged. We have Crowe listed on the return flight plan. You're cleared. Have a good dock – the slip is clean of souls." Pause – static. "Man, you guys have been out on the spiral arm for a while! Control out."

Those lousy bastards, thought Zaz. Orion couldn't change the return flight plan, especially after they'd left for Sidus. Zaz and his crew were listed as a returning compliment. They'd beamed Earth a return flight plan message the moment they knew Zaz had lost his ship. So Orion hadn't thought of everything after all. Maybe they would have made it back without the blackmail threat. He had to know about one other thing before he disconnected from Long Beach Control.

"Achilles 27JS here, Control, do we have any other incoming traffic for the port facility?"

"This is Port Traffic Control. That is affirmative. We have a return flight notification on a corporate liner that will fill slip one-twenty-four in about fifteen minutes. I suggest that you clear that chimney vector to make room."

"Captain Zachary Crowe, Achilles 27JS, confirmed on that traffic, we're on our way down."

He knew it. Orion Industries had followed them!

Dendy clapped her hands. "They hound-dogged us here. Now, if we just knew whether or not they'd rigged this ship for an accident before the jump. That would put the last nail in their coffin."

"I *know* they wanted to sleep us for good," said Carl. "I'd look for something connected with a pod accident. It's either in the main database program or an external device."

"They wouldn't leave any evidence in the main computer system that could be recovered," said Samantha. "Look for something that could interact with the pod cycle without leaving a trace. Find something you could erase easily."

Out of curiosity, Zaz turned on a panel and brought up the service archives, locating the automech schedules. He scanned the data. There it was – all the automech units had been activated just before jump. Except one. According to the specs, the off-line automech was perfectly functional, but shut off and strapped into a dead cradle. He used the manual override on the automech to fire it up for analysis. The data showed green across the board.

"So that's how they were going to do it," Zaz said to the room. "They programmed an automech to sabotage the sleep chambers. But they had a change of heart at the last moment, otherwise we wouldn't be here."

"They're a pretty ruthless bunch," said Dendy. "Why the change of heart?"

"Vanity," said Zaz. "Let's just say I gave them a big pandering spiel smothered in apologies. It was the last conversation I had with them after our little act was over. I gave them the impression we'd knuckled under. Gable must have changed his mind after my speech. He probably sent a com to the Achilles at the last moment. A subordinate wouldn't know how to deprogram an automech. But they sure as hell would know how to cradle one and shut its power supply off. Somebody goofed."

"You sound plum fixed on this, boss," said Galoot. "You really think it was going to go down like that?"

"Yes, I do. What's one of the best ways to bring a company jump ship into Earth orbit with a dead crew? You claim an automech went berserk and fouled the sleep cycle. Then you make sure the automech commits electronic suicide to hide the bug."

Galoot wrestled with a too small seat harness that wouldn't cinch. He finally gave up and tied a knot in it. "Just to be on the safe side, boss, I'll pull the daddy board on that unit after we dock."

"You do that. If that automech had murder on its mind, it will show up in the programming. That's our evidence. Blue Five is the rogue machine."

"What if it was just a hiccup in the self-destruct, but then decided to go boom all of a sudden?" asked Carl. "I'd rather clear that up right now. Hold the show until I get it out." Carl left his couch then sped back to the service area.

Five minutes later he returned with a circuit board, which he slipped into his tote bag. "Okay, I've got the goods. Here's the kicker, those automechs are six months newer than ours – two models up on our old machines – totally top of the line."

"What's the significance?" asked Samantha.

"Simple. They can't say I rigged a board that I don't know anything about."

Zaz brought the ship into the atmosphere. He activated the repulser field and let the ship drop. They came down through the clouds, picking up descent speed. The calculations were perfect, except Zaz had not allowed for 25 years of construction additions to slip 121. Having not read the new slip profile map, he landed the Achilles on top of an empty warehouse. He shut the repulser field off. The ship settled with the screech of crunching metal.

Samantha stifled a laugh. "That went rather well. Next time I'll drive."

Dendy threw her straps off. "Awe, the hell with it. How else are they supposed to know that Planet Janitor is back in town?

Remember, this is the planet where we can't do anything right, so that means everything's perfect. Speaking about imperfection, would somebody please get Silver Two. He's Planet Janitor property."

They gathered their belongings then climbed out the emergency hatch and jumped down onto the crumbling warehouse roof. Galoot followed, Silver Two slung over his shoulder. They slid the rest of the way down onto the tarmac. Zaz looked at the Achilles. She sat at a cocked angle on a heap of corrugated tin and broken framework.

A small knot of Port police and technicians ran toward them. One man was out in front, speeding along in a convertible hover sled and furiously waving a clipboard over his head. He pulled to a halt and stood up in the small vehicle. Zaz thought he recognized the man, but he wasn't sure. Then he heard those inevitable words:

"You are in violation of destroying Port property by failing to dock with sufficient clearance in proximity to permanent structures." The Port Inspector read several more code violations while Zaz nodded his head and said, "uh, huh," a lot.

Having been activated and placed on its feet, Silver Two said, "May I be of service, sir?"

Zaz gave the Port Inspector his thumbprint and a retina scan to comply with the violations. Then he said, "I'm a busy man. The checks are in the mail."

"Checks were expired from circulation eighteen years ago," cried the Port Inspector. "Wait just a damn minute – it's you! Of all that is unholy and indecent, it's *you* again. You have fines! Dozens of fines, compounded with interest. No, wait. You can't leave – I decree it!"

"When Henry Gable of Orion Industries docks," Zaz called over his shoulder, "tell him he'll know where to find me."

The Planet Janitor crew walked across the tarmac. Several port employees shouted at them, some threatening bodily harm. But no one stopped them as they passed through the security gate. Zaz concentrated on keeping his legs moving steadily, taking in deep breaths of planet Earth. Ah, the fresh air; it would quell his cryo headache. Either that or he would drink at least two bottles of Champagne to numb the pain. He felt the heavier tug of Earth's atmosphere, even with the weight he'd lost.

Upon entering the spaceport bar, Zaz led his crew back to the private booths. One table in particular had special meaning – the place where he'd first met Gable. They sat down and unburdened themselves. Silver Two stood obediently at the edge of the booth.

A thin, silver-haired waiter appeared at their table. He planted his hands on his hips; his eyes were cold, disapproving. Zaz thought his expression could have said, *They look like barbarous Triton miners who haven't seen soap and water for six months. And they'd brought their pregnant space trash with them!*

Andreas, smelling of rose water and starch, shook a finger. "This will never do. You don't have a reservation." He paused, scrutinizing the faces of the crew. "Oh, my goodness!" He stared at Zaz. "Is that you, Zachary? Oh, my! It *is* you!" Tears welled in his eyes. He shook out a handkerchief to dab his face. "It's been such a long, long time!"

"Set 'em up, Andreas," Zaz boomed. "You still know what we drink, right?"

"Oh, I certainly do. But I am not the regular waiter anymore, I am the manager... oh, never mind."

Carybell, with a large smile widening across her face, announced, "I'm a real botanist with Planet Janitor." She proudly pointed to her breast patch. "See?"

"My dear, I am more than impressed and shall not erase that fact from my mind."

Galoot thumped the table with a ham-sized fist. "I'm telling you if I don't get some alcohol down my neck real soon I'm gonna erase something around here plum fast."

Andreas disappeared like a wisp. A moment later he returned with the full inventory of drinks. He told the crew it was on the house.

*   *   *

Zaz had not yet finished his first bottle of Champagne when he noticed a small crowd of people pushing their way through the bar, heading toward their private booth. Henry Gable was in the lead, followed by three Orion executives and two security guards.

Gable stumbled up to the table and bowed awkwardly, favoring Zaz with a lopsided smile. The man was a wreck; his ponytail had come undone, his suit was not pressed, and he was sweating profusely. A guard shoved a chair under him the moment he bent to sit down.

Gable caught his breath, trying to rub a sticky eye open and talk at the same time. "I hope I'm not too late, Mr. Crowe. I'm very sorry for the foul up." He spoke in rapid bursts. "I was wondering if we could make a deal, if it isn't too late. It isn't too late, is it? I hope that we can settle this matter, if you know what I mean. We're here to honor our end of the deal – providing that the deal is still on. You haven't mentioned anything to anybody, I hope? Like I say…" The vice president of Orion Industries droned on with promises, apologies, bribes and numerous other certainties.

Zaz nodded at Carl. Car unzipped his jumpsuit and reached around to his backside. He zipped back up, holding the small object. He rolled it around in his fingers, drawing Gable's eyes.

"Oh my," said Andreas, who stood by awaiting an additional drink order.

Carl grinned. "I would have had you pull it out, Gable, but we're in a respectable joint."

Zaz looked at the frazzled vice president. "I suppose the *Majestic Sun* is parked in orbit over this port facility. I'll also wager that's the fastest emergency jump you've ever made." It felt great to rub it in.

"Yes, she is in a holding pattern as we speak," Gable choked. "The entire fleet is here. Look, I have the resources to give you anything you want. All you have to do is name it. Just please deactivate that device now."

Zaz nodded again. Carl ran his tongue over his lips, then used the end of his fingernail to trip a tiny switch on the device. But he didn't hand the device over. Instead, he pulled a small circuit board out of his tote bag and held it up against the overhead light.

"I'll just bet you that I can find some real dangerous programming in this automech circuitry." said Carl. "And I'll bet that evidence could wrap you up in the courts for years. Hell, it just might get you hauled in for attempted murder."

Henry Gable did not look directly at the object. He ran his finger around a moisture ring on the tabletop. "Well, that can be part of the negotiation, too. Look, we could have but we didn't. Besides, I can claim that you sabotaged the programming to set us up."

"Won't work," said Carl. "We don't know anything about the tech codes on those newer models. You might as well ask me to cipher God's computer."

Gable's excuses and bribes were running out like water through an open sluice gate. "All we wanted was a little cooperation. We're not as heartless as you think."

Dendy cocked her head. "That's funny, we were just debating that. None of it looked good for you."

Zaz thought he had let Gable sweat long enough. He held up a finger. "First, you'll give up the rights to Georgian Sidus and let nature take its course. Then you'll dismiss all of your contractors and laborers from this assignment. You're all here, and you have no cleared property on Sidus, anyway. Secondly, I have some port fines that need to be paid, with interest."

"I have no problem with those conditions," said Gable. "The contractor fleet vessels were only a few minutes behind us."

Zaz held up a third finger. "Last but not least, I lost a pretty damn good ship in this deal through no fault of my own. You'll deed the *Majestic Sun* over to me, signing the transfer of ownership right here and now."

Gable rose up from his seat. "You can't do that! She's a brand new company flagship. I christened her myself!"

"Yeah, and I'll bet you bought it with stockholder's money," said Zaz. "I'm sure they'd like to know that. Either you agree with those terms or the whole world finds out about what you've done."

"I can let you have a freighter or a smaller company liner without too much problem."

"It's going to be the *Majestic Sun,* or you'll have to get used to a complete lifestyle change inside a federal penitentiary. You'll be eating prison grog and working in an automech mill for the rest of your life. The choice is yours. I know which way I'd go."

Gable sat down woozily. He made a half-hearted attempt at snapping his fingers. An executive slid a document case next to the vice president's elbow. He brought out a flat-screen zip-scanner and punched in an entry. The device spat out a hardcopy document. He signed and thumb-printed it. One of his executives witnessed the transaction by applying his thumb-print. Gable pushed the title across the table.

Zaz looked the document over then nodded to Carl. Carl handed the receiver to Gable, but kept the automech board firmly in hand. "We'll keep this for insurance purposes. Dishonoring the deal will get attempted murder chargers slapped on ya."

Henry Gable dropped the tiny receiver on the floor and crunched it with his heel. He tried to contain a trembling voice. "Now if you don't mind. Where is the charge hidden on my, er, *your* ship? How did you get it on board? I've lost the hand. I would at least like to know what cards beat me."

"I knew when you arrived that protocol scanners hadn't changed much. They still don't use them on pregnant women or individuals with serious medical conditions because of the X-ray penetration. One of our gals brought the package in."

"We scanned the entire ship," said Gable. "We *couldn't* have missed the proximity device."

Zaz looked at Gable, unable to mask his disgust. "When was the last time you hugged your father, or even paid him a visit? Check your dad's float chair – Carl stashed it under the seat."

Gable's one open eye rolled to the back of his head. He looked as if he were on the verge of a stroke.

*   *   *

The party in the spaceport bar went on all night. Acts of lascivious contact abounded, including some nudity when several unidentified patrons began dancing on the bar tops. Several bottles had been broken over numerous heads, and that was before the fight started. Andreas was bound to a chair, forced to suffer the kisses of several inebriated women. A Port Inspector wound up taped to a joist beam.

In the end, it took three Port Authority police officers and seven bar police to forcefully evict the Planet Janitor crew from the premises and onto the street.

CHAPTER TWENTY ONE

ODYSSEUS RETURNS

ZAZ HELD DENDY'S HAND as he led her past the latched gate and up the narrow walkway around the old two-bedroom stucco home. He reflected on the numerous changes to the property: the yard still held a riotous fruit salad of blooming flowers, only now a profusion of ivy creepers had squirmed up the walls, clutching the little house in a fond embrace; numerous new ponds shimmered, fed by the trickle of fountains and sheet rock waterfalls. There was a new addition on the left wing of the residence – a greenhouse. The largest hardwood trees had skyrocketed in height. The air brought a hundred fragrant scents, but one stood out more than any other – honeysuckle.

He'd called a half dozen times but repeatedly got the same message – the phone code had been unlisted for nine years. He couldn't even find them in the current cyber directory. The only way to find out if his parents were still alive was to check their last known address. Now that he was here, he was afraid of what he might find. The place had changed so much; he suspected the home had new owners. That could only mean that they had... He didn't want to think about it.

Dendy watched as a hummingbird fluttered through the air and hovered near a birdfeeder attached to the front porch. "I love it,

Zaz," she said. "They say that a home is a reflection of its owners. If that's true, and if your parents are still here, they must be beautiful. It's like a little piece of paradise."

He took a heaving breath for courage and then followed the small stone walkway that led to the rear of the house. The last time he walked this path he'd had his back to his parents, leaving on the longest journey of his life. He also remembered the parting words his father had said to him: *We'll meet again, son. Godspeed to you and your crew. We love you.*

He would give anything to hear those words again.

As Zaz rounded the house, a large white gazebo came into view. It was an intricately fashioned, high-spire structure of white timbers and scrolled latticework. Carved angels gawked from the support posts. A wind chime tinkled above the entrance steps.

Zaz froze when he saw movement. There were two people on the deck, sitting in lounge chairs. A thin woman with sun-colored hair had just brought a cup to her lips. She stalled, listening to the soft-spoken words of a man who sat on the edge of an adjoining chair. The man glowed with a deep tan; his lush brown crop of hair waved in the slight breeze.

Zaz cleared his throat loud enough for the couple to hear him. "Either the two of you are trespassing, or you're the new owners of my parent's house."

The couple turned their heads at the sound of Zaz's voice. The woman got up slowly and stared at the intruders in her backyard. She wore a loose blouse that ruffled in the breeze, but her silk pants clung tightly over shapely legs. Upon seeing Zaz she dropped her cup.

The man rose from his seat and stepped in front of the woman, protecting her with an arm. He walked down the gazebo steps, gracefully balancing his weight.

"What do you want?" asked the man.

"I want to know what you are doing on this..." Zaz let the words hang, studying the couple further.

Dendy raised a flat palm to her forehead to shade her eyes. She gripped her mate's arm. "Wait a minute."

Zaz squinted against the sunlight, dumbfounded. As incredible as it seemed, he was looking at Donald and Ruth Crowe. They were not the father and mother he'd left behind. He saw two people who had been transformed, revitalized beyond his wildest dreams. Neither of them looked a day over 30. It was like some time machine had taken away the worst years of their lives. The couple looked fit, brimming with vitality. In the bright sunlight that shined on their faces, not one wrinkle or liver spot was evident.

Life Extend.

Zaz's voice caught in his throat. "Mom? Dad?" He wiped a tear from his eye. He suddenly realized that his straggly long hair and beard might have given his parents cause for suspicion. He still looked like a grungy Triton miner who hadn't seen soap and water for six months.

Donald Crowe said, "My boy? Oh, mama, it's our boy! Zachary!"

Zaz met his father with a crushing embrace. Don Crowe tried to speak, but cried instead, unable to contain his emotions.

Ruth Crowe dashed to her son's side, wrapping strong arms around him. Then she turned to Dendy. Taking the hands of the small girl, she spun her around in dizzying circles. "Oh, Zachary, she's absolutely adorable!"

CHRIS STEVENSON has been a native Californian for most of his life, until recently moving to Sylvania, Alabama. His career has spanned such occupations as automotive mechanic and service manager, government security officer, and newspaper reporter and editor. At the age of 34 he discovered *Twilight Zone Magazine* and got the urge to write short stories. Shortly after, he entered the L. Ron Hubbard Writers of the Future contest and placed amongst the finalists. Since those early days, he has published two non-fiction books, sold six novels, numerous short stories to the major slick magazines, and hundreds of newspaper and science articles. The only thing he hasn't published is a screenplay, which he doesn't plan on drafting anytime soon. His fondest wish is to continue with his writing career and produce the ultimate breakout novel.